The Woman Who Fell

Praise for Matthew Frank

'A clever, compelling spiderweb of a plot'
JANE CORRY, bestselling author of *My Husband's Wife*

'A gripping murder story . . . Frank brilliantly maintains a balance
between the demands of a complex plot and his character's
difficulty in returning to civilian life'
SUNDAY TIMES

'Outstanding characterization, passion, perfect dialogue
and pinpoint plotting'
CRIME REVIEW

'Seriously good . . . a tightly plotted thrilling page turner of a book'
JAMES OSWALD, author of the Inspector McLean Series

'Nail-bitingly tense plotting, with characters you can't help but
root for' SUSI HOLLIDAY, author of *The Last Resort*

'*The Woman Who Fell* is the best book in the Joe Stark series by far.
A truly brilliant mystery that builds to a thrilling climax'
JAMES BENMORE, author of the Dodger trilogy

'The definition of a page-turner'
HOWARD LINSKEY, bestselling author of *The Chosen One*

'Well researched and totally convincing'
SUNDAY MIRROR

'A gripping thriller, packed with dark twists and unexpected
turns, which kept me guessing until the very end.
Perfect for fans of *Slow Horses*'
JESSICA BULL, author of *Miss Austen Investigates*

'Thrilled to discover what Joe Stark's been up to.
This series is fantastic!'
CLAIRE WILSON, author of *Five by Five*

'Joe Stark is such a terrific hero . . . the writing is top-notch, the
action sequences are superlative, the characters crackle off the
page and the dialogue whips like bullets in the dust. Read it!'
SARAH HILARY, award-winning author of the
Marnie Rome series

By the same author

If I Should Die

Between the Crosses

The Killer Inside

The Woman Who Fell

MATTHEW FRANK

PENGUIN BOOKS

PENGUIN BOOKS

UK | USA | Canada | Ireland | Australia
India | New Zealand | South Africa

Penguin Books is part of the Penguin Random House group of companies
whose addresses can be found at global.penguinrandomhouse.com

Penguin
Random House
UK

First published 2024
001

Copyright © Matthew Frank, 2024

The moral right of the author has been asserted

Set in 12.5/14.75pt Garamond MT Std
Typeset by Jouve (UK), Milton Keynes
Printed and bound in Great Britain by Clays Ltd, Elcograf S.p.A.

The authorized representative in the EEA is Penguin Random House Ireland,
Morrison Chambers, 32 Nassau Street, Dublin D02 YH68

A CIP catalogue record for this book is available from the British Library

ISBN: 978-1-405-93076-5

www.greenpenguin.co.uk

MIX
Paper | Supporting
responsible forestry
FSC® C018179

Penguin Random House is committed to a
sustainable future for our business, our readers
and our planet. This book is made from Forest
Stewardship Council® certified paper.

*To Bignose & Titch, for always being there with
the bright side of life.*

Out of the night that covers me,
Black as the pit from pole to pole,
I thank whatever gods may be
For my unconquerable soul.

In the fell clutch of circumstance
I have not winced nor cried aloud.
Under the bludgeonings of chance
My head is bloody, but unbowed.

Beyond this place of wrath and tears
Looms but the Horror of the shade,
And yet the menace of the years
Finds and shall find me unafraid.

It matters not how strait the gate,
How charged with punishments the scroll,
I am the master of my fate,
I am the captain of my soul.

William Ernest Henley, 'Invictus'

Prologue

Tears . . . Karim Mansour wiped his cheeks, angrily . . . as fruitless as prayer. Weeping would no more undo pain than piety prevent it.

Prayer had not saved Amina from cancer, nor tears restored her. Prayer had not curbed their beloved Hassim's belligerent patriotism, nor tears returned him from whichever trench in Kuwait had become his grave, over fifteen years ago now. How many sons had Saddam's tyrannical ambition interred? Or America's wars of liberation?

And now, this . . .

Karim's fingers trembled in the straw, picking out another fragment, another piece of shattered history. Babylonian vases, unearthed with his own hands; painstakingly cleaned, verified, catalogued, displayed and at terrifying personal danger, saved from the sickening post-war museum lootings in 1991 and 2003 . . . With these hands, these fingers, now dusty and stained with futile tears.

Saved, until now.

Enough collateral damage for the corrupted officials to dismiss it as just more looting, but this was a targeted theft; yet another stripping of his nation's priceless artefacts by those too wealthy to be stopped and so impoverished of soul as to be despised.

These thieves had struck gold.

The soldier shifted, uncomfortable in his heavy battle gear, unused to Al-Baṣrah's 46°C summer heat. The 2003 looters had stripped out the storerooms' air conditioning, and the reconstruction effort had more photogenic priorities.

Soldier . . . hardly more than a boy. Hardly older than Hassim had been. The gun and uniform looked too real for the face, as if he should be standing there in a child's military costume, clutching a toy rifle.

Not American. British. The flag badge too small to stand out much on his camouflage, too stained with imperialist blood to ignore. But then, was not Iraq a part of the ancient Babylonian empire, as steeped in blood as all? Was it wrong for a historian to look on the history of his country, his world, with horror? The boy watched the door, on edge, new and unspoiled as yet by the unceasing war he'd joined; latest in the line of mankind's murder of mankind, stretching back unbroken through time.

But then he slung the wicked assault rifle across his middle, stepped over and crouched near Karim, and began wordlessly searching the straw with careful fingertips protruding from fingerless combat gloves. He picked out a fragment, inspected it, and added it to Karim's growing pile.

Karim stared, but the boy continued unabashed.

There was a word stitched into a badge on his uniform. Karim's written English wasn't what it had once been, before tyranny and liberation's vacuum cut his country off from the world of cultural and academic exchange. His studies in London seemed a lifetime ago. Too many lives ago . . .

S-T-A-R-K, he spelled out the word in his mind, reaching deep to recall its etymology. Strong. Resolute. Brave? A fitting name, perhaps, for a boy-soldier far from home, setting aside his war for a short time to help an old man sift through dust for fragments of a life.

PART ONE

Eight Years Later

I

Yes, it was a nice staircase.

Beautiful even.

Architecture wasn't really Fran's thing but as staircases went, the Tulip Stair, with its sweeping spiral of white stone steps and elegant tulip motif balustrade, picked out in striking Regency Blue, was probably worth its prominence on the brochure in Fran's hand. *The first centrally unsupported helical stairs constructed in England,* apparently. Primary feature of the Queen's House; *Grade 1 Listed, Scheduled Ancient Monument* and oldest building of what was now the National Maritime Museum – along with the Old Naval College, Royal Observatory and Greenwich Park – designated the *Maritime Greenwich World Heritage Site,* glittering jewel of the Royal London Borough of Greenwich, London, UK, thank you very much.

The ornate black-and-white patterned floor was not, however, much augmented by the fatal impact of a middle-aged woman, nor by the darkening blood pooled around her mis-angled corpse.

Humanity in a nutshell. What one created, another hastened to despoil.

And another had to clean up.

Okay, the scene of crime officers would bag the body

and some other poor sod would scrub the floor, but sorting out the mess of how a highly respected curator of the British Museum plunged to her death on the opening night of a major exhibition, that was now Detective Inspector Francine Millhaven's bloody job.

Lucinda Drummond. Fifty-seven, according to her Wikipedia bio. Big deal, apparently. The kind of expert that arty history shows liked to call upon. Voice for Radio 4, face for TV. Inevitable media storm.

Nice heels, thought Fran, staring disconsolately at the body. Dress, too – or had been. The kind they probably didn't even bother making in Fran's size. Maybe the formerly elegant, clever, successful woman had simply caught her sparkling hem on her killer stilettos and tripped right over the tulips. Luck had a way of catching up with you in the end. Or maybe an unfair portion of life's blessings had simply become too burdensome to bear and she'd thrown herself over in solidarity with the sisterhood of the dumpy. Maybe Fran could chalk this up to karma and bugger off home.

More likely, the marks on the woman's arms that Marcus had already pointed out were defensive wounds. But the kicker was the scream. Singular. The person finding the body. No one so far had reported hearing one preceding it. And no one fell unwillingly to their death without audible protest, unless incapacitated first.

'Another late night,' Marcus added now, as the photographer got to work.

Another late night. She'd lost track of who'd used that excuse more often now. Between her job and his. Enough to crush any relationship. To start with perhaps, part of the charm. Spontaneity. Inbuilt distance. At some point it had become a frustrating impediment. Now an excuse, masking the cracks. 'I'll call you tomorrow.'

She watched him nod and leave. Marcus Turner. Forensic pathologist, doctor, nice guy. Nearly father to her child – a point of pain that neither of them seemed able to get past.

She looked up the stairs again, picturing the victim's fall. She shook her head, blinking to dispel the image. Another ghostly impression. According to the brochure, the blurry photo by some sixties clergyman indicated the staircase was haunted – in the way of such clumsy mis-exposures. Doubtless some spook-freak would 'sense' the screaming spectre of Lucinda Drummond soon enough. Give it a year, thought Fran, when tonight's tragedy started selling more tickets than it deterred. Maybe six months.

The greater mystery was how the killer had come and gone.

The ground-floor level where Lucinda's downward travel had ended in fatally abrupt deceleration opened only onto the Great Hall, where the great and good had been enjoying fizz and canapés before the scream. The landing above opened only onto the balcony that circled four sides of said hall. You could access the balcony from other sides, but not without risk of being seen by one of the hundred people below. From the balcony level the stairs continued up to the roof, but the door out was firmly locked, with no sign of tampering. Same for the windows. And the circular fanned roof-light atop had no broken pane or abseil rope. That just left the stairs spiralling down to the basement undercroft. Blood had already crept partway down the stone steps. They emerged below into the inescapable finale of any museum tour, the gift shop – one end of a long white-plastered corridor, with the narrow visitor's entrance, ticket desk, side rooms, toilets, and a bare brick cloakroom behind a black velvet curtain – plus a second door to the outside, acting as the catering company's entry. Mostly staff down here; at the far end, the other, less floral, boringly straight staircase.

'Bag,' said one of the SOCO marshmallows, pointing out a sequinned clutch bag beneath the body as they rolled it onto its back, straightening broken limbs in readiness for the body bag. The photographer snapped.

'Let's have a look inside,' said Fran.

The SOCO carefully emptied the contents onto the evidence tarp. Couple of bank cards. Taxi receipt. Lipstick and foundation. Index cards for her speech. Nothing to indicate that Lucinda hadn't expected to survive the night.

'Got names and details, Boss,' said Phil Williams, appearing at her elbow. He and his fellow detective constable, John Dixon, had been corralling the party guests and staff for two hours. 'No one saw or heard her fall. No one recalls anything or anyone suspicious. A lot of people eager to get home.'

Join the club, thought Fran, suppressing a yawn.

Where the bloody hell was Stark? she thought for the umpteenth time. He was supposed to have been back a *week* ago, and if there was one thing a night like this needed, it was a detective sergeant to leave in charge so a detective inspector could get some sleep. She sighed, inside. Outwardly, she ground her teeth. One had to keep up appearances. 'Right. I'd better have a word with the principals before we let them all go.'

Stark stirred, the sounds and smells of a busy Tripoli dawn blending with the strange wanderings of dreamscape.

A soft chill suggested a breeze from the Mediterranean north rather than Saharan south. The blanket might not have been enough, were it not for the warm shape beneath it with him.

Sunsets brought relief from the arid afternoon heat; balmy evenings and cool nights warmed with cheap whisky, tangled limbs, passion and sweat, the sunrise soft and soporific. An old mattress on rough wooden pallets, in the ruins of a bombed hospital. A strange sort of paradise.

From the pace of her breathing, he sensed Gabrielle was awake.

Opening one eye, he found her watching him, flawless ebony skin creased with amusement around bottomless brown eyes.

Her smile widened into an inviting grin. 'Don't go.' The same words with which she'd instigated last night's faux argument and enthusiastic rapprochement. She wasn't about to let him leave without another round.

Stark suppressed a smile. 'I have to.'

She made that uniquely French sound of disparagement, halfway between a harrumph and the word '*bouf*', making it sexy in the way only a Frenchwoman could. ''Ow can you leave, not knowing when or if you'll return?'

'We've talked about this. I have commitments.'

'And London needs another policeman more than we need you here?' she dismissed his position. 'Just when things are finally starting to function. We need you more,' she stated as fact.

Starting to function was a low bar. If this was what functional looked like, how had anything been achieved before? Stark had arrived a year ago under the general banner of logistical support, expecting to be driving trucks and humping boxes, but within a week was leading the rag-tag security team and sweet-talking supply routes through the ever-changing factional borders of the local militias, with a smile, a rudimentary mish-mash of Arabic and Italian, and a Glock 19 at his belt.

Too often, the 'supply' was casualties.

That's where he'd met Gabrielle, as he carried a young boy with a thoracic bullet wound and thready pulse directly into the ER. A small woman in oversized scrubs and no-nonsense authority. She'd found him asleep on a floor several hours later. The boy had been stabilized – a close thing.

The hospital was barely supplied, lit or staffed, and it was drowning in patients, from sick to injured. Gunfire was a frequent soundtrack, with occasional detonations for harmony. Gabrielle and the other Médecins Sans Frontières volunteers had augmented the few remaining local doctors and nurses, but all were at constant breaking point. Any O-negative staff, Stark included, had donated all the blood they could reasonably do without – and more. For a region not officially at war, the ground situation was dire. A good day was fuel for the generator, lights in the operating theatre, with a supply of fresh saline and clean bandages. Stark had helped jerry-rig power and water to the one autoclave left intact after

8

some recent air strike levelled the rear of the hospital. The whole thing felt like shouting at the storm, but what else was there? The soldier digs his foxhole, then looks to see where he can be useful next. A step at a time, one loss or win at a time, until the storm took you or retreated, leaving you standing, hoarse but defiant. That was the job. Now he was caught between two storms. 'It's out of my hands.'

'Your hands,' she scoffed. 'Are they not full here?' She shifted her body against his to make her point, a twinkle in her eye behind the mock-indignation.

Stark smiled, taking one of her hands in his. So small and smooth against his, almost childlike in fineness. Surgeon's hands, skilled in life over death. So different from his . . . scarred by war, skilful in death over life . . .

'No, no, no,' Gabrielle scolded him gently. 'No sad thoughts. Not for you, *chéri*. You who will love and leave me, leave us all and fly home to your police and their . . . *ingratitude*. To your *rain* and *roast beef*.'

Stark couldn't quite keep a straight face.

Gabrielle hid her own laughter beneath a growl of disapproval, sliding her lithe form over to straddle him, pinning his wrists with her limited weight. 'You dare laugh at me?'

Stark felt a fresh pang of regret. What was he really flying home for, in the end? Where even was home? What could he hope to find or achieve in that swamp that he couldn't surpass here, where his skills were surely in greater need? Nothing but the knowledge that he'd run away, hidden, let people down. Nothing but stubborn pride.

9

The faux anger in Gabrielle's expression softened into a quizzical kind of sadness. 'Don't go,' she repeated, softly, almost but not quite pleading. Hers was a world of constant change, rarely knowing when the next meal might come, let alone who would be around to share it. Where the solace of another might be shared, but never last. The most real of worlds, where pleading was too often futile.

If his other life was still too fraught with conflicting forces, he could simply quit and return out here, where he could finally breathe, but he could no more promise her that than reveal the other grim appointment that called him back to London.

Stark knew that one kiss would lead to another, and more . . . and to the weakening of his resolve. But he also knew from experience that sometimes a kiss was all there was, and the regret of moments lost was ever-haunting. London was a city of regrets, and as Gabrielle lowered her lips to his, he'd happily never set foot there again.

She murmured approval, but crow-black wings flitted across the azure sky above, with a carrion cry . . . the shriek of jets overhead, and screaming . . . the air pulsed in violent shock as the ground heaved . . .

He jerked awake, banging his head as the giant military C-17 bounced and dipped, massive tyres shrieking against the ground and biting, the airframe lurch-adjusting from crosswind to runway, engines wailing into reverse to scrub speed, blood-red interior lights flickering, web-netted cargo shaking, and the other souls, strapped to the perimeters, laughing or grimacing . . .

And then all settled into the regular physics of the earthbound, and the huge craft slowed and taxied to the disembarkation point of RAF Brize Norton. The same base where he'd arrived home, barely alive, after his final deployment; not that he'd been conscious and able to remember that. The same base through which so many had arrived home in bandages or flag-draped coffins. Ready to disgorge Stark back into the rain-lashed UK to face his various fates.

The first thing his phone had to say on the subject, after connecting to the UK network for the first time in over a year, was that Fran's patience had run out about a hundred messages ago.

'I can't believe it,' he said for the third time.

Fran dug deep for patience. It was nearly midnight. The exhibition coordinator who'd found the body had hardly stopped crying long enough to say anything useful and now this guy, Adrian Fairchild, was clearly still in shock.

Late fifties, early sixties. Tall but slightly stooped. Handsome in his day, but fading. The careworn face of an academic but with enough pride for a good suit and shoes, decent haircut and trimmed beard. Distinguished. Credible. The definitive expert witness polished for trial, minus the detachment. But he appeared to be the guest who knew the victim best, putting him firmly on Fran's list for tonight. 'So, you've worked together how long?'

'On and off, twenty *years*.' He shook his head, staring at the floor. 'But we've known each other since Cambridge. She was an undergrad when I was completing my PhD. My research assistant for a while.'

'And now she's your boss, or was.'

He shrugged, still staring at the floor. 'We were peers

for years. When the head curatorship came up, she got the job. It needs someone media-friendly these days. Lucy was always a star. Egyptology, you see – much more publicity than my line.'

'Which is?'

'Well, I've dabbled broadly in my time, but my most serious scholarship has been in ancient currency.'

'Money?'

'In simplistic terms. Rare metals and gems, but also barter-able commodities, right back to shells and beads. Fascinating stuff but less glamorous ... apart from the occasional unearthed coin hoard.'

Fran was already bored. 'No hard feelings then?'

Now he looked up, recognizing her insinuation. 'What? *No.* No, nothing like that. We were *friends.*' He put his face in his hands again. 'What are we going to tell Libby and Ryan?'

'Her children?'

He nodded. 'All grown up now, lives of their own, but they were close.'

'And the father?'

'Simon? I don't suppose he'll shed a tear. Left Lucy for a younger woman when the kids were small. Probably done it again by now. Lives in LA, last I heard.'

'You have contact details for them?'

'I already gave Libby's number to your colleague.'

'They've probably already asked, but can you think of any reason or anyone who might have wished her harm?'

'No. The very idea is *absurd.* Lucy was a *good woman.* She brought nothing but light to the world. This must've been an accident.' His red eyes suggested he *had* shed tears. His hands were shaking and he looked pale.

Fran made a mental note to find out if anyone had seen this one leave the hall around the time of Lucinda's death. Not only the innocent could be stricken by the magnitude of murder.

If Fran could have her way, she'd round everyone up, confiscate their clothing, and swab every hand for DNA evidence, but she didn't have probable cause – and with a guest list like this, and her luck, one or more of them would have the Commissioner's personal phone number. Someone at the Met would have advised on the security of the exhibits, and you could bet the higher-ups were closing ranks already.

'Detective Inspector Millhaven?' asked a steadier voice.

Fran's eyes climbed wearily past the kind of shoes and suit made in your size only if you had the cash and connections, to the face of a man used to both. Sixties, groomed, tanned, handsome and knew it. 'For my sins, Mr . . . ?'

'Zedani.' He offered a smile no one should comfortably summon after midnight with a body in a bag. 'Patron.'

'Of the arts?'

'Indeed.'

'Is that like a donor, or sponsor?' There was a banner in the Great Hall, listing the various companies using this exhibition to shine their brand. She didn't recall the name Zedani on it.

'For my sins. I'm told you're in charge here?'

Nothing in his demeanour suggested he found issue with a woman of colour being in charge, but Fran was willing to give him the benefit of her distrust. A slim, pretty, manicured woman in her late twenties hovered at his elbow. Too little bling for a trophy wife. Fran settled on assistant, but didn't rule out mistress as well. The slab of muscle behind them sat firmly in the security deterrent column. So, this Zedani was the kind of man that attended invitation-only exhibition openings with an entourage.

Zedani followed her eyes. 'My indispensable PA, Kat, and my personal security, Jan.'

'Your person needs securing at a museum gala?' Fran recognized the absurdity of the question even as it left her lips, given the reason for her presence.

Zedani smiled graciously. 'One never knows.'

Presumably one never knew when one might need a helping hand from one's glamorous assistant too, thought Fran. DC Williams hovered behind them with an expression that didn't so much apologize as say *over to you, Boss*. 'And how can I help you?'

'I was just wondering when we might all go home. I seem to have been deputized to ask. There's a lot of tired and upset people back there, some of them quite elderly.'

All of them more sober than they'd expected to be, in every sense. The caterers had replaced the champagne with water and shared out the remaining canapés. Fran had been too busy to nab any and hoped these perfect people couldn't hear her stomach grumbling. She gave a quiet sigh, fighting the urge to tell Deputy Entourage to get back in line.

'All names, contacts and photos taken, Boss,' said Williams, recognizing her look.

'Then yes, Mr Zedani, I think we're about done for tonight.'

If only that were true, she thought.

All those present had been warned not to discuss what had happened outside these walls, so naturally the second she let them all go, the news would leak.

The Family Liaison officer was already here, waiting for her.

The real work would begin in the morning. But tonight, she had bad news to deliver.

2

'Well, you can scrape that hipster crap off your face for a start,' said Fran brusquely, squinting in the low morning sun as she met Stark at the station's tradesman's entrance, with evident disapproval. His crisp suit, shirt and tie passed muster, but a sun-bleached beard and tan hardly projected the contrition one half of this reunion thought was required.

Groombridge watched with interest from the shade of the canopy. A year on from her promotion, Fran was still learning that it was the detective inspector who generally got the least sleep between the midnight corpse and the morning investigation meeting.

'Where the bloody hell have you been?' she demanded, irritably. 'I've messaged you like a thousand times!'

'Indeed,' replied Stark, levelly.

'You were supposed to be back a week ago.'

'I emailed you I was delayed.'

'Saying you'd be back *yesterday*!'

'My flight was diverted.'

Fran waited pointedly for further explanation, but Stark could outwait a stone. After the fatal shooting hearing had cleared and reinstated him, his request for a sabbatical had been waved through by Superintendent Cox without question. His subsequent emails had simply said he was getting some sun. 'You look like shit.'

'While you're radiant as ever,' he smiled.

A fleeting shadow dimmed her ire, which she masked with a decent harrumph. 'Congratulations. You've taken less than ten seconds to remind me what a maddening git you really are.'

'I've missed you too, Detective Inspector.'

Groombridge smiled. Stark looked relaxed. Tired, maybe, but healthy. Whatever he'd been doing, the break appeared to have done him some good. This could finally be the start of something long overdue. Dawn after the storm. Hope of the distant harbour where he, if he wasn't dashed on the rocks first, might finally relinquish the wheel. Fran had handled promotion to inspector well this last year, though with relatively simple cases only to test her. The next tempest was never far beyond the horizon. Hammed had done a passable job as *acting* and, finally, *qualified* DS in Stark's absence, but his transfer to Lewisham a fortnight ago couldn't have come soon enough in Groombridge's opinion. Fran still had a lot to learn. Nothing got easier with inspector rank. A new DI needed an indomitable bagman, not a passable one. Fran needed Stark. The plan for them both to pass their exams and move up to DI and DS respectively hadn't factored in Stark taking a year's sabbatical.

'Well, you're back a day late for a shitter of a case,' said Fran, 'and I'm confiscating your damn passport.'

'Not sure she trusts you not to disappear for another year,' grinned Groombridge, stepping from the shadows.

The fleeting expression on Stark's face suggested that perhaps she was right not to, but then came a broad smile. 'Can't make any promises, Guv.'

'Who of us should?' He shook hands. 'Nice tan, Detective Sergeant,' nodded Groombridge, 'but the Super might take the whiskers as a challenge to his moustache. I'm sure he'll want to say hello, as will half the station, but first there's Fran's "shitter" of a murder to solve.'

Category-A Investigation.

Senior Investigating Officer: Detective Inspector Francine Millhaven.

A year of seeing her name on the file as SIO. Eventually it had to stop feeling like a bad joke, thought Fran. Like a terrible mistake she should've corrected immediately, now compounded with each reoccurrence.

A feeling hardest to shake when briefing the press, though she did think she was starting to get the hang of that. Better than abysmal at least. Picturing your audience naked was an appalling thought, and it still generally felt the other way around. But there was a world of difference between reporting on yet another teenage stabbing or gang-spat shooting – the media barely glancing her way – and a respected, attractive, white TV pundit having plunged to her death at a posh party. There shouldn't be, but there was. And after this morning's meeting, she'd doubtless face a fuller crowd.

It was a good job Stark had snuck in the back way. The nation's favourite decorated hero. The longer the vultures didn't know he was back the better. Indefinitely, if possible.

Wishful thinking. The leaks of the past had been plugged – with DI Harper gone and his puppet master, Deputy Assistant Commissioner Stevens, 'retired' and still fighting for his pension after the press scandal – but if Stark's gauntlet of greetings downstairs was anything to go by, word would soon get out.

Tomorrow's problem, she thought. Right now, she had a large whiteboard with two photos at the top: Lucinda Drummond, alive and well-to-do, the image copied from her multiple online hits, and then crumpled in death from last night. An email from Marcus relayed preliminary findings.

Time of death consistent with finding of body.

No apparent alternative cause of death, yet.

Marks on her arms likely defensive wounds, but nothing under her fingernails.

Marcus could've phoned instead, but he hadn't. Neither had she, and the whys and wherefores of that had no place in her head right now.

Fran felt the familiar stirring of anger. That was good. Elegant middle-aged women deserved every bit as much of her indignation at their deaths as poor teenaged boys whose lives were cut short in pointless territorial grievances. Murder was the grossest of thefts, and nothing stoked Fran's fire faster than injustice. Except, perhaps, slowness, non-compliance, incompetence – and a number of irritating individuals she kept on a mental list.

Her underlings waited for her to bestow wisdom. Well, Williams and Dixon waited to be bossed at least. Stark just waited. And Groombridge hovered at the back, waiting for her to mess up. Both on the list, of course, along with Marcus.

'So,' she said, after summing up the basics, 'thanks for coming in on the weekend. Good luck chasing the over-time pay. Anything new on the overnights?'

'Nothing yet, Boss,' confirmed Dixon.

Fran noted Stark smile. Her rise to DI had presented a nomenclature problem. To this team, Groombridge would always be *Guv*. She put up with *Ma'am* from those outside this room only. Then Dixon had recalled Stark saying *Boss* was the term army rank and file used for their lieutenants, and that had an acceptable ring to her. He clearly found that amusing in some twisted military way.

'Right,' she started. 'Immediate family consists of a son and daughter, both grown, plus a sister in Australia. No living parents. Family Liaison have contacted secondary relatives. Judging by the growing crowd outside, the press have picked up on the online leaks. It's down to the people in here to remember that Lucinda Drummond was more than a face on Nerd-TV. She was a person, with a past and hopes of a future. A friend, colleague and mother. Right now we have one hundred and thirty-one suspects, and that lot outside aren't going to give us much time. Start with the timeline and then move on to the party guests, while I go feed the hacks.'

3

'Back for good?' asked Groombridge, staring down from his office window at the press awaiting Fran. It was good to see him back where he belonged – not usurped, as he'd been the last time they'd seen each other – but he'd never shied away from blunt questions.

Stark kept a step back. The window had reflective privacy film, but the instinct to hide from the press was ingrained now, and if the media got wind of his return it would distract from the case. But celebrity claustrophobia aside, part of most soldiers' decompression after front-line deployment was adjusting to windows. Glass was never a great idea when a mortar round or IED might send it ballistically inward. Drafts and noise became a comfort. The bomb-deglazed hospital had felt a lot like a forward operating base. The office felt like a trap.

Talking of traps, Fran hated public speaking. She thought she lacked DI Harper's stature and DCI Groombridge's gravitas, but she didn't see her own power. A short, mixed-race woman didn't make SIO in this man's world without standing her ground, and experienced press hacks could tell forthright from fraud. It felt bad to pick up their relationship with half-truths. His flight had diverted, but deliberately, to drop off casualties in Geilenkirchen, the NATO airbase in Germany, but the instinct to withhold was ingrained too.

'We'll see.' Stark could be open with Groombridge in ways he could never be with Fran. Indeed, experience had shown there was little use dissembling. The DCI's penetrative stare could be discomfiting even when it appeared focused elsewhere.

'Well, you'd better take this . . .' Groombridge slid open his desk drawer and passed Stark an envelope. 'Damn thing's been cluttering up my desk long enough.'

Stark slid out the pristine warrant card wallet and flipped it open: *Joseph Stark, Detective Sergeant.*

That was going to take some getting used to.

He hardly remembered sitting the exam now. He'd certainly been in no fit state after the horrors of the night before. Bloody-minded pride, as usual. He'd left the country long before the results came in.

'We need you here,' stated Groombridge, watching him. 'Fran needs you.'

Stark didn't know what to say to that. He was just one man. He had sacrificed willingly, but the world had taken more, bringing terror and peril to those he loved most. To the *one* he loved most. Only time would tell if this was too soon for him to attempt a return. 'That's kind of you to say.'

Groombridge didn't miss the dodge. He hadn't once asked where Stark had been for the last year. Part of Stark being honest with him was that the wily DCI knew what questions not to ask. Instead, he sat at his desk and turned the case file to face Stark.

Lucinda Drummond. Fifty-seven. Divorced. Son and daughter in their twenties. One sister. A family bereaved.

Grieving friends and colleagues, readable between the lines. '*She* needs you.'

'Right,' muttered Fran under her breath so the desk sergeant didn't overhear. 'Nothing to see here. Move along.'

Taking a deep breath and shoving open the doors, she stepped as purposefully as she could to the top step of the station stoop, and opened her leatherette folder like a lion tamer uncoiling her whip.

'Good morning. As you've already been reporting, units from this station were called to Queen's House at a little after eight last night, where the body of a woman in her fifties was found dead, apparently from a fall. We are, for the moment, treating her death as suspicious, pending a full post-mortem.'

A barrage of calls erupted. Among them someone clearly saying the victim's name.

Fran held up a hand for quiet.

Groombridge insisted she was getting better at this, but the various times she'd done this over the last year had been generic South London cut-and-paste to the hacks. This one had a TV celebrity and a World Heritage Site.

Groombridge generally cautioned patience. Fran found growling inwardly seemed to be her best strategy for that – and for not gibbering like a fraud. Looking down from the stoop helped too. What she lacked in height she addressed with elevation, and what she lacked in confidence she tackled with intransigent brevity. The Groombridge book again – decide what to say, say it, and get offstage. Not one word more than necessary. Scraps for hacks. And time your announcements as close to the hour as you could so they had to trot off to file their copy or pontificate to camera. She could already spot one or two glancing at watches.

'I can now confirm the victim was fifty-seven-year-old Lucinda Drummond –'

Another barrage of questions. Fran waited with her best resting-indifference face until they trailed off.

'The family have been informed, and we would ask that you respect their grief at this most difficult time.' Though I might as well ask a pack of hyenas not to cackle over a carcass, she thought. 'The Greenwich Major Investigation Team have formally opened an investigation and we will share more information as progress allows. That's all for now.'

Thespians say, leave them wanting more.

Coppers usually had little choice.

As the press dispersed, Fran saw one journalist linger, and her heart dropped.

Gwen Maddox – freelancer for one of the hipper online news feeds – infamous for bagging Stark's one and only press interview and, more recently, for forcing the resignations of Met Deputy Assistant Commissioner Rupert *Shithead* Stevens and his mutually corrupt media mistress.

Fran remained suspicious of the former and grateful for the latter, but the last thing she needed was an investigative reporter that actually investigated. 'Isn't this sort of ambulance-chasing a bit beneath you now?'

Maddox shrugged. 'Well, I saw a juicy story crop up in my old stomping ground and just couldn't help myself.'

'Or you've been blacklisted for sinking one of your own along with one of ours.' An occasional willingness to swim against the tide of populist regurgitation might win you Pulitzers, but probably not friends.

'Corruption is corruption, whichever side of the line. And if everyone likes you, you're not doing your job,' added Maddox, implying that was probably something Fran not only knew from experience but would herself say.

The fact that she was right on both counts only made it worse. 'Okay, well, for the record then, no further questions.'

Maddox nodded, amused. 'Not even off the record and unrelated?'

Fran stared back, distrustfully. 'Then what would be the point?'

Maddox smiled, a hand tucking her natural red hair behind a delicate ear. Too young and pretty. Fran was thinking that about too many people these days. 'I was just wondering whether you've heard from our mutual friend?'

Fran kept a straight face. 'I don't think either of us is in the right profession for friendships, let alone mutual ones.'

'Yet here we stand, mutually concerned. No one has seen him in over a year. He changed his mobile number and email, after . . . what happened.'

'And only gave his new ones to the people that mattered, I guess,' said Fran pointedly. She still didn't understand Stark's relationship with Gwen, but she was easily attractive enough for suspicion, and it gave Fran some pleasure to know Stark had ghosted her too.

'His family won't talk to my kind, for obvious reasons. Even me. As a reservist he still has to register contact details with the MoD but they just stonewall. I tracked down Major Pierson who would only confirm his where-abouts were *known*, but I got the impression she was worried about him too. Do you know where he is?'

Fran allowed herself a silent moment of smugness. 'If I did, it wouldn't be my business to share it with you. He took a sabbatical. It's no one's business where he's been.'

'Been, or is?' Gwen's eyes narrowed slightly.

Damn! 'Either.'

'I just want to know he's all right.' Those hazel-green eyes softened with what did appear to be concern.

Fran clenched her jaw against traitorous empathy. 'As far as I know he's fine, by his skewed standards.'

'You've spoken with him?'

'No comment. Look, we both know he's as stubbornly private as he is uniquely irritating, so why don't you stop worrying about Joseph bloody Stark and go file your juicy story.'

'There he is . . .' said Superintendent Cox, looking up from his desk as his long-serving, suffer-no-fools PA, Marjorie, showed Stark in. 'At long last.'

'Sir.' Stark received the incoming handshake with as much of a smile as a summons to the general's office permitted.

'Welcome back, welcome back.' Cox shook Stark's hand vigorously. 'Looking good. Bit of sun. Back, fit and strong, by the look of you – though Mrs Cox would force-feed you a meal or three. Ready to fight the good fight?'

'As ever, sir.'

'Splendid. Splendid. And congratulations on the promotion, *Sergeant*. Not before time. First of many, I'm sure. Got to keep you here as long as we can before HQ comes calling to poach you. Makings of a great team here. Greenwich Major Investigation Team needs you. National attention after that last case of yours. *International.*'

Too much attention by half, thought Stark, who'd evaded more than enough press attention before flying away.

His thoughts must've shown in his eyes. Groombridge always insisted there was a sharp copper's mind behind Cox's bluff exterior. 'Well, that's all done with for now,' smiled the senior man, slapping his arm encouragingly. 'Don't make any plans to disappear again. I'll give DI Millhaven orders to handcuff you to your desk, if she has to.'

'Sir.'

'Good. Well, marvellous to have you back where you belong. Plenty to do, I hear. Plenty to do.'

4

'You back for good this time?' asked Fran.

Family Liaison had obtained keys and the alarm code to Lucinda's home from her daughter, and Fran had co-opted Stark to accompany her. When she didn't immediately start the car's engine, he sensed an ambush.

When he failed to immediately respond in the positive, her hands tightened on the steering wheel. 'I can't be doing with you buggering off again. You can't be half-in, half-out. Not in this job.'

'I know.'

'You've had a break. God knows you deserved one, and I hope you had fun or found inner peace or whatever else you went looking for, but we need you back, here, *really* here.'

Stark thought he detected urgency beneath her usual pre-emptive strike against contradiction. Her step-up to DI responsibilities would have been hard enough, without a denuded team.

'I'm here,' he replied. For now. Two weeks till his appointment with Major Pierson. After that . . .

Fran stared at him, but it had been a year, and some of the confident delight with which she habitually interrogated him seemed to have dissipated.

Giving up for now, she started the engine and ten-point-turned out of the overcrowded car park into the

London traffic, with her usual brand of righteous impatience.

'Nice car,' he commented.

'Tight gits at Central Procurement couldn't keep stalling after I waved a DI card under their noses.'

It wasn't really much of a step up from her last one, but . . . 'Best try to keep this one free of bullet holes,' he suggested, straight-faced. Doubtless she still blamed him for that.

'Piss off.' It seemed she did. 'You'd better get on to them for one of your own, if you're sticking around. Unless you fancy booking out that shitty little blue pool car for the rest of your career.'

A marker. To benchmark his commitment to stay.

He typed Lucinda's address into the sat nav. Fran glanced at him from time to time as she drove, likely checking to see if his PTSD hyper-vigilance could cope with the passenger seat. They had history there. Stark had travelled dodgier streets than these since last they'd shared a car, but still had to fight the tension of transit – the vulnerability instilled by time spent knowing that your armoured vehicle might survive a blast, but not necessarily without rattling its contents to ragu.

'You in touch with Kelly?' she asked as they made their way west. 'Please don't tell me you ghosted her too, after everything . . . ?'

'I'm not much of a one for postcards.'

Fran shook her head in disbelief. 'And there was me thinking it might've shaken some sense into you.'

It had certainly shaken him. 'She needed a break too.' A clean break, from him and the peril he'd brought her.

'You're an idiot.'

'So I'm told.' His mother, chief evangelist on this topic and the guilt-tripping stakes. His sister came second and was raising his nephew and niece in the faith. Fran was a relative newcomer to the church, by comparison, but no less devoted.

But again, she let it go. They say the sign of a true friendship is picking up seamlessly after time apart. Stark and Fran were something else. And his self-imposed exile appeared to have altered whatever that was. Perhaps they'd get back to where they had been. Perhaps not. Nothing stayed the same.

'Your other girlfriend was asking after you. The reporter.'

Gwen? Surely she couldn't know he was back *already*. 'When?'

'After this morning's press circus. Don't worry, I didn't let on you were back. It's none of my business how you keep them all keen.'

'Funny.'

'Is there anyone you *did* tell where you were?'

'Mum. Sister.'

'And Major Pierson?'

Stark glanced at her, wondering whether she'd got that from Gwen, or arrived there all by herself. The last thing he needed was either of them talking to Major Wendy Pierson.

Fran waited in vain. 'Tell me you at least ghosted your God-awful shrink too. I can't stand that woman.'

'Really?' he said dryly. 'She'd be crushed.'

Fran and Hazel's single meeting appeared to have been

enough for both of them. Stark was happy to let that topic go, along with the rest.

Lucinda's house was relatively modest, though with London prices an academic probably had to be doing pretty well in the punditry stakes to afford anything freehold. At least the Home Secretary didn't hit you with below inflation pay deals or freezes, thought Fran.

Inside was well ordered, clean, and awash with photos and objects suggesting extensive travel and curiosity. A curator's home. Pictures of the children, Libby and Ryan, through childhood holidays to graduations. Only one early family shot showing the ex-husband. Fran would've drawn devil's horns and a tail on him, if it was her. Or just burned him in effigy. If she didn't do something soon, Marcus might move on too.

Nothing obvious appeared out of place or untoward.

Upstairs was much the same. Main bedroom tastefully decorated, with more objets d'art and photos. Fitted wardrobe stuffed with the kinds of clothes and shoes Fran could only dream of – if she was a foot taller, two stones lighter and three times richer. At least three outfits she'd have killed for lay rejected on the bed. A woman dressing for a special occasion without the slighted expectation of it being her last.

The other two bedrooms were still the kids' rooms. One neat and feminine, one male and cluttered. Single beds.

'Empty nest,' commented Stark.

A middle-aged woman, more hopeful of visiting offspring than guests. Two young people robbed of a mother to greet them home. A pang of loss sliced through Fran.

Reminding yourself that you'd have been a terrible mother didn't always help. 'Let's go speak with the fledgelings then.'

We're very sorry for your loss.

Comfortless words. The only words possible.

They sounded so hollow from Fran's mouth that Stark could not bring himself to add to their echo.

Libby Drummond did not thank her for them. 'You think someone killed her.' She glanced between Fran and the hovering Family Liaison officer, a quietly reassuring sergeant called Don Reynolds.

'It's too early to draw conclusions,' replied Fran, evenly. Another platitude.

'But you're treating Mother's death as suspicious, or you wouldn't be here.'

'You're *wrong*,' said Ryan Drummond forcefully. 'Everyone *loved* Mum. No one would want to hurt her. It's impossible.'

Denial. Stark knew the first stage of grief all too well. The anger came next. He could already see it, starting to simmer behind the boy's eyes.

Lucinda's children had a long road ahead of them.

Children no longer. Both in their early-to-mid-twenties, good looks diminished by present circumstance, Ryan a year or three younger than Libby. The latter resembled the mother more, though the boy had more of her eyes. Both wary at what the presence of the detective branch represented.

At a glance from Fran, Reynolds pitched in. 'As DI Millhaven says, it's too early to say anything much, but we have to keep an open mind. As I explained earlier, there are just questions we have to ask.'

'Formalities,' said Libby, coldly. Her mother reduced to a tick-box exercise. She'd moved past denial already.

She did most of the answering. They didn't recognize anyone on the event guest list, apart from Adrian Fairchild, a family friend of many years. They didn't know of any reason anyone might want to harm their mother. Her life was too busy and eclectic for much in the way of routine, but they could think of no indication of disquiet in her recent activities, behaviour or demeanour. This tragedy appeared to have been visited upon them out of the proverbial blue sky, and was all the more crushing for it.

Ryan's eyes were darting impatiently by the end. Libby looked rigid with pent-up exhaustion. Stark doubted either would sleep much tonight. That part carried through all five stages of grief.

Libby looked at him for a moment, but what she was thinking, he could only guess.

5

First thing that morning Stark had automatically reoccupied his old tiny desk, sandwiched between filing cabinets and the photocopier.

Returning now with Fran, he found his meagre work accoutrements relocated to the larger desk formerly occupied by Hammed, by the window, with its own noticeboard and coat hook, and space to lay files out rather than stack them up.

'You're not the new kid any more, Sarge,' said Williams.

'Coffee, black, one sugar, Sarge?' asked Dixon.

Stark could tell they were trying not to laugh. 'Piss off, the pair of you.'

Williams saluted. 'Pissing off back to work, Sarge-yes-Sarge!'

And so it begins, thought Stark. It was going to be strange – but no stranger than being unceremoniously plucked from your fellow army privates and told you're a lance corporal and you damn well better run and sew this stripe onto your tunic before you're charged with presenting out of uniform. And that, it seemed, was that. The new world order. Everything in its place. Stark's life seemed to be defined by change.

'Don't expect me to treat you any differently,' said Fran, lifting a considerable weight of files and paperwork from her desk's usual backlog in-tray and placing it in his.

'Wouldn't dare to dream, Boss,' smiled Stark.

A lunch at your desk day.

Dixon fetched sandwiches and took turns with Williams on the coffee run.

Once he'd triaged Fran's delegated backlog pile into things that could be left for now, things that ought to be done now, and things that you could only hope no longer mattered, Stark joined in the rest of the team's legwork. And if it was no secret that he sometimes found solace in monotonous tasks, he was in the right place today.

The timeline was relatively simple. The taxi receipt had no time next to the scribbled semi-legible date, but a quick call had confirmed the approximate times Lucinda was collected from home and deposited outside Queen's House, corresponding with the time the exhibition coordinator welcomed her in. She'd mingled with the growing number of guests until it was time for her to prepare to make her speech inaugurating the exhibition, a broad collection of maritime objects on loan for one year from the British Museum to augment the House's renowned collection of paintings. It should have opened to the public this morning. Disappointed ticket-holders still mingled outside, peering at the police tape and the solitary uniform, who was growing increasingly tired of repeating his apologies to stuffy academic types and overseas tourists of varying national stereotypes.

At 19:30 Lucinda had withdrawn to a basement room, provided for her to prepare.

When Lucinda failed to reappear at the allotted time of 20:00, the coordinator had gone to find her. And succeeded.

Most of the assembled worthies and staff had little difficulty recalling where they were at the moment of the scream.

That was at 20:04. A thirty-four-minute window of opportunity.

There was only one door into the Tulip Stairs on each of the three landings: undercroft, ground floor and first floor.

The ground-floor door from the Great Hall where the guests were gathered was obscured behind a huge promotional cloth banner emblazoned with the names of key sponsors, masking the grandest exhibit – a dramatic series of ship's figureheads dating back through centuries – intended to be revealed when Lucinda cut the ribbon, dropping the banner to the floor. The banner also covered a small flight of stairs leading down to a door that opened onto the vaulted tunnel that bisected the ground floor where the house had been built spanning the original road to Woolwich – presumably so the Queen in question could alight from her coach without being rained on – today the central feature of the famous colonnades linking it to the later buildings. This door now served as a fire exit, with a night latch to allow egress but deter entry. But the latch snub button had been in the hold-open position, allowing free access. An ideal route for a killer to slip inside and go up the Tulip Stairs out of sight behind the banner ... There were CCTV cameras *outside*, covering the colonnades and showing both entrances to the tunnel, but they had captured no such assassin coming or going.

CCTV *inside* the Great Hall showed four people slipping behind the banner, shortly before the killing: the museum's exhibition coordinator and Alex Zedani, with his PA and bodyguard. The coordinator reappeared a minute later. The Zedani trio only reappeared after the alarm went up. According to initial interviews, they were outside in the tunnel the whole time. CCTV didn't cover the tunnel itself. Three connected people, whose only alibi was each other.

Fran had already placed their names at the top of the board.

The first-floor door was only accessible via the balcony around four sides of the Great Hall, highly visible, and covered by a camera – again showing no one.

The lowest-level door opened onto the main basement corridor. Off it was the room set aside for Lucinda to prepare, the staffroom used as temporary kitchen by the caterers, the cloakroom, toilets and a number of storerooms, confirmed as locked by the museum staff and the first uniforms on the scene. Caterers, guests, all coming and going and, lacking priceless artefacts at that level, camera-free.

So, aside from the self-alibiing Zedani trio, the suspect list included just about everyone else.

The initial assessment of Lucinda Drummond's level of injury suggested a fall from a considerable height, possibly beyond the first-floor landing, suggesting she'd retreated upwards, towards the roof exit – a literal dead end. But not one of the hundred-plus people the other side of the Great Hall door had heard her accelerated descent *towards* their floor. Possible defensive marks made resolute suicide less likely than foul play. So why was the only scream heard that of the coordinator finding Lucinda's body?

Stark had been taught several ways to ensure an enemy

died soundlessly. Good fun in basic training. Less so in special forces training. In practice, his kill-count had all been with guns. Easier to live with in some ways. Harder in others.

Some guests reported hearing a bang over the background classical music and the hubbub of chatter, but dismissed it as something being dropped somewhere. So far, that sound did not seem to have been caught on any phone camera audio – these people were not generally the selfie or vlog generation – but estimates put the alleged impact between five and twenty minutes before the scream. That narrowed the approximate TOD window to between 19:44 and 19:59, but for now they were scrutinizing the whole thirty-four minutes.

Establishing where everyone was during that time was a painstaking task, divided up between the detectives. CCTV covered the Great Hall. Snippets of phone video and photos began to come in, to be catalogued and scrutinized in the hope of seeing who was where when, and perhaps even catching someone behaving suspiciously, but while the party guests were for the most part congregated in the Great Hall, the seventeen staff were not. Miracles were possible, theoretically. But none had manifested by the end of the day. And after the cataloguing would come the follow-up interviews.

'Pub?'

Stark looked up from his work to find Fran staring at him, with Dixon and Williams spectating. 'Jet lag,' he offered by way of apology.

Fran huffed, unimpressed. 'Lightweight.'

*

Jet lag was half a lie. The time difference to Tripoli was only two hours, but the stopover in Geilenkirchen to drop off casualties – in need of life-saving treatment Gabrielle and her colleagues could only *wish* to provide – had extended the four-hour flight into fourteen. And a C-17 wasn't exactly first class. Time was, Fran would have twisted his arm all the way to the bar of The Compass Rose after a Saturday shift, even without a burning need to know where the hell he'd been for a year. Perhaps promotion had redirected some of her innate nosiness into more necessary channels. Or another sign of reticence.

Lights still off, Stark closed his door, set his keys down gently in the bowl on his kitchenette counter and stood a moment in the stillness.

Street light crept in through the balcony sliding doors, street noise whispering behind. His little pocket of privacy. No Kelly cluttering his world with her chaos and light. No Pensol, passed out on the sofa. No one but him. His natural state, turned unnatural by reckless forays into the lives of others. Ghostly eddies of warmth in his chill refuge. Sanctuary turned strange; the stale air of a tomb sealed shut for a full rotation around the sun.

Probably too many poetry books on the shelf.

He glanced at the antique walking cane, hanging on its hook by the front door, with its royal history and hidden sting. Like everything else in the flat, neatly in its place. Apart from his kitbag on the floor where he'd dumped it in the early hours this morning.

He should unpack. Wash desert dust and sweat from worn clothing. Begin the process of filing away the blood and tears in his worn mind. Cultural linguistics placed the past behind and the future ahead, but there was a difference between past and passed. Stark's past was always present, inescapable – carried forward in ever-increasing mass, pressing down on every thought and step. There was no reset, only recollection; grinding to the grave.

Cheery.

Puffing out his cheeks, he flicked the light on.

Leaving the bag, he tried calling Gabrielle. She'd cut through his maudlin nonsense. But the mobile coverage out there was patchy on a good day, forcing him to leave a message. Safe home, et cetera.

A message was better for now. She'd demand reassurance that he was coming back out to her, to the 'real work'. Lucinda Drummond's family might insist policework was real too. Stark's opinion, were he not too tired to form one, seemed frivolous. Immediate immersion in a serious case hadn't factored in his plans. The road ahead was never clear, but one thing always seemed true, every fork presented a decision on who to let down.

Talking of which, there was an email on his phone from Major Pierson, checking he was back in Blighty, checking he was ready for their appointment, checking he wasn't going to dick her around like the colossal pain in her arse he was – to paraphrase.

Ignoring it, he opened a kitchen drawer to peruse the selection of takeaway menus, but eating alone now felt somehow pointless. Exhausting. Opening a cupboard instead, he stared at the two whisky bottles. The half-full Royal Lochnagar Selected Reserve Highland Single Malt for rare celebration, and the half-empty cheap blend for everyday rumination.

He poured three fingers of the latter into a tumbler, necked it, and called his mother.

The usual blend of theatrical surprise and relief, admonition, and demands to know when he would visit. 'Have you called Kelly?'

'Before calling you . . . ?'

'Before it's too late. Now you're back . . .'

'I've moved on, Mum.'

'To your doctor friend? You said that was just a casual thing.' She managed to not make *casual* sound sordid.

'Kelly moved on to her own doctor friend, remember. I don't know why you're still banging on this drum.'

'I don't know why you're not.'

Because sometimes you had to face the reality that someone could stay in your heart but not in your life. He could never fully explain the reasons to his mother, without worrying her more, though she was no fool to his holding back. Eventually extracting himself, he went through round two with his sister, Louise, who at least had the decency to complain almost as much about her husband and children as she did about her brother.

Duty done, he poured three fingers more, slid the balcony door open enough to let the sounds and smells of London wash over him in the cooling breeze, pulled the army blanket from its wooden chest, and crashed out on the sofa, thinking of blue sky, laughing brown eyes and warm ebony skin . . . but drifting into dreams of cornflower-blue eyes, soft with love, wet with tears, wide with fear and forgiveness.

6

'I didn't like this one much,' said Fran, tapping the photo of Alex Zedani on the board, cradling her umpteenth coffee of the morning. 'Too cool by half.'

Stark let his eyes roam over all one hundred and forty-one photos, with names and mini-bios jotted beneath. Ninety-nine party guests on the left; staff on the right, subdivided into the Queen's House event manager with her twenty-three staff, and the external catering manager with his seventeen. All taken the night before, with varying degrees of cooperation. Expressions from weary, through alarmed, to downright cross at being lined up for identification and mugshots. But it was the only hope the police had of tracking everyone across the building's thirty CCTV cameras. None on the Tulip Stairs or in the undercroft, of course. The universe usually sided with DCI Groombridge and all army training officers in the opinion that nothing worthwhile ever came easy – to paraphrase some more. Otherwise what would be the point of underlings? 'Shall I take all these other photos down then?' he asked.

Few people could pull off a glare and eye-roll as comprehensively as Fran. 'Well, who's your money on?'

'I'll take the butler.'

'Hilarious.'

But the point remained. There was, so far, nothing

42

solid to elevate any individual to the level of suspect. That would take meticulous sifting and/or blind luck. This was Fran's least favourite part of any investigation. She'd want to be doing something, chasing down leads, haranguing informants, interrogating suspects. Interviewing witnesses would do, but times one hundred and forty-one . . . Stark suspected her frustration would boil over soon into double figures.

The second board had the timeline and mind map of salient information, in Fran's neat lettering, though the picture taking shape thus far remained fuzzy at best. She'd made no move to pass the marker-baton to her new sergeant, and Stark wasn't going to ask. Underlined twice with an exclamation point was the TOD window. That, combined with CCTV, was adding to the number of photos with a black marker dot beneath – those in sight the whole time. Sixty-two so far. Red dots indicated those out of sight during some or all of the window – several staff and nine guests, so far. The rest either had no dot yet, or a question mark where the footage on them was unclear. Follow-up interviews would hopefully confirm which of the catering staff were in the kitchen the whole time. On the night, their manager had been adamant they were all too busy to slip away and murder a guest, but he'd been too worried to be reliable.

And that was all still assuming no external assassin had somehow slipped in and out. With cameras covering every door and both ends of the tunnel, that seemed impossible.

'Needle in a poxy haystack,' muttered Fran.

Not for the first time, Stark wondered what he was doing here, a cog in the needle-hunting machine, with all life's complications, far from the simplicities of sun and war. A certain shrink he knew would have an opinion on that last sentiment.

Fran blew out a breath. 'Right, well, Family Liaison need someone from the investigation team at the body ID so we can green light the post-mortem. Sounds like a detective sergeant kind of job.'

Stark blinked. 'You don't want to go?' Before Stark had left, Fran would surreptitiously volunteer herself should any visit to the Home Office mortuary be required. Stark had no idea if her clandestine relationship with Marcus Turner was still a thing. He didn't imagine being Fran's secret boyfriend was a position many could long endure, but if anyone had the spine and humour for it, it just might be the unflappable pathologist.

She ignored any inference. 'I'm far too important now.'

'So the rumours were *true* . . .' Marcus glanced up from his grisly work on someone's mortal remains. 'The prodigal returns.'

'Trumpets sound and flowers spring from my footsteps,' replied Stark.

'So I've heard. Belated congratulations, Detective *Sergeant*.' Marcus held up his nitrile gloves in habitual apology for not shaking hands. 'Good to have you back. Got a bit of sun, from the look of you. Sea as well as sand?' he asked, meaningfully. He'd taken voluntary turns of his own in the sun and sand of UK Army Camp Bastion Field Hospital in the past. Stark had never asked the degree to which such experiences had driven Marcus to turn his medical skills to pathology. The dead didn't

44

scream and thrash, bleed out, or cling imploringly to lives beyond saving or forever impaired.

'Plenty of entertainment,' replied Stark.

Marcus let it go at that. 'Straight back in the deep end then.'

'There's a shallow end?'

'One hears rumours.' Marcus smiled, phlegmatically. 'Drummond ID?'

'A DS's job, according to my new DI.'

'Eager for a preview, I expect?'

'You know Fran.'

'If one can claim to know another in life,' smiled Marcus, giving nothing away. 'Or in death. But Lucinda Drummond is next up, if you want to stick around for the grisly bit?'

'Sounds delightful. What's the skinny so far?'

'Temperature-determined time of death coincides. Scratches and sub-dermal haemorrhages on the forearms I pointed out to Fran at the scene, consistent with grappling defence. Another on the upper right hip; size, height and angle consistent with impact with the stair balustrade.'

'Possible defensive marks, plus silent fall, makes it more likely pushed than tripped?'

Marcus gave a facial shrug. 'Assuming my investigations exclude cardiac arrest or stroke – though the impact damage may mask the latter – both of which could also account for silence. And in the apparent absence of an impact or knife to the throat, or strategic stab to the diaphragm or lungs.'

'Decent punch to the guts is enough,' commented Stark. 'Can't scream winded.'

Marcus looked at him. Their army training had been along very different lines. 'I'll double-check for signs.' Glancing at the clock, he pulled the sheet up over the corpse and peeled off his gloves, cap and gown into the clinical waste bin just as his assistant appeared to signal the arrival of today's audience.

'So, at best, involuntary manslaughter, at worst, murder,' said Stark, following.

'That's your department. This bit, sadly, is mine,' added Marcus entering the brightly sunlit reception to greet the FLO, Reynolds, hovering with Libby and Ryan Drummond, plus another man Stark recognized as Adrian Fairchild. He looked different in the flesh to his photo on Fran's board, Friday night's shock replaced with Sunday's fatigue. He looked like he'd barely slept a wink more than the siblings. Hard to get the image of a murdered friend out of one's mind.

But the most striking change was the puffy bruising and closed cut beneath his left eye.

Reynolds introduced Libby and Ryan Drummond to Marcus, leaving Stark aside, keeping it simple. Fairchild hung back too, turning to offer a hand for Stark to shake. 'Adrian Fairchild. Offering what support I can,' he explained. 'Known them since they were born. Can't believe they have this to go through. Heartbreaking.'

'DS Stark.'

'Oh, yes . . .' Fairchild's good eye widened in recognition. 'The one from the news last year. And before that, of course. I thought I'd read you'd *left* the police?'

'Just a sabbatical.'

Fairchild nodded. 'Don't blame you. Awful business. Your girlfriend caught up in it too? Terrible.'

That pretty much summed it up, apart from the girlfriend bit. 'Been in the wars yourself?'

Fairchild felt his injured left eye, with a wince. 'Slipped in the shower. Can hardly sleep or clear my head, after . . .' He rubbed at his temples, suggesting a headache on top of his woes. 'Will you catch whoever did this?'

Stark watched the bereaved offspring talking to Marcus. 'We'll try.'

'But isn't it true that half of all homicides go unsolved?' asked Fairchild in a low voice, so Libby and Ryan might not hear.

Less than a third, in London at least, but it used to be one *ninth*. Who would've thought yearly police funding cuts might result in less policing? Stark didn't share this insight with Fairchild. 'We do better than some people think.'

The academic watched him for something more reassuring.

Marcus came to Stark's rescue. 'This way . . .'

They followed.

The awful formalities unfolded.

The room with the glass panel. The curtain pulled back like the worst possible theatrical opening night. Marcus's careful masking of the worst damage. The nods, the tears, the directionless recriminations. The forms to sign. Both siblings glancing at Stark. Libby's eyes demanding answers he could not give. Ryan's demanding retribution he could not promise.

47

Fairchild wiped the tears from his own eyes and led them out.

'Never gets any easier,' said Marcus, watching them leave with Reynolds. 'Nor should it, I suppose. All we can do is try to provide answers.'

Indeed, thought Stark, letting out a long breath. Too little. Too late.

'What do you mean, they're not here?' fumed Fran.

The catering company owner shrugged apologetically. 'Many of our staff are casual, augmenting their incomes around whatever else they do. We keep a broad book. Some of them are better at picking up their phones than others.'

'But you told them to keep themselves available.'

'I did, but it's Sunday. Maybe they didn't want the money. Those that *are* here are expecting me to pay for their time,' complained the manager.

'We appreciate you doing your civic duty.' Fran smiled thinly over her irritation. She'd come to the caterer's premises to interview seventeen staff, not fifteen, and to rub it in even more, the manager failed to quail before her ire as much as she would like. 'Tyrone Pook and Nathan Goff?'

'Drivers and loaders. Tyrone's okay but hardly the sharpest tool in the box. Nathan's just a tool. Work-shy. Barely reliable.'

'We'll need their contact details.'

When the manager looked hesitant, she reiterated that this was a murder investigation, not a social call. The manager made the mistake of glancing at Dixon, as if seeking a higher, *male* authority. Fran could bristle with the best.

'Unless you'd like to come down the station for a conversation about obstruction?'

That cut through his male prejudice.

The subsequent interviews took time. Carefully cross-checking who was where, doing what. Five of the staff hadn't left the kitchen. One of the museum staff had already confirmed remaining with them. The catering manager and five others were identifiably serving drinks from a trestle bar in the Great Hall throughout the TOD window, under the watchful eye of the event manager.

A further five catering staff came and went with platters of canapés, taking the main *non-tulip* staircase to and from the kitchen. Leaving aside today's two non-attendees, Goff and Pook – whose sole purpose seemed to be to drive, load, unload and otherwise just sit in the main catering van – those present today insisted they'd diverted nowhere else, apart from the WCs, or outside for a smoke or vape, and the TOD window was their busiest period. It would've been hard for them to slip away, with the rest of the museum staff stationed throughout the museum, directing guests to the WCs, and in readiness for guiding them through a building packed with priceless artefacts after Lucinda's speech. All on camera.

Fran would not be alone in wishing there'd been a camera on the Tulip Stairs or in the adjacent corridor. The killer was either lucky or observant.

Fran scribbled the maths on the corner of her pad. So far it appeared all twenty-four museum staff were accounted for. The catering manager and ten of his staff too. The five canapés profferers were each in the hall for most or part of the TOD window.

Inconclusive.

Time for background checks.

Starting with Tyrone Pook and Nathan Goff.

'Right,' said Marcus, snapping his gloves into place. 'Let's take a look then.'

It was cold in the room, with a background scent that might remind most people of a butcher's shop but reminded Stark of darker places. Squeamishness wasn't his problem; more its lack. He'd seen too much death to be repulsed.

He stared at the mortal remains of Lucinda Claire Drummond. Not the mother carefully arranged for identification, with her worst injuries tastefully masked for the grieving family, but the cold corpse, bare and broken, laid out for forensic scrutiny. Stark saw only indignity, and theft – of vitality, hope, happiness, future, of mother and friend. The most unforgivable of crimes, beyond restoration or reparation. One he himself had committed in the crucible of war – fathers, sons, brothers. All combatants – a debatable distinction, but real to any soldier.

He imagined her doubled-up, gasping, desperately scrabbling to fend off her attacker, shoved over the balustrade and plunging in silent, breathless terror towards inevitable death, imagining all the years she might have lived – the works, experiences, relationships and love she'd been robbed of. You'd think he'd be used to death by now. That the lives he'd seen lost and taken himself would long since have inured him to this deep sadness and indignation.

They hadn't.

The heinous banality of murder boiled his blood.

In his role as spectator the next two hours of Stark's life would not linger in the memory with any fondness, as Marcus and his assistant went about their business with professional detachment, speaking jargonese for the benefit of the recording throughout.

'Well,' said Marcus eventually, straightening up to acknowledge Stark for the first time since the ordeal began. 'So, to summarize: in fine fettle for her fifty-seven years on this earth. Fit. Healthy. Non-smoker. Heart of a regular runner. Liver of someone with a balanced relationship with alcohol. No indication of drug use. No history of mental illness, anxiety or depression. No prescription medications other than HRT following peri-menopausal onset eight years ago. No indications of poison ingestion, injection or absorption. No obvious signs of violence, aside from the possible defensive wounds to the forearms.'

Stark took his cue. 'No *obvious* signs . . . ?'

'Indeed,' said Marcus. 'Nothing under the nails to suggest fighting back. Mild ligament damage to the left ankle suggests twisting, high heels on a stone stair possibly. And here,' he said, pointing to a graze on the hip, 'angle and shape consistent with the stair handrail, suggesting impact with rather than climbing over. All supposition, of course. Catastrophic damage to the skull, skeletal structures and upper internals; impacting the floor with the rear-right head and shoulder. Cause of death massive brain damage, broken neck, ruptured aorta, heart and lung damage,' he recited, as if dictating a shopping list. 'Floor-induced sudden deceleration trauma. Quick at least.'

'And the *un*-obvious signs?'

Marcus pointed to the belly. 'Not sure I'd have spotted it without your lead. The belly tends to dissipate impacts, reducing bruising, especially post-mortem development, and the internal bleeding pooled into the cavity, but some subcutaneous capillary damage here,' he said, pointing to where a flap of skin had been temporarily peeled back, 'appears to confirm the hypothesis of blunt force trauma.'

'With?'

'Impossible to be sure, but if you wanted to, you might interpret a pattern consistent with the bony prominences of a fist.'

'But not conclusively?'

'No.'

'Man's or woman's?'

'I couldn't say. I might request a second opinion from a colleague in the US who's conducted some research into this, see if they might offer firmer conclusions.'

'But, for now, she may have twisted an ankle on the stairs. She definitely hit the handrail hard, so may have toppled over, and she was struck in the belly, but we can't say punched.'

Marcus smiled, guessing how unhelpful Fran would find the news. 'Good luck with the boss.'

7

Fran shot the messenger a look of displeasure in response to his inconclusive report.

Stark shrugged, knowing that annoyed her. Funny how much he'd missed this.

She made no enquiry into the health or otherwise of a certain forensic pathologist she may or may not have a romantic interest in. Further speculation on that front seemed frivolous as Stark added Lucinda Drummond's latest photo shoot to the board. The Y-shape incision from shoulders to belly, the defensive marks, the hip bruise and, for what it was worth, the 'subcutaneous capillary damage' that may or may not signify a punch to the guts – none of which delivered any certainty about what happened, let alone who was responsible.

During their absence, Williams had managed to add a few more black dots to the board of ninety-nine guest photos. Fran's return added the same beneath most of the staff.

Tyrone Pook and Nathan Goff's photos soon got red dots.

CCTV showed them leaving their van and going inside during the TOD window, and it didn't stop there. Checks showed both had received youth cautions for shoplifting, with Goff graduating to six months in a Young Offender Institution and being flagged up as a person of interest in a number of unsolved burglaries and one mugging as an adult. Stark decided to take their photos downstairs.

'I was beginning to think reported sightings of you yesterday were marsh gas or weather balloons!' exclaimed Sergeant Ptolemy when he saw Stark.

'He's too important now to visit us below-stairs types,' suggested Constable Peters.

Nick Ptolemy and Jane Peters. Seemingly inseparable. A platonic romance worthy of much station jocularity, and bearing consistent professional dividends. Both happily married outside work, by all accounts – presumably to saints. British police didn't really have 'partners' like their American cousins, but it was widely recognized that Ptolemy and Peters were the station's pre-eminent team in uniform.

Stark looked apologetic. 'You know I'm not one for emotional hellos.'

'Or *goodbyes*,' protested Peters. 'Where the hell have you been? Sunning yourself in Tahiti while the rest of us sweep streets, no doubt. And then you swan back in without a word, with a *beard* and *DS card*! We really need to work on your communication skills.'

Ptolemy ignored his colleague's verbal incontinence and shook Stark by the hand. 'Good to have you back, wherever you've been. Marianne will be glad to see you. She's out on a training day.'

Constable Marianne Pensol, rookie to Peters' mentor, as Peters had been to Ptolemy. The only other person Stark had texted before leaving. But after what she'd witnessed, he wasn't at all sure she'd be as glad to see him back as Ptolemy assumed. It took several more minutes of banter and gentle avoidance of Peters' prying to get the subject off himself.

'See, like I said, too lofty to stray below-stairs unless he needs something,' joked Peters.

'Don't know this Pook,' said Ptolemy, looking at the photos. 'But Nathan Goff . . . I had him for shoplifting and vandalism when he was thirteen or fourteen. Wouldn't learn his lesson. Young Offenders Team tried, but . . . I remember his mum's face when Nathan got a spell in YO. Came out of it worse than he went in, as so many do. Questioned repeatedly as an adult, but never enough to charge him, slippery sod. What's he done now?'

Stark rubbed his whiskers, in thought. 'Proximity to a possible murder, and failure to turn up to work.'

Groombridge frowned at the two photos promoted to the top of the board, above the other red dots. 'Prime suspects?'

'*Only* suspects, so far, really,' admitted Fran.

'Ptolemy didn't fancy Goff for murder,' said Stark. 'Strictly small time. And Pook has no adult flags. But CCTV shows them out of their van, heading inside, for twelve minutes during the TOD window.'

Groombridge nodded. Ptolemy generally knew his stuff. 'Any sign?'

'Left them voicemails,' replied Fran. 'If they don't call back tonight, I'll ask uniform to knock on their doors in the morning. Failing that, family and friends.'

'And failing that, the press,' sighed Groombridge.

'Persons of interest?'

He shook his head. Too soon. 'Help with inquiries. If they don't materialize. Other red dots?'

'Nine and counting. I want to finish the footage analysis to be sure, before we re-interview.'

Groombridge nodded again. Patience was a new look on Fran. Experience overcoming instinct. Stark's influence too, perhaps. He'd waited too long to get them both to this point. If only Joe would stick around long enough to let this grow into what it should. They both looked tired and wired. The look of real detectives at the end of a long day – sensing the edges of the jigsaw taking shape but dissatisfied with progress. 'Forensics?'

'We've got fresh victim's fingerprints on the stair handrails near the top, but no one else's recent,' said Fran. 'Hairs, fibres and the usual dirt collected from her clothes et cetera, but nothing to compare them with yet. No sign of a break-in at her home, and we've caught no intruder on camera. It has to be one of this lot.'

Groombridge looked at all the photos. 'And you like this guy, Zedani, because he was polite and self-assured?'

'You know how that rubs me up the wrong way,' replied Fran, eyes darting pointedly at Stark. The list of personality types that rubbed Fran up the wrong way was long, and Stark somehow managed to fit most. 'And who brings their trophy PA and bodyguard to a museum exhibition?'

'They alibi each other?'

Fran gave a for-what-that's-worth gesture. 'Zedani went outside for a vape and phone call, but was out of camera shot for a while.'

'But they were together the whole time.'

'So they say. All innocent, or all in it together.' Fran

shrugged and tapped another photo. 'Didn't much like this one either.'

Groombridge peered closer at Adrian Fairchild. 'Too upset at the murder of his oldest friend? Too nice to her kids . . . ?'

'Man outshone by younger woman and previous underling,' suggested Fran.

'Something, I suppose,' admitted Groombridge.

'Looks a bit more mugshot-classic today,' added Stark. 'Left eye shiner with cut beneath. Slipped in the shower, he says. Lack of sleep.'

Welcome to the club, thought Groombridge, silently. 'Better keep sifting the rest. See if we can't find someone with a stronger motive.'

Fran nodded, disconsolately. 'Pub?'

Groombridge made an apologetic face. 'Paperwork.'

Fran looked to Stark. 'Pub?'

He mirrored the DCI's expression. 'Shrink.'

'Logistics and security?' said Dr Hazel MacDonald, clinical psychotherapist, long-suffering, trying to decide between incredulity and exasperation. 'For Médecins Sans Frontières? In Libya?'

'Yes.' Concision was Stark's therapy default.

'Where they are having another civil war?'

'They need doctors.'

'Who need logistics and security?'

'More than ever.'

'And a regular year out, travelling, wouldn't do?'

'Goa, tie-dye and finding myself . . . ?' he scoffed.

Good point. If there was anyone in the world more

solidly rooted in himself than Joseph Stark, Hazel had yet to meet them. He had a fixedness that defied life's floods to part around him, for all they pummelled him in their elemental vexation.

The effect of his penchant for dark poetry was obviously back too.

She resisted the urge to stretch her back. Managing her thoughts through a long day of back-to-back appointments sometimes forced her to sit too stiffly. She was, to be frank, bored with most of her current crop. It had taken a lot of work to achieve this, with the particular goal in mind of a long-awaited holiday.

And now Joseph Stark was back. By far her least boring patient. Whose idea of a holiday was clearly somewhat different to hers.

He'd disappeared over a year ago, after the latest traumatic impact on his cratered life, with just a short text.

Going away for a bit. Look after Kelly and Pensol for me. Cheers, Doc.

His parting thoughts had been for Kelly, his ex, and Pensol, a colleague. Both collateral damage in the universe's apparent grudge against him. The last she'd heard from him until another text this morning on a new number.

Hey, Doc. It's Stark. New phone. Back in town. Not sure how long. Could use a tune-up. Can you fit me in?

Booked solid, she'd typed back. *How urgent?*

She skipped any pointless enquiry or admonishment. For him to request a 'tune-up' could signal an ominous creak in his emotional dam, and she didn't want to put him off. He was probably her most reluctant patient too. In his world, help was something given, not asked for, and sympathy was for the devil. But he turned up anyway, did the work in his own way, took his medicine, because it had to be done – because the only thing more unconscionable than offloading your shit on someone else was surrender.

You tell me. Anyone else might've added a wink-face emoji, but not Stark. Answering questions with questions was the tool of her job he mocked the most.

Ha ha.

Download backlog. Crossroads looming, he'd replied.

Stark's downloads were never boring, and his crossroads often existential, so here they were, face to face again, as the setting sun poetically cast the walls of her sanctuary blood red.

May you live in interesting times, went the ancient Chinese curse.

During the course of their relationship, she'd watched him fight and rail through the stages of grief, depression, heartbreak, two hospitalizations and worse. She'd seen him taut with fury, lean from over-exertion, and a heartbeat away from death. But sitting before her now, he appeared . . . relaxed – by his standards – tanned, healthy even. No sign of his walking stick and little evidence of his limp. The kind of transformation normal people might only achieve with weeks of pampering in some spa resort. Hazel recalled the tattoo on his right shoulder. A tiger at rest was still a tiger.

'Perhaps not,' she conceded.

'Call it escapism,' he added, with a sly smile, knowing she'd enjoy the provocation.

Plenty of holiday destinations had nightlife, beer and girls, but he could get those at home. 'Some people might say what you call escapism amounts to an existential crisis.'

'Or a death wish.'

Another provocation. 'No. You passed that point atop that clocktower, a year and a half ago.' And the crow he'd added afterwards to his left shoulder stood as testament to that, in his skewed way. A watcher, for both darkness *and* light.

'So you insist,' he replied, though he knew she was right. 'Another classic symptom of survivor's guilt then?'

It always did come back to that. 'I suppose what matters, as ever, is what you'd call it?' A question for a question.

He smiled. Perhaps he'd missed her too. 'Making myself useful?'

'You don't feel useful here, in everyday life?'

'Would you call my life *everyday*?'

'A matter of degrees, I suppose.' Trauma victims sometimes talked of relearning how to live a normal life. Stark's version seemed to be to take each new normal as it confronted him, bloody but unbowed. If not master of his fate, he would damn well remain captain of his soul. 'As is being useful. Something you needed to be, but couldn't here.'

He allowed his face to concede the point. 'I needed a change of scene.'

'That, I understand,' conceded Hazel in return. 'But you've been away over a year.'

'I was benched temporarily, after the shooting. After that, I took a sabbatical.'

The press had recorded that 'Officer X' had been cleared in the subsequent hearing, the shooting declared to be in legitimate defence of life. 'How did Fran take that?' Hazel couldn't help a smile at the thought.

'I texted her just before take-off, then turned my phone off.'

'For a year?'

'I let her know I was okay, from time to time.'

'But not where you were.'

'She's a worrier.'

She certainly took an excessive interest in other people's business, thought Hazel, who believed Fran would make nearly as *interesting* a patient as Stark. 'She forgiven you yet?'

'Catches yet to manifest.'

'And Kelly? You drop her the occasional sit-rep too?'

He didn't look away in shame. That wasn't his way. He wore his shame inside. 'Clean break. She's safer with the good doctor.'

His voice betrayed none of the pain that sentence surely cost him. Kelly's safety took precedence over his happiness – and it seemed, from what Kelly had confessed, hers too. On paper, Dr Robert Laithwaite seemed a better prospect than the much-damaged man of duty sat here, but Stark had taken the decision out of Kelly's hands.

'They're still together?'

He shrugged. 'Online stalking's hardly my thing.' He didn't do social media at all, even before the Media-with-a-capital-M targeted what little privacy he still clung to. But he must ache to know, for all his pious self-denial. 'She didn't say anything to you? After . . . ?'

After being abducted into the twisted games of a monster. Or after her knight in shining armour stepped aside before she could tell him she still loved him. 'She declined a follow-up. Adamant you needed me more than she did.'

Stark sat back. 'I hope that's true.'

'She's as stubborn as you are.' Made for each other, Hazel didn't add.

He nodded all the same. 'The hardest part is admitting you need help, right?'

Indeed. Plenty to circle back on there. 'Well,' Hazel said, with a deep breath. 'I suppose that's a start on the download backlog. What about *crossroads looming*? London law enforcement versus Libyan logistics?'

'That's about the sum of it.'

'And the thing you're not telling me?' Getting to the heart of the matter was never quick in their sessions. Part obstinacy, part amusement. Always reasons within reasons, like the concentric walls of a castle – any single cause enough for therapy in most people.

'I could be down the pub with colleagues right now.'

'But instead, you came here for a tune-up.'

He looked out the window for a moment, his expression faraway and sad, then down with a sigh. 'Remember Major Pierson?'

Hazel did. And her reappearance in Stark's life spelled trouble, as Stark now confirmed. So much for the universe leaving him be. 'You're right,' she admitted. 'Your life isn't normal.'

He sighed deeply. 'Not by choice.'

That half-truth followed Stark all the way out from Hazel's sanctum into the evening air.

Like it or not, his choices had contributed to the

62

outcomes he'd both endured and inflicted on others. To bleat about one was to deny the other. Perhaps blithe abstention was the only path to a carefree life, but he couldn't countenance the waste. The obliviousness.

Of course, one of the outcomes to be endured included the truth of Fran's prediction that the crappy old Ford Fiesta he'd used a year ago would be the only option available to him out of the station's limited pool of unmarked cars.

It wasn't a nice blue. It wasn't electric blue or cobalt, metallic, or even good old-fashioned navy blue; it was *meh* blue. A fitting reminder of Fran's demand for commitment from him. And if he needed any other assurance of karmic imbalance, a call from the station as he pulled into the basement parking beneath his block of flats put paid to hopes of a relaxing takeaway and an early night.

'Maggie?' Matriarch of the station control room, who prided herself on knowing just about everything first, and finding out the rest by fair means or foul.

'That you, sweetie?' Harmless flirtation was her default setting.

'In the flesh.'

'No point buttering me up with innuendo, mister. Gone – with no goodbye or so much as a postcard. You're still in my bad books.'

You and everyone else's, he nearly replied. 'I'll make it up to you.'

'That's what they always say,' she sighed, theatrically. 'But then it's straight back to take, take, take.'

'The lament of the vast-hearted, Maggie. And are you calling to give, give, give?'

'See . . . ?'

'Box of choccies and a bunch of flowers?'

'Promises, promises . . .'

'And in the meantime?'

'In the meantime, I thought you might like to know who we have in the drunk tank.'

8

Cell Six. Royal Hill's designated drunk tank, on the happy occasion when only one was needed. Farthest from the custody sergeant's desk. Close enough to hear the singing, abuse or vomiting, far enough to diminish the smell. After a look through the peep-hole, confirming that Nathan Goff was going for the hat-trick and they'd get nothing else from him, Stark had reviewed the arrest sheet, called to inform Fran, and gone home to bed.

Now it was Fran's turn. Goff hardly looked pleasant company this morning either, slouched in Interview Room One with sweet tea and a bacon butty, nursing a hangover and a grudge. Picked up by uniform, staggering across busy roads, yelling abuse at drivers, after being ejected from a local pub for getting rowdy. Now sober and sullen.

To make matters better, however, uniform had also brought in his partner in work-absenteeism, Tyrone Pook, alarmed to find two coppers knocking on his door at sunrise, now sat in Interview Room Two, looking pale to Goff's green.

Fran glanced at the mirrored window, picturing Stark's granite stare beyond. News of his return would leak soon enough, but exposing him to the grieving family was less risky than letting a potential suspect, with few qualms about selling a story to the press, set eyes on him.

Goff's bullish demeanour bore out Ptolemy's description. Sallow complexion, acne, cropped hair; nine stone, soaking wet. Tattoos up both arms and creeping up through the neckline of his beer- and vomit-marked Millwall T-shirt. You'd probably peg him for a racist gobshite, were his IC3 friend not stewing in the next room.

Just a gobshite then, thought Fran.

'What happened to your hand?' she asked, nodding at Goff's right knuckles, split and bruised.

'Banged it.'

'On what?'

Marcus had forwarded Stark an email from his colleague in the USA, confirming that *from visual evidence, the subcutaneous capillary damage was consistent with a punch hypothesis* – science speak for definitely maybe.

Goff shrugged. 'Dunno.'

Fran glanced at the arrest sheet: causing a disturbance, drunkenness, abuse, endangering traffic, at a push. Ejected from The Anchor pub. Didn't say anything about fighting back. She made a mental note to ask the arresting officer if they fancied affray. Stark said punching a silk-clad woman in the guts wasn't likely to split one's knuckles, but Fran had ordered swabs taken all the same. 'Listed here, among your personal effects, is nearly a thousand pounds in crisp new twenties. Rather a lot for a night out in the pub?'

'Man's got a right to splurge his hard-earned.'

'Earned . . .' Fran wrote the word down on her pad, with a question mark. 'Why didn't you show up at work yesterday, after your manager emailed you?'

'Didn't see the email.'

'Or a guilty conscience?'

'What for?'

'Murder springs to mind.'

He shifted in his seat, any nerves masked with a front of weary impatience. 'First I heard about all that was when you lot turned up and started taking names. Knew it wouldn't take you long to pick me to blame.'

'We're talking to everyone who was there.'

'Yeah,' scoffed Goff. 'How many of 'em down here under caution?'

'I read you your rights because, with the state you were in, you may not have remembered them being read to you last night.'

'So you bang me up for having a drink, then start trying to pin a murder on me.'

'No one is pinning anything on you, unless you've anything you'd like to confess?'

Silence.

'For now, we just want to hear your side of things so we can decide whether to rule you both out as suspects.'

'Both?'

'You and your friend, Tyrone. He's in the next room, waiting to speak to us voluntarily.'

The news that Tyrone was about to tell his side had the desired effect.

A momentary surprise and thoughtfulness. 'We're not that close.'

'He got you a job.'

'If you say so.'

'I'm simply repeating what your manager told me,' said Fran, evenly.

Goff just huffed.

'So why don't you talk me through the evening again.'

Goff's impatience resurfaced. 'I told you – we unloaded and waited in the van, like always.'

Fran made a small show of checking her notes. 'We have you both on camera, leaving the van and going inside at seven forty and leaving again twenty-five minutes later carrying a catering box, just one minute after the body was discovered.'

'Went in for a piss,' replied Goff, seamlessly. 'And to see if there was any scoff we could nab.'

'Had the munchies, did you?'

'The what?'

'I've heard you're partial to a surreptitious joint while you're waiting around.'

He shook his head. 'Says who? My boss? He's full of shit. Got it in for me.'

'Why?'

Goff shrugged. 'Jealous of my good looks and sex appeal, I suppose.'

'You get that a lot, I'm sure,' replied Fran, dryly. 'So you deny it?'

'Yeah. That would be unprofessional.'

'And illegal, whilst in control of a vehicle. Even a parked one.'

'Exactly.'

'And was there any scoff to nab?'

'Nah. Too early for leftovers.'

'So you went to the loo, to the makeshift kitchen, saw nothing of suspicion or note, and went back outside. And everyone else we speak to will corroborate this?'

'Co-what?'

'Confirm your story.'

'Yeah.'

'Tyrone too?'

'Well, if he doesn't, he's a liar.'

'Really? Why should he lie?' Fran let that hang in the air a moment, but Goff just shrugged again. 'People lie to hide the truth, Nathan. So what would Tyrone want to hide?'

'Nothin'. S'just an expression.'

'Hmm . . .' Fran looked thoughtful. 'Come to think of it, he did look pretty nervous when we told him you were going first. Almost like he was worried you were going to offer him up to save your own skin.'

'Bullshit,' replied Goff, crossly. 'We've done nuffin' wrong, neither of us.'

'And yet a woman is dead. Almost certainly murdered. And here's you two, on the spot, both with criminal records.'

'I ain't got no adult record. Maybe I was a bit naughty as a kid, but I seen the error of my ways, officer. Anyone says otherwise is a liar.'

'There's that word again . . . liar.' Fran jotted it down at the bottom of her notepad, beneath a long tally of largely illegible drivel, in clear capitals with an exclamation mark, underlined and circled to draw his eye. Goff knew she was fishing, but even those lacking any conscience could sometimes feel the weight of guilt. And he knew they'd be talking to Pook next. 'Well, I suppose I'll find out.' She looked up with a smile. 'I always do. Let's take it from the top, shall we . . . ?'

*

Tyrone Pook was an altogether healthier-looking specimen. Lean but filled out. Not quite handsome, but close enough for anyone willing to overlook the dullness of his eyes and wits.

Unfortunately, he *did* corroborate. Almost word for word. And claimed to know nothing of Goff's arrest or wad of cash.

'And you saw nothing out of the ordinary while you were inside Queen's House?' asked Fran again.

He shook his head.

'And you didn't see this woman?' She tapped the photo of Lucinda Drummond.

'No.'

Either he was telling the truth or he was sticking to the agreed story. He did look nervous, but innocent people did that too – the age-old problem in policework. Fran was never sure whether to blame guilty people for trying to look innocent, or everyone else for trying not to look guilty in the face of police questioning. If you arrested everyone with a guilty conscience, you'd just be weeding out the psychopaths by omission. 'Did you see any other party guests?'

'I told you, I can't remember. I don't think so, but it all went crazy after . . .'

'After this woman was found murdered, with you and your criminal-record-friend, Nathan, in the vicinity.'

'I don't know nuffin' about that, I swear. We was *outside*.'

'Not the whole time. *Not* when we believe she was killed.'

'We was *outside*, I *swear*!'

'Thing is, Tyrone, people swear things to me all the time, and as often as not they're lying. Your pal Nathan sang the same tune, and I think he was lying too. So again, any idea why he was out on the lash last night with an unusually large wad of cash in his pocket?'

Tyrone shook his head. 'No. He said something about getting some cash. Maybe he got lucky at the bookies, or sold something.'

'When did he say this? About coming into money?'

'I dunno,' said Pook, retracting. 'At work, maybe.'

'Before the night at Queen's House?'

'Yeah. Maybe.'

'Yes, or maybe?'

'I dunno.'

'Maybe after?'

'Maybe.'

'Maybe the next day?'

'Yeah, maybe, I *dunno.*'

'You saw each other the next day?'

'No.'

'You spoke on the phone?'

Tyrone looked like he'd lost his place in the script. 'I can't remember.'

'What about yesterday?'

'I can't remember.'

Fran stifled a sigh. Some criminals were genuinely too clever by half. Most thought they were cleverer than they were – a category that she'd place Nathan Goff in – but some were just too dumb to realize there was any other way to be. Tyrone Pook sucked IQ out of the room.

The pair seemed a perfect fit for a bungled robbery, but murder . . . ?

If MMO was the yardstick, the *means* was ubiquitous gravity and *opportunity* went with proximity, but Fran couldn't see the *motive*. Lucinda didn't appear to have been robbed or molested, and attempting either in their place of work seemed too stupid even for Goff and Pook.

But there was something . . . a waft of bullshit. Fran's copper's nose twitched with it. But if she wasn't sure they were killers, what *had* they done?

A few rounds of repetitive questioning unveiled nothing.

'Maybe they're guilty of nothing more serious than an occasional spliff at work,' she said afterwards, as the team rewatched the interviews.

'Or maybe they're a pair of low-life twits on the pilfer, and she confronted them,' said Williams. 'Sometimes motive is just stupidity.'

'Killed her by accident, maybe?' suggested Dixon.

'After a punch in the gut to silence her,' said Stark.

He was right. Murder or manslaughter would depend on the forensics and might ultimately come down to that point, and how persuasive the forensics proved to a jury, thought Fran, meaning trying to keep her mind away from expert-witness-extraordinaire Marcus, and the lengthening silence currently separating them.

Right now, she'd nothing on the pair of them but proximity and Goff's general shiftiness. As SIO, the next move rested with her – along with any fallout.

'Okay,' she sighed, 'get ready to release Goff on pre-charge bail, slowly, while I sound out our chances of a search warrant for both their homes. Give Pook a lift home and see if he'll voluntarily let us bag up whatever he was wearing on the night from the CCTV image. We into the victim's bank accounts yet?'

'Warrant came through last night, Boss,' replied Dixon.

'Good. See if she withdrew a grand in cash in the last few days.'

'Boss.' Williams and Dixon set to immediate compliance, as they knew she expected.

Progress-wise, things weren't especially rosy as afternoon rolled around. Lucinda's financials raised no red flags, and no thousand-pound cash withdrawl.

The catering manager and two waiters had confirmed seeing Pook and Goff on the scrounge for food, with Pook hanging around while Goff went to the loos, but that neither counted them in nor out.

Tyrone Pook was so relieved to be dropped off at home that he not only agreed to let them bag up his clothing, but also to search his flat without a warrant.

A few hours of determined cross-checking who might have seen who, and when, suggested the nine red dots might drop to six, but it would take numerous re-interviews to firm that up, and memories hardly got more reliable with time.

'He even helped us tidy up after,' said Williams later. 'I felt so bad, I almost got the Hoover out.'

'Nothing incriminating then?' asked Groombridge.

'Only of a low income and poor domestic habits, Guv.'

They all looked at each other. People with things to hide didn't wave the police into their homes unless they'd had plenty of opportunity to remove evidence first. Pook had had a day. But had he been removing anything?

'Shoes and clothing on their way to Forensics,' said Fran. 'But even he's not stupid enough to cough up his clothing if we're likely to find Lucinda Drummond's blood or hair on it. Hadn't even cleaned them.'

Nathan Goff had not been so cooperative. And Fran's warrant request had been rejected. Insufficient probable cause. Not without whittling down the other red dots some more.

They'd released him on police bail and driven him home.

He hadn't invited them in. So now he could be removing evidence.

Stark watched Fran grinding her teeth.

Groombridge subjected Fran to his *teaching-moment* look. 'So, what's next?'

9

Fran wasn't one of those people who ever paused to wonder what a museum looked like behind the scenes, because she wasn't one who ever thought of going into one.

Growing up in a large, cash-strapped, mixed-race family, attending a cash-strapped, ethnically diverse state comprehensive school in a borough historically swallowed up by London because Surrey wanted nothing more to do with it, did not ignite much fascination in historical objets d'art. Croydon had a museum, like it had a library and a town hall. A fancy cluster of red brick and stone that young Francine was barely conscious of, let alone curious about, only noticeable because it looked so out of place among the traffic, concrete and glass.

But of all the museums she'd never thought of entering, this one would've topped the list.

The vast British Museum, with its imposing spiked iron railings and classical stone columns, dominating a block of the northern West End, made everything around it look shamefully out of place. It sang of imperial power. Her ever-cheerful Jamaican father would kiss his teeth and go sniff out some back-alley joint with authentic jerk chicken, reggae and rum instead. And her white British mother had too many day-to-day problems to ponder the past. As a part-descendent of slaves, standing in the showroom of imperialist loot, Fran's

75

overriding urge was to handcuff the most senior person she could collar.

But the most senior person was dead. And here was Fran, being escorted into a labyrinthine basement by a person of interest.

She should've brought Stark.

Not that she couldn't handle herself, she thought firmly, tracing the shape of the ASP baton and pepper spray through the walls of her handbag. But Stark was . . . reassuring. Which was odd, considering the number of times she'd nearly been killed in his proximity. But, while Groombridge insisted everything was hunky-dory now Stark was in the DS slot, the team was still two DCs understaffed, with miles of legwork to cover, so she'd sent Stark to speak with the victim's kids again, now the news had settled in. He was better at that. Even so, if she didn't get some hooks into him quickly, he might disappear again. And despite an upbringing which, from the little he discussed such things, may have been even more impoverished than hers, this place would probably be the backstage pass of his geek dreams.

Too late now.

If she disappeared down here, wrapped in some mummy bandages and put on silent display in a sarcophagus, he'd blame himself like he did for everything else; so at least there was that.

'This way . . .' Adrian Fairchild held a door open for her and followed her through.

Having him behind her gave her the shivers, and she stood aside until he was again leading the way.

He'd met her in the imposing central, glass-roofed

Great Court, with a welcoming smile, but there was something irksome in the way he'd led her into the restricted zones. A little proprietary smugness, which did little to dispel the suspicion that Lucinda's demise might be the perfect way to reopen the debate about whether the somewhat *less* public face of the resident Curator of Ancient Currency was just the person to fill her shoes in this troubled time.

Though it had to be said that, right now, he hardly looked the face of respectable dependability.

The bruised face Stark had reported had begun its imitation of the colour chromatography experiment she only remembered from school because she'd seen too many black eyes since. 'A slip, you said?' asked Fran.

'In the shower,' he shook his head at himself. 'Stupid. I've not been sleeping well, since . . . as if the headaches weren't bad enough.'

'Your fingers too?' She nodded to the man's left hand, with the pinkie and ring finger splinted together. Stark hadn't mentioned that.

Fairchild looked at his hand, despondently. 'Hurt myself worse that I'd realized. Numb, I suppose. But it really started hurting last night. Went to A&E this morning.'

He did look exhausted.

Of course, guilt and fear of arrest could keep someone up just as effectively as grief or an injured hand.

A 'staff only' door and a flight of stairs brought them down to a very different face of power. Had she ever tried to imagine it, this is what it would have looked like. A maze of narrow, artificially lit corridors, countless doors with numbers and nameplates and a million more bits of other people's history, removed, categorized, labelled and stashed away.

Fairchild's office at least had some natural light, albeit from a high, grimy window. Every other inch of wall was shelving with glazed wooden doors, containing books she probably couldn't understand and objects she couldn't name.

Next time, she thought, you're coming to my gaff. Interview Room One.

'So,' he said as they settled either side of his desk, 'how can I help?'

'I just need to go over your movements. Help us eliminate you from our lines of inquiry.'

His face said he would like that.

His answers aligned with those given on the night. He'd been at Queen's House most of the day, double-checking the exhibits, security procedures and arrangements for the opening, after a busy week's installation. He'd joined the English Heritage exhibition coordinator to greet the chief patron, Mr Zedani, and treat him to a private tour. Then he'd taken part in greeting the main body of guests, though schmoozing wasn't much in his skill set. He'd checked in with Lucinda when she arrived, to make sure she had everything she needed, but then left her to it. After a brief spell of butterfly small talk with some of the guests, he'd retreated outside for air. It had been a gruelling week, and a glass of champagne had worsened rather than relieved his habitual headache. He blamed himself for not knowing better. He blamed himself for not being inside when it happened, and not staying with Lucinda throughout. He grew emotional as he spoke. He still looked tired. Frayed.

'We have you on CCTV appearing outside via the door used by the caterers, off the main basement corridor, several minutes before the body was found, but there was a period of time between you leaving the Great Hall and appearing outside. Sixteen minutes, in fact. Long enough for murder.'

He didn't look shocked at the accusation, nor particularly appalled, just dismissive. 'You can't possibly believe that.'

'It doesn't matter what I believe at this stage. I'm paid to suspect.'

'The scientific method,' he smiled. 'Theorize, test, surmise. Perhaps our jobs are alike in that regard.'

'And there was more than one reason a person might need some air.'

'I popped into the loos down there on the way.'

'For sixteen minutes.'

'I was feeling unwell. My head. Occupational hazard of the workaholic, I've come to accept. Cool water on my face and closing my eyes for a while sometimes helps. A toilet cubicle is often the handiest refuge.'

Fran sometimes found the same herself, but usually to stop her head exploding with rage. 'But from my perspective, you were unaccounted for, within easy reach of the Tulip Stairs, at the time of death.'

Fairchild's face fell. 'I've thought the same thing, over and over. That if I'd just gone that way, looked in on Lucinda to ask how her speech was ... I might have prevented . . . but she preferred to be in her own space at such times, and my head was bad. I just didn't *think* . . .'

Fran kept her face impassive, aiming for inscrutable. Sixteen minutes. So far, it appeared that most people who'd used the toilets had done so on arrival, when dropping off coats and bags at the adjacent cloakroom. Right now, Williams and Dixon were following up with the museum and catering staff, with photos of the guests who still had red dots. After that, they'd have to do the same with the guests themselves. Fran really didn't know what to make of Fairchild, but the footage showed him pacing up and down outside, then leaning his back against the wall, rubbing both temples with his fingers. A man with a bad head perhaps. Or a man agitated by what he'd just done.

He shifted uncomfortably in the silence. 'I . . . I still can't believe this is happening. I keep thinking she'll knock on the door, with her glasses on her head and pencil through her hair. It's unfathomable. Such a . . . *waste*.' He looked up at Fran, as if remembering himself. 'And the kids . . . Libby, Ryan. *Awful*.'

'You're close?'

'Not especially. There was a time, I suppose. But they're grown now. But I've known them since before they were born.'

'It was good of you to escort them to the pathologist.'

'Least I could do. I'm godfather to Libby. More in the birthday and Christmas presents and look-out-for-my-kids-if-anything-happens-to-me way than anything churchy. Neither of us subscribed to theistic nonsense, but Lucinda was a meticulous planner. Covering the bases, to use the baseball idiom. One never thinks tragedy will actually strike, until it does, I suppose. So here I am. Lucinda's insurance policy. Though how on earth am I supposed to help them with this?'

A rhetorical question. One Fran had little answer to.

'I understand they're waiting for the body to be released before they can arrange the funeral,' said Fairchild. 'Any idea when that might be?'

'There'll be an inquest. In murder cases that can take weeks.' More often months, she didn't add. In the worst cases, years. 'Has there been any talk here about who gets her job?'

Fairchild looked briefly appalled. 'There's been an emergency board meeting. They'll appoint an interim, I expect. Leave the bigger decision until after things have quietened down.'

'Might it be you?'

'I suppose. I'm trying not to think about it. Right now, I'm just trying to make preparations in case the board and insurers decide the Queen's House exhibition should be cancelled.'

Fran couldn't tell whether cancelling or pressing on appalled him more. A black eye and busted fingers might not recommend him overly to the board, but to all outward appearances, he seemed the very model of grief. She also couldn't decide what it was about him that she didn't trust. Then again, that was pretty much how she felt about everyone.

Fran placed photos of Nathan Goff and Tyrone Pook on the desk. 'Do you recognize either of these men?'

Fairchild looked closely. 'No. No, I don't think so. Are

they suspects?' he asked, looking again, as if willing it to be them.

'We're narrowing down our lines of inquiry.'

'Can you tell me anything about how the investigation is going?'

'No,' she said, levelly. 'I think that will do for now. Please don't leave town.'

10

'Thank you for seeing me.' Stark ran his fingers through his beard, glancing around, grateful for seats tucked near the back from which he could see the door. Busy places could still set him on edge, but it was more the chance of someone snapping a shot of him for social media than pulling a gun or S-vest trigger that had him scanning the mid-afternoon café crowd.

Libby Drummond shrugged politely. 'Sergeant Reynolds has been very kind, but he didn't say there'd been any new leads.'

'Sometimes it's hard to tell what might be a lead until the picture clears.'

'That doesn't sound promising.'

'I try to avoid promises in this line of work.'

'The crime isn't always solved?'

'No.'

She studied him as the waitress delivered their coffees with a chirpy instruction for them to enjoy, whether they liked the drinks or not. 'I don't know whether I should applaud your honesty or accuse you of apathy.'

'Perhaps just wait and see.'

'And in the meantime, you're sorry for my loss.'

Ouch. 'For what it's worth.'

'Hmm.' She studied him as she popped two pills from

a blister pack and swallowed them with a sip of hot coffee. 'Sorry. Bad head. Trouble sleeping.'

'Understandable.' Stark didn't imagine it was much easier losing a parent suddenly in your twenties than at the age of eleven, as he'd been when his father passed. Or comrades in war. The best consolation one might offer was that life's losses should make you value the gains – but as the losses accumulated, you started to wonder. A tally in both sides of the ledger wasn't conducive to peaceful sleep.

'Have we been de-prioritized? A sergeant instead of an inspector?'

'For some reason, DI Millhaven thinks I'm better with the bereaved.'

'She doesn't think the scars will put people off?'

'I couldn't say.' The beard masked some of the jagged scar running from his jawline round to his temple, where it had faded over time, but the tan re-highlighted it and the others. Funny how little he noticed them now. How the stranger in the mirror had overwritten the boy he'd once been. Libby was looking at the burn scars on his hands too, and the half-missing pinkie. And those were just the visible opening lines of the tales of war etched on him. It was a good job she couldn't see the rest.

'Perhaps you have kind eyes.'

Weary, angry perhaps. Gabrielle said *autre part*. Only Kelly had ever said kind.

'You're the one from the news,' said Libby. 'You were a soldier before you were a policeman.'

Technically, he'd been a policeman first, then both at the same time, or taking turns in the Territorials, but it didn't matter enough to say. Soon the army side of his life would be over, once and for all. Perhaps that shouldn't matter any more either. A nod was the best answer for now.

'You won a medal. The Victoria Cross.'

Olympians won medals. Soldiers were awarded them. A distinction that mattered, but a personal one, so he didn't correct her.

'Weren't you supposed to be getting another one, for that shooting on Greenwich Clocktower?' she asked.

He shook his head. 'Press rumour.'

'And that thing last year, with your girlfriend . . .' Libby looked appalled as the memory came to her, then even more so as she noted his slight recoil. 'I'm sorry. Painful memories.'

Stark demurred, with an attempted smile. 'All in the past.'

'Are you still together?'

'We're not here to talk about me.'

The sadness crept back into Libby's face. 'No. I wish we were. The only interesting thing that's happened in my life is a C-list celebrity mother, and now this . . .'

Stark almost said he was sorry, but they'd covered that ground.

Libby nodded. 'Does it get in the way of your work, being famous?'

It got in the way of a lot of things. 'Sometimes.'

'Mum loved it when people recognized her. I suspect you don't.'

'There are worse things, I suppose.'

'Like being shot at?'

Or indeed *being* shot, thought Stark. Or blown up, tasered, punched, kicked, cut . . . or detaching yourself from the woman you love because you're too dangerous to be around. It was a long list.

Libby appeared to sense the small talk had taken a wrong turn. 'So, what did you want to ask?'

'Background really. Had you noticed anything unusual in your mother's recent behaviour, emotions, movements?'

'Your inspector already asked that.'

'Sometimes it's better to ask again, after the initial shock.'

Libby stared at the cooling coffee. After the initial shock, nothing got easier. 'No. Not that I noticed. But I don't live there any more. Ryan does, when he's not pissing away his time at uni, but he's not one to notice how other people are feeling.'

'I'll have to call him to ask again.'

'Good luck with that. He's still too angry. He still thinks this is a mistake. An accident.'

'That no one would want to hurt your mother. What do you think?'

'I don't know. She was successful. Maybe she'd trodden on someone's toes? But it's hard to imagine a crime of resentment or passion. As far as I know, she didn't owe gangsters money or lead some dangerous double life. She was just Mum.'

'How would you characterize her relationship with Adrian Fairchild?'

'Adrian? Why? Surely you're not saying he's a suspect?'

'No. We're really still at the information-gathering stage, trying to eliminate people from our inquiries. I was just struck that he accompanied you to identify your mother. Obviously, it went beyond being a purely professional acquaintance.'

'Not as far beyond as he'd have liked.'

'He had feelings for her, you think?'

'Unreciprocated.' Libby sipped her coffee. 'They were together once, did you know? Back in their uni days. He was the wise older post-grad, she the wide-eyed fresher. Nearly a year, apparently. They'd laugh about it, mutually agreed separation, they'd call it, but really it was just Mum moving on. Serial monogamy. I loved my mum, but she had a ruthless streak. Relationships, jobs . . . always eyeing up the next opportunity. It may have been my useless dad that cheated, but Mum isn't the angel people see on TV –' She stopped and corrected herself, '*Wasn't*.' She took a moment to collect herself.

'And never remarried.'

'No need. She'd got the children she wanted, the house, and the means to support both while she climbed the career ladder. After that, just flings I think.' She studied him. 'Now you don't know whether to applaud my honesty or accuse me of disloyalty.'

'Perhaps I'll wait and see.'

That earned a smile. The first he'd seen beyond the photos in her mother's house and on social media. A pretty smile, briefly soothing grief-worn eyes.

'Ryan would deny everything I just said, of course, but good luck asking him. Flew out to Ibiza yesterday, with his infantile pals. Claims he's a DJ, if anyone asks, but we both know he's handing out flyers and getting legless. Leaving me to deal with everything here.'

Stark knew this from Reynolds. If the siblings' alibis hadn't checked out, Ryan wouldn't have made it through airport security. But it was frustrating nonetheless.

'Anyway,' continued his sister, wearily. 'Ryan runs from everything, including being honest about Mum, or "Uncle Adrian". Thought the sun shone out of his arse when he was younger. Too self-absorbed to spare two thoughts now.'

'But you didn't think the sun shone from Uncle Adrian?'

'He was nice enough, I suppose, growing up, but by the time I was old enough to realize why he was hanging around Mum all these years, I started catching him staring at me too, finding excuses to talk to me, complimenting me on how much I looked like her.'

'Creepy?'

'A bit, yeah. I would only have been around thirteen, fourteen? I never told Mum. She'd probably have told me to be flattered. Attractiveness was something to be utilized, in her view. She could be a bit . . . I don't know . . . lacking in empathy, I suppose. It wasn't that she couldn't understand why people didn't see everything her way, more, I think, that she just didn't *believe* them – that there was any other way to see things – if that makes sense.'

'I think so, yes,' nodded Stark, thinking of a certain detective inspector of his close acquaintance, but also a little about himself – the intransigence that underpinned the wall between himself and others. Kelly, not least.

Libby tilted her head slightly, perhaps sensing his passing sadness. 'Are you going to ask me whether I think he could have done it?'

'I am now.'

'No. I don't think so. I think, at heart, he's weak.'

And she'd perhaps grown up with a weak father and brother to recognize the kind. But weak people could crack, and unrequited love could sometimes spark jealous rage.

'He ever have any money troubles you know of?'

'No, I don't think so. And he bought that big house a few years ago. Showed off pictures. Not very bachelor pad. I can't really think of anything unusual about him. He's just Adrian.'

'Okay. Changing subject, did your mother ever mention Alex Zedani?'

'Her golden goose. Mum would joke that money didn't buy you taste, but it sure helped.'

'You ever meet him?'

'No. I had my fill of museums early. Long before she got her hooks into him.'

'They ever get personal, do you think?'

'She never said so, but she keeps that side of her life to herself. He'd be her type, I suppose.' More misuse of tense. Emotion bubbled up and she shook her head, blinking back tears. 'Someone else you're trying to eliminate from your inquiries?'

Stark nodded. For completeness, he also showed her photos of Zedani's PA, his bodyguard, and Nathan Goff and Tyrone Pook, but there was no reason to think she'd know any of them, and she didn't.

'Can I ask *you* a question?' she said as he slipped the photos back into his folder.

'I suppose.'

'If, hypothetically speaking, you *were* single, would you

be allowed to . . . socialize, with the daughter of a murder victim?'

Stark got the distinct impression socialize meant more. Grief could make people do or want things they might otherwise not, but the firmness of her gaze suggested she'd something of her mother's reported directness. He smiled apologetically. 'Definitely not.'

'What about after the case is closed?'

'Still frowned upon.'

'Mmm . . .' She smiled faintly, perhaps filing away his equivocation. 'Perhaps I'll just wait and see.'

11

'You're a hard man to pin down, Mr Zedani.' Fran took a seat on the opposite side of the wide modern desk in the plush penthouse office of Horizon Logistics. The floor-to-ceiling glass wall looked north across the turgid Thames at the sunlit glass offices on the opposite north bank.

'This was the only opening in the diary,' said Kat, the glamorous assistant, primly.

'I'm sorry,' Zedani replied. 'My schedule is packed at the best of times, but as you can imagine, Lucinda's death has sent out something of a shockwave. The exhibition has yet to open to the public, and a lot of people are perturbed. Some are calling for it to be scrapped.'

'Coffee?' asked Kat.

'Hot, dark and bitter,' replied Fran, earning a faint smile from Zedani.

Snog, marry, avoid? thought Fran, watching his handsome, earnest expression. All three in that order – rinse and repeat.

Stylish tea and coffee pots steamed, ready on a modernist side table, with matching accoutrements. No biscuits, sadly. Kat proffered a cup and saucer. Fran just took the cup.

Kat smiled with perfect white teeth, returned the saucer, and sat in a chair to the side of the desk.

Fran placed the coffee down to cool. 'I'll need to speak with you separately, if you don't mind.'

Another smile. No teeth, no eyes. 'Mr Zedani insists I sit in on all his meetings to ensure nothing is missed.'

'Are you his lawyer?'

'No –'

'Then please wait outside until I'm ready to speak with you.'

At a faint nod from her boss, Kat smiled tightly and left, clipping elegantly out of the office on killer heels to match her killer skirt and blouse, closing the door silently behind her.

Zedani sipped his own coffee, appearing amused. 'She'll take that personally.'

'There goes my perfect streak of pleasing everyone all of the time,' replied Fran, deadpan. 'What's she going to do, strike me off your Christmas card list?'

More amusement. He really was far too suave. The chiselled looks of a model for active older men's clothing; greying temples, but you knew there were washboard abs beneath the argyle sweater. No wedding ring. Throw in the wealth and style and you had the fantasy sugar daddy. A thirty-year age gap might seem worth bridging to an ambitious personal assistant.

'You might get the cheap coffee next time.'

Fran sipped hers. It was amazing. 'This better not be the kind of beans that've passed through a cat. No pun intended.'

'How about we leave that one a mystery?'

'I hate mysteries.'

'I would've thought them your stock-in-trade.'

'My trade is *solving* crime.'

'Of course. Well, that brings us to the point. You have questions.'

'I do. How well did you know Lucinda Drummond?'

'Quite well. We first met at a charity fundraiser, perhaps five years ago? She called me a flippant philanthropist, saying I needed to give more and get serious. She could be very direct.'

'You like that in a woman?'

'I like that in anyone.'

'How would you define your relationship?'

'Cordial.'

'Not friendly?'

'In my experience, money and friendship rarely mix well. Lucinda needed me. In my way, I needed her. Neither of us made any secret of it, so we got on very well.'

'Why did you need her?'

Zedani smiled patiently. 'Philanthropy is a lot more complicated than dropping a pound in a rattling collection box. The tax implications alone can make one's eyes water, and it's not just about giving money; it's about giving time, lending credence and publicity, and above all choosing a cause you feel passionate about. Lucinda was the perfect dance partner. Her loss is a tragedy on so many levels.'

'Did your relationship ever stray beyond the professional?'

'Were we lovers?' He frowned, but whether at the notion or her impertinence she could only guess. 'No.'

'She was a very attractive woman.'

'She was. But relationships and money don't mix well either.'

And you probably prefer a thirty-year age gap to a ten-year one, thought Fran, wondering if Kat was listening in through an intercom, or just holding a glass to the door. 'Did you do it?'

'Trip up many hardened criminals with that cunning question?'

'My luck has to change one day.'

The seamless smile returned. 'The real question is what possible reason could I have to want to?'

'In *my* experience, reason doesn't always come into it.' But he was right. And when you were struggling to narrow down those with means and opportunity, motive was key.

'I hope you're not about to tell me not to leave town? We have a meeting in Cyprus on Friday.'

'We?'

'Kat and myself, meeting some shipping partners.'

'And Jan?'

'Possibly. The security detail rotate.'

'You book this before Lucinda Drummond's death, or after?'

'*Planned*, rather than booked.' Zedani smiled, without pretention. 'I hate to appear ostentatious, but my work forces me to keep a modest aircraft on standby in the Docklands.'

'Poor you,' said Fran, unwilling to believe *anyone* bought a private jet because they were *forced* to. Especially not when they had a hot PA they could impress with a nice overnight getaway.

'Back on Saturday.'

'Make sure you are.' As much as she wished otherwise, Fran had no powers to prevent him leaving town or country without arresting him and a judge setting conditional bail. TV cops didn't have to put up with this shit.

Zedani tilted his head, amused. 'You can't seriously consider me a suspect?'

'The three of you are among those unaccounted for at the time of the murder.'

'We've told you where we were.'

'Tell me again.'

He paused just long enough to demonstrate that compliance was down to his beneficence and not any authority on her part. 'We arrived early so the exhibition coordinator could indulge me with a private tour. Patronage having privileges.'

'This tour included Adrian Fairchild.'

'Yes. He was heading everything up, from the British Museum side.'

'How well do you know him?'

'We've met. Over the years.'

'That's it?'

'I mostly deal with Lucinda.'

'The organ grinder, not the monkey.'

'I wouldn't put it quite like that.'

'What's your opinion of him?'

Zedani mused for a moment, doubtless wondering what to infer. 'In so far as I have one . . . competent?'

'That's it?'

'Lucinda seemed to rely on him for a lot. The art of leadership is to surround yourself with good people to delegate to. Lucinda was a very busy person. I suppose Adrian was reliable.'

Competent, reliable people could come to feel put-upon and undervalued, thought Fran. 'So, after the tour?'

'Other guests were filtering in. And Lucinda. I spoke with her for a few minutes.'

'How did she seem?'

'Happy.'

'Not nervous or agitated in any way?'

'No. Public speaking was half her job. Plus the TV work. No, she actually bent my ear about sponsoring an exhibit tour swap with the New York Met. Quite shameless really. Then she went off to schmooze and I asked the coordinator if there was somewhere private I might withdraw to make some business calls. She suggested the carriage tunnel, showed us the way, and left us to it. I believe Kat has already sent call logs to your subordinates, with a request for discretion. Commercial sensitivity, you understand.'

One of the caterers who'd gone outside for a vape had confirmed seeing Zedani's group in the tunnel. 'When did you come back inside?'

'After we heard the scream.'

'The call logs showed you finished nearly ten minutes before that.'

'I'm afraid after that I sought solace in the last remaining refuge of a wicked lifetime smoker.' He smiled wryly, pulling a vape from his pocket.

It looked about a hundred times more expensive than the ubiquitous market-stall jobs likely used by the caterers, but probably lacked their thrilling risk of spontaneous pocket combustion.

'Did the three of you remain together that whole time?'

'Yes. Kat never leaves my side.'

'Does she hold it for you when you pee?' It was an unpleasant thing to say, but there was only so much charm Fran could stomach.

His smile cracked just a little. 'Within reason, obviously.'

'And your bodyguard . . . ?'

'He does follow me into the loo, if we're out and about, but I don't think he's the type to peek.'

'Jan Zieliński. Polish?'

'I've never asked.'

'Why do you need security?'

Zedani gave a pained expression. 'I'm wealthy and visible. And my business often takes me to less secure parts of the world. There have been issues in the past. Now our insurance company insists. As something of a key worker, they consider my death or kidnapping a risk to the business.'

'And what exactly is your line of business?'

'Logistics.'

Fran treated that with a level stare, then flipped back a few notebook pages to her advanced notes. 'The detailed organization and implementation of a complex operation? The activity of organizing the movement, equipment and accommodation of troops? Or the commercial activity of transporting goods?'

'The third, achieved by the first,' he replied. 'Shipping mostly, but we provide an end-to-end service, so air, road and rail, packing, unpacking, storage, preparations, permits, border control. Everything to get our client's goods safely from A to B.'

'Over the horizon.' Mostly through the Black Sea and Suez, via the Mediterranean.

'Indeed.'

'Lucrative?'

'Very.'

'Why the arts, for patronage?'

'A fascination with history, a passion for beauty.'

'With a little calculated tax planning?'

'It doesn't hurt.'

'You could just build a few orphanages?'

'We do that too.'

'Save the elephants?'

'I'll have Kat add them to the to-do list.'

'Well, when you're done there, apparently hedgehogs need help too.'

'Noted.'

Fran felt his charm sneaking up on her again and stamped it down. 'So none of you slipped inside, behind the big banner, to the Tulip Stairs?'

'Neither individually, nor together.' He smiled, patiently.

'I should say that, right now, it looks like the three of you are probably the only people present who could have accessed the stairs without risk of being seen.'

'Then whoever did, risked being seen.'

Fran cheerfully let the smugness of his reply rub her up the wrong way. 'You might find this amusing, but in my experience mutual alibis can mask mutual interest, and you appear wealthy enough to buy silence – or, indeed, to procure a murder.'

'You're suggesting I sent a bodyguard I barely speak to, and Kat, all fifty kilos of her, as assassins? Or I killed her myself and paid for their silence?'

'I've seen stranger.'

'Then I pity you and those in your line of work. I may be a successful businessman, but I try not to let that get ahead of ethical behaviour.'

'Most people try,' nodded Fran. 'But sometimes money gets things done that ethics can't. And the problem is, people who'll sell their loyalty or silence can't be trusted not to change sides to avoid prison time.' She'd be interviewing the PA and bodyguard next.

'I've nothing to hide, Detective Inspector.' It looked like Zedani's patience was finally wearing thin too.

Fran kept her smile to herself and placed two photos on the table. 'Do you know either of these men?'

Zedani looked at Pook and Goff. 'No. Who are they?'

'I'm not at liberty to say.'

He made a facial shrug, and glanced at a watch that probably cost a year of her wages. 'In that case, was there anything else?'

12

Kat appeared with suspicious alacrity. If she hadn't been listening, Zedani must have a call button under his desk.

She showed Fran into a separate meeting room.

Fran declined a second coffee.

Katherine Hamilton-Smythe.

Private school snootiness but Daddy insists she get a proper job, was Fran's guess.

The PA's answers matched her boss's as flawlessly as her make-up and hair, but without the charm. She could doubtless turn it on for anyone of consequence but Fran was beneath her interests. She recognized Fairchild, but not Goff or Pook.

'How would you describe your relationship with Mr Zedani?'

'Professional.' It was the first personal question, but clearly one she was rehearsed in.

'Purely?'

'I don't like what you're implying.'

'I'm not implying, I'm asking. He is an attractive, wealthy, unmarried, older man. You're a beautiful, smart, young woman. Ambitious too, I'd surmise. It would hardly be a first.'

'We are not romantically involved.'

'Such arrangements are often more transactional than romantic.'

'So now you're calling me a whore?'

Fran really wasn't making any friends here today. But for some reason she leaned towards believing the girl. 'Forgive me. In a man's world, my job often requires me to ask questions I'd rather not. I imagine yours is no walk in the park either.' The girl's face barely defrosted at the sisterly offering. Fair enough. Fran wasn't really in the mood to make nice, and she wouldn't lose sleep if they didn't part as pals. 'So if, for example, your wealthy boss and/or his rather lethal-looking bodyguard had slipped back inside for a few minutes, between finishing his calls and the alarm being raised, I imagine it could be hard for a subordinate like yourself to resist lying for him.'

Kat's eyes narrowed. 'I'm not lying.'

'He certainly has the money to reward silence,' continued Fran. 'And if he'd just proved himself a killer, he might have the menace to scare you into it too.'

'I'm *not lying*. Why would he want to kill Lucinda?'

'That certainly is a question,' mused Fran, seriously. 'And another is, if he did, what's to stop him deciding to ensure your silence permanently?'

Kat stood, her smile at the cutting edge of businesslike. 'I think we're done here.'

The bodyguard wasn't much help either.

He wasn't close with Mr Zedani, it wasn't that kind of job. He was only needed when Zedani was out and about, though here in the UK the risk was probably negligible. He mostly drove and stood about. He'd worked for a London-based company, Temple Security, for around five years, after serving in the Polish army. Special forces, he emphasized in his accented English.

He had a scar on one cheek, like an old Action Man toy, and smaller ones on the backs of his hands. His knuckles were calloused, and the way he moved suggested the muscle wasn't just for show. A spiderweb tattoo peeped over his shirt collar.

There appeared to be a brain behind his eyes, but tempered by terseness.

Quiet and capable, in ways you wouldn't want to see. Perfect for this job. If Stark was here, they'd probably square up to each other until the air cracked with testosterone, then grin and go get drunk without ever speaking a word. Whether Jan Zieliński would dive in front of a bullet to save his client, only he knew. He wasn't protecting the Queen.

Stark would probably do it to save a cat.

Fran quite liked cats. You had to admire that level of wilful independence and shameless freeloading. Perhaps she should get a cat. Damn sight easier than a boyfriend – or a baby.

'Are we finished?' asked Zieliński.

Fran blinked back into the now. 'Have you ever killed anyone?'

Now it was Zieliński's turn to blink. 'I was a soldier for sixteen years. I served alongside your British SAS in Iraq and Afghanistan.'

'Is that a yes?'

'Yes. Many enemies.'

'Civilians?'

'Not that I know. What has this to do with your dead lady?'

'Well, I'll tell you. I have a dead lady, as you put it. I have you, a trained killer, alone with your very wealthy employer and his subservient PA, as the only three people present who could've made it to the scene of the murder and back without fear of being seen.'

'You think I killed her? Why would I?'

'Money.'

'You think Mr Zedani paid me to.'

'And paid or threatened Kat to keep quiet.'

Zieliński was already shaking his head. 'You're *pomylony . . . crazy lady*. Why? Why would he?'

As ever, the same question. 'I don't know, yet. But the question you should be asking is what's to stop him looking at you as a loose end now too?'

Zieliński appeared unfazed. Water off a duck's back to a man who'd faced combat.

Fran was glad to step outside, drawing a deep breath of industrial-grade London air, laced with a whiff of Thameside ooze. It was at times like this she wished she smoked. If for no better reason than it must be so much easier to be an angry badass when you can drag down half a cigarette and then grind the burning ember beneath your heel and stalk off in a cloud of exhaled fury.

Instead she settled for calling the office.

Dixon proved his constant luck by picking up.

'Someone better find me a motive. Because I may not be able to use thumbscrews on suspects any more, but I'm pretty sure I can on you lot.'

13

'So where are we?' asked Groombridge, as the team reconvened at the end of the day.

'The Zedani trio still back each other up,' said Fran, reporting the keys points. 'But a three-legged alibi with self-interest and money involved looks shaky to me. I left them with some undermining thoughts on each other. Next time, we interview them on our turf.'

'That'll bring in the lawyers,' said Groombridge. 'And without any kind of motive to wave at them, they'll be away in their limo before their tea goes cold.'

Fran nodded sullenly. 'Fairchild's sticking to his headache story. Grief seems genuine, on the surface, but he's still out of sight and in proximity for half the TOD window.'

'The daughter didn't have a lot of time for him,' said Stark, relaying Libby's thoughts.

'So Fairchild carried a torch for Lucinda for over twenty years,' mused Groombridge. 'And perhaps had started to look at the daughter as a replacement? Add in professional jealousy, and there's scope for motive in there perhaps.'

'I might go one better, Guv,' said Williams. 'One of the girls from the cloakroom check-in said things had gone quiet after the initial influx of guests, and her colleague had gone to help upstairs. Then who should walk in and retrieve his briefcase, but Adrian Fairchild. That room *does* have CCTV, but we hadn't reviewed it yet because it doesn't cover the route to and from the crime scene. So . . .' He dialled up the file on his screen. 'Here we have Fairchild walking in, handing over his ticket. The timestamp says 19:33. The girl fetches a black brief-case with a tan stripe from the rack behind, and hands it over. Fairchild leaves at 19:35, but returns and checks it back in at 19:45, before appearing on the cameras outside a minute later.'

'So his sixteen minutes drops to ten,' said Fran. 'Still seems like a long time to spend in the loo.'

'And what did he want his case for?' asked Dixon.

'Headache pills?' suggested Stark.

'But here's where it gets really interesting,' said Williams, fast-forwarding to 20:04. 'The cloakroom attendant looks up sharply from her phone at the reported time of the exhibition coordinator's scream.'

Onscreen the girl looked around and cautiously approached the curtain, peering out, then went out. A couple of minutes later, the curtain twitched and then opened a little. A black-gloved hand and black sleeve reached in and flicked off the light switch. Briefly silhouetted against the corridor light, a figure slipped inside. By the time the camera readjusted to infrared, the curtain was closed, but the now monochrome footage showed a figure in dark trousers, jacket, shoes and gloves, with no apparent markings, grey hoodie pulled up over a black baseball cap, with the hood drawstring tied tight to cover the whole face other than the eyes.

Head down the whole time, the figure looked around

furtively and pulled out a phone and turned on its torch function, the beam sweeping the room and then shining directly at the camera, blinding it.

As the beam moved off and the camera readjusted, the figure could be glimpsed searching the racks and coming away with what looked a lot like the same briefcase Fairchild had just re-deposited. The curtain twitched open again, light briefly silhouetting the figure again as they slipped out.

'Now *that*,' grinned Dixon, 'is what I call suspicious behaviour.'

Groombridge peered closely at the still-frame printout of the figure that Williams was sticking to the other board. 'Nathan Goff or Tyrone Pook?'

'Build looks better for Goff,' said Fran. 'Savvy enough to counter a camera, and cover his face and any identifiable markings.'

'Reasonable doubt surfacing – again,' nodded Groombridge, referring to Goff's streak of avoiding prosecution.

Williams asked the pertinent question. 'But enough for probable cause?'

Stark flicked through the files he'd brought with him. Light reading, while they waited.

The duty judge was obviously having a busy night. Groombridge was persistent, then persuasive, then patient, albeit reluctantly. Fran looked ready to punch someone. Warrant requests required two officers present. Stark had come along because Groombridge suggested it, but also because knowing she wasn't strictly needed would ratchet up Fran's irritation amusingly, while going home to his lifeless flat would highlight his lack of a life more harshly than he felt ready for yet.

The warrant finally got signed, but the thinness of probable cause meant it came with a requirement to knock and be let in, within daylight hours.

Groombridge suggested a drink but conversation proved stilted. The Compass Rose pub – adopted second home of the Royal Hill Police Station – was too quiet. The case had been talked out already. Fran was in a mood, seeming not to want to go home either, and unwilling to talk about why. Stark readied himself for an inquisition into where he'd been for the past year, but none came. After a single round, they called it a night.

Back home, Stark downed an Indian takeaway and a beer, took the cap off the cheap whisky but then put it back on and went to sit out on his balcony, listening to the ceaseless city noise. The night was warmer, but still felt chill as he wrapped the scratchy blanket tightly around his shoulders and closed his eyes, to picture the rooftop sprawl of a warmer, faraway city with different sounds, different smells, different air.

Somewhere distant, whether in that city or this, he thought he heard a crow caw.

It took him a moment to rouse and recognize it was just his phone.

But the dark tidings of the call gave the portentous corvid the last laugh.

14

Blue lights greeted Stark on the stroke of midnight outside Valiant House, a sixteen-storey seventies block of flats, typical of the type, directly overlooking Charlton Athletic football ground. Outwardly ugly, inside something nasty awaited.

It was always difficult with flats – where to draw the evidence line? Obviously, tape off the flat in question, but the communal areas . . . ? Residents typically protested at having to be escorted back and forth, and God help you if you had to seal off the lift.

Dixon was already there.

Fran was waiting for their call, once they'd had a first look.

Station stalwart Sergeant Tony Clark greeted them at the entrance to the flats, with a grin splitting his weather-beaten face. 'Morning, DC Dixon, for those of us all too familiar with this ungodly hour. And who's this beardy reprobate with you then?'

'This would be Detective *Sergeant* Stark,' replied Dixon, smiling.

Clark nodded appreciatively. 'About time too. Welcome to the three-stripe club, you crazy young fool – I don't suppose we'll keep you for long. But club rules: newbie buys all the other sergeants a drink.'

Stark grinned. 'You just made that up.'

Clark affected mock outrage. 'Irreverent youth – ask DI Millhaven, if you don't believe me!'

'She was a sergeant when she moved here.'

'She still stood her round. Buying drinks for the Inspectors' club now, of course. Champagne and single malts, I expect. Well,' Clark sighed, smiling, 'the world turns, for all our stubborn wishes. And what they say about feeling old when the policemen start looking like kids applies double for sergeants and triple for inspectors,' he laughed. 'Take my advice, Dixon. Stay close to this one. He'll need a sergeant of his own soon enough.'

'Not me,' said Stark. 'I work for a living.' Stark was no more likely to seek inspector rank than he'd have been to seek an army commission.

'That's just what Mike used to say,' replied Clark, with ominous certainty. There were probably as few people who'd call Groombridge by his first name as there were on close enough terms with Stark. 'So, while we've still got you . . . Rosie's after shift, tomorrow?'

Stark glanced up at the monolithic building. 'Doesn't seem likely.'

A grim nod from the weather-beaten sergeant suggested that drinking time might be in short supply for a while, as well as sleep. 'Nasty one. Neighbour reported bloody footprints in the hallway. First responder PCs found they led from Nathan Goff's flat, forced the door, then called it in. Another resident reports three men in dark clothing and motorcycle helmets tailgating him in through the main front door, around ten. Too nervous to challenge them. Good job he didn't, from his perspective.'

'CCTV?'

Clark nodded to the camera beneath the entrance canopy. The rust on its dangling innards suggested considerable time had passed since some feckless twonk had stoned it to death.

The lift had no camera. It was taped off now.

'Nasty one . . .' said Dixon, with a hint of dread, as they climbed the stairs to the ninth floor. Notoriously weak of stomach and seemingly impervious to Fran's exposure therapy, here he was, answering the call, off to greet another bloody corpse, trepidatious but resolute. That said, this being their first time alone since Stark's return, he'd said nothing beyond exchanging obvious pleasantries, hesitant to encroach on Stark's notorious privacy.

'You can wait outside if you like,' Stark offered.

'Nah . . . we've seen worse, I expect.' He glanced at Stark, probably remembering that whatever he'd witnessed, Stark's overseas deployments were likely to have surpassed it.

The corridor outside the victim's flat was taped off too. Residents of the adjacent flats had already been ushered outside, while arrangements were made to put them up with family, friends or in hotels.

Strategically placed SOCO stainless-steel stepping stones protected the bloody footprints, partials only – perhaps more than one pair, with similar but blurred tread patterns, fading with each step – while scene of crime officers did what they did.

Goff's flat was on the wrong side to enjoy the views of the football ground, but that was the least of its property-value problems now. One SOCO introduced herself as Assistant Crime Scene Manager – one of Geoff

Culpepper's minions, new to Stark. 'Photographer is finishing up, but pathologist is running late.'

'Can we take a look?'

'Brief.' She supervised their donning of anti-contamination gear with hawk-like scrutiny, and only when completely satisfied led them inside. 'Watch where you tread. Touch nothing. Face masks and gloves at all times.' An officious young woman, Stark guessed her to be around his age or younger, perhaps recently promoted out of her depth, like him.

Nathan Goff's flat was dingy, and it looked like the only attention the original seventies decor had received in the intervening years was the steady accumulation of wear and grime. Glances into the slovenly bedroom and squalid kitchen made Stark's army-induced OCD prickle.

The hallway carpet was worn to the weave, beige once, perhaps, but now grey with ingrained dirt. Multiple bloody bootprints ran from the living room, petering out towards the front door, forcing them to tread carefully along more SOCO stepping stones. Forensic arc lighting from the living room hurt Stark's eyes, but not so much as the scene inside as his irises adjusted.

Dixon had been partially right – there *were* worse things to see. This body was relatively fresh, male, adult and whole, give or take. Stark had seen worse on all counts, but Dixon had not, took one look, clamped a hand over his mouth and staggered from the flat as fast as wobbly legs would carry him.

Stark stared at the gory remains, and dialled Fran. 'Our one murder just became two.'

PART TWO

15

The victim had been tortured.

The callous brutality of that chilled and disgusted in equal measure. In Helmand, Stark had found the body of a local, suspected by Taliban militants of supplying the British troops with coffee beans. By comparison, this guy had got off lightly. But only by comparison.

Nathan Goff.

It might take forensic testing to confirm that. He may not have enough whole teeth left but prints would not be a problem, once his fingers had been collected up from the floor. Goff had been gaffer-taped to a cheap dining chair, arms strapped behind him, gagged with more tape and what looked like his own sock from his one bare foot.

Everybody breaks. Even with training and bloody-minded resistance, it was only ever a matter of time. Goff didn't strike Stark as a stubborn hold-out. For an interrogation to go this far the torturer either asked questions the victim could not answer, didn't believe the answers given, never had any intention of stopping even when they had answers, or never asked a single one. The only mercy in this sick-fest was the chance that Goff might've passed out before his throat was cut.

Stark was almost shocked at his own dull detachment on witnessing this scene, having been bound in similar fashion himself only a year ago, at the mercy of the merciless. Dixon's was the more human response.

'Are you *the* Joseph Stark?' asked the young CSM.

His beard might not match the tiny image on his warrant card, but the name was unmistakable. She had pretty eyes above her mask, but they watched him with more distrust than interest. Everything about her said she hated letting anyone into her crime scene. SOCO were often thus, which put them on the side of the angels in Stark's book. 'I think that's a frame of reference thing. Prints?'

'Gloved. So far at least. And the way the bootprints are smudged suggests disposable overshoes. Looks like your killers came prepared.'

'Is there a detective sergeant in the house?' called a familiar voice. Marcus, back in marshmallow garb. 'Not sure I was hoping to see you again so soon. No DI Millhaven?'

'On her way.'

Marcus nodded phlegmatically, still offering no clue as to whether he and Fran were still entangled. It didn't sound hopeful. 'Nasty one, I hear. DC Dixon looking positively pale outside.'

Stark nodded to the bloody mess. 'Not pretty.'

Marcus surveyed the carnage. 'Photographer done their bit?'

The CSM nodded. 'He's outside if you need him back in for specific indicators.'

'Right then, no rest for the pure of heart,' breathed Marcus, pulling his mask up into position. 'Cause of death unlikely to hold many surprises, and I understand time of death might be sometime before midnight . . . ?'

Stark turned his attentions back to the flat. There wasn't much to suggest that Goff was still the low-level thief Ptolemy suspected, but the best way a thief could avoid conviction was by not keeping their loot around too long. It didn't look like his killers had taken much interest in his 'belongings'. If they'd been looking for something, they'd asked for it rather than ransacking the place. What it might've been, to provoke such violence, and how someone low down in the food chain like Goff had it, were the obvious questions. Drugs, might be the first thought, were it not for the fact that two nights ago this guy had been shifting catering supplies at Queen's House when Lucinda Drummond was killed.

There was a laptop, open, bloody fingermarks on it. Stark tapped a gloved fingertip on the corner of the space bar, but got only a log-in screen.

'Tech might get that open,' said the CSM.

They both glanced at the floor. The laptop had a fingerprint scanner.

'Don't suppose you've come across a black briefcase?' asked Stark.

'No. Important?'

'Could be.'

'Want us to widen the search?'

He was about to defer, when he remembered he now had the power to make such a suggestion. He'd have to answer to Fran if it blew the budget, but . . . 'Please.'

She ticked a box on her clipboard and made him sign.

Fair enough.

Stark looked around, despondently. All in all, not much to show for a life.

The only remaining stand-out feature of the room was the litter of envelopes scattered across the carpet as if violently discarded, some bloody, all identical: Dosh4Gold.

Prepaid receptacles for a cash-for-gold postal service – in recent years the simplest way for burglars to fence gold jewellery.

Dixon had made it all the way outside before puking.

'Look at it this way,' said Stark. 'Next time you say you've seen worse, it will probably be true.'

'Only probably,' muttered Dixon, smiling wanly, 'knowing my luck.'

'*Joe?*' Stark wheeled round, to find Marianne Pensol beaming at him, pristine in her uniform, a happy sight indeed. 'I heard you were back.'

'I heard *you* were back,' he replied. Before his disappearance, her return to work had been in doubt, after her convalescence from a bullet wound had descended into a period on his couch trying to get her head straight.

'Not long after you left.' Her smile turned crooked. 'Saw Hazel and the others a few more times,' she said, referring to the trauma recovery group therapy sessions he'd coaxed her into attending. 'And Nick and Jane looked after me. But I never got to thank you.'

'No need.' Her smile was enough. After what she'd seen him do a year ago, he was just glad she didn't recoil. She looked well. Indeed, there was no point beating about the bush – she looked great, he thought with a pang of regret. Life was a series of missed chances.

'Are you all right?' Pensol asked Dixon, who was still looking positively green.

'I'm fine,' said Dixon, unconvincingly.

Stark winced. If there was one thing John Dixon did not need right now, it was the compounding embarrassment of a pretty face.

'Right,' said Fran, marching up to Stark. 'What the bloody hell have you done with our prime suspect?'

16

If there was one aspect of this job Stark was glad never to have confronted before, it was this. Informing the family. He'd been there shortly after, muttered the standard commiseration, but never this . . .

He stared at the shabby 24/7 launderette, dawn-lit in the unloved end of a litter-strewn London street, not a mile from where Nathan Goff's body had been bagged up barely six hours ago. According to Nathan's extensive record, he had a mother. She needed to be told she no longer had a son. And for now at least, for all his sins, that fell to Stark.

They'd tried her home. A neighbour said she was here.

Both the army and police had specially trained officers to deliver the news families dreaded. But while, in the army, it was the officer's job to write the letter of condolence and explanation, offering some answers to the worst questions imaginable, in the police it was the senior investigating officer's job to *ask* questions. Or in this case, their sergeant, Fran having taken some uniforms to knock on Tyrone Pook's door.

The Family Liaison officer would do the talking, but the mother needed to see a face from the detective branch, to know that even her low-life son's death was worthy of investigation, if only by a detective sergeant with the ink still drying on his promotion and barely three hours' sleep behind his eyes. Some images were not easily pushed aside, and the quantity of whisky required would have left him still abed. He doubted very much he'd be buying the sergeants a round at Rosie's tonight.

Inside, the oversized drums rolled, spun or tumbled according to their cycle. The diminutive woman feeding them shuffled about, oblivious to the policeman sitting in his car opposite. Single mother, abandoned by the father when Nathan was three, left to raise a boy alone on scraps of sub-minimum wage, only to see him slide into a life of larceny, and now this.

A rap at Stark's window startled him. The FLO, Reynolds again, stood back as Stark climbed out. 'Didn't expect to see you so soon.' He shook Stark's hand.

'Bad penny, I suppose,' said Stark. 'Shouldn't you be with Libby Drummond?'

'If you think CID is short staffed, try Family Liaison. Besides, you have to give them space to grieve.'

'Ibiza far enough?'

Reynolds nodded. 'I think my babysitter thing was getting in the way of their sibling sniping. She seems nice enough, but he's a bit of a brat, to be honest.' Reynolds followed Stark's eyes to the launderette. 'First time?'

Stark nodded.

'First one's the worst,' Reynolds sighed. 'But so are all the others.'

It took a special kind of officer to volunteer for FLO duty. When Stark tried to imagine it, his mind skittered to all the mothers, fathers, wives or children he'd personally bereaved. He'd never, to his knowledge, taken a life he'd not take again, but lack of remorse was not the same as lack of regret. War drew brutal distinctions.

Talking of which, Major Pierson had sent him another email, raising her impatience to DEFCON-3. Another excruciating conversation to be had.

Mistaking his expression, Reynolds placed an encouraging hand on Stark's shoulder. 'Don't look so worried. Remember your training – kindness first, questions after. Follow my lead and you'll do fine.'

Stark's phone rang while they were putting Mrs Goff into Reynolds' car to take her home. She was in shock. And at this stage, she didn't yet know what horrors her only son had endured at the end.

Stark stared at the caller ID. Mum. If he was the kind of person that attributed specific ringtones to individual callers, this one would be a klaxon. Fran would be a soldier yelling *Incoming!*

Watching Goff's bereft mother now, he felt a pang of guilt pressing reject.

It took his mother less than ten seconds to presumably huff to herself that, no, she didn't wish to leave a message after the tone, then curse her wastrel son and call again.

This time he hit the preselect message: *In a mtg, can I call you back?*

She wasn't quick at typing, so it took a full minute to come back with: *IMPORTANT!!!* All her texts arrived in capital letters. If challenged, she'd claim she couldn't fathom how not to, but a surfeit of exclamation marks suggested she preferred it that way.

Reynolds drove Mrs Goff away.

Stark waited until he was sat in his car, then took a deep breath, before calling back. 'Hi, Mum.'

'Don't you "hi, Mum" me, you misser of boats . . . you boat misser.'

It was going to be one of those calls. 'Mum, it's barely eight in the morning.'

'And what other son gives their mother such sleepless nights and fretful mornings?' she demanded, thereby adding the fact that he'd barely been to bed at all to the long list of things this son-of-war could never tell her. 'I warned you this would happen.'

He rubbed at his aching temples. 'What would happen?'

'I told you to call before it was too late. But just because a girl has said yes, it doesn't mean she can't change her mind, if you act fast.'

'Mum. I love you very much, but if the next words out of your mouth don't start filling in the context, you might as well be having this conversation on your own.'

'She's *engaged*, you dolt. Kelly. She's going to marry that good-for-nothing doctor, if you don't *do* something!'

Stark's stomach gave a twist. He'd been hit with bullets and bombs, blades, punches, kicks and tasers. This shouldn't be so bad. It was, after all, everything that he'd wanted for Kelly.

'Did you hear what I said?'

'Yes.' And much as it should've been expected, the news still came as a gut-punch in the dark – one he probably deserved. There was a reason one unfollowed one's ex online. But . . . 'Wait, how do you know this? Have you spoken with her?'

'No! You made me promise not to! It's *online*. On her social media. Well, not hers, his!'

'His?'

123

'Yes. Bold as brass. Relationship status. *Engaged!*'

So Robert had popped the question. It really wasn't Stark's business. If anything, it was remarkable it had taken another year. Stark certainly had no right to feel hurt or shocked. But he retained the right to be shocked at his mother. 'You follow my ex-girlfriend's new boyfriend on social media?'

Shame, in her book, wasn't something a body should dwell on. 'Well, I followed her, then him. Then after . . . what happened last year with you, and all the press hounding her for her side of the story, she shut down all her social media. Learned that trick from you, I think.'

Not exactly. Stark never had a social media footprint to suspend. Never his thing, even before all the public interest in him. But after the fresh interest in him last year, some journos had got hold of his private email and mobile number, forcing him to change both. Which his mother had somehow taken personally, despite her being the first person he'd updated.

'Anyway, you being home made me check,' she continued, 'and there it was, with a close-up photo of a whopping great diamond solitaire on her hand! So what are you going to do about it?'

Feel sick. Berate his stupidity. Curse his luck and all the steps that had brought him here – all the inescapable decisions and events, horrors, triumphs, fury and fate. What else was there? 'Nothing, Mum,' he said flatly, refusing even to sigh. 'It's none of my business.'

'None . . . ? How can you say that? You love her, and she loves you. Don't you dare deny it. What can he offer that trumps that?'

Safety. Security. Affection, unfettered and unclouded by storm. Sleep-filled nights and fret-free mornings. A clear path away from Joseph Peter Stark, he thought solemnly. Peace. 'She did love me, Mum, I know that. But she loves him now, so I have to wish them every happiness.'

That caused a brief moment of apoplectic silence down the line, of which Stark took full advantage to declare that he was in the middle of something with work and had to hang up.

17

'Early start,' observed Williams, coffee in hand, eyeing Stark's handiwork.

A second incident board had been dragged from the clutter corner, with a photo of Nathan Goff, alive, pinned to the centre-top. Photos of him dead were pinned below, among crime scene photos printed from Stark's phone ahead of the professional ones.

'*Jesus*,' Williams winced, 'who did this guy piss off?'

Stark nodded thoughtfully. 'That does seem to be the question.'

'Tell me you didn't let John see this.'

All Stark could offer was a mea culpa face.

Williams winced, peering closer. 'Need a chat with this one,' he said, tapping the side photo of Tyrone Pook, fellow catering company worker and old schoolfriend, according to Goff's mother, who'd helped get Nathan the catering company gig. 'Still unaccounted for?'

Stark nodded. 'Fran banged on his door first thing. No sign. She's had his phone pinged but it's suspiciously off grid. She's gone to try his family. Uniform have his photo.'

'Want me to make a list of any known *arse*-sociates, Sarge?' asked Williams, with a wry smile.

'If you'd be so kind, Detective Constable.'

But would Pook show up alive or dead? Or merely

confused by their search for him? Had he killed Nathan Goff and/or Lucinda Drummond? Was he in danger himself?

Williams peered at a scene photo. 'Dosh4Gold? Goff was up to his old tricks, after all, then.'

Stark indicated the labelled evidence bags on his desk, containing un-bloodied envelopes, some used, with transaction receipts for small amounts of cash in return for small items of gold. 'Domestic thievery doesn't normally get you killed though – not like this anyway.'

'Unless it's failing to pay for your drug debts?' speculated Williams.

'Small quantities of cannabis found, and a few pills, assumed MDMA, but nothing to suggest he was into anything much above personal use. Unless he'd got into something bigger but his killers took it with them . . .'

'Morning,' Dixon called out, entering with four takeaway coffees in a cardboard holder, and a bakery bag. He looked like he'd not slept well. His eyes avoided the photos.

Stark didn't blame him. He'd worked on dozens of boards, if rarely one so gory. But he'd never started one himself, until today. He yawned deeply and took a coffee. Five mornings ago, he'd woken in the arms of a beautiful French doctor and had bidden farewell in the knowledge they might see each other again in a fortnight, or maybe never. 'The world turns, for all our stubborn wishes,' he sighed.

'What was that?' asked Williams.

'Nothing.'

Fran bustled in, dumping her jacket and bag on her desk with perhaps more than the usual venom she directed at the world for her lateness. From her eyes, Stark could swear she'd been crying. A brief glare suggested he mind his own business. 'No sign of Pook, either at his mum's or his brother's. Start getting a list together of known associates.'

'Boss.' Williams kept his face straight.

'FLO with the mum?' she asked Stark.

'Yes.'

'Okay, get on to the pathologist and get her over there for the formal ID?'

It made sense for a DI to delegate this to her new DS, but if Fran wouldn't even say Marcus's name, maybe she really had been crying.

Fran turned her glare to the new board. '*Christ*. How the hell does this bloody mess link to Lucinda Drummond?'

Stark indicated the arrow at the top of his board pointing to Fran's, with a big red question mark.

She made a face. 'I blame you.'

'It's that consistency I flew home for.'

'I thought that was just to remind me what a pain in the arse you are.' She stared at the board. 'Seriously, whatever happened to nice, simple open-and-shut cases?'

'Whoever said life got simpler with seniority?' said Groombridge, behind them, making Fran jump.

Fran wasn't below glaring at him too. 'Stirring pep talk, as ever, Guv.'

'Sugar-coatings are for the people out there,' he nodded through the grubby window, 'not the people in here.'

'I must've missed that little gem in the inspectors' manual.'

'It's assumed the requisite level of cynicism is baked in during the sergeant years. What do reckon, Joe?'

'Hard to imagine my sunny disposition giving way, Guv, but I'll keep you posted,' replied Stark.

Fran gave a small harumph. 'That's just his polite way of saying he hates being a sergeant as much as I hate being an inspector, and it's all your fault.'

'I think we all know what's more true is that overt resentment is *your* way of showing begrudging gratitude,' smiled Groombridge, sagely. 'So you're both welcome. And with you both finally where you should be, you'll have Joe's support from below, and me freer to shelter you from crap cast from above. The bit in the middle is your problem now.'

Fran turned her overt resentment up a notch. 'You know we all secretly hate you, right?'

'No, you don't.' He smiled, to rub it in. 'So . . .' he said, with a single clap of his hands. 'In the immortal words of Juliana of Norwich – all things are well, and all manner of things shall be well . . . but there's still the *un*necessary sin to be dealt with.'

Stark smiled, as if this were something witty, but it was lost on Fran.

'Ergo, DI Millhaven and DS Stark, run me through your boards, if you'd be so kind.'

One hundred and thirty-one black dots – visible on camera or accounted for throughout.

Four question marks – people they thought they'd traced but needed to double-check. All of it would have to be double-checked. But at least now they had a fair idea who to ask, and what.

Six red dots. Six people out of sight during all or part of the thirty-four-minute window of opportunity.

Alex Zedani – wealthy patron of the arts, pillar of the business community, too charming by half. His personal assistant, Kat-short-for-Katherine Hamilton-Smythe – too slim and pretty by half. And the bodyguard – a trained killer. All outside so Zedani could indulge his vaping habit while on business calls, confirmed only by each other. The exhibition coordinator confirmed letting them out, but then leaving them to it. Opportunity, but no apparent motive.

Adrian Fairchild – old colleague and friend, the way he told it, but professional and romantic jealousy might lurk beneath. Outside, nursing a purported headache, for some of the window of opportunity, but in the loo with his briefcase for the rest? Time for some harder questioning there.

And then Nathan Goff and Tyrone Pook, the catering roadies. There to drive, unload and reload the catering vans, and largely superfluous in between, sitting in their vehicles. The catering manager said he'd smelled dope on them in the past but never caught them in the act. Both on camera, going inside shortly before the window of opportunity, and leaving shortly after the scream was heard. Both with juvenile previous, Goff's more serious, but for thievery, not violence.

Now Goff, possible purloiner of Fairchild's briefcase, was dead; brutally murdered. And his school pal, Pook, was suspiciously absent. That had to put him top of the board for now. Fran wouldn't have pegged him for favourite, but then people often didn't look like killers until they did.

The only one of the six with obvious potential was special forces turned bodyguard, Jan Zieliński, and, by extension, his slimy boss, Zedani. But wishing didn't make it so.

Six names she could work with. Backgrounds, interviews, forensics; she could sift the truth from the lies. But Goff's murder . . . that added *facets*. Just a different name for angles, according to the Groombridge font of unhelpful aphorisms. All Fran saw were complications.

And this morning's one-sided row with Marcus hadn't exactly helped, having to sit in her bloody car outside to wipe away tears of frustration before coming inside. Wanting to scream. Whoever said life got simpler at all? *Ever?* she thought, grinding her teeth and stepping out onto the stoop to feed the press.

'Good morning. As you've already reported, at around eleven last night officers of this station responded to the concerns of a resident of Valiant House in Queen's Park, where they discovered the body of a male in his twenties. His family have been informed but we are not releasing his name at this time, pending formal identification. His death is being treated as suspicious.' Hard not to, considering, she didn't add.

The baying questions erupted, including the one she'd prepared for. 'I can confirm we *are* investigating a possible link to the death of Lucinda Drummond on Friday evening, but I can't comment any further, and I must ask you to refrain from speculation while the investigation unfolds.'

Fat chance of that, she thought, spotting Gwen Maddox, near the back, eyeing her thoughtfully but staying out of the cackling questions.

The hyenas soon sensed there'd be no more flesh on the bones this morning. They had their straplines and ten-second clip for the 10 a.m. news. But Fran felt Gwen's eyes follow her all the way inside.

'Finding your feet again?' asked Marcus, conversationally, as one of Reynolds' junior FLO colleagues guided Nathan Goff's weeping mother out of the viewing room, her only son's body identified by his battered face and tattooed arms, the tattoo on his throat covered for obvious reasons.

Stark watched the door close. 'Waiting for the ground to stop moving, as usual.'

'Yes,' agreed Marcus. 'It does seem to do that a lot.'

Stark spotted an opportunity. 'Everything all right with you?'

Marcus tilted his head. 'Goodness. Are we straying beyond small talk?'

'Could be.'

'Is this you asking?' Anyone who knew Fran might suspect her hand at work.

'Entirely.'

'Sparked by . . . ?'

'Fraternal concern. A feeling.'

'Shifting ground?' mused Marcus.

'Hard to tell.'

'Yes,' nodded Marcus, ruefully. 'It so often is.'

So there was something wrong between them. Star-crossed lovers. God knows, Fran wasn't likely to make it easy. 'SNAFU?'

Marcus smiled. He had enough military background to know *situation normal – all fucked up.*

'Anything I might help with?' asked Stark, unsure what that could possibly be.

'Thanks, but you're best off out there beyond the mine-field, I think.'

'Minimum safe distance?' scoffed Stark. If Fran had one.

'Now we're straying into areas a gentleman doesn't discuss.'

'Understood.' What else was there to say?

They both stared through the glass as Marcus's assistant materialized to wheel Goff's remains back into the main mortuary for the post-mortem.

'Not sure we're going to move much on cause of death,' commented Marcus. 'But I'll let you know what I find.'

18

Stark was halfway back to Royal Hill when his phone rang. SOCO. 'Hello.'

'DS Stark, please.'

He almost corrected the S, as when he'd been bumped to acting-sergeant in the army. 'Speaking.'

'This is Yasmina Patel, CSM from the Nathan Goff bloodbath.' The eagle-eyed crime scene manager, calling to update him on her initial findings, which didn't amount to much so far. 'We're still cataloguing a few items of suspicious provenance, but no hits yet on the stolen items database. Some points of interest though: no bloody knife or sign of whatever they used to remove the fingers, so perhaps they brought their own tools. As we thought, the bloody footprints indicate the killers wore disposable overshoes as well as gloves, so they came with a plan. You might assume they brought overalls too.'

To make blood-spot evidence less likely, further indicating cold-blooded intent.

'The footprints do give hints of rugged tread patterns,' continued Patel, 'perhaps indicating boots – walking, military, motorcycle. Varying patterns. Two size elevens and one size twelve, indicating males, possibly tall.

'We found some spare keys in a kitchen drawer, but no main set in the flat or on the body. Outside, we found his postbox locked but empty, but we found his post in a nearby front garden, including two more Dosh4Gold envelopes ripped open, but with cheques still inside. Looks like gold was his preferred loot.'

So I wasn't the only one who took an interest in what he might have stolen, thought Stark, unsurprised.

'But the real reason I'm calling is, you asked about a briefcase?'

'You found one?'

'We widened the search area to nearby properties and scrubland. Found a case under sacks in bins behind the adjacent low-rises. Empty. But in another bin we found paperwork appearing to belong to –'

'Adrian Fairchild.'

A moment's silence suggested he had somewhat burst her balloon. 'Lucky guess?'

'It certainly helps connect some dots. Thanks.'

'Want us to process it all for prints and DNA?'

'Drop an email to the SIO, DCI Millhaven, to confirm, if that's okay.'

Patel agreed to, and rang off.

Stark was stopped at a red light. He pictured the case boards in his mind's eye, mentally adding a line linking the photo of Adrian Fairchild with that of Nathan Goff.

But that still didn't make him Goff's killer.

Fairchild hardly fitted the bill of the brutal butcher.

Nonetheless, he'd made no mention to the police of a missing briefcase. If, as seemed likely, Goff had stolen it from the Queen's House event, was that why he'd been killed? If so, what could possibly have been in the brief-case to bring down such brutal retribution on his head? And how had the killers found him?

A horn tooted behind, alerting him to the fact that the light had turned green. Stark pulled into a side street and dialled the office.

Dixon answered.

'John, how did you get on with Dosh4Gold?'

'I'm sorry, Mr Goff, but as I said, once your items are received and passed to our assaying team, you must await the formal offer before either accepting it or requesting return of your items.'

Dixon had run aground on Dosh4Gold's sandbank bureaucracy earlier, and it seemed the script hadn't changed. Stark's patience was wearing thin. In the last few days he'd twice witnessed the grief of a bereaved family forced to endure the horror of identifying the remains of a loved one – first of a loving mother, then of a wayward son. And with every degree of anger came a sting of accusation for the lives *he'd* taken, however justifiable.

At this stage there seemed little point reiterating to this next-level arse-scratcher that he was not Nathan Goff – but he did so, all the same. The chances that anything from Fairchild's briefcase had been made of gold seemed slim, but they needed to explore the angles before confronting him about it.

'And have you tried submitting your request through our online customer services page?' asked the misnamed enquiries manager, a little sniffily.

'No, because this is not a customer matter,' replied Stark, with false calm. 'As my colleague and I have both explained, this isn't the owner asking for their bling back, this is the *police* asking for evidence pertaining to a *homicide investigation*. So we thought it best to call direct.' A decision Stark was rapidly regretting.

Fran hovered nearby like a wasp, less interested in the picnic than stinging someone. It was a good job she wasn't on this call.

'I see . . . okay, please hold while I check . . . ahh, yes, our records show two telephone requests for the return of your item.'

'Including this one?'

'I'm sorry?'

'Two calls, including this one?'

'No . . . this is the *third* call. I also see nine-forty this morning and . . . eleven forty-three last night.'

Stark paused. 'Both requesting return of the item in the envelope?'

'Yes.'

'Which was what exactly?' Such a detail had been beyond the authority of the mere enquiries *assistant* that Dixon had run foul of earlier.

'Er . . .' There was a long pause. 'One gold coin.'

Stark sat up, exchanging a look with Dixon. 'Okay . . .' he said slowly. 'So, can I just ask, when you pre-declare that you're recording all conversations for security and training purposes . . . is that for real?'

It wasn't Goff's voice.

It had taken all of Stark's experience in dealing with the intransigency of British Army Quartermasters to negotiate past the Dosh4Gold enquiries manager to someone able to cut the crap – a senior manager with army background, who recognized Stark's name.

The coin was now on its way to the station and the recording had been emailed to them.

Accented English. Eastern European, or Russian perhaps. Ptolemy had already confirmed it definitely wasn't Nathan Goff's second-generation South London lingo. Tyrone Pook was also London born and raised, so unless Goff or Pook had put on a fake accent, it seemed Stark might now have a recording of the killer's voice bang in the middle of Goff's TOD window.

Some perps were careless. Some just didn't care. Given the state of Goff's remains, this felt more and more like the latter. They'd taken enough care to use a burner phone – not currently switched on – and hadn't given an email address.

We really needed to speak to Tyrone Pook, thought Stark.

As if in answer to that thought, Williams' number popped up on his phone.

'Thought I'd take a run at Pook's place with uniform while Fran went for a warrant,' he explained. 'Knocked on some doors. Maintenance guy showed us in, and the first thing we noticed was a busted lock. Neighbours say they hadn't noticed it. Not the most salubrious block in town. But a couple of them said they heard some noise in the night, somewhere around two. Good enough for probable cause for a look-see, in my book. The flat's been turned over, but not like anyone was really looking for anything. Portable electronics still here, TV, DVD, games console . . . but the bedroom looks more like someone was packing in a hurry, clothes drawers open, half empty, with pants, socks and T-shirts on the floor. No sign of a passport. My guess is Pook got spooked, packed and ran, and maybe just in time. We're sealing off the flat now, then I thought I'd try his family again.'

He was, Stark realized, asking permission. 'Good idea.' He told Williams about the Dosh4Gold lead and sent him the voice recording to play to the family, just in case they recognized it. He did the same with Reynolds, asking the FLO to play it to Goff's mum. Then he called Fran to let her know the warrant was no longer needed.

Whilst this saved her wasting more time, she predictably focused on the precious minutes already lost.

God help Marcus, thought Stark.

'Alert the ports?' suggested Dixon.

Stark nodded. This latest development perhaps made it appear less likely that Pook had killed his mate Goff and more likely that he'd escaped a similar fate, but the only way to be sure was to find him – before anyone else did.

When the bike courier arrived from Dosh4Gold's fortified smelting works in Tilbury, an hour later, Stark gloved-up, opened the envelope, tipped the contents into a clear evidence bag, sealed it shut and inspected it. By now it had been handled by God knows who, but DNA comparison could be a long game. A single gold coin hardly seemed motive for what had been done to poor Nathan Goff. Stark had expected a gold sovereign, such as a generous grandparent might give an infant for their birth year. Nice, but still a poor price for a man's life.

It wasn't that.

There was no hallmark, no date and no sign of Her Majesty the Queen. It was larger, fatter, irregular, blob-like, with a worn, bearded and crowned face on one side and a punched indent design on the reverse. Beautiful but rudimentary – and by the look of it, very old.

The kind of antiquity a curator of ancient currency like Adrian Fairchild might be interested in. The kind of thing someone might badly want back.

Perhaps Goff had tried to extort a ransom and walked into a trap, ending up back at his own flat answering difficult questions. But then why had he sent it off for smelting? Greed? Bank the cash value and try a fake ransom on the off chance?

Whatever the answers, Goff's action appeared to have fatally backfired.

Stark stared at the coin.

The Met had to have people he could ask about this.

19

The Met Police Arts and Antiquities Unit was buried in the bowels of a dishevelled building several streets from Scotland Yard, in a single windowless room with noisy pipes and missing ceiling tiles. Three desks, stacked with teetering files, fought for space with filing cabinets. A small fridge and kettle had evidently been squeezed out into the corridor, clearly prioritizing extra space over fire regulations.

The officer he'd spoken with on the phone was not only too busy to come to Greenwich, she was evidently too busy to meet him in reception or spare him more than a cursory glance when he finally found his way down here alone. Whatever Stark had expected, DC Sophie Swan was about as far from a tweedy professor as Indiana Jones was from any kind of professional archaeologist. No older than him, hair tied back, pretty face unembellished by make-up, the most succinct description one might offer in the context of her surroundings, was neat. He would not have been surprised if she had identical Einsteinian outfits for each day of the week, to save time. She waved at an empty chair with barely a glance, industriously forking colourful salad into her mouth from a Tupperware container while scanning emails.

It was 4 p.m. Perhaps she'd been divorced from sunlight down here so long that she'd lost track of lunchtime.

Stark considered pulling a chair closer, but her personal

zone of tidiness was clearly fighting a losing battle with the box files stacked on every surface and covering most of the floor.

'It's not what most people expect,' she stated, eyes still scanning. 'Those who even know we exist.'

'Thank you for agreeing to meet me. I can see you're busy.'

'Busy?' She rolled her eyes, but that seemed about as far from her screen as they were likely to stray. 'At any one time, we're cataloguing over fifty thousand stolen artworks, and that's just London. We also have to coordinate with regional teams and the international market. The US have over four hundred trained officers, not counting twenty dedicated FBI agents. We have two DCs led by one DS.' She tutted, stabbed what could only have been a terse response into her keyboard, hit send and clicked to open another email. 'Every time there's some political emergency we get shut down and seconded for months, sometimes longer, and there's the constant threat of being *permanently* defunded in the name of austerity. All this in a country with a twenty per cent share in a fifty *billion* dollar art black market. So, the only reason I'm sparing you two minutes is the photo you sent, and we don't get many celebrity visitors down here.'

'I'm hardly a celebrity.'

'You're the closest thing we're likely to get.' She finally glanced up. 'A word from you and we might actually get a line of press interest.'

'I don't do endorsements.'

'But you know the press. That online reporter you sold your exclusive to.'

'I gave an interview. I didn't *sell* anything,' replied Stark, starting to get annoyed.

'Well, perhaps you can give me her number, and I'll give her another free exclusive.'

'Look, if you're too busy, perhaps I can speak with someone else?'

'See anyone else here?' she asked, waving her hand around. 'No, because they're out doing the job of twenty officers each, without a lick of overtime pay. Sod forty hours maximum, we don't even have time to get signed off with stress.'

'Well, if you think I'm wasting your time . . .' Stark stood to go.

'I hope you *are*,' she said bluntly. 'The last thing we need down here is more work. Let's have a look then . . .'

Stark decided discretion was the better part of valour and wordlessly passed her the evidence bag.

She peered at the coin through the plastic, felt it, pulled out a jeweller's loupe to inspect it more closely, and sighed. 'Damn.'

'Damn?'

'Where did you get this?'

'A low-level thief tried cashing it in with Dosh4Gold.'

She blinked. 'Then tell them to pay more attention to what they steal, before they send it off to the smelters.'

'He'll have a few lifetimes on the karmic ladder before he can put that lessen into action.'

'Dead?'

'Very.'

'Then perhaps whoever killed him knew what this was really worth.'

'Which is more than its weight, I assume.'

'You could say that.' She clicked through files on her computer until she opened a photo for him to see. An identical coin, laid next to a millimetre rule for scale. 'To your stupid thief, a few hundred quid. To Dosh4Gold, double that. On the black market, it depends who's buying, how much they want something they can never show off publicly, and how desperate the vendor is to get rid of something this hot, but anywhere between fifty thousand and a million. But to any curator with scruples, priceless.'

'Seriously?'

'Well, I'm no expert.' She shrugged. 'We buy the brains in – if and when anyone's prepared to sign off the budget. But if this is what it looks like, the real question you should be asking is, where are the rest?'

'Time to release the names,' said Fran.

'That a statement or a question, Detective Inspector Millhaven?' asked Groombridge's measured voice through her phone.

Everything was a test with him. She was the senior investigating officer. 'The mother has ID'd Nathan Goff. The press will find his name, whether we give it to them or not. As soon as it's out there, it's true that our chances of finding Tyrone Pook un-spooked are gone, but his disappearance suggests he passed spooked some time ago – or worse. If he's not already dead somewhere in a puddle of his own blood, and missing his digits like Goff, he's the only red dot left to re-interview. I don't see any benefit in waiting longer.'

'Time to shake the tree?'

'Exactly.'

'You've prepared the press release?'

'First thing this morning.'

'Then if that's your recommendation as SIO, I concur.'

And with that ringing endorsement, he was gone.

She rang Williams to tell him to send the release. No point waiting to deliver it from the station steps, like her self-aggrandizing predecessor. Fran had suffered her fill of Gwen's ilk for now – and this way, Pook's face would just make the evening news.

Her stomach growled again. Coppers learned to eat on the go, but the culinary snob in Fran made that hard, and the guilty pleasure she took in pastries didn't make her any more likely to make love with the light on. Not that lighting was the current issue.

'The international arts community is going to have a shit-fit,' continued Swan, rubbing her temples as she stared at the coin. 'Everyone thinks the Nebuchadnezzar Hoard was melted down.'

'Babylonian?'

She looked up in surprise, surveying him. 'Very good. I had to look online. One of only twenty-three found buried in a clay urn, prize Iraqi heritage before they were stolen from a museum. There's nothing like them, apparently. Before they were found, everyone thought the earliest proper coinage, not bullion – that's ingots – was around 560 BCE, with the Lydian gold stater.'

'Stater?'

Swan shrugged. 'It's about how they're made, apparently. A modern coin is struck between two obverse die,

145

leaving two proud images, heads and tails. But a *stater*'s reverse side is struck with an incuse punch, stamping an imprint – usually some form of pattern, image or script. Anyway, the most common, like a Persian daric, might fetch two to four thousand at auction. A rarer Croesus stater in good nick might go for sixty-plus.'

'Croesus, as in rich as . . . ?'

'Exactly. But the Nebuchadnezzar staters proved to be hundreds of years older . . . larger, less sophisticated, but completely unique.'

Stark stared at the evidence bag, imagining what would have happened if he'd not asked for it back. 'So either one or more escaped the melting pot, or someone's found a twenty-fourth.'

'More likely the former,' suggested Swan. 'A find like this would be hard to keep quiet. But either way, unfortunate for your dead thief.'

'But someone who knew what they'd actually got, might badly want this back.'

Swan nodded. 'Especially if they had the other twenty-two. Of course the real prize was the mask.'

'Mask?'

'The Mask of Kings. Nebuchadnezzar the First . . . founder of the dynasty. Unearthed with the coins. Stolen at the same time but recovered weeks later, thank goodness. Culturally priceless.'

'Wait a minute . . .' said Stark suddenly. 'These weren't all looted from the Shu'aiba Museum storage building outside Basra, were they?'

'Yes.' Swan stared in surprise. 'How on earth would you know that?'

Memories swam ... of six weeks escorting curators from the Basra Museum Project in their search for a suitable site to home what little had survived the looting and destruction after the 2003 Coalition Invasion years earlier. Of an oven-hot warehouse in the Iraqi summer, and an old man kneeling in the ruins of broken crates and shattered pottery. Stark had volunteered. A bit of extra deployment pay. Fraught with danger on the roads but a cushy secondment compared to seven months in a front-line combat outpost that followed. A chance to give something back, mend something instead of destroying, or so he'd thought. The project had eventually settled on the once-opulent Lakeside Palace, requisitioned by Saddam in the eighties to keep his wife out of the way, but not before the temporary storage facility was raided.

Looting, was the official Iraqi verdict. It had seemed more like targeted theft to Stark, but his opinion was never sought. Ancient urns, gold coins – and a mask. That was all he was told. But he could still picture that poor man in shock, collecting shards of ancient earthenware as if each were the death of a child ... 'I think I was there.'

'You were *there*? In Basra?'

'In the warehouse, just after the looting, if that's what it was. Long story.'

Swan held open her palms, impatiently, to indicate her surroundings. 'You'll note that I've stopped everything else I was doing.'

'Wait a minute,' said Stark, with a sneaking suspicion he knew the answer. 'You said you buy in expertise. Who would you call in about this?'

20

Stark stared at the board, joining the red dots, so to speak.

Lucinda Drummond and Nathan Goff, dead. Tyrone Pook missing. And now, in the middle, Adrian Fairchild.

There was nothing definitively linking Fairchild to the Nebuchadnezzar stater, but the proximity of the rarest of coins to the nation's foremost ancient coin expert would seem an improbable coincidence, even before the brief-case linking him to Goff. Did this leapfrog Fairchild over Pook into the prime suspect position? Had he, in fact, disposed of Pook too? A mild-mannered academic might turn killer, in desperation or passion, but to do what was done to Nathan Goff . . . ? It didn't feel right. No judge would sign a warrant for them to search Fairchild's house.

Prime person of interest, then.

Stark un-popped a marker and wrote POI under Fairchild's picture, and then, after a moment's hesitation, added a wavy line across the top of all four pictures, ending in an arrow, where he added a photo of the coin and a question mark.

There was still something or someone missing from this picture.

The only thing they could be sure of was that someone had probably gut-punched Lucinda before shoving her off a height, and someone had tortured and butchered

Nathan Goff. Both of them had pissed someone off. Whether that was the same person, remained uncertain.

'Holy crap,' breathed Swan next to him, peering at the crime scene photos of Nathan Goff. 'Someone really wanted that coin back.'

So it seemed, thought Stark.

'Who's this?' demanded Fran, entering and looking Swan up and down with a default expression of distrust.

'Long story,' replied Stark.

'Then give me the short version, and make it snappy.'

Stark stared at the new photo, conscious of both women staring at him. Taking a deep breath, he blew it out slowly, deciding on the best opening to annoy Fran. 'Okay . . . how much do you know about Ancient Mesopotamia?'

'This coin appears to be one of twenty-three looted from an Iraqi museum warehouse along with a priceless cere-monial gold mask,' explained Stark's new BFF, DC Swan, of the *who-knew-we-even-had-one* Arts and Antiquities Unit.

On first impressions she looked like someone who didn't get out much and preferred it that way, addressing the room like a dogged teacher who knew for certain it was *her* time *you* were wasting. Fran had automatically filed her under *dislike – mitigations pending*.

'The latter was later recovered and is on display in the rehoused Basra Museum,' continued Swan, 'but the coins were never seen again. While there is a lucrative inter-national black market for such treasures, it was assumed that with the dire socioeconomic state in Iraq at the time, they were most likely melted down for base gold. This one turning up now will cause a major stir, and the powers-that-be will want radio silence until it's been authenticated. Adrian Fairchild would have been the man we called in for that, which might explain his involvement. One of the trickiest elements of the black market is provenance and authenticity.'

'Are you suggesting there might be forgery in the otherwise whiter-that-white black market in stolen artworks?' joked Williams theatrically, earning a glower from Fran. It was all very well goofing around in-house, but not in front of guests.

'Who'd have thought, right?' nodded Swan. 'But it does mean there's money to be made for the unscrupulous expert. It's not all that surprising, therefore, that second only to follow the *money* in what – if we were funded in any meaningful way – we might call our "investigations", comes follow the *expertise*.'

'So Fairchild is bent,' said Dixon.

'Could be. But you don't have enough to haul him in – and if you ask him about the coin, you tip your hand.'

'But if we get lucky, it's Fairchild who turns up, boasting a dodgy Russian accent,' said Fran.

'Leading us to your cunning plan,' mused Groombridge, with zero apparent enthusiasm.

'They don't know we have it,' Fran explained, unnecessarily. In the year Stark had been gone, she'd somehow forgotten how quickly she could come to regret listening to him.

The DCI stared back levelly. 'I do understand the cunningness of the ruse.'

'Once they do, the chance is gone.'

'And the timeliness.' Groombridge looked at Stark. 'This has the feel of one of *his* ideas.'

Fran shrugged. 'And you know I hate any idea that wasn't mine, especially his, but the potential upside is appealing – and if it goes wrong, we all get to blame him.'

Groombridge looked to Swan. 'And you're on board with this?'

Swan shrugged. 'Doesn't risk the coin we've got. Might lead us to more. And if it all goes wrong, I'm happy to blame Stark too.'

'You have any spare bodies you can call in to assist?'

'It's probably too soon in our working relationship for me to scoff derisively, sir.' She met his scrutinizing gaze with no apparent fear. She reminded Fran of Stark in that regard, which was not much of a mitigation.

Groombridge steepled his fingers in thought, likely filing Swan away for later consideration too. 'Then we'd need some uniforms.'

'Already spoken with the three Ps, Guv,' said Stark. 'Just need sign-off on the overtime and equipment.'

Fran held her breath. She wasn't at all convinced this was a good idea, but sometimes a sledgehammer was exactly what you needed to smash a nut.

'Okay,' said Groombridge. 'Talk me through it . . .'

Valiant House loomed into the light-polluted sky, its monolithic charmlessness turning slowly from sunset gold to blood red, as if the stain of Nathan Goff's brutal exsanguination were leeching out to remind the onlooking coppers why they were on a stake-out below.

Stark closed his eyes, but the crimson lingered like red

desert sands burning into the eyeballs, the dry-mouthed waiting, searching every sound for the bullet's betrayal or mortar's whine, the sweat and constant alertness. He re-opened his eyes and shook away the past. This was London, not Helmand.

Briefed by Stark, the ex-army supervisor at Dosh4Gold had willingly agreed to message the party pretending to be Nathan Goff, claiming that a delivery driver had returned the item to the given postal address that evening. As long shots went, this one was three Hail Marys, but with little else to go on, Groombridge had reluctantly agreed. If there was any chance at all that Goff's killers might return to the scene of the crime, it had to be taken. But now that it was in motion, the cunningness of the ruse was confronting the reality of self-doubt.

'John *Dixon* . . . ?'

The incredulity in Ptolemy's voice brought Stark's thoughts back to the car. Rewinding the background chatter in his head, he found Constable Peters musing on the notion of matchmaking Dixon with Pensol.

The pair in question were sat in Dixon's unmarked car in a nearby street as backup or pursuit; a suggestion of Peters' that suddenly sounded less than innocent. Her appetite for gossip and matchmaking was shameless, but generally kind. 'He could do a lot worse,' she shrugged.

Pensol could do worse too, thought Stark – and she had, after a bullet had sent her into the same spiral of booze and self-loathing Stark himself was probably still climbing out of. Dixon had more to him than people generally thought.

Ptolemy still looked bemused. 'But what happened to fixing her up with Joe here?'

When Peters had conspired to match Pensol with Stark, two years ago, he suspected it was born out of Pensol's own partiality. But whether or not Dixon's green-gilled ignominy in the early hours of this morning had somehow sown fresh seeds of romance in Pensol's heart, it clearly hadn't gone unnoticed by Peters.

'*He* happened, didn't he?' She rolled her eyes, pointing a fork-skewered chip at Stark. 'Before his subsequent disappearing act. I mistook him for a nice guy. Safe pair of hands. Turns out he's a walking lightning rod for trouble.'

Unsafe to be around. Stark smiled at her jibe but it rang too true for genuine amusement – as his ex, Kelly, had found out to her cost.

'And marriage proposals,' added Swan, digging half-heartedly with her wooden chip-fork, as if hoping to find some salad beneath. 'How many was it they reported in the news, after that clocktower thing . . . ? And weren't you supposed to be getting another medal?'

The fact that someone he'd never met before today knew such things about him made Stark shudder.

Peters grinned. 'Yeah, what happened to that, Joe?'

'Trouble cancels medals.' Another half-lie, to paint the world a little greyer.

'There goes *our* chances then,' declared Ptolemy. 'Makes you wonder how we let him talk us into this little excursion.'

'Anything for a free bag of chips,' grinned Peters, chomping into the last of the pickled onion she'd demanded to seal the deal. Stark supposed, in America, it might've been a chilli-dog or doughnuts. Small price to pay to have Royal Hill's finest to keep him company on a speculative stakeout. They'd have come without the freebies, of course, but it never hurt to grease the wheels of friendship – or in this case, the arteries.

'And people think this job's all about the glamour,' muttered Ptolemy, who'd been in uniform long enough that his waistline and face both showed a level of resentment towards yet another lump of sub-standard greasy horror eaten leaning against a police car as curtains twitched and the occasional passer-by eyed them with uncertainty or outright hostility.

'You'd rather be circling Thamesmead, waiting for kids to brick the car?' asked Peters.

'I'd rather be in Rosie's with Stark here buying the sergeant's round.'

'Tony made that up,' said Peters, laughing.

Ptolemy acted appalled. 'Don't listen to her, Joe, she's a troublemaker.'

Stark chuckled. 'I'll admit, it does sound more fun than sitting here hoping to cross paths with whoever did for Nathan Goff.'

'Assuming they're stupid enough to show up at all,' said Peters. Assuming Stark's plan wasn't as stupid as Fran was now insisting. 'Least this way we get a bit of rom-com with our chips. Stoke the nascent flames of station-crossed-love and all that. Call it dinner theatre.'

'You're incorrigible,' scoffed Ptolemy, disapprovingly. 'Anyway, I thought Dixon *had* a girlfriend.'

'Not a particularly *friendly* one, is what I hear,' mused Peters. 'That right, Joe?'

'My only intel is a year old,' he side-stepped.

Peters just shrugged. 'Do him good to rub shoulders with a *nice* girl like Marianne.'

Perhaps it would, thought Stark, but he was ill-qualified to judge Cupid's aim. 'You're asking the wrong person.'

'You're not fooling me,' grinned Peters, crumpling the greasy paper wrappings into a nearby bin. 'You're an old romantic at heart, just like me.'

'I've been called worse, I suppose.' Old for his years. High mileage. Broken down. All common themes of his shrink sessions, as well as stubbornly self-flagellating with a self-appointed pre-Galilean opinion of his place in the universe and responsibility for all its orbiting disasters, manifesting in survivor's guilt, duty martyrdom and an unhealthy dose of saviour complex – apparently. And all that before they got on to the impact on his *romantic* relationships. Pensol, like Kelly, was better off beyond minimum safe distance – outside *his* minefield. Perhaps it would do *her* good to rub shoulders with a nice guy like John Dixon, but matchmaking was Peters' forte, not his.

'Not in the press,' said Swan, fastidiously folding closed the paper around her lightly sampled chips with evident distaste. 'That's why *I'm* here. You may consider yourself above celebrity endorsements, but getting your shiny name next to the recovery of one of the Basra staters might just keep what's left of Arts and Antiquities breathing stale basement air for another year.'

They did a quick radio check with 'the lovebirds', plus Fran and Williams, parked around the corner on the approach road, before settling into his car. Peters made a point of taking a back seat with Swan. 'Front for the *sergeants*.'

Stark wound down his window to shed the clinging aroma of chip fat and pickled onion. The day was giving up its warmth rapidly into the still night. The hum and wails of London added texture to the fume-laden, silty air. He found it all strangely soothing. Eyes fixed on the distant, dimly lit base of Valiant House, his mind wandered from Peters' cheerful quizzing of Swan's apparently non-existent personal life to distant places in brightly lit pasts. His pasts. Past versions of himself.

He thought of Gabrielle, wondering if she too might be enjoying a moment's peace, shedding the struggle, if only for a time, to sink beneath the wind-waved dunes into that pre-dream state so akin to memory.

'Sigh of a heavy heart?' asked Ptolemy.

'Or a distant one?' suggested Peters. 'He was *miles* away. I knew it,' she cheered. 'There had to be a girl, for you to pass over sweet Marianne. What's her name, Joe?'

Stark suppressed another sigh. 'Fate.'

Peters harrumphed. 'Don't think I won't get her name out of you.'

But before she could try, the radio crackled with Williams' voice.

'Biker just pulled up.'

21

Long shot or not, they were now recording a suspect onscreen.

The camera – battery operated, motion sensitive, concealed in a bush overhanging the postboxes and linked via an obliging resident's WiFi to Stark's phone – had seen Valiant House residents come and go, but this latest visitor could best be described as furtive.

Stark's phone screen showed the infrared image of a figure in black looking around, then stepping up to the postboxes outside, pulling out a key and opening Nathan Goff's. Male, from the size and shape, wearing an open-face motorcycle helmet but with sunglasses and one of those snood-scarves designed to hook up over the nose to keep out the cold, bugs or facial ID.

'So much for Plan B,' tutted Ptolemy.

'I was always more of a Plan A kinda guy,' said Stark, climbing out of the car as Peters radioed the others.

'*Plan A, go, go, go!*'

Stark was running. The titanium in his hip usually had a thing or two to say about that sort of thing. But if life in uniforms taught you it was easier to beg forgiveness than permission, then life with old injuries meant sometimes you just had to do now and ache later.

Out of the corner of his eye he glimpsed Williams and Fran converging on the same point, but his eyes stayed fixed on Valiant House, the stationary black motorbike, engine still running, and the black-clad biker inspecting the mail. So much so that he barely registered Dixon's voice shouting urgently through the radio about another bike, nor the sound of another engine, until a second motorbike shot between Fran and Williams, scattering them to the ground, and tore across the pavement to cut off Stark. Ptolemy shouted something behind him. Ahead, Biker One froze, then ran – away from Stark, down the ramped access to his waiting bike.

That was all Stark had time to see before diving beneath something being swung at his head by the second rider as the bike ripped past him. Shoulder-rolling straight to his feet, with more than one stab of pain, he spun to see the bike slew round in a broad skid. A motocross bike, sturdy, powerful, agile. All black, like the rider. No decals, no brand, no plates – identical to the first. Biker Two paused, side-on, dark glasses fixed emotionless on Stark. The engine revved. And again. Clutch-out, it ripped the ground another vicious scar, and launched back towards Stark, a crowbar in the rider's hand.

But Stark had his answer to hand. A police-issue ASP baton. Twenty-one inches of telescopic steel.

First, it was about biology. Timing. When to breathe, move, swing. When to twist, and thrust. The crowbar cleaved the air, close enough to feel how near it came to cleaving his skull. The ASP skewered into the front wheel.

After that, physics took over.

The ASP bit into its target, just failing to take Stark's

hand off but successfully sinking its solitary fang into the wheel, and by association, the bike and its rider. The former flipped fully twice, and bounced another three times. The latter hit the ground two metres further along but took it like a pro – staying curled and loose, letting the leather, armour and helmet do their job, letting the roll dispel the energy.

Peters, Ptolemy and Swan lay sprawled, as bike and rider must've spun between them.

And then, like some Vegas conjuring trick, a third identical biker materialized, revving in from nowhere and skidding to a halt by his fallen triplet, bellowing something unintelligible. Miraculously, Biker Two was the first to their feet, though it looked like it cost them, gripping Biker Three's arm and swinging onto the pillion seat behind them. By the time the cops were all upright, both remaining bikes and their three riders were away off up the street.

'*Suspects fleeing on two bikes, north on Valley Grove!*' Stark barked into his radio for Dixon and Pensol.

But a single car didn't stand much chance against two bikes.

'*They got past us on the pavements,*' announced Dixon's voice, followed by his calls to Control for patrol assistance, then a minute later: '*Lost them! They cut south through Maryon Park.*'

More radio traffic.

Stark's mind was already picturing the park exits in aerial view. Too many. Control was repeating out the details to all patrol cars. They might get lucky. But this had stopped being a vehicle pursuit. Helicopter was their only hope, but a call came in that India Two was busy elsewhere and India One would take too long to get airborne. India Three would be in the service shed. One of the three always was.

If it weren't for the adrenaline coursing through him, Stark might have sighed or cursed, but his brain was still on high alert, scanning for threats, cover and casualties.

No incoming.

Enemy withdrawn.

No one on the ground.

Five standing.

Last full measure of devotion given, the ASP lay bent nearby.

The fallen bike was still revving loudly on its side, cowlings shattered, forks bent, front alloy wheel shattered.

Stark limped over and turned off the engine, straightened up and rolled his bad shoulder. A diving roll over a once bullet-shattered scapular had seemed like a bad idea even as he was doing it. The problem with begging forgiveness afterwards was that the more you did it, the angrier the oft-overridden protests of his body became.

Not as furious as Fran appeared, currently wordless with rage.

'Well . . .' grunted Swan, dusting down her clothes. 'Plan C it is then.'

Groombridge stared at the shattered remains of Plan C in an evidence bag.

The mini GPS tracker they'd hidden inside the Dosh-4Gold envelope in place of the gold coin. Backup, in case the perps got away, in the hope of tracking them to their lair. The app on Stark's phone had shown it travelling only as far as Maryon Park, where it was found crushed beside the opened envelope.

Perusing the other exhibits on the fold-out table, he wondered why he'd even bothered trying to go home earlier. Wasn't the point of having a DI and DS beneath him that he didn't get called out to crime scenes late at night? 'So much for the budget-007 gadgetry.'

Stark wisely said nothing.

Dixon and Pensol had returned empty-handed. Uniform cars had arrived within minutes, a chopper minutes later, but the bikers were long gone. Fran had charged back to the station to redirect her frustration at anyone in the traffic camera suite. The set of keys found dangling from the postbox lock were a match for Goff's spare set, linking this incident to the murder, but that was hardly news.

'So, aside from this wreckage, all you have to show for your efforts is bruises, one broken bike with no plates or visible VIN numbers, video footage of a covered face and riders in black fleeing on black motorbikes at night in a world where high-vis black is de rigueur in motorcycle safety-wear.'

Anyone else might've had the decency to shift in discomfort at his tone, but Stark could outstare a tank barrel. 'I think crowbar-biker-guy had a beard poking out the bottom of his helmet, Guv. Brown.'

'Like every other self-respecting biker.'

'Yes. Otherwise that about sums it up, Guv.'

Groombridge gave this the dull stare it deserved. 'So we're agreed, the potential upside has failed to materialize, and we all get to blame you.'

'Fran's way ahead of you on that one, Guv.'

Quite how this had become a competition to see who could keep the straightest face was a mystery, but Groombridge wasn't budging first, especially in front of a stranger. 'And you, DC Swan, who's more foolish – the fool or the fool who follows them?'

'Constables follow orders, sir,' replied Swan, levelly.

Groombridge suspected she'd suffered enough fools to know how this game was played. According to her sergeant, during their brief phone call earlier, as the Met's most under-recognized specialist unit, few came to the AAU and even fewer stayed. Swan had been there six years. Dedicated, smart, no one's fool. 'Well, your DS Roberts says you can stick around to help us look for more of these coins, but since DS Stark has already nearly killed you with a flying motorcycle, I thought I'd ask your opinion.'

'Change of pace from my basement, sir.'

'It's the sudden accelerations you have to worry about with this one. Don't say you weren't warned.' He looked at Stark. 'How's the hand?' There was an ice pack strapped to his right hand with a thick bandage. Damn fool was lucky the ASP hadn't broken bones.

Stark turned it back and forth, flexing his fingers. 'Nothing that would stop me cheerfully punching that rider in the face with it.'

'Well, at least wait till he removes the helmet,' suggested Groombridge. With anyone else he might have bothered to articulate further disapproval, but Stark's immunity to hierarchical critique was among his best and most annoying qualities. 'So how do we feel your first outing as a DS is going?'

Stark thought about that for a second. 'About average.'

'Right,' Groombridge sighed to hide his smile. 'Plan A was to apprehend. Plan B was to capture a face on camera. Plan C was to trace the suspects with GPS. So what's Plan D?'

Stark had seen Groombridge testing Fran too often not to know his part. 'Traffic cameras, local CCTV, door-to-door and TV appeal. Forensics on the bike, crowbar, envelope and smashed tracker. And Adrian Fairchild.'

22

'You sure about this?' Fran stared through the one-way glass into Interview Room One, where Stark and Swan were running through the rights and preambles with Adrian Fairchild and the lawyer he'd called a minute after they'd shown up.

Groombridge's eyes didn't leave the glass either. 'He's your bagman. It's your call.'

Fran made a face and sipped her coffee, suppressing a yawn. Dawn door-knocking was good for discombobulating your suspect, but that worked both ways. But that wasn't what was irking her. Fairchild looked rattled, but from the moment they showed up it felt like he'd been dreading this. In other words, expecting it. She itched to be in the room, picking him apart, but Groombridge had quietly asked whether she'd consider letting Stark take first crack. Just one of his innocent little thought-bombs. He'd been her mentor for years. Now she was Stark's.

Stark looked like he'd slept, at least. He looked well. Something seemed to have changed in him during his absence. Fran couldn't say why, really, but he seemed less out of kilter with the world in general – though still with hers, of course. Or was it really her out of kilter? Probably both. 'He's earned his sergeant's stripes. Now he needs to learn what they mean.'

Groombridge nodded, sagely. She needed to learn that

her inspector's pips meant sometimes letting her sergeant kick open the door. Point made. 'Everything okay?'

Here we go, she thought. 'Peachy.'

'I meant, outside work?'

'I know.'

'Wanna talk about it?'

'No.'

He knew about Marcus. The daily paranoia over whether anyone had noticed her burgeoning belly bump or nausea had eventually forced her to fess up. The miscarriage had come a week later. Not uncommon in geriatric pregnancy, they said. Geriatric, at thirty-nine, and didn't she feel it. Weeks of wondering how to break it to Groombridge, of worrying what the hell would happen with her job, of waiting for the merciless morning sickness to stop, of growing closer to Marcus, of starting to believe in a different life, and then . . . Her knuckles whitened around the mug handle.

Yesterday morning, doubtless in desperate hope of reaching through their fog, Marcus had tentatively asked whether she'd like to try again, and she'd snapped at him, and he'd been infuriatingly nice about it until she'd screamed and stormed out. When she'd finally made it home last night, there was a note saying sorry. But no Marcus, no call, no text. So, no, she didn't want to bloody talk about it. If she started down that road, she'd end up on Dr Insufferable's couch next to Stark!

How did people do it – the normal masses, ambling blithely through life high on hopium? And why couldn't she?

'Fair enough,' said Groombridge. Nothing fatuous

about his door always being open. She knew that already. And he knew there were subjects he shouldn't press. He nodded towards the glass. 'What do you reckon?'

Fran watched Fairchild, fidgeting. Five minutes alone and she'd have him blabbing every secret he'd kept since he was five, but Stark . . . ? He had sharp edges that worried her, but empathies she could hardly fathom. And she didn't know Swan from Eve.

No sign had been found of last night's bikers. The press had gobbled up her visual aids this morning, but so far only a trickle of callers. Bikes were just too ubiquitous, even speeding through parks. Until they found them, the briefcase and coin were the only links. Initial background on Fairchild had found nothing untoward, but they'd hardly started digging, and Fran's gut was telling her he was involved, knowingly or unknowingly.

She blew out a breath. 'Depends on the lawyer,' she said.

Stark studied the lawyer.

This was a voluntary interview, but under caution. They'd offered the duty solicitor. Fairchild had turned up with this guy. Expensive suit, quiet observation, barely a word wasted. And depending on how honest his client had been with him in their time alone, he probably knew everything Stark didn't, making this a fishing expedition where the fish could see your fumbling nets coming. Perhaps that was why Fran had suggested he lead the interview, though Groombridge was the more likely culprit. Everything a teaching moment. Sink or swim.

Still, half a morning for the interviewee to conspire

with their lawyer was half a morning for the interviewers to strategize.

'What can you tell us about this?' He slid the coin across the table.

Fairchild leaned forward to peer at it. 'May I?' At a nod from Stark, he picked up the evidence bag to look closer. 'Goodness. This . . .' He frowned. 'Where on earth did you get this?'

'We'll come to that. Can you tell us what it is?'

'Of course.' Fairchild's smile felt a little supercilious. 'Well, I can tell you what it *looks* like.'

Stark raised his eyebrows, indicating for him to continue.

'This would *appear* to be one of the oldest coins in history. A gold stater from the time of Nebuchadnezzar the First, Babylonian king around eleven hundred BCE. This is believed to be his face in profile on the obverse side, though of course it's hard to tell one bearded king from another, with his dynastic lion mark on the reverse stamp. Caused a hell of a debate. They predated any other coin found, by around four hundred years, and those are all electrum, a natural mixture of gold and silver common to that part of the Middle East, not solid gold like this. But you couldn't argue with the dating. The urns they were found in, the strata, and of course the mask.' He glanced up and explained. 'The Mask of Kings. Same gold, same workmanship, same everything, a rare face-on personification, and very clearly cast with cuneiform identifying it as Neb One. Do you mind . . . ?' He plucked the reading glasses from his lawyer to use as a magnifying glass, to inspect the coin more closely. 'But this is a fake. All twenty-three were looted after the Second Gulf War in

Iraq, melted down in the philistine heat of greed. A shocking loss. Irreplaceable. The only blessing was the mask was recovered.'

'You think this is fake?' asked Swan.

He looked at her as if she were a child with her hand raised in class. 'Yes. Believe me, I'd know.'

'How?' asked Stark. He'd been through this with Swan.

'Well, the size, shape, weight, markings, wear, patina . . . all look about right, from memory, but they can all be faked. Sadly, while the people that stole them didn't know or care that gold could be worth more than its base weight, other people know that base weight might carefully be fashioned to resemble something more. I'd need to take it back to our labs to be sure, if that's okay?'

'How?'

'Would we be sure? Initially, check for modernity in the wear, deliberation, there are clues, and of course compare them to photos of the originals, each with unique defects and variance. Look for particles, patina, for radiocarbon dating. But these would only confirm my hypothesis. If any of the twenty-three had survived, they would have been found with the mask or have resurfaced by now. Most likely, they would have been ransomed back to the Iraqis. But the men convicted of the theft all confessed. The coins were melted down. The Iraqi police have thorough methods, as we might shudder to know.'

Methods for extracting confessions, regardless of guilt, thought Stark. They were hardly alone in that. 'But if none of that *did* prove your hypothesis, you'd try uranium–thorium–helium dating?' asked Stark, following a crash course from Swan.

Fairchild blinked in surprise. 'Indeed. And with a small and potentially valuable sample I'd use one of UCL's ultrasensitive mass spectrometers. Anyway, I'd be very happy to run the tests,' nodded Fairchild earnestly. 'Even as a fake, this should be in the museum. So –'

'It stays here,' Stark interrupted bluntly.

Fairchild blinked at his tone.

The lawyer re-donned his glasses, alive to the change in mood.

Stark placed a photo of the very dead Nathan Goff on the table, facing them. 'Fake or real, this stater is evidence in a murder investigation.'

Fairchild recoiled in horror.

'Do you know this man?' Stark placed a photo of a living Goff adjacent, so Fairchild could hardly look at one without the other.

'No, I don't believe so. I think your inspector already showed me a photo of him, and another. Who is he?'

Stark placed a third photo down. Lucinda Drummond, dead on the floor below the Tulip Stairs in a pool of her own blood. Switch and bait. 'Let's go back to the evening of Lucinda's murder.'

Fairchild winced again. 'Is this man connected with Lucinda's death?'

Stark ignored the question. 'Queen's House, the night of the exhibition opening . . .'

Fairchild's reluctant regurgitations matched his previous statements closely enough, but his eyes darted again and again to both murder scene photos, his voice wavering. The lawyer said next to nothing, but stood ready to jump in at the first sign of any slip.

'Did you lose anything at the party?'

Fairchild stiffened, perhaps in anger. 'Aside from a life-long friend and colleague, you mean?'

'Aside from that.'

'I don't know what you mean.'

Stark let that hang for a moment. 'You don't recall losing anything?'

'No, I don't think so . . . ?' He searched Stark's eyes for a clue, but finding none, tried Swan's.

'You didn't perhaps lose this?' Stark added a photo of the briefcase laid open on a tarp with a police evidence tag.

Fairchild's eyes widened. 'My *briefcase*? Heavens, where on earth did you find that?'

'So this is yours?'

'Well, it looks like mine. But mine had an ID tag.'

'Had?'

'Well, it . . . went missing, of *course*, from Queen's House that night . . .'

Self-contradiction. Police interview gold. 'You just said you didn't lose anything.'

'I forgot, with everything else . . .'

'You didn't report it stolen?'

'I wasn't . . . I just assumed someone had taken mine by accident and would return it once they realized. There seemed to be a lot of unclaimed bags and coats. I suppose people just wanted to go home.'

'You didn't try to recover it?'

'There were more important things to worry about.'

'Was there anything of value inside?'

'Not really. Paperwork.'

Stark laid down a matching photo of the recovered contents. 'Nothing else?'

'No.'

Liar, thought Stark. Fran said she could tell when someone was lying in an interview, but Stark suspected that was because she thought everyone was. He wasn't so certain. People did lie, all the time. The little white ones were daily practice for the monstrous black whoppers. And people under police caution were naturally nervous. But if forced to declare, Stark would say Fairchild was lying now. 'Nothing of value?'

'My client has already answered that question,' chimed the lawyer.

'How much do you charge?' Swan asked him, out of the blue.

'I'm sorry?'

'Per hour? How much?'

The lawyer straightened. 'I don't see that's any of your business.'

'It is, if we decide it is,' riposted Swan, undaunted. 'Is Mr Fairchild footing your bill, or someone else?'

'Again –'

Swan cut him off. 'How much is your house worth, Mr Fairchild?'

Fairchild's eyes were ping-ponging. 'What's that got to do –'

'It seems a nice big house. In a lovely area. Much nicer than I'd expect an academic to afford, even one occasionally retained for expert advice. I know the Met's Arts and Antiquities Unit hasn't needed you since before my time there, but I certainly know we've never been able to pay much, compared, shall we say, to the *private* sector.'

His eyes widened slightly at the revelation that Swan had skin in the game. 'I had family money.'

'Did you?' Swan fixed him in her gaze. 'We have a little motto in the AAU – follow the money, follow the expertise. We're getting good at both.'

Fairchild licked his lips, glancing at the lawyer, who said, 'I'm sure you are. But may I remind you this is a voluntary interview?'

'Under caution,' nodded Swan. 'Would you like us to rewind the recording to the bit where we explained that to you both?'

'How much would this be worth if it were real?' asked Stark, indicating the coin.

Fairchild was starting to look rattled. 'Impossible to say.'

'Priceless?'

'Yes, I suppose.' He rubbed his temples between thumb and fingers.

'To the right buyer,' nodded Stark. 'Which, if it wasn't the Iraqi state, would have to be someone less scrupulous. DC Swan here's department is focused entirely on the scruple-free trade in stolen artefacts and treasures, and the numbers she's quoted me are eye-watering. Easily enough for someone stumbling across the operation to find themselves in danger.' Stark slid Lucinda's photo closer to him. 'Easily enough – *were* this real, and not fake, as you in your expert opinion insist – for someone to really want it back . . .' Stark laid down more photos of Nathan Goff, his bloody bindings, his slit throat, broken teeth, mutilated hands, finger-strewn floor. 'Not to mention being *really* unhappy with whoever lost it.'

'Enough to cause that person to slip in the shower,' said Swan, indicating Fairchild's bruised face and splinted fingers. 'And be distinctly unnerved if that person was then questioned by the police . . .'

All the colour had drained from Fairchild's face.

His lawyer saw it too. 'Have you any charges to bring at this time?'

Stark ignored him. 'We can offer you protection, Adrian.'

'Is my client under arrest?'

'Take your time, Adrian. If you're caught up in this, we may be your only chance of getting out alive.'

The lawyer stood, buttoning his immaculate jacket. 'We'll take that as a no.'

23

'We should've arrested him,' said Fran.

'What for, exactly?' asked Groombridge. 'Do we miraculously have evidence tying him irrefutably to either murder that I was unaware of when we discussed this earlier?'

'No.'

'And does anyone in this room seriously believe that man is capable of ripping out teeth or cutting off fingers?'

'No, but you saw his eyes, Guv. That man has a guilty conscience.'

'So do most people.'

'Twenty-four hours in the cells away from that lawyer and he'd be telling us why.'

Perhaps, but they didn't have grounds. Fran was just venting. Groombridge looked at Stark and Swan. They'd done well. Stuck to the plan, and from Fairchild's reaction, hit a nerve. 'What do you two say?'

'Not sure it makes much difference,' said Swan. 'We sowed the seed in his head. But from my AAU perspective, if the rest of the coins are out there, we probably lost any chance of recovering them the second Goff stole this one. The black market is jittery as fuck. It's swoop or bust. The second we surrender the element of surprise, we lose.'

'Joe?'

'I think we should've held him, Guv,' said Stark. 'Maybe

he'd have cracked, maybe not, but my jab about people being unnerved was real. If any of this is what it looks like, the moment we pulled him in we put a target on his back.'

Groombridge nodded. 'Agreed, but the lawyer took that out of our hands. In one hour, twelve or twenty-four, Fairchild would walk out of here. Only he really knows if that makes him more safe, or less. Maybe that's the best we can do for now.'

Fran's face looked suitably displeased. Stark's impassive, but alert. All as it should be, thought Groombridge. And Swan looked like a handy addition. 'A big fat coincidence can still be just that. The coin is a possible, one might even say *likely*, link between Fairchild and Goff, and both of them were on hand at the death of Lucinda Drummond. But proximity doesn't prove connection. Only Fairchild knew her, as far as we're aware – and as far as we know, neither had a firm motive to kill her. So, what is it I always say?'

'Bugger this, let's go down the pub?' suggested Fran.

'We don't know what we don't know, until we do,' he corrected her. In other words, get digging.

'We've found the expertise,' said Swan

Stark nodded. 'Let's look for the money.'

That sort of thing wasn't quick.

Recent government rhetoric about tackling money laundering on the oligarch scale may have prompted some banks to cooperate with police warrants at something above glacial speed, at least with clients of no real consequence, but you still needed the warrant.

So Groombridge went with Fran again. Nathan Goff had been murdered in his flat while they waited for a warrant to search it. They weren't taking that chance again.

Warrant in hand, the bank coughed up Fairchild's accounts.

Certain things stood out.

Firstly, that Adrian Fairchild, mild-mannered academic, was by most standards well off. The accounts showed his museum wages arriving, along with a dribble of earnings from his publisher for a dry-sounding scholarly book about ancient currency, written some years earlier, but very little money appeared to be going out. Utility bills, some house repairs, but no mortgage payments in recent years, and very little in the way of everyday purchases or supermarket shopping.

Then came the red flags. Two payments from a numbered account in Cyprus, seven years ago, two months apart, both for £20,000. Just over a year later, the same thing, and six months after that, twin payments of £50,000. Shortly after, the bulk of the money was transferred into his mortgage account, paying off the outstanding balance. Then another forty grand. Some weeks later, Fairchild booked a holiday to the Cayman Islands, towards the end of which, the forty grand was transferred from his UK account to a numbered Cayman Island account. A year later, the address registered to Fairchild's account changed. He sold the modest, three-bed terrace in Finchley to buy his current palatial, detached Edwardian villa in an altogether more salubrious area of Muswell Hill at twice the price, with no new mortgage – the balance appearing briefly in his UK account from the

Cayman Islands bank – five times the forty grand he'd sent the other way.

'Family money, my arse,' muttered Swan.

Proving that would be harder, if not impossible. Cayman and Cyprus were part of the ever-growing international hide-your-dirty-money-here laundry club. Notable other examples of which included the British Virgin Islands, Gibraltar, Jersey and Guernsey – all pipelines for laundering money into Britain. Neither the government nor the banks were keen on cooperation at that level of consequence.

Nevertheless, if there was one conclusion to draw from all this, Williams summed it up perfectly. 'Fairchild looks bent as fuck.'

The third interesting item of note was that the day after Lucinda Drummond's death, Fairchild had gone into his bank's local branch and withdrawn £10,000 in cash without prior notification. The bank had apparently been only too willing to cooperate with such a valued customer.

Fran disappeared upstairs with Groombridge to update Superintendent Cox before his meeting with divisional command, and pave the way for a search warrant for Fairchild's fancy home. Swan was helping Dixon and Williams in the CCTV suite, still poring over the wider traffic camera footage from last night to see if they could pick up the missing bikers.

Leaving Stark with no excuse but to make an uncomfortably overdue phone call.

The case was gathering profile. A search of Fairchild's

home would alert any press not already onto his questioning, and link him directly to Lucinda Drummond. The carpet of flowers outside her house was growing daily, and her face was still on every news channel. Sooner or later, someone was going to spot the unwilling celebrity policeman beavering away in the background.

Better Gwen heard it from him.

'Libya?' Gwen's tone down the line sounded like Doc Hazel's, without the professional restraint. 'You do realize there's not one tub-thumping jihadi alive who wouldn't give his grandfather's Kalashnikov to nab you for a game of Behead the Infidel Online with Britain's most prominent war hero?'

'I adopted a cunning disguise.'

'Of a white guy in a cap and sunglasses.'

'Plus beard, to be fair.'

'Did the MoD know? Major Pierson must've been shitting kittens!'

'She's a worrier.'

'You didn't tell her till your boots were sandy, did you?'

'I meant to, but I was running late for my flight.'

Gwen sighed. 'Didn't we talk about you being more careful last time we spoke?'

Stark sensed the inevitable sobriety creeping in. 'Stuff happens.'

She huffed a laugh. 'To you. That was my point. Did Fran know?'

'No comment.'

'She lied to my bloody face.'

'I'd say don't take it personally, but only because I have to say it to everyone she talks to. After your story on

Stevens, you're probably her favourite reporter.' In the same way that a crocodile might be the pond-dweller she accorded the most wary respect.

'I'll leave room for her Christmas card among all the others I expect to receive from the Met,' said Gwen, wryly. Many in the Met would have cheered the downfall of DAC Stevens – but many had to hastily un-hitch their wagons from his star, and reporters didn't feature on many cops' lists to start with. 'So, you back for good?'

'People do seem to be asking me that.'

'And?'

'Undecided.'

'Flying visit? Just in time to visit the palace on the Queen's birthday?'

The cloud that threatened to shadow him to the grave. So much of his year away had been about drawing a line, trying to move on, move past. Past the traumatic events that had the public baying for him to receive another medal, past Kelly and the horrors he'd brought to her door, past all the blood and fury of his past. 'You'd be the first to hear.'

'Even if that were true, you'd start the call with the words "off the record", just like you started this one. I mean, thanks for the year-late update and everything, but an exclusive I can't use is worse than none at all. People are going to notice you're back.'

'I know.' Now it was his turn to sigh. 'But the longer that takes the better.'

'For you maybe. While I catch hell for not knowing first.'

'Sorry.'

'I'll add it to your tab.'

The list of times she'd not gone to print with a story about him was growing. One early exclusive wasn't going to cut it forever. 'Till next time then.'

They'd not long hung up when Williams wandered in with a fistful of empty mugs. 'Coffee?'

'Please.' He held out his empty mug to the collection, pleased of the distraction. Thinking of which . . . 'Is John still with that same girl?'

'Commandant Tracy?' Williams nodded. 'Can't be long before she pops the answer. Why?'

'No reason.'

Williams let that go and left as Stark's email pinged with a fresh message from Fairchild's bank with several batches of twenty-pound-note serial numbers from which the £10,000 withdrawn by Fairchild was likely taken.

Stark thought for a moment, then went down to the custody suite. Pulling the booking sheet from the night Goff had spent in the drunk tank. Released without charge, the wad of twenties he'd been splashing around had been returned to him, but as a matter of procedural propriety the booking officer had photographed Goff's belongings. Just distinguishable, was one outward-facing serial number.

There was an undeniable thrill to racing across Tower Bridge under blues and twos, but all Fran could think was that she'd sat with Fairchild just hours ago, when she could've been cuffing him.

Fairchild lived north, forcing Fran to fight her way across the river with the assistance of lights and sirens.

But if there's one thing a born-and-bred South London police officer likes, it's waving a flag north of the river. Borderline excusable. They weren't responding to a call, merely going to question a suspect, but if the DCI in the passenger seat didn't object, that was good enough for the DI driving.

It felt reassuring to have Groombridge along. Like all the times she'd driven them to scenes as his sergeant. But of all the times she'd wished for his input and guidance over the last year, he showed up today for the collar. Not to steal her thunder – he wasn't like Harper – more likely just his own inability to fully relinquish the wheel.

She couldn't blame him for that. Fairchild knew victim one. The gold coin and briefcase appeared to link him to victim two, also suspicious, but the ten grand cash withdrawal definitely did – and to pay for what, the day after a murder? Add in the international money, and Fairchild was firmly top of the leader board. Somewhere out there, if he was still alive, Tyrone Pook might fill in some missing pieces, and he remained a suspect himself, but right now Adrian Fairchild was prime.

The judge had agreed. Waiting for warrants was perhaps the most frustrating thing Fran could endure, but the murky financials had thankfully sped things up, and so here they were, Arctic-bound.

Groombridge had asked nothing further about her well-being, thank God. And Stark sat silently in the back, so she didn't have to endure his threat-assessment body language. The only reason Danger Man didn't flinch at her driving was that his whole body was already rigid. Bumming around beaches for a year didn't seem to have unwound him much on that score. So the only comments about route were her own complaints about people's idiot inability to get out of her way fast enough.

'Shit.' Stark's voice behind her.

'What?' she asked, but then saw it too — above the rooftops not far ahead, a faint column of smoke rising into the dark sky, lit from below by flames of gold.

'*Watch out!*' cried Groombridge as three motorbikes tore past them in the opposite direction before Fran could do more than flinch.

'*Fuck,*' she hissed, grabbing for her radio, but Groombridge was already on it, barking to Control and any cars in the area to look out for the bikes. '*Fuck . . .*' she breathed again as the sat nav directed them round the final turn.

Smoke belched skywards as flames licked from a shattered ground-floor window, light from the others suggesting the fire was spreading.

A local uniform car was just pulling up too.

Stark was already out of Fran's, hearing Groombridge behind him, radioing for the fire brigade, as he ran towards the house.

Flames were also visible through the small pane of glass in the front door.

Shattering glass and a fresh roar of oxygenated fire from above let him know the conflagration had reached an upstairs room.

'*Joe!*' called Groombridge, but Stark was already darting round the corner of the house. A small window was broken, the glass fallen inwards, rather than blown outwards by the fire. A downstairs toilet. But the glow inside confirmed fire in the hallway beyond. Without slowing, Stark vaulted the side fence, scraping his midriff on the timber and landing with a grunt as the shock wave through his bad hip sent him tumbling like an assault course newbie.

Rolling to his feet, he saw smoke billowing out through the open fanlight of a side window. At the rear, a large French window showed the kitchen filling with more smoke, lit by the fire in the hallway beyond.

And a figure, prone on the floor.

The window was modern double glazing.

Stark cast around, eyes fixing on a large plant pot containing a small topiary lollipop tree. Wrapping both arms around it, he hoisted it with bent knees, straight back and protesting hip, and heaved it sideways through the toughened glass in an avalanche of tiny ice cubes.

A fresh roar of flame followed the crash, and a wall of heat hit Stark like the opening of a furnace door.

Shielding his face with one arm, he pushed his way through the crazed peripheries and ducked beneath the choking smoke, now billowing halfway from ceiling to floor.

Dropping to hands and knees, he scrambled across the wooden flooring to the victim.

Adrian Fairchild.

Unmoving. Unconscious. Lying in a wide pool of slick-black tar, more soaking through the ripped shirt covering his abdomen.

Two vertical stab holes.

Stark felt for a pulse but his hands were slippery with blood.

The smashed French window was venting more of the smoke, but fresh eddies reached deadly fingers down towards them, with a scorching touch.

Taking a final stinging breath, he grasped Fairchild's collar . . . and dragged.

24

Fran yawned deeply.

Hardly respectful, but a day spanning a dawn knock to a smouldering midnight crime scene clearly assisted her in not giving a shit. It was never hard to spot when Fran was cross, only to identify any particular hotspot in her cosmic background vexation. But something other than work was definitely upsetting her. Groombridge had been watching this fuse simmer for a while now, suspecting a certain Home Office pathologist lay at the heart of it all. One thing was for sure, Fran didn't want to talk about it.

He stifled his own yawn.

Two local constables leaned against their uniform car, watching the firefighters starting to roll up their hoses, but their eyes kept straying to him and Fran, with the usual enthusiasm reserved for out-of-borough CID bringing trouble with them. Their own inspector had turned up, demanding answers, disliking the ones offered, and heading off to a warm bed.

'I should've gone with Stark,' muttered Fran, cradling a tea one of the Brigade lads had brewed up.

Groombridge sipped his own, wincing at the sugar but glad of it. Alice would forgive him the lapse. 'We're needed here.'

Or would be, eventually.

The fire was out, wisps of smoke still drifting out but

the embers doused. Two-thirds of the house had escaped the flames but would take a long while to dry out. The Brigade specialist fire investigators were gearing up to enter. After them, SOCO would take their turn.

A long night lay ahead.

Fran grunted. Waiting around wasn't her forte.

Groombridge stared at the smouldering house; before this evening, it had been an attractive, large well-maintained Edwardian villa in a nice street. According to local uniform, there had been burglaries here in the past, but most of the properties now had decent-enough alarm systems, including this one. That didn't deter all low-life scrotes from a hasty smash and grab. Most burglaries happen in daylight, after an exploratory ring on the bell. Burglary while residents slept remained the riskier prospect. But evenings, when people were most likely to be both at home and awake ... If the odds that this was a burglary interrupted seemed beyond a coincidence already, the fleeing motorbikes lengthened them further.

There were no reports of the suspect bikers being pulled over, but in the briefest of glimpses Groombridge was sure they matched the description from Valiant House, though the captured black bike appeared to have been replaced with a red one.

But unlike Nathan Goff, Adrian Fairchild hadn't been taped to a chair. His teeth were unbroken, his fingers non-detached and his throat un-cut. A double stab to the lower abdomen and a burning house had been all the perps thought necessary. It might yet be. But he'd departed this place just about alive, thanks to Stark's quick reactions and battlefield training – finding the barest pulse and assuming control, ordering his seniors around, stemming the flow of whatever blood Fairchild had left until the paramedics arrived and going with them in the ambulance, leaving Groombridge and Fran to pick up the pieces.

The fact that he'd not called yet to say whether Fairchild had arrived at the hospital alive didn't bode well.

Fairchild succumbed to blood loss in the ambulance, but plasma and CPR had delivered him to the Whittington Hospital, where a defibrillator jump-started him into the operating theatre . . . four hours ago and counting.

It was out of Stark's hands now.

He stared at them, cupped around the machine coffee that one of the nurses had pressed on him. Too hot and sugary. Now too cool. Heat dissipated into bloody hands.

He should get cleaned up.

Not much he could do about the soot and blood on his suit. Knees, cuffs, everywhere. But he should drink this cold coffee and go wash his hands. There was literally nothing more he could do, but washing the blood off while the man's life hung in the balance felt like washing his hands of him. The tiredness talking. Post-adrenaline crash.

How many times had he crashed out in corridors in the last year, while Gabrielle and the other doctors took over with their surgeons' hands? Life over death . . . Taking his phone out, he pulled up her number. But 2 a.m. here meant 3 a.m. there. With a bit of luck she was sleeping, away from the blood and sorrow.

A shiver snaked down his spine.

Looking around, he felt like he was being watched. Judged.

He necked the cold coffee with a shudder, tossed the cup into the nearby bin and stared at his hands – stiff with dried blood, scarred by past fire, and stained by past blood loss and bloodshed.

Blinding light exploded in his peripheral vision, followed by the recoil of secondary detonations.

Stark was on his feet in an instant, hands feeling for a rifle that wasn't there, eyes scanning for muzzle flash or the telltale spark and bark of a mortar.

The lone member of the paparazzi grinned, cradling his thick-lensed camera with its mounted flash, and high-tailed it through the door and away.

Stark didn't give chase.

The bomb had detonated. The butcher's bill would be counted.

He looked down again at his blood-soaked attire.

A pair of green plastic clogs clopped to a halt in front of him. A sombre-looking male surgeon in crumpled scrubs. 'Detective Sergeant Stark?'

25

'So what do you want to tell the press?' asked Superintendent Cox.

Reports of the fire had quickly been linked to Adrian Fairchild and jumped from local to national breakfast news. No news was as irresistible as bad news, as far as the press was concerned, and the longer they went without a statement, the more interested they'd get. 'Man attacked in own home remains in critical condition. No name,' replied Groombridge.

'His name's out there already,' replied Cox. 'Someone left him for dead. We should worry about what they'll do when they realize he's still clinging on.'

'Enfield have him under guard in hospital with armed response outside, sir. If the riders are stupid enough to come at him there, they'll be caught. No need to confirm Fairchild's name before we know where he sits on the suspect scale, and while we've so little idea what's really going on and who we're dealing with.'

'Reasons to be cheerful . . .' muttered Fran darkly.

Groombridge ignored her. 'Weapon was likely the kitchen knife SOCO found on the floor, matching the empty slot in the wooden block of siblings nearby. Hose water washed away much hope of forensics. Signs of forced entry via a side window, house turned over, bedside tables, men's jewellery box empty, no signs of cufflinks or whatever. No watch, wallet or phone found on the victim.'

Cox nodded. 'Window dressing.'

'Best guess,' agreed Groombridge. No one thought this was a real burglary. 'Fire looks to have started in a small study. Investigators say it was probably ransacked, then set alight.'

'Looking for something? And no way of telling what or if they found it.'

'No way of asking, either, while they keep him on life support,' added Fran, evidently still disgusted that the doctors had put Fairchild's chance of survival ahead of police questioning.

'Looks like someone wanted Fairchild dead,' said Groombridge. 'And before that they wanted something he had. Evidence of antiquities smuggling feels most likely. The fact that he escaped the same torture as Nathan Goff suggests he'd offered it up quickly. The killers had to know his connection to Lucinda Drummond would raise suspicion, but either didn't care or knew that avoiding conviction was all about sowing doubt – that this might have been a random break-in gone bad and three men on bikes just happened to be nearby.'

Cox nodded. 'And Stark?'

'Minor smoke inhalation. Told him to clean up, sleep in and keep his head down, sir,' said Fran.

'Dry cleaners will raise an eyebrow at his bloody suit, I should think.'

'Probably used to it, sir.'

'Indeed.' Cox pursed his lips. 'And the press attention too.'

'Sadly so,' nodded Groombridge, though for all the reasons Stark had found himself plastered over the tabloids and TV news in recent years, he wasn't sure how anyone might get used to it. The hyenas would be after more than scraps from Fran this morning. 'At least the blood wasn't his this time.'

'Small blessing indeed.' Cox stroked his moustache with finger and thumb. 'So we've two murders and one attempted, all connected by the opening night of the Queen's House exhibition. A missing catering van driver. An ancient gold coin that our nearly dead, possibly suspect, expert said was fake, and only supposition on how they might fit together.'

'That's about the sum of it, sir,' nodded Groombridge.

'Much chance our suspect expert will suddenly regain consciousness and explain what the hell is going on?'

'Doctors weren't hopeful, according to Stark. Miracle he made it through the first surgery, apparently. Another today. If he makes it through that, who knows?'

'Then unfortunately,' Cox puffed out his moustache, 'I'd say you've got your work cut out.'

'So . . . ?'

His mother was using that tone today. Initially to berate him for showing up on the morning news covered in blood again. And then, once reassured, to tell him that Kelly had texted her to ask if he was okay. So now his mother had Kelly's new number and wasted no time in forwarding it to Stark.

'So what?'

'So, you should call her.'

'I really don't think I should.'

'She's worried about you. Believe me, I know what *that's* like.'

'Then by all means, text her back that I'm fine.'

'But you're not.'

'It wasn't my blood.'

'And you know that's not what I mean. So what are you doing about it?'

Stark closed his eyes, silently cursing the universe and all its makers. 'What exactly do you think I should be doing?'

'Urgh,' she exclaimed in disgust. 'Something. *Anything*. While there's still *time*.'

'I don't see how this has anything to do with time or me.' Or indeed how this call had descended into another polemic on his refusal to intervene in Kelly's love life. 'As I said before, it's no longer any of my business.'

'Kelly Jones will always be your business, and you hers. *Lord*, I can't believe I raised such an idiot son,' she cried. 'First into any fight but the one that counts. She was the *one*, and you know it.'

He did. But those more experienced in such matters said there wasn't just one person for everyone. Stars aligned in the sky might still be crossed in time. Or worse, a gravitational danger. If received wisdom insisted there wasn't just one perfect person for you, then heartbreak was nature's way of teaching you not to fuck up so badly next time. His mother called it cowardice. Maybe that was right too.

'She moved on, Mum.'

'You *forced* her to.'

'I did what I thought was right.'

'You always do. That's your problem.'

'I was hurting her, Mum. Every day, inch by inch. And even after we split, I put her in mortal danger. I can't be with her.'

'Because you love her.'

'Yes. *Okay*. But it didn't work out. That's life.'

'And you only get *one*, unless you've gone all Buddhist on me, in which case I hope you come back as something with more sense.'

'Thanks,' he joked, 'but I think we both know that, karmically speaking, my score isn't high.'

That caused a pause, and a change in tone. 'You're too hard on yourself.'

'You just called me an idiot, more than once.'

'But a big-hearted one. That counts. And I'm allowed, because I love you. And you deserve to be happy, so don't expect me to drop this.'

After a further ten exhausting minutes of her version of love-bombing, she finally rang off.

Stark turned the TV back up as a picture of Adrian Fairchild appeared next to Lucinda Drummond's and Nathan Goff's, followed too quickly by his own.

A passer-by had filmed the paramedics trolleying Fairchild from his house to the ambulance and posted it online, not realizing they'd caught the famously missing Joseph Stark on camera. Some hours later, a friend/follower commented with a *Hey, isn't that #JoeStarkVC with a beard?*, and before long it was trending. A paparazzi photographer had picked up on it and rushed to the hospital in time to catch Stark, covered in blood and soot. Presumably it had taken till morning to negotiate the best deal for their 'art'.

Video and photo were now viral, the news anchors had all suddenly remembered the unforgettable news from a year ago, and were cheerfully speculating about where he might have been, from some top-secret military mission to the psychiatric ward.

He glanced at the text that had beeped in his ear while his mother chewed it off.

What's the point in saying you want to remain hidden if you're then going to swan about with a flashing sign over your head?

First Fran's call, rousing him from sleep with none of her usual delight, then his sister and mum, an expletive-laden email from Major Pierson, and now Gwen texting – a positive queue of condemnation. Stark puffed out a despondent sigh, typing back. *Stuff happens.*

Barely a minute passed.

Next time you say off the record, I'm hanging up.

Fair enough.

Just cos a building's on fire, doesn't mean you have to run inside. There are people for that you know, with training and all sorts of nice PPE.

I'll try to remember next time.

Any of the blood yours?

For once, no.

Well if I see you I might well punch you in the nose, so there's still time.

You know I'm a high-profile national military treasure and MI5 probably screen my phone for threats?

I'll just join the queue then.

All the more reason I should hide out at home. There were already paps on mopeds outside.

You won't though, will you?

Can't.

FFS! At least put a bag over your head or something. Cap, sunglasses and beard are a bust.

Bit late for that.

Idiot! Gotta go. Tell Fran she did okay.

Stark would do nothing of the kind. Fran's press conference had been painful to watch. The plan to withhold Adrian Fairchild's name had gone out the window with the viral video outside his house, but all the hacks seemed interested in was Stark. Yes, he had returned to work, she revealed. No, he was not injured. No, he had not fought off knife-wielding attackers, this time. No, she would not comment on where he had been, nor on his health, personal life or state of mind, and no, she would not comment on his prospects of receiving another – *unspoken expletive* – medal. It was a masterclass in how to wind Fran up. That she hadn't erupted was a miracle, doubtless negated by an explosion of expletives when she stormed back inside. She'd already texted, blaming him, so mentioning Gwen at this point would soothe her the way petrol soothed a brush fire.

He stared at his hands. Scrubbed clean. Yet he'd slept. No triggered dreams, no waking flashbacks. No bullets or bombs, ghosts or screams, no itching of the old burn scars that a fresh encounter with fire sometimes triggered. Perhaps there was a sixth point of the curve – denial, anger, bargaining, depression, acceptance . . . then numbness. Something to discuss with Doc Hazel. More fun.

He'd tried Gabrielle's number again for her allocation of disapproval. Still no answer. He was starting to worry that she hadn't at least messaged him back – not for romantic reasons, but general security protocol. He'd tried a couple of the team out there but had to leave more voicemails.

He glanced at the clock.

R&R was all very well, but there was work to be done.

Stark dreaded the day that one of the press worked out he had a back way in and out of his flats through the bike store.

His car was still at the station from yesterday evening, so he cut through backstreets towards town on foot. The roads were already clogged, the shops bustling with people going about their busy lives. An urban fox had met its end beneath uncaring wheels in the high street. People walked past, looking at or away with equal distaste. Black wings clattered as a crow hopped to a standstill on the pavement, eyeing the carrion, weighing the odds of darting between the stationary traffic to snatch a morsel.

Stark eyed other pedestrians to reassure himself that they saw it too.

He shuddered.

Suddenly, and for no reason he could account, the hairs on the back of his neck stood up again. Without altering his gait, he began scanning – rooflines, corners, reflections. It took a moment to realize what he was doing, and to mock himself for the madness – in broad daylight. The worst it would be was another paparazzi, not an insurgent with an IED trigger.

That was when he made his shadow.

Madness aside, it seemed for all the world that he'd picked up a tail.

For all that his common sense scoffed, every other sense screamed louder: he was being followed, but not by anyone with a camera . . . ?

He began counter-surveillance without thinking. Subtly slowing, fishing out his phone to read a text, letting something in a shop window catch his eye and stopping to go in. Each time the man in an innocuous grey donkey jacket and flat cap would continue about his own business or pass by without a glance, and yet each time he reappeared shortly after, behind, across the street, even in front. They didn't teach skill like that in paparazzi school.

What the hell . . . ?

Stark placed his faith in home-ground advantage. Turning casually down Turnpin Lane, he slipped into a shop he knew had a secondary door directly into the covered area of Greenwich Market itself, where traders were noisily erecting stalls or setting out their wares. Moving quickly through, he slipped off his coat and ducked into another shop to wait. It took several minutes for his tail to reappear, scanning slowly for him. His economy of movement, patient focus and skills said professional, special forces, or maybe spook. But why on earth . . . ?

Then Stark saw his face.

As a girl exited the shop he glided out alongside, moving as if they were together. Even altering his gait to disguise his faint limp, he would only have seconds before his pursuer picked him out. But it was enough.

He pressed the end of his new ASP baton into the small of the man's back and spoke quietly. 'If this were a knife or gun I'd be away in the crowd before anyone noticed you fall.'

The man didn't bother to turn. 'And if I was here to kill you, I'd've used a feckin' rifle,' he replied in his thick Glasgow brogue. The same brogue with which he'd lashed Stark across the Brecon Beacons and up and down Pen y Fan on special forces training. 'When did you make me?'

'Across from the church. Why are you here, Tink?'

'You recognize me then? I'm flattered.'

'I'd know that nose anywhere.'

The man turned now, a broad grin across his weather-beaten face. 'So you feckin' should, you broke it.'

'But why is it here, following me around?'

'To see if you remember a damn thing I taught you. Come on, you owe me a pint.'

26

Few people could comfortably order a pint of stout at
10:15 in the morning, but Staff Sergeant Douglas Bell was
old-school Regiment – SAS – raised in the worst slum in
Glasgow, weaned on whisky and Buckfast, or so he claimed,
and indifferent to all forms of disapproval. Unfortunately,
the best that cosmopolitan central Greenwich could offer
him this early was a brew, but he sat eyeing the hipster-
ridden Blue Door Café with the cheerful disapproval of a
soldier on incursion deep behind enemy lines only to find
nothing but untrained, underfed and poorly armed con-
scripts, feckless and doped to the nines. Easy pickings.

Tink, short for Tinker, was, by UK military standards,
a staggeringly polite nickname for a man called Bell, but
rumour had it that an officer who'd tried calling him End
had abandoned the notion after suffering a series of
unfortunate and wholly inexplicable embarrassments.
There were many rumours about Tink, and he had several
nicknames among selection candidates – none of them
repeatable in polite company, and none ever spoken
unless you could be absolutely sure you were at minimum
safe distance, and even then, at a whisper.

The man himself preferred to regale anyone who
would listen with the fine history of highland Bell's, and
the name's personal suitability to him in its origin from
the French word *bel*, meaning comely and agreeable.

He had been among the euphemistically named Directing Staff during Stark's training and ignominious exit from special forces selection. During his jungle-training phase Stark had contracted malaria, the mild symptoms of which he had put down to fatigue or flu, and hidden. Weeks later, in the final stage back in Blighty, during Escape and Evasion across the Brecon Beacons in freezing rain and Second World War clothing, the illness had taken hold. During the Tactical Questioning that followed, the fever had spiked and, in his delirium, Stark became the first man ever to break out of TQ, breaking Tink's nose along the way – being eventually cornered twelve miles away across the icy moor in nought but his pants, and forcibly restrained by four bemused, and by this time distinctly unamused, DSs.

'I argued for you to stay,' admitted Tink, to Stark's astonishment. 'But the Regiment is the Regiment. I was looking forward to beasting the shit out of you the following year – you wouldn't have pulled the Grey Man twice, ye sly shite. But you never showed.'

Almost as bad as drawing the attentions of the Directing Staff for being consistently slow, was being consistently fast. The key to survival, and ultimate selection, was to ghost through unnoticed – the Grey Man. 'I went travelling instead.'

'A nice wee spot of Afghan sunshine, aye. How's the hip?'

'Why are you here, Tink?'

'I told you, to see if you still have the skills.'

'For what?'

'A job offer.'

'I have a job.'

'Aye, and dashing into burning buildings is all very well, but they hardly ever let you shoot people any more; where's the fun in that?'

Stark's identity as the shooter in last year's sensational case was a closely guarded secret, nevertheless widely speculated about in the press. But this still didn't make sense. 'I'm not fit for the Regiment; we both know that. The only reason I'm still on the reserves is because they want to wave my bauble around.'

'Who said anything about the dear old army?'

'You're out?'

'Only way to get my hands dirty a few more times before Queen and country put me out to pasture.' He slid a business card across the table.

'StoneTower?'

'Indeedy.'

So that was it. StoneTower were the UK's largest private security firm, supplying everything from close protection to celebrities, to military training and fully equipped 'training' units to unstable allies across the globe. 'Mercenary?'

'Private Security Contractor,' grinned Tink. 'Boots on the ground where the Crown can't go. I pick the jobs, the men, the kit and the time. You wouldn't believe what they're paying for ex-Regiment. I should've done it years ago.'

'But I never made the Regiment.'

Tink waved his hand dismissively. 'You were top of the feckin' class and you know it – don't play the shy shite with me. Tell me you don't miss it.'

Stark hesitated in spite of himself.

'And did I mention the money . . . ?'

'The Queen's shilling was privilege enough.'

Tink smiled. 'We're not morally bankrupt sell-sword wankers. We work for the good guys.'

'This isn't TQ, Tink.'

'Sure, and it ain't carrot and stick,' nodded Tink, 'because there's no feckin' stick. I'm not working you for more than name, rank and number; I'm cutting your hands and feet free and opening the cell door. It's a fun world out there. I spent the first year on "train and assist" with the ANA special forces on the Durand Line.'

The mountainous border between Afghanistan and Pakistan. Where training and assisting the Afghan National Army was a brief with plenty of wiggle room for hunting Taliban leadership hiding among the Pashtun, confirming targets for unmanned drone missiles, painting them with laser to guide in smart bombs, or taking them out in person. The quiet side of Coalition drawdown – continuing the decapitation strategy, with deniable assets. Dangerous and lucrative work for those crazy or greedy enough to try it, and about as much fun as the right kind of soldier could wish for.

Tink read Stark's thoughts and shrugged unapologetically. 'It's what I trained to do. You too. Shites like us – we've unfinished business out there. You can never leave a war behind. Tell me I'm wrong.'

'I'm sorry but I cannot answer that question,' said Stark. The only response other than name, rank, serial number and date of birth that a candidate was permitted to offer during Tactical Questioning.

Tink sat back and chuckled. 'Anyway, I'm getting too old for that shit now. And that limp you mask probably makes clambering over the Hindu Kush a thing of the past for you too. I transitioned into protection. That's where the

202

real glamour is anyway, and not all the primaries are arse-holes. Money for old rope – sprinkle a bit of military common sense and Gucci gear and they think you're Captain-feckin-America! And going back to the shilling . . .' He pulled the card back and wrote a cash sum on the rear.

Stark stared at it. 'A year?' It was more than he'd earn in three.

'That's just your basic. It's double during deployment,' grinned Tink. 'Seriously, tell me everything you've done in the blues this week, then tell me this doesn't sound better.'

'Give me a cigarette,' demanded Fran.

'You don't smoke,' Stark reminded her, levelly.

'I'm starting.'

'I don't either.'

She tutted. 'I thought all troubled ex-soldiers smoked.'

'How long have you known me?'

'Too long.' And probably never long enough to work him out. 'You're supposed to be my bagman, pandering to my every whim.'

'Tell me to go bum a cigarette off someone inside and I'll go.'

'Why are you standing out here if you're just going to be unhelpful?'

'You said you needed some air.'

She had. Completely out of character. He'd probably complied just to see what stupid bloody thing she came up with next. He wasn't even supposed to be in, but she'd found him at his desk an hour ago and left him to it. She stared at the parked cars. The rear entrance canopy was the only place they could stand out of sight of the press photographers milling beyond the gates like *Dawn of the Dead-hearted*.

She took a deep breath of good old-fashioned South London air – gritty with car fumes and sun-baked tarmac. Probably the equivalent of a cigarette, but with less satisfying contrarianism. Better than that North London rubbish at least. Everything north of the river felt alien: the City, the West End, the shoppers, tourists, attractions, fashions, and the air. The breath turned into a yawn.

Stark waited, patient as a stone, immune to yawn contagion.

Fran eyed him, levelly. 'You made me look like an obstructive cow in front of the press this morning.'

'I thought whack-a-mole was your favourite game'

'That's not the point.'

'You're right,' he nodded, impassively. 'Unforgivable.'

'If you didn't keep doing such stupid bloody things, they'd lose interest in you.' Stupidly brave – save the day and occasionally her life – kind of things.

'One can only hope.'

Fran made a face. 'I've changed my mind. I think I *can* be doing with you buggering off again.'

He smiled, a faint laugh. 'Funny, I just got a job offer at six times the pay.'

'*Hilarious.*'

'I'm in demand.'

'What's stopping you then, mister big-pants?' she said crossly.

'Aside from the predictable working hours and blame-free culture here, you mean?' he repaid, dryly. 'Maybe it's all the rewarding work we do?'

Added to public hostility, press intrusion and the hellish cost to your love life, thought Fran. *Fuck*. Ideas above his station were Stark's natural territory, but before she could dwell on his scarier transferable skills her damn phone rang. She thought about declining, but it was the SOCO main line.

'Yes?'

'DI Millhaven? SIO on the Fairchild case?'

'Speaking.'

It was a techie from the team that had attended Fairchild's house, with curious news about Fairchild's home computer. Despite being burned almost beyond recognition, last night's SOCOs had expressed hope of recovering the hard drive. Apparently 'the enclosures were pretty good at protecting the platters', which Fran took to mean the magic metal discy innards. But the news wasn't good. 'Wiped?'

'Yep, everything gone.'

'But not by the fire.'

'Before the fire.'

'Can't you guys find deleted files, ghost copies and all that?' said Fran, pretty much exhausting her knowledge on the topic.

'If it's not been overwritten, sure, but this laptop's hard drive is dead. No data, no operating system. Nothing but junk.'

'Junk?'

'Junk data. Wall to wall, random gobbledegook.'

'Deliberate?'

'Well, there's no fingerprints, but short of a massive magnet, the only way a drive gets this dead is if somebody floods it with junk.'

'And how would they do that?'

'Plug in a cleaner. Available in all serious computer stores, so the kind of people who don't leave all their user names and passwords in a drawer can wipe their data before ditching it in landfill for who knows who to pick over. Just plug in your thumb-drive and press kill. You can do it remotely, if the machine is powered up and connected to a VPN – or someone else can, if they hack you.'

'But easier in person,' said Fran.

'If you're an amateur. Could have done it himself, of course. But with his antique hardwood desk charred to hell but mostly intact, guess what we found in the drawer?'

'User names and passwords?'

'Bingo. And it gets worse. Wanna guess what we found when I used those passwords to log into his cloud storage?'

'Nothing.'

'Bingo. And it'll take a warrant and some heavyweight badgering to get those Silicone Valley fucks to go looking for ghost files. Easier for them to just say "sorry, already overwritten".'

'Great.'

'Oh, I'm not done yet . . .'

Fran was already moving this git up her to-slap list. 'Go on.'

'Wanna guess what I found when I remote logged on to his work computer at the museum?'

'Nothing?' Fran gave the expected response, already deciding that if he said bingo again she was going to lose her shit.

He said bingo.

27

'We're gonna need a bigger boat,' said Williams, staring at the third whiteboard crowding out the office, scrounged from the main CID office, loaded with photos from the Fairchild crime scene and growing background notes.

'We need a bigger crew,' said Dixon.

'We need a break,' said Stark. Morale and crew rotation were the sergeants' job and these two had been hard at it all day, digging further into Fairchild's background. But so far the murkier side of it remained hidden in the Caymans.

That still left the ten grand in cash. The cash withdrawal happened the day *after* Lucinda's murder, meaning the money wasn't in the briefcase, so how had any of it reached Goff, and where was the rest? Payment for a hit seemed too far-fetched for most tastes. Ransom for the coin was the more likely scenario. The thousand Goff had been found drunk with wasn't found with him in his flat. Pocketed by his killers, most likely. Maybe the other nine grand had been too. But this was all guesswork. Goff was dead. Fairchild all but. Tyrone Pook was still AWOL without a trace. Stark yawned into a sigh. 'We've done all we can for today. You two get off home.'

Neither of them argued. Williams might just make it home in time to kiss his kids goodnight. Dixon might make it home in time to keep Commandant Tracy mollified. Swan had gone back to her office to liaise with her DS and see about authenticating the coin now the pre-eminent expert was in a medically induced coma. Groombridge and Fran had departed via updating Superintendent Cox upstairs, and hopefully making a case for seconding some help.

But someone had to stay in case the uniformed officers running the door-to-door and witness call lines up in Enfield came up with any questions or answers, and he'd had the only semi-lie-in. Plus the later he stayed, the thinner the herd of bike-riding paparazzi downstairs might become.

Unfortunately, as his head became less crowded, Tink's offer muscled its way back in.

The grizzled old soldier had laid it on thick, only accepting Stark's excuses that he had to get to work after Stark promised to try and meet him for last orders that night. Staying late got Stark out of that, but aspects of the offer *were* tempting. Companies like StoneTower had a place in the world. The primaries they protected could be angels to arseholes, but there was a chance he might wangle a deployment protecting NGOs trying to do some actual good, like he'd been doing for Médecins Sans Frontières and Gabrielle, but with the resources to do it properly. But he couldn't pretend that the less protective side of things wasn't tempting too. The chance to get back to what he did best, taking the fight to the enemy, unencumbered by rules or restraints – exactly how the SAS had started life in the Second World War Sahara. Unfinished business, just like Tink proclaimed.

An email from Fran interrupted that dark reverie.

Forwarding on one from Fairchild's mobile phone provider responding to the request for his phone records. Cross-checking Fairchild's call logs against known numbers, and unknowns – exactly the kind of tedious job Fran knew suited Stark. Army OCD, she called it, but it went back further. Losing one's father in childhood quickly taught you to pick up your own socks and get your homework done. *Enjoy!* No smiley face. Her little revenge for however he'd irked her most recently.

Thanks, he emailed back.

He was jotting down caller IDs when he noticed three calls from an unknown number on the day after Lucinda Drummond's death. Putting the new number into the system, it came up as unregistered. Pay as you go. A burner.

In American TV crime dramas, the cops seemed to have instant access to call logs, and locations – not to mention live feeds from every CCTV camera in the universe, and instant facial recognition wizardry to boot – enabling them to find criminals in seconds. In reality it took an hour just to fill in the request forms for one SIM number. But if you were a low-life demanding ransom or blackmail money, a burner was one way to go.

Typing made his bruised hand ache. Flexing it, he let out a long breath and closed his eyes, leaning back in his chair to stretch his back and roll his sore shoulder.

'This help . . . ?' asked a voice. Pensol, standing in the doorway with two takeaway coffees and a bakery bag. 'Cinnamon rolls. I'm on lates this week. Heard you'd volunteered for the graveyard shift. Thought you might use a pick-me-up.'

'You're an angel,' said Stark, eyeing the pastries,

hungrily. The coffee helped too, but so did the company. He felt thankful, given where they'd started and everything they'd been through, that she could still bear to sit with him. Possibly the only woman in his life not in the disapproval queue.

'You okay?' she asked.

There was no short way of answering that properly. 'In my way. You?'

'In mine.' She smiled. 'Better than when you came to my rescue.'

'Wasn't it you who came to mine?' The thought of how easily the events of a year ago might have turned out differently gave him the shivers all over again.

'Hardly.' Her eyes, after gazing around without much focus, settled briefly on the boards and their macabre photos. She looked away.

'Glad you came back?' he asked.

'Most days.' An honest answer.

'Always wanted to be a copper?' Not something he'd ever asked her before. A question that usually drew derision within these walls.

But Pensol nodded. 'My favourite doll was a Police Cindy. Tell anyone that and I'll kill you. My dad was uniform, twenty-five years. Retired two years ago. I can tell he still misses it. Tried to talk me out of it though. Tried twice as hard after I got shot.'

'I can imagine.' His own mother never missed a chance to remind him that *both* his careers had got him shot. What would *she* say to the StoneTower idea?

'I think it's worse for him than Mum,' continued Pensol. 'Maybe that's part of why I struggled so much ...

after. People expected me to give up, but . . . I couldn't imagine doing anything else, I suppose.'

A more common sentiment than most police would admit to, Stark suspected. 'There's good people here.'

Pensol nodded thoughtfully. 'John seems nice.'

'He is.' Stark was trying to work out how to tell her that while John had a girlfriend, the consensus was that he needed a nicer one. But before he could come up with something he was forced to answer the phone. 'Greenwich MIT . . .'

'Hi, is DC Williams there?' A Scouse accent.

'No, this is DS Stark. Can I help?'

Fran stared at her freshly cooked, healthy, nutritious, delicious meal for one, with enough for a second in a Tupperware ready for the fridge.

This was her life. This was how she'd lived for years. This tiny kitchen, her sanctuary and solace at the end of every day on the job. Hit-and-miss cross-cohabitation with Marcus had destabilized the routine, denuded her fridge of fresh ingredients, and generally been a damn nuisance. Life was complicated enough.

She should seize this opportunity to end it and be done, refocus on what mattered – work, home-cooking and family. She should call her parents, her brothers, go spoil her nieces and nephews with fun-aunt disregard for parental norms, book a flight to Barbados, visit aunts, uncles, cousins and kids, real cooking, sun and rum. She should go back to being herself.

But right now, *herself* faced two murders plus one attempted but still in the balance, connected God knows how. Every time someone rose close to prime suspect, they turned victim. Another potential suspect/witness was missing, possibly dead as well. The only three remaining suspects alibied each other, albeit partially supported by phone records. She'd need something firmer to get them in Interview Room One – and with her luck, they'd turn up dead the moment she found it.

She'd love it to be Alex Zedani – you just couldn't trust people who smiled that easily while clearly making money hand over fist – but there really was no motive. Her own money had to be on Tyrone Pook, hopefully on the run rather than dead in a ditch. Please let it be him, she thought. Let him turn up and confess, so she could book that flight.

Yes, she thought firmly: work, food, family and *sun*.

She closed her eyes and savoured the aroma steaming off the plate, but before she could take a bite her phone lit up with Stark's name.

'You know that thing where you call me late at night or on my days off with some breaking news that I have to drop everything for . . . ?' he said, with too much irony.

'I hate you so much right now.'

'Not for long.'

'This better be good.'

'Merseyside Police just picked up Tyrone Pook trying to board a ferry to Belfast.'

28

Prisoner transfer was a nightmare to organize at the best of times, and Pook's case wasn't cut and dried. *Wanted for questioning in connection* in London didn't immediately trump *arrested for presenting false documentation to the Ports Authority* in Merseyside.

The Liverpool to Belfast ferry wasn't an international border. As generations on every side of the Troubles knew to their cost, Northern Ireland remained part of the United Kingdom. Stark's old paratrooper friend, Maggs, could attest to that personally. But Pook's agitated and furtive manner had drawn the attention of the Transport Police, and challenged, he'd offered a false ID. His brother's driving licence and bank card.

At no point during Williams' conversations with the worried family had the brother mentioned any contact with Tyrone. That was a conversation for later.

What wasn't, was where Tyrone was going and why. And the only way to avoid waiting, was to go ask.

Fran had insisted on taking her car, but with Stark driving, declaring that his propensity for sleeping in vehicles was as annoying as his passenger-paranoia, and there was no way she'd risk driving three hundred miles with either excuse for silence.

Conversation had hardly proved flowing though. Historically, she might have berated him over his romantic failures, but that was a topic she was clearly avoiding. And she'd already said her piece on his reappearance distracting the press.

She'd turned on the radio, but tutted as the London DAB stations faded into the rear view, cursed at the inane Radio 1 DJs, scoffed at fuddy-duddy Radio 4 and clicked it off again in irritation.

Thankfully, she'd fallen asleep somewhere around Birmingham.

They pulled up outside Birkenhead Police Station shortly after 1 a.m., Fran jerking awake, masking disorientation with accusation. 'One ironic smirk and I'll have you demoted to street sweeping.'

'Wouldn't dream of it, Boss.'

The desk sergeant was not much impressed to receive visitors at this hour, but figured it was okay to make it the custody sergeant's problem. The custody sergeant had been forewarned of their arrival but was reluctant to get off his arse to set the sleeping prisoner up in an interview room. Fran took his reluctance and threatened to insert it where he might not like it. The supervising inspector was called, swore a bit, and went back to sleep. The duty solicitor proved even harder to rouse, so it was nearly two hours after arriving before Fran and Stark were sat with instant coffees as a tired-looking, wary Tyrone Pook was led in and deposited opposite them by a muttering custody sergeant.

'Do you remember the rights I read you at the beginning of this interview?' asked Fran after an inauspicious start. 'In particular, the bit about harming your defence if you fail to mention anything during questioning you later rely on in court?'

Pook nodded.

'For the tape, please.'

'Yes.'

'So you realize that includes lies, right?' she said pointedly. 'Look at me,' she said sharply, repeating it three times until he complied. 'I'm not your friend here. We're not here to play good-cop bad-cop. I'm *hates being lied to, especially at three in the morning after being forced to abandon dinner and drive up here into the Arctic bloody Circle* cop, and he's *silently seething, trained killer* cop. So I think we should run through those questions again, don't you?'

Fran had sat opposite hardened criminals, black-hearted villains and one psychopathic serial killer, and the one thing they all had in common was, they all knew silence worked. Tyrone Pook looked exhausted, scared and way out of his depth. The duty solicitor looked half asleep and twice as disinterested. Both of which meant the simplest form of interrogation might be her best chance – blunt repetition.

'So, again, Tyrone, you fell out of touch with Nathan Goff after school because, in your words "he was trouble", but you bumped into each other last year and he swore he'd gone straight and just needed a chance. You helped him get work with the catering company. Correct?'

'Look, I'm tired, man. I told you all this.'

'Yes or no.'

'Yes.'

'So you've been working together when called upon for over eight months, and you've become friends again.'

Pook shrugged wearily. 'Not like best mates or anything. Just a work mate.'

'You'd socialize outside work.'

'Yeah, a bit, but . . .'

'So when did you start accompanying him on burglaries?'

A side swipe. Pook blinked and shook his head. 'Nah, nothing like that. I never. I wouldn't –'

'Wouldn't when he asked?' interrupted Fran. 'How many times did he suggest it?'

'It's not like that –'

'When did you become aware that he was just as deep in criminality as he ever was – deeper, in fact?'

'I ain't no criminal.'

'You smoke cannabis together.'

'Yeah, well, but –'

The solicitor placed a cautioning hand on Pook's arm.

'Yeah, well, but?' Fran hardened her glare. 'Cannabis is a Class-B drug under the Misuse of Drugs Act 1971. And don't you dare say *personal use* to me. We've searched Nathan's flat.' She was careful not to say that they'd found less than a quarter-ounce of weed and half a dozen ecstasy pills, hardly a Columbian Cartel drug submarine. 'So you take illegal drugs together, including during work hours – work that includes driving commercial vehicles.'

'Nah, it's not like that . . .'

'So what is it like, Tyrone?'

Silence.

'I'll tell you what I think it's like. I think Nathan has dragged you into his world, bit by bit. I think you've been working your arse off for a pittance while you've seen him waving around magical windfalls of cash and saying how easy it was. It probably started small, keeping lookout. No harm in standing in a street, right? He probably told you it was harmless, all those rich sods in their posh houses, everything insured, everything replaceable.'

The lawyer looked about to jump in, but lacked specifics to object to, so Fran pressed on.

'But once you take that first ten-pound note, it's all over. Too late to worry about whether that gold necklace was a family heirloom, an irreplaceable memory of a beloved grandmother, or the rest of that jewellery the collected memories of places been, people seen, gifts received, the birthday earrings given by a child to their mother.' Pook was all but squirming now. 'How long before you saw him smashing open children's piggy banks? All those coins, painstakingly collected, all those five-pound notes from birthday cards? Easy money.' It looked like her words were hitting home. 'Never mind those children crying themselves to sleep, asking their parents whether the bad men were coming back. Never mind those parents shuddering at the thought of strangers rifling through their bedrooms, staining their intimate worlds, that lingering dread of no longer feeling safe in your own home. Never mind, eh? They're the *haves* and you and Nathan are the *have-nots*, right? Easy money?'

It actually looked like Pook might cry.

Good, thought Fran, fiercely. How many burglaries had she attended in uniform? She wasn't making any of this up, and Pook's reaction said she'd guessed right. 'But you finally bit off more than you could chew. You finally stole something too valuable. Am I right?'

Pook was staring down, shaking his head. 'It was Nathan.'

'It was Nathan,' repeated Fran. 'And now he's dead.'

Stark silently slipped a photo of Nathan Goff's bloody corpse across the desk. Pook recoiled in horror.

'They smashed his teeth out, Tyrone. They cut off his fingers, one by one, and when they were finally done, they cut his throat. And then they went looking for you, didn't they?'

Pook looked like he might puke. 'This is all Nathan's fault!' he spat, finally cracking. 'I told him it was a stupid *fucking* idea! I should never have listened to him. I wish I'd never fucking seen him again!'

29

'You know that being SIO means the buck generally stops with you, vis-à-vis being woken at four in the morning,' muttered Groombridge groggily, sitting up and speaking quietly. He was attuned to the vibration-only setting on his phone, but sadly so was Alice, and speaking quietly seemed only polite. 'Have you found another suspect dead or dying?' he asked, levering himself out of bed with a suppressed grunt and heading for the stairs. Much as he might complain, if Fran had news to share it was usually worth hearing.

'Alive and kicking.'

'Pook?'

'The very same.'

'Where are you? Are you hands-free?' She had a liberal attitude on that front that she needed to curb before some surly traffic cop pulled her over or a pap snapped her driving one-handed. The top brass were increasingly touchy about bad press like that.

'Stark's driving. We're just on our way back from sodding Liverpool. Bloody UNESCO need their eyes tested. Place was barely passable in the dark.'

'I sense a long story,' he sighed.

She actually summarized it quite neatly. Hyperbole and profanity removed, it boiled down to this – if Pook were to be believed, he and his pal Goff had gone inside Queen's

House the evening of Lucinda Drummond's death to relieve themselves and scrounge for food, as they'd already stated. The bit they'd missed out was that while Pook was in the makeshift kitchen, Goff had overheard raised voices from a side room off the corridor. Peeking in, he'd apparently seen a man wearing white gloves in the act of showing a woman something gold. The man had popped the golden object into a small orange box and put it into his briefcase. The woman had grown angry and exited the room, the man following. Goff had played innocent, walking past them towards the toilets, but turned to see the man follow the woman into the base of the Tulip Stair.

Minutes later, Goff had watched the man come back out and duck past the curtain into the cloakroom, seeing him emerge again without the case.

But before he could work out how to bypass the attendant, a heartrending scream had brought people running, and he'd persuaded Pook to act as lookout while he swiped the briefcase and hid it in one of the catering boxes.

After that, Pook said he'd bottled it, wanting nothing to do with a briefcase linked to a possible murder.

But three nights later, Pook had received a call from Goff, telling him they'd hit the jackpot and he should come round immediately for his cut of the cash. Thousands, apparently. In hindsight, Pook had thought Goff sounded strange, but he'd assumed he was wired on something. Drawn by a possible windfall, he'd walked round to Valiant House, pressed Goff's number and been buzzed wordlessly in through the main entrance, but as he approached Goff's door he'd heard voices inside and a muffled scream. Turning on his heels, he heard the door open and glimpsed someone chasing him. The lift doors had closed so he took the stairs, pursued the whole way. A man, masked, large, wearing white disposable overalls splattered with red.

Escaping into the night, he'd run all the way home, packed a bag and fled.

He'd stayed with his brother that night, but the next day had seen news of a murder in Valiant House. Panicking, he'd set off in the hope of making it to Belfast, where he had a couple of old friends. When Fran told him that his own flat had been broken into shortly after, he'd gone white.

Groombridge sat in his dark kitchen for a while, mulling it all over. Nothing to say it wasn't all complete fabrication, but Fran sounded convinced. He'd review the interview video himself in the morning, then support Fran in her bid to have Pook transferred south.

Assuming it was true, the man with the briefcase had to be Adrian Fairchild, the woman Lucinda Drummond, but Pook hadn't seen for himself. The only person left who might know for sure was Fairchild himself. They certainly had plenty of ammunition to question him with. But according to his doctors, it was still uncertain if he'd wake up, or how much of his blood-starved brain might have survived if he did.

Blowing out a sigh, Groombridge levered himself off the chair and crept back upstairs and settled back into bed as stealthily as he could.

'Tell her she's off the Christmas card list again,' muttered Alice.

*

Wired as she appeared from updating Groombridge on speaker during the car journey south, the lull of the Birmingham ring road had closed Fran's eyes again soon after, leaving Stark to his own thoughts until they reached the early rush-hour traffic of inner London just before seven, the morning sun stabbing between buildings.

She jerked awake, somehow managed to blame his driving for the crick in her neck, and settled into grumbling about hunger, traffic and her haste to get back to the office. 'Where are we?'

'Euston.'

'That near the British Museum?'

'Ish.'

It was a syllable he somewhat regretted as he watched her drive away, leaving him the best part of a mile north of the museum. The walk did, however, afford him the chance to load up on caffeine and calories in a kooky little café while pondering the events of the last few days, and to try Gabrielle's number again, away from Fran's prying ears.

No answer still.

There were a hundred and one reasons for comms drop in a war zone, most of them relatively benign, but it was the others that were becoming harder not to dwell on. So he dialled Jergen's number. His trusted number two in Libya. Still out there, filling Stark's boots. Also ex-military. A big no-nonsense Berliner, useless at blending in, terrific at being overbearing. No answer. Voicemail could be unreliable, so he typed out a quick message.

Jergen. No answer from Gab. Drop me a sit-rep when you can. Cheers, Stark.

Not much else he could do for now. Blowing out a sigh, he necked the dregs of his cooling coffee and walked the remaining distance to the museum. It didn't open till ten, but a warrant card and inflexible tone got Stark to the security office where the senior night guard greeted him with a nod. 'Wondered when you lot would show up. How's Professor Fairchild doing?'

'Officially, no comment. Unofficially, no change.'

'Hmm.' The guard yawned, near the end of his shift. 'Can't say I really know him. Passing ships. But some of the day-shift lads said he was all right. Shocking, him and Professor Drummond in one week. Connected of course, but no comment, right?'

'Right. They get on?'

'Couldn't say. You'll have to ask the upstairs types. Day manager will be here in an hour, if you want introductions. One of the late-shift lads was bound to have seen him that night.'

'That night?'

'Night he was attacked. He was here for a bit.'

'Two nights ago?'

'Wednesday, yeah. I check entry–exit logs when I clock on at midnight, see who's in the building . . .' He set about his computer until he pulled it up. 'See, Professor Fairchild swiped in eleven-oh-three, and out again forty minutes later.'

Around the time he was actually suffering cardiac arrest in a racing ambulance. 'Is that unusual, people coming and going so late?'

'We're an academic institution,' said the guard, as if that explained away all eccentricity.

'You have video?'

'Sure.' This took a little longer to pull up. 'Here . . .'

The man entering used a pass that logged Fairchild's entry, but unless he'd grown a foot taller, put on three stone of muscle, pulled back from the brink of death and been in two places at once, it wasn't him. Plain black baseball cap, thick brown beard, black jacket and trousers, biker boots. Same leaving. Crowbar-biker-guy. But, barring further analysis, that was it for now. No face visible. 'Why do you guys never think of mounting your cameras on walls instead of ceilings?' asked Stark.

The night guard correctly identified this as a rhetorical question.

30

'How much sleep did you get last night?' asked Fran.

Stark looked at her. 'Whilst driving you to and from Liverpool?'

'None. Exactly. And the night before, what, two or three hours?'

'What's your point?'

'Just admit that you're tired.'

'I already did,' said Stark, refusing to rejoin the game.

'Yeah, but you're just saying that to get me off your back,' insisted Fran. 'We both know you're too stubborn to really admit it.'

'I have admitted it. I'm hanging on my chinstrap. I don't know what more you want from me.'

'Some outward sign.'

'What for?' He didn't sigh. He didn't snap at her, he didn't argue. That's what made this so much fun.

She'd dumped him near the museum with three object-ives: check Fairchild's office, bag his wiped computer and anything else useful and deliver it to the station by taxi, and go home to sleep. Instead he'd turned it into a three-hour-long SOCO circus and ended up back here, briefing the team and mucking in. And it was exactly that ingrained, dogged, never-quit soldier crap she just couldn't resist poking. Better than dwelling on the case – or worse, life. 'Because that's what tired people do,' she persisted. 'They show they're tired. They yawn and look sleepy, they get irritable.'

'I'm irritated right now.'

'They show it.'

'Who are these people you're referring to?'

'Normal people. *That's* my point.'

'I think you lost the point, along with the plot, some while back.'

Fran harrumphed and changed her angle of attack. 'She's cute,' she nodded towards Stark's new BFF, Swan, on her phone in the corner. 'In an off-duty dominatrix sort of way.'

'I could put a word in for you,' replied Stark, dryly.

'You're deflecting again. You should ask her out.'

'Just how much coffee have you drunk this morning?'

'No need to get all arsy. Just making conversation.'

'*Right* . . .' said Groombridge, marching in at speed. 'Thank you all for waiting. I've just got back from Scotland Yard with the Super, where I've been updating divisional command on the latest developments, so I thought I'd better come straight back here and acquaint myself with what they actually are. So, Fran . . .'

Fran stood to address the troops. They did look tired. Especially Stark. It had been a morning of legwork after a long night, and if she was riding the rickety caffeine train, he must surely be close to derailment, but there he sat. 'Okay, so we've all watched Tyrone Pook's confession. We're told he's now signed a transcript. So we think the coin came into the possession of Nathan Goff via the stolen briefcase of Adrian Fairchild, renowned expert in ancient coinage. We don't know where *he* got it, or who from, but we can suspect *why*, given that its value on the black market depends on expert authentication. What we don't know for sure is how the killers found Goff, but, Joe . . .'

'We've just heard back from the service provider,' said Stark. 'The burner phone calls placed to Fairchild's mobile the morning after Lucinda's killing triangulate on Valiant House, so it looks like Goff placed those calls from somewhere in or around his own block of flats. Our best guess is Goff got Fairchild's number from the paperwork in the briefcase and called to demand a ransom for the coin, despite already posting it off to Dosh4Gold – or to blackmail Fairchild for killing Lucinda Drummond – and somehow led his killers to himself.'

'Idiot,' commented Williams. No one said *serves him right*. The photos on the board behind Fran precluded any such thought.

'No burner phone or SIM was found with his body or nearby,' continued Stark, 'but if that was how the killers found him, they may have taken them to cover their tracks.'

'I have an alternative theory on how they found him,' said Swan. Fran waved her to present it. 'It's common practice, when shipping antiquities, to box them with a GPS tracker. Even more so, on the black market. The little orange box that Goff described to Pook could've been one of these . . .' She stuck a printout to the board of a dayglo-orange Peli case with a digital keypad. 'Available in multiple sizes. Tamperproof. Programmable digital lock. Integral GPS. Just the thing for your paranoid black marketeer.'

'So how did Goff get it open?' asked Dixon.

'Tamperproof isn't the same as arsehole-proof. Brute force, plus a hammer and chisel or jemmy.'

'Fairchild strike anyone else as the kind of bumbling academic that would stick the combination on the lid on a Post-it?' said Williams, dryly.

'So maybe Fairchild killed Lucinda, though we still can't be sure,' said Dixon. 'Then Goff gets in touch to black-mail him for it, or ransom the coin. Fairchild hands over ten grand but gets a punch in the face instead of his coin back.'

Williams took up the baton. 'So then he has no choice but to confess its loss to the clients, who send the Black Riders round to break his fingers to make sure he's not lying, check the orange box GPS and head round to Goff's for a game of What the Fuck Have You Done With Our Coin? And when they realize *we* have it and we're talking to Fairchild, they decide he's a loose end.'

'But how was Lucinda Drummond involved?' asked Dixon. 'Was she part of it, or were she and Fairchild argu-ing because she'd caught him at it?'

'All questions we'll put to Fairchild if he wakes up,' said Fran. 'But right now the doctors won't say how much longer they'll keep him in an induced coma.'

'And if they can't wake him up, or there's no one home . . . ?' You could always trust Williams to ask the uncomfortable question.

Fran had no answer. 'I guess that leaves us with you, Bingo.'

'I have a name,' complained the computer tech.

He'd been doing a lot of complaining since Fran had

arm-twisted his boss into sending him over. 'And if you manage to get through the next few minutes without incomprehensible jargon, I might bother learning it.'

He wasn't some spotty geek or basement potato. He was dressed like a regular human being with a regular haircut, but he did have a goatee beard on a face too young to carry it off, and that was enough for Fran to keep her prejudices in place.

Bingo stood up reluctantly. 'In layman's terms,' he said, in a way that left no one present in any doubt that he was calling them stupid, 'someone who knew what they were doing systematically binned Adrian Fairchild's digital footprint.' He looked at Fran, as if to say, was that simple enough for you, or should I spell it out phonetically?

'How do you know?' asked Williams, who cared about computing about as far as his twelve-year-old daughter could explain it to him, and probably just wanted to see if he could provoke Bingo into using an acronym.

'Because I know what I'm talking about,' replied Bingo, with a glance at Swan, who'd been called by her name and gone unquestioned. 'Because the same software was used to wipe Adrian Fairchild's home and work computers. Because while it overwrites the drives with gobbledegook, it does so in a pattern unique to the –' he stopped himself on the cusp of some jargon – 'to its own code. And because they also took the time to wipe his cloud storage, both work and private email accounts, and whatever arcane social media platforms someone his age might have fumbled their way onto.'

'This wiping software,' asked Groombridge, 'does it offer any clues? On origin, perhaps?'

'Russia.'

'Russia?'

'Leading brand. State-owned. For some reason they don't trust the American versions. If you have the computer's login details, you just plug and go.'

'And if you don't?'

'We've seen versions packaged into an email virus ransomware, but that requires the receiver to click on the *I'm an idiot* link. There are backdoor hacks, if you've clicked on *no I don't want to install the latest security updates because I'm an idiot*. Or you can force your way in, but that usually takes the hardware manufacturer's complicity or next-level cyber-craft, usually state-sponsored. In Fairchild's case, he *was* the kind of bumbling academic that leaves all his logins in a drawer next to the computer, though he might've just offered them up at knifepoint.' He sat down, suggesting his efforts to dumb things down had exhausted him.

'Round of applause for Bingo, everyone' said Fran, rising to silence. 'Well, having been in Fairchild's museum office on Monday, I have to concur with Stark's insightful conclusion that the huge mess he found today wasn't sudden-onset academic untidiness. But despite it not being set on fire, Bingo's non-digital colleagues can't tell us what, if anything, was taken. So . . .' She looked to her audience for deductions.

Dixon obliged first. 'So this is all about that coin? If it's genuine.'

'And whoever's been paying Fairchild to authenticate it for them,' added Swan, 'along with possibly more antiquities, going back years.'

'Only the bastards raided his home and workplace, swiped any evidence and wiped his computers to destroy any research or communications he may have made over those years, to cover their tracks. Anything that might highlight what he's authenticated for them before, anything that might lead us to them now,' concluded Williams.

'Anyone fancy wheeling Fairchild's bed out into the hospital car park as bait?' said Fran.

The room went silent, until Stark spoke up. 'Then I guess it's back to the Black Riders, and Plan D.'

PART THREE

31

Plan D.

Williams took local CCTV and door-to-door. Dixon the traffic cameras. Swan brought the mighty weight of the Arts and Antiquities Unit to bear on trying to prove Adrian Fairchild's links to the illegal trade. That left forensics.

'Someone did a job on the bike,' said Geoff Culpepper, Senior Crime Scene Manager. 'Other than you, that is. Original black colour, not re-sprayed, but everything else – decals, maker's badge, plates, and not just the usual VIN numbers embossed on the engine casing, but the ones hidden inside the cowlings – all removed.'

'We checked on HOLMES,' said Stark. 'No reports of three of this make and model being stolen nationally, together or within days of each other.'

'I think I can say why,' said Culpepper. 'There's no sign of it having been souped-up, but there's no real need, as it's pretty high-end for the type. Ideal getaway job. Except for the tyres. According to the website, this model comes with tyres more geared towards off-road use, but the tyres on this one have been swapped for urban/off-road hybrids. And this is where it gets interesting – these tyres are Turkish.'

'*Turkish?*' said Fran. 'Stolen vehicles normally *leave* the country, not the other way around.'

'Indeed.' Culpepper turned to his notes. 'Good news is, we picked up a partial print. Bad news is, it doesn't flag up any known ne'er-do-wells. We've sent it to the lab but it's hit and miss whether they can recover any DNA. I'll let you know. Nothing so far off the crowbar, envelope or your broken GPS tracker. Whoever handled those was wearing gloves. Tracker looks like it was ground beneath a boot. Not a lot to go on really.'

'Hard to tell what is or isn't a piece of the puzzle until it fits somewhere,' replied Stark, earning an eye-roll from Fran.

'Don't start with the Groombridge-isms,' she muttered. 'I hit my positivity ceiling several coffees ago.'

She had a point.

Stark stared at the shattered bike and crowbar that had nearly taken his head off – hoping the rider's protection gear hadn't soaked up all of the crash.

Ptolemy, Peters and Pensol had been busy on the door-to-door with Williams, and canvassing people around Maryon Park, but with its various exits the search pattern spread too quickly. From there you could head back to the roads or cross into Charlton Park, then Woolwich Common, Shooters Hill and Oxleas Woods, Eltham Park, Avery Hill Park and on and on outward. London was a patchwork of grey and green from the air, making off-road hybrid bikes the perfect getaway vehicle.

But the riders were down one steed. Maybe they got their bikes from Turkey of all places, but unless they had a ready supply, they'd have had to secure the red replacement more locally. Stark had Dixon looking for any similar bikes stolen in the last three days. In the meantime, the public incident line had finally offered up a possible sighting of interest.

At the north-east end of Woolwich Common, a curved road called Circular Way had long since been gifted a set of kerbs and bollards to stop it being used as a cut-through by anything bigger than a cycle – effectively turning it into a car park for anyone desperate enough to park their vehicle where it might be broken into, largely unobserved, which in London meant almost anyone *with* a vehicle, which may or may not include many residents of the walls of five-storey brick flats opposite the southern end.

Signage declared Circular Way a dead end 'Except Cycles'. There was an overgrown ditch all the way along to prevent anyone taking to the grass. The perfect place to ditch pursuing cop cars. Scanning around, Stark could see no CCTV cameras on the nearby roads or buildings. The lack of through traffic, and the relative seclusion, made it a useful spot to loiter. Regular smatterings of toughened glass, reduced to cubes, stood testament to the risk of parking here, but one of the people willing to risk their car's windows had called the hotline.

On the night of Stark's 'Coin Sting', as Fran was now calling it, a white Luton Van – possibly a Ford – with no memorable business or hire company decals had been parked at the southern end of Circular Way, making it tricky for the caller to get their car out. Nothing particularly suspicious in itself, but the caller had seen Fran's TV appeal and recalled that the guys around the van had been using its tail-lift to load a large, black off-road-type motorbike.

Fran looked around, making a face. 'Pity they didn't memorize licence plates for fun, like certain ex-military freaks.'

Stark ignored the jibe. If the perps were here, it added to an emerging pattern of thoughtful planning and execution, but even false plates would've given them something to track on ANPR cameras further afield. They were going to have to add the location and van description to the TV appeals, leaflet every car parked along here, and go door-to-door on the flats. Stark watched a number 386 bus trundle past. 'If I yawn and get irritable now, will you give me a hard time about it?'

'Yep. So let's start with a sergeant lesson.'

The sergeant lesson was a reminder of whose job it was to rotate the resources, to make sure everyone was operating at, or as close as possible to, peak performance, including oneself. Or, in Fran's words, 'Get some sleep before you fall down, numpty!'

Stark had spent most of his army life as a corporal, so delegation came naturally, and the move to sergeant the same. But what a corporal or sergeant *didn't* do was slope off to bed, assuming their underlings were nailing their tasks. That was the officer's prerogative, but Stark very much doubted that Fran's year in the police equivalent, at inspector level, had made her any more comfortable with switching off either.

Nevertheless, the TV appeals, car leafleting and door-to-door were delegated. But he still checked his emails from home. And after the work ones, the less fun ones. One from his mother, pointing out that if he wasn't going to call for two days, he might find time to email, and that she'd messaged Kelly back, but not what she'd said. One from the bank, extending the overdraft he never used. One from his credit card, extending his limit just in case he ever felt like using it. And last, but the least pleasant, one from Major Pierson, now at DEFCON-2. The thing with problems that couldn't be delegated, was they couldn't be postponed indefinitely either.

That said, a curry and two beers later, shoes off and eyes closed, he was starting to see an upside to both delegation and procrastination.

This was usually the moment when a call from Fran derailed his R&R.

So when his phone rattled him from sleep several hours later, he rubbed his eyes, expecting to see her name on the screen, but it wasn't.

'Jergen?' Using the sat phone rather than his mobile. Not a resource he'd expend lightly. One hour ahead made it five in the morning there. Stark was already sat bolt upright. 'What's wrong?'

'*Non, chéri, c'est moi.*'

'Gabrielle?'

'*Oui.* Though now I find you care more for Jergen than me. You never call, you never write!'

'I've been calling. I've left messages.'

'The government bombed the cell towers to hamper the militants,' explained Gabrielle. 'We're taking turns on the sat phone.'

'And you decided to take yours at four in the morning?'

'I know you never sleep.'

And for her to be calling at this hour meant she'd been

up half the night, saving or trying to save a life. He didn't ask which. 'It's getting worse?'

'We've been without mains power for a few days, and rationing generator fuel while Jergen tries to get more past the roadblocks. We need you here.'

'I'm sorry,' he replied dully, all too easily picturing the chaos she was dealing with.

'*Pah*, keep your sorry,' she scoffed. 'You do what you must, always. Do it and come back. Then show me you're sorry. Assuming you live that long. One of the other doctors tells me you are on the news reports, saying you were hurt.'

Great. So now his infamy was grown so large as to add to her worries halfway round the world. 'It wasn't my blood.'

'Good. I didn't let you go back there only to get incapacitated.'

He almost laughed at that one. 'You know me.'

'Too well. You are not careful.'

'I do what I must.'

'Ha. You are not funny either.'

'So my inspector tells me.'

'And the army? Your deal with Major Pierson? You are resolute?'

'I don't see a better choice.'

'Doing what you must.'

Indeed. And she was right – it wasn't funny. 'But you're okay?' he asked.

'Now he pretends to care,' mocked Gabrielle. 'The soldier with his girl in every port.'

'That's sailors.'

'*Pah*. Have you seen her?'

Kelly. They'd been pretty up front about things. Gabrielle had someone back home, but they were apart so often they both accepted flexibility. She wouldn't label it as an open relationship, polyamory, or even just Parisian *je ne sais quoi* – she felt no need to label it at all. And she knew about Kelly. 'Why do people keep asking me that?'

'The past is never passed. Is that not what you say?'

'I think I got that from a fortune cookie.'

'I have another for you – life is short.'

And she would know. 'My mother suggests I convert to Buddhism to hedge my bets.'

'Hedge . . . ?' She paused. 'Never mind. I only have a few minutes. We have injured incoming. Tell her you love her still. If she deserves you, she'll wait.'

'She's engaged to someone else.'

'Ahh,' said Gabrielle, sadly. 'Then you made her wait too long.' She made no excuse for the contradiction. Life was too short. 'And now my time is up also. We need to recharge the batteries. Will you be more careful?'

'I'll try, if you will.'

'I will. *Au revoir, chéri.* Come back to us.'

'I'll try,' he said to the call-ended symbol, not sure if it was a lie.

It was so good to hear her voice, to know she was safe, but the guilt of absence felt all the heavier, and his so-called commitments harder than ever to balance. One at least he could answer before he tried to go back to sleep. So thinking, he returned Major Pierson's latest email volley with one only marginally less insulting. The fact that his deal with Pierson wasn't funny in the least felt all the more reason to seek a little cheap amusement in it.

32

'You look better,' yawned Dixon, gratefully accepting a takeaway coffee from the six-cup cardboard carry tray in Stark's hands, and unhooking the bag of assorted pastries from his little finger.

'Slept like a baby, thanks.'

'Say that when you've lived through three babies,' said Williams.

Stark couldn't picture parenthood, but he did feel better. Hearing from Gabrielle had lightened one load, and he'd managed to fall asleep again after a while. He felt more like his old self these days. Less like the guy that slept badly and woke tired. If he could only get his mother and Major Pierson off his back, he might really sleep like a baby, if never like an innocent. Or maybe not, he thought, staring at the boards. Lucinda Drummond, broken. Nathan Goff, butchered. Fairchild left to bleed out in his burning kitchen. No one should be able to sleep after seeing those images.

'You still look like shit,' said Fran, entering, and eyeing their shared smiles with suspicion. 'What?' she said, taking a coffee and selecting a pastry.

'Tyrone Pook is going before the magistrate in Liverpool today, Boss,' reported Dixon. 'If he pleads guilty to the ports offences, he'll be bound-pending-sentencing up there, meaning if we want to speak with him again it'll be another long drive. Adrian Fairchild is still alive, but there's indication of further internal bleeding. If scans confirm, he'll need to go back under the knife.'

'Great,' she sighed. 'Maybe we'll find the three bikers dead next, and then we can file this whole case under *nobody knows*.'

'On that line – cars all leafletted, press release updated, door-to-door got going an hour ago,' said Williams. 'Nothing yet.'

'And the buses?' asked Stark. Seeing the 386 bus trundle past last night, Stark had noted that its route joining the A225 from Woolwich Common Road would be pointing its dash cam directly at where the caller had said they saw the bike being loaded onto the van.

'Footage requested. They said it might take a few hours.'

'Take longer than that to scan through it all,' muttered Fran.

'Not sure I've any better news,' announced Swan, stood in the doorway with an armful of files and a laptop balanced atop.

Stark would've helped, but Dixon beat him to it. Indeed, John seemed encouragingly attentive. Perhaps Pensol had competition.

'I've been trying to link the early payments Fairchild received with suspected black-market transactions,' she explained. 'There was a theft of ten electrum staters from the Turkish museum several years ago that Interpol thought they'd traced to Cyprus, supposedly bound for the UK, around the time of Fairchild's first windfalls, but they lost track. I've got nothing coinciding with the second round, a year later yet. But around the time of the fifty-grand payments, after that, there were rumours of a Mesopotamian dagger on the move, in Turkey, but nothing more. In truth, there's dozens of rumours circulating at any time. If we could get into his Cayman account for more transactions, we might build a pattern, but . . .'

'What about the Cypriot account?'

'Same thing. Numbered accounts are sacred, and we don't have anything like enough to request freezing it, let alone peeking inside.'

So again, it seemed the most realistic way of cracking this case relied on finding the three bikers.

'HOLMES flagged up a bike theft in Dartford on Wednesday,' said Dixon. 'Same make and model. Red. Morning after you wrecked the black one and hours before you saw two black and one red speeding away from Fairchild's burning house. No witnesses or CCTV though.'

And so again, it proved a long day, getting nowhere slowly, each member of the team revealing their frustration to differing degrees, with Fran at one end and Swan at the other, for whom opening case files was a far more common occurrence than closing them. She spent the day deep in files, emailing and on the phone, half the time liaising with an Interpol counterpart in fluent French Stark could only loosely follow.

Pensol turned up, offering to help with the bus camera review, after which poor Dixon's attentions did appear somewhat torn. When, later, his head began to drop, Stark took mercy on him and sent him home.

Williams clung on, saying he'd rather see out the day and then spend time with his family, than miss them by sleeping early. So it turned out to be him that chimed up later. 'Okay,' he announced. 'Three eight six is the magic number.'

The dashboard camera on a 386 bus had captured a white Luton van parked in Circular Way on the night of the Coin Sting. A Ford. Checking the next bus, ten minutes later, Williams found the same. And the bus after that: the same van with a black bike on its tail-lift while another waited adjacent, with at least three men visible.

And one night earlier, the night of Goff's murder, he found the same van in the same place. And in one still from *that* night the van's licence plate was discernible.

Predictably a false plate, stolen off a car in Erith, but still traceable on ANPR cameras. Hundreds of fixed locations on arterial roads, plus fifteen hundred or more operated by Transport for London to monitor the capital's various Road User Charging schemes, mainly the Central Congestion Charge, Low Emission Zones and HGV safety permits. Not counting those on most patrol cars, pop-up DVLA checkpoints, and hundreds more monitoring car park pay schemes and the like, all of which the Met might access. Big Brother really was watching. But he'd sworn an oath to protect, and he policed by consent. That had to mean something.

'Gotcha,' crowed Williams. 'East on Plumstead Common Road. Then again on the two-oh-six, Boxley Road . . .'

It took a while, but by the end of the day, they'd traced the Luton Van coming to Circular Way from an ANPR camera near Erith in the neighbouring borough of Bexley, on both nights in question. They were now looking at the traffic cams.

Four Ford Lutons had been stolen in the capital in the last year, one in the Dartford-Erith area, but that case was closed with no leads. And that didn't account for the fact that the van might have been stolen earlier or elsewhere.

In the meantime, the door-to-door had come up blank so far, but a couple of people had responded to the car leaflets, saying they'd seen the van on the night of the Coin Sting. And one of those had a dash cam. The footage was emailed over, and it clearly showed two bikes and three riders with their helmet visors up. All you could really say was they appeared Caucasian or Middle Eastern – one with wisps of brown facial hair. But there was a fourth man. Maybe the van driver? And you could see his face. Not very clearly, but a breakthrough nonetheless.

That was the good news.

The bad was that Fairchild had deteriorated and been rushed back into surgery to repair a bleed. He was back in the ICU now, but his odds of recovery had taken a fresh blow.

Fran treated the press to an update, batting away all questions about Stark. 'Your girlfriend didn't ask after you this time,' she told Stark, meaning Gwen. 'You piss her off?'

'Not intentionally.'

'So that's a yes.'

'It pisses her off knowing things she can't print.'

'Can't?'

'I trust her.'

'You told her you were back, off the record, then inadvertently outed yourself to her competitors?'

'In as many words.'

Fran huffed amusement at that, but it didn't make much of a dent in her broader suspiciousness. 'You ever tell her things she *can* print?'

'I had nothing to do with the exposé on DAC Stevens.' The corruption scoop that had sunk one of the third-ranked officers in the Met, and a persistent threat to Greenwich Police Force and Royal Hill Police Station. They both looked at Groombridge through the glass wall to his office, neither voicing their suspicion that he might have been the one who'd taken down Stevens through Gwen.

'That's not a full answer,' said Fran.

'How about no comment? Gwen *really* hates that one.'

Fran made a face. She didn't like minding her own business any more than Gwen Maddox.

Stark's phone pinged. 'Ah ...' he said, reading an email.

'What?' demanded Fran. 'I know that look.'

'Mmm ...' mused Stark, clicking open the attachment and scanning it slowly to annoy her.

Fran peeked at the screen. 'UCL?'

'University College London. I emailed them, asking for a list of all the times Adrian Fairchild booked time on one of their ultrasensitive mass spectrometers – and guess what?'

Fran stopped trying to read his screen and stared impatiently at him instead, eyebrows raised in her *hurry up or die* expression.

Stark pointed at particular dates. 'Seven years ago – between the first two payments into his account. Six years ago, between the second two payments. Several before and since, but those two, and more in recent years, were all booked late at night, see? After midnight, early hours. According to the accompanying email, the machines run 24/7 because they cost so much. Late at night usually indicates a last-minute booking, but it's also handy for scanning stuff you'd rather other people didn't see.'

Fran nodded. 'Can you use them by yourself, or do you need a techie?'

'If you're trained – and Fairchild has been for years.'

'Do the machines store results?'

'I asked. The email says not. Researchers can be proprietary. They tend to save results directly onto their own drives. Cut-throat, I guess.'

'So we can't tell what he scanned.'

'Especially since someone wiped his digital life,' said Stark, pointedly. 'Probably after taking a copy. But look at the last slot: one in the morning, on the day of the Queen's House exhibition.'

'He tested something *that morning*?'

'Looks like,' agreed Stark. 'Want to lay odds it was the coin?'

'Lying *bastard*! Not only had he seen it before, he'd been to test whether it was fake or real. I wonder which.'

'Or which answer he feared more?' mused Groombridge, manifesting behind them.

'Either way,' said Stark, 'less than eighteen hours later, he argued with his boss, Lucinda, about something small and golden, shortly before she was found dead.'

Groombridge nodded thoughtfully. 'Good work.' He

glanced at the wall clock: 6 p.m. 'Okay, enough for today. We've been at this eight days straight, and it's Saturday night. I've signed off on the hours so far, and there'll be more to come, I'm sure. Joe, pick someone to cover tomorrow, and the rest of you come back on Monday. But first, one compulsory drink in Rosie's, my round. After that, it's up to you.'

33

Sunday announced itself with a mild hangover.

Stark's wouldn't be the worst.

Fran had been tucking it away. Dixon had reappeared and circulated between their table, which included Swan, and the uniform group Pensol had joined, laughing with Peters, who Stark now suspected of direct interference.

Whether or not he was following tradition, or starting one, Stark saw only the upside in buying a round for the sergeants, and then another for luck. They were good people, and it never hurt to oil the engine room. So he also bought one for the cluster of uniforms that had been driving the door-to-door.

Dixon had volunteered to take the Sunday shift, but of all those in the MIT, Stark truly had nowhere better to be. And with a sausage, bacon and egg baguette and steaming tea from the local café, there were worse ways to start one's day.

Fairchild's best prognosis was that he hadn't died in the night. But it was still a toss-up whether he'd ever wake to help them join the dots.

That left the van driver. Stark stared at the printout. The face wasn't that clear, but probably recognizable. And from the footage, he was tall and heavyset. So far no one in uniform could put a name to him. If only that facial recognition camera wizardry so popular in TV dramas were real, they'd be kicking down his door by now.

Their best chance of finding the driver was finding the van, but with a description out in the press, the van was probably being resprayed, dismantled or burnt at this very moment.

He finished his breakfast and stood in front of the incident boards.

Fran had dismissed his offer to tidy them up as 'army OCD'. Fair enough. But she wasn't here today, and if giving permission wasn't her style, begging forgiveness wasn't his. So he took down the photos with black dots beneath and carefully transcribed the associated notes into the case files. Progress, even if Fran refused to concede it aloud.

He left the red dots at the top, and next to them lined up the driver and three men in bike helmets with red question marks where names should be. Then he condensed everything across all three boards, until the salient points stood out, and stared at the wiped-clean area he had created on the central board.

So far, *follow the expertise* had taken them from Mesopotamia in the eleventh century BCE to a north London ICU bed, via broken earthenware in a baking Basra storeroom and Lucinda Drummond's fatal fall. *Follow the money* had laid a trail from Cyprus to the Cayman Islands via a London bank, but no further. And *follow the motorbikes* had laid a trail from Turkey to Erith, via Nathan Goff's bloody corpse, the yellowing-purple bruise on Stark's hand, and a Luton van.

Using a different colour for each, he plotted the routes in a triangle and stood back.

Then he plucked a photo from the red dots and stuck it in the middle of the triangle.

Someone with money.

Someone with trade connections through the Mediterranean, Suez and the Black Sea – therefore including Cyprus, Turkey and the Middle East – and expertise in moving things across borders.

Someone Fran would be delighted to see in the centre frame.

'Alex Zedani.'

The rest of Stark's morning was spent liaising with Bexley station on the search for the Luton van, while finding out more about Alex Zedani and Horizon Logistics.

Aside from their London HQ, they had offices in Istanbul, Sevastopol, Athens, Eilat, Tangier, Paphos in Crete and Limassol in Cyprus.

If anyone really wanted to ship stolen motorbikes from Turkey to the UK unseen, Horizon Logistics could probably manage it. But why would you?

Why, was a big question here, but there were so many others.

If Zedani was somehow involved with the coin, was he buying, selling or just smuggling? He claimed an interest in historical artefacts, but was he a collector?

Was Fairchild selling his expertise to Zedani, or to a separate seller or buyer?

Who sent the three Black Riders to try and retrieve the coin from Nathan Goff? Zedani or the separate party?

Who really pushed Lucinda Drummond off the Tulip Stairs, and why? Had Adrian Fairchild tried to involve her somehow? Or confess to her? Or had she been involved all along? That was something Stark hadn't considered before. In all the outrage at her killing, had anyone stopped to think she might be dirty? His instinct said she wasn't, but who really knew? Were they all at Queen's House to meet, or was that just coincidence? Had she become an impediment, or just seen or heard something that made her a risk?

Or had she just been the victim of a flash of jealous rage from the man she'd left in her wake, both romantically and professionally? Or had they argued and parted, only for Zedani or his easily capable bodyguard to slip into the stairwell and topple her over the ornate balustrade?

And these were just some of the *known* unknowns. The unconnected straight edges of the jigsaw – with something hidden in the empty centre?

Stark's headache had crept back in, and he was just about to seek out more coffee when the desk phone rang, with news from the incident line.

Yusef Mohamed.

The dash cam footage of the supposed van driver hadn't been clear on ethnicity.

Now they knew. Turkish. Second-generation immigrant.

Photos in his family's cramped home spoke of pride in the only son. Two younger sisters had been shooed from the room by the mother as the father showed Stark in.

Tea was offered and declined. Stark was more thirsty for facts. 'And this is definitely your son, Yusef?' he said, showing them the printout again. The same one fed to the press. The same one his concerned parents had seen, to prompt them to call the hotline.

Nods from both.

'And you say he's missing?'

'Over two days now.' The father's English wasn't great. 'He went to work on Thursday, but never came home.'

'Is that something he's done before?'

'No. No. Yusef is a good boy, a good man. He works hard.'

'Where did he work?'

'Lots of different places.'

An unhelpful answer. Stark glanced at the time. He shouldn't leave the office empty too long, even with the desk line diverted to his mobile. 'Sorry, but could you narrow that down?'

'He drives,' said the mother. 'And moves things, guards things. He's strong and brave.'

'Who does he do these things for?'

They looked at each other. They didn't know.

'Does he wear a uniform? With a logo?'

Nods. The mother went to get something and returned with another framed photo. Yusef, grinning, big arms around his laughing sisters as if tickling them. He was wearing black cargo trousers and matching bomber jacket with orange lining and a logo.

Temple Security.

The same company as Zedani's bodyguard, Jan Zieliński.

*

It should have been obvious that a company called Temple Security would have an immovable gatekeeper.

GDPR legislation, she insisted, prevented her from divulging employee information. Stark explained that he wasn't after personal details, merely confirmation that Yusef Mohamed was an employee.

She remained unmoved. It was a Sunday, she pointed out needlessly, so there was no one present with authority to help.

Stark considered driving over there and explaining some of the finer points of the Police and Criminal Evidence Act 1984 to her, but guessed that beneath her stupidity lay deeper layers of incompetence, and it would be more fun to watch Fran try in the morning. After calling to update her, he shared Yusef's details with uniform as a missing person and person of interest. The afternoon passed without actionable intel, before he locked up the MIT office for the night and set off.

He had somewhere worse to be.

'You look tired,' said Doc Hazel as he took his usual seat opposite her, ever eschewing the couch of cliché.

'That a personal opinion, or professional?' asked Stark.

'An observation.'

'Are you going to ask me how I feel about it?'

'Okay.'

'Tired.'

'Bravo.' She smiled. Warm-up dealt with. 'So how are you – aside from tired?'

'Frustrated. When Fran first called this a shitter of a case, she had no idea . . . Every time we think we might be working out what's going on, something else bad happens.'

'You're taking it to heart?'

'You mean, obsessing.'

'That's not the description we use, is it?'

'My difficulty in accepting that not everything is my fault or responsibility,' he smiled. 'Pathological omnipotence delusion?'

'You're right,' she smiled. 'Obsessing is pithier.'

He nodded. 'But no, I don't think so. No more than anyone would.'

'Faced with death and injustice?'

'I suppose.'

'But you have a different relationship with those things than most.'

And he'd spent the last year . . . what? Running towards that, or from it? 'There's other stuff going on.'

She listened while he downloaded the gist. He expected her to fixate on the news of Kelly's engagement or Tink's job offer, but she picked something else. 'Tell me about the flashbulb moment. With the paparazzi.'

'It wasn't my blood.'

'That's not what I was asking.'

'I know.' He took a moment to gather his thoughts. 'We were on a night raid once, outside Tikrit, searching a property intel suggested was being used as a base to lob mortars into our FOB. Turned out to be a trap. The ATO missed an IED they'd left for us and lost his leg. Then we came under small-arms fire and got pinned down. He kept saying sorry, over and over, as if his mistake had hurt me, not him. I did what I could, but he was barely alive by the time we got him to an LZ for MedEvac. He died in the chopper. Blood loss. I remember staring at my hands when we eventually got back to the FOB. I was too tired to go wash the blood off, too wired to sleep. I just sat there against a wall, staring at my hands. And then a mortar round detonated a few metres away.'

Hazel waited in case there was more. 'So it was like that?'

Stark nodded. 'Pap was lucky I didn't have my rifle.'

She nodded slowly. 'Which I suppose brings us on to your old pal Tink's job offer with StoneTower.'

'You've heard of them?'

'Not always favourably.'

'It's the kind of work that generally only makes headlines when things go *un*favourably.'

'Tempted?'

'Yes. I could make a difference, do what I'm good at.'

'And retire in ten years or less.'

'You know that's not it.'

'Or get yourself killed.'

The perennial survivor's-guilt/death-wish conversation. 'Or that.'

Hazel tilted her head. 'A simpler life, then.'

'Perhaps.'

'What is it you say – in war everything is simple but every simple thing is hard?'

'You think I'm looking for ways to avoid real-life complications.'

'Are you?'

Of course. Logistics and security in Libya. Private security. Far from the complications of home. 'Running away.'

'You know I'd never call it that.'

No, but she wasn't wrong. He'd spent the last year in a war zone with a pistol at his hip, but trying to do good. This was different. It wasn't about the money. It was about the rifle. Redressing a different imbalance.

'And what about Kelly?' asked Hazel, joining painful dots. 'Tempted there?'

'She's moved on. What should I do but wish her well?'

Hazel wasn't here to answer the questions. 'Still, it hardly seems fair. Given all your sacrifices.'

Stark shrugged. 'Fairness is an aspiration, not a given. And who's to say Robert doesn't deserve her more?'

Another unanswerable.

Hazel nodded. 'So, you're at a crossroads. Behind you, Kelly. Ahead, your police career. To the left, saving lives with Gabrielle, and now to the right, taking up arms again. So, what is it to be?'

34

'Monday again,' said Williams. 'Back to work for a rest after a long one-day weekend with the family. Thanks,' he added, as Swan doled out the coffees – everyone's preference correct from memory. 'You can stay.'

'No, I won't bloody hold,' spat Fran into the phone.

The labs had just confirmed no foreign DNA found in the swabs taken from Nathan Goff's knuckles last week, and she was channelling her cheer into the Temple Security Human Resources department. She'd made it past the gatekeepers to some kind of line manager and was getting into her stride. Normally, this might be when everyone else in the MIT office kept their heads down behind their screens, but a strange gallows fascination seemed to have crept in.

'I was told you could help. Can you help? Because I have your name written here on my pad, and if you can't help, I'm going to come there and bang on the door of the biggest, glassiest, highest corner office in your building and tell the occupant that you've been obstructing a multiple-murder investigation.'

Heads in the MIT office nodded in appreciation of a point well made.

Fran listened, then scribbled on her notepad, before hanging up with the most perfunctory of thanks.

Now everyone ducked their heads.

'So,' she announced, 'Yusef Mohamed was an employee

of Temple Security until about two months ago. They let him go when his immigration status came under question. Failed to get his leave-to-remain paperwork correct in the post-Brexit confusion. The people at Temple assumed he'd been deported by now.'

'His family never mentioned this,' said Stark.

'Well, they're probably in the same boat,' said Williams. 'No pun intended.'

'No, I mean they said he was still going to work every day.'

'Maybe he was pretending,' said Dixon. 'Ashamed or something.'

'Or maybe he got a different job,' said Swan.

There was only one way to find out. Fran jiggled her car keys.

Stark spoke to the father again, letting Fran and Swan speak with the mother and daughters in the next room. They compared notes outside in the car, afterwards.

'The mum says Yusef had changed two months ago, working more randomly, seeming more tired and stressed,' said Fran. 'He told her he'd been promoted.'

'The father said the same,' confirmed Stark.

'And the sisters,' nodded Swan. 'But the eldest says he had a second phone he kept hidden, that when she caught him using it, he claimed it was a new girlfriend. A white girl. Non-Muslim. The parents wouldn't approve, apparently. Only now she says it hadn't sounded like a romantic call.'

'We haven't found his regular phone, let alone a second,' said Fran.

'No, but it was on her birthday. She's given me a time, and the location is here.'

'So we can check the towers,' concluded Fran, nodding appreciatively. Meaning she'd let Stark check the towers. Triangulation could give them a thousand numbers to sift through.

'Anyway, last week he suddenly got agitated at something on the TV,' continued Swan. 'The news. The sister says he looked scared but wouldn't talk about it. That was Wednesday morning.'

'The day after his dipshit Coin Sting fiasco,' said Fran, indicating Stark. 'Same day I told the press about the Black Riders.'

'Exactly. She saw Yusef talking angrily into the second phone before he took off.'

'So maybe he drove the van and Black Riders to Circular Way on both nights, oblivious to what they were buzzing off to perpetrate,' said Fran. 'But he sees the news and puts two and two together – and makes fear.'

Fran gave Yusef's name to the press.

Some of the hacks even managed a few pertinent questions about the case, between fishing for Stark updates.

Gwen Maddox kept quiet. Given her past exclusive with Stark, she could easily find the questioning turned on her and whether she had known he was back – and if not, why not, et cetera, et cetera.

Fran left them all to it.

She took Dixon with her to sit for the warrants, and as soon as she had them in her hand, she harried the bank and phone companies for Yusef's details.

The bank statements showed his last pay cheque from Temple Security corresponding to when they said they'd let him go. Since then, the only deposits were in cash. Roughly weekly, amounts varying. A lot like someone was paying him off the books. But who, and for what – beyond driving motorcycle maniacs off to butcher thieves and swing crowbars at coppers? What they didn't show was any activity on his account since he was last seen.

And neither did his phone records. A ping showed the number still non-contactable. Call logs showed it was last used on Wednesday morning, before his sister said he'd been upset at something on the news. Fran's appeal for information relating to the murder of Nathan Goff and three motorcyclists in black. But his sister said Yusef had used a second phone for the last two months. He'd made a call with that, hurrying into his room and closing the door, then left the house immediately afterwards. There was no second phone registered to Yusef, so a burner. His primary phone's location services were switched off, but the cell tower triangulation data showed it travelling at walking speed to Westcombe Park Railway station, and then at train speeds on the overland line towards Dartford, but switching off before the train reached Erith.

The same pattern proved true for the afternoon before that, the Coin Sting fiasco, and the one before that, Nathan Goff's murder. But on those two occasions the pattern reversed, later that evening, as Yusef returned home. Further analysis showed the same pattern over the last two months on what would doubtless prove to be all his work shifts.

So, Yusef's new job appeared to involve him being paid

in cash, turning his primary phone off to mask his location, and using a secondary burner phone.

'Dodgy as fuck,' commented Williams.

Only Wednesday appeared to be a one-way trip.

Some hours later, London Transport's CCTV network confirmed Yusef boarding the train at Westcombe Park, and disembarking at the station before Erith, at Belvedere.

Street cameras traced him on foot disappearing into the Belvedere and Erith Marshes Industrial Estate, a fractal maze of assorted light-industrial, warehouse and wharf buildings. Tracing him further was going to involve knocking on countless doors for countless more hours of security camera footage. The daunting nature of which was somewhat curtailed by a call from the Marine Policing Unit.

Bodies from the river weren't always easily identifiable, but this one's deficiency in the face department wasn't mother nature's work so much as over-enthusiastic tooth removal. The missing fingers were another clue, but it was the slit throat and concrete block tied round one ankle with nylon rope that sealed the deal.

'I guess we'll be treating this one as suspicious,' said Stark.

'Yours?' asked the police boat captain.

Fran sighed. 'Maybe.'

Although still part of the Thames, the Swanscombe Marshes fell outside Greater London, under Kent Police's jurisdiction, but their Search and Marine Unit seemed confident the tide had probably brought the body to them from the capital, and checked the Met's missing persons list.

The body had been stripped naked. Clothes, wallet, phone, all hidden, buried or burned somewhere, but aside from the missing elements, the body matched Yusef Mohamed's description close enough for the river unit to call Stark. The family might have to inspect what was left for distinguishing marks to confirm that. Fran wasn't looking forward to asking them.

'Whoever weighed the body down forgot to allow for bloating,' explained the boat captain. 'Increases the buoyancy. Can take a day or three to resurface, depending. Judging on when it was spotted, outgoing tide had carried it east.'

'From where?' asked Fran.

He shrugged. 'I can put you in touch with an expert, but the number of factors involved . . . it's informed guesswork.'

Fran stared out across the water. The evening sun glinted off the broad curve of the Thames, turning turgid brown to glittering silver, but the body and fetid mud banks dispelled any illusion of beauty.

She wasn't in Kansas any more.

And now, in addition to a murdered TV celebrity and low-life thief, and a dodgy antiquities expert in a coma, they had another connected homicide.

'Someone call for a pathologist on this fine evening?'

Fran turned to find Marcus, doing his best impression of someone with no reason to avoid eye contact. God, she missed the maddening sod. She'd stupidly allowed him to breach her solitude, and now the sanctuary of her limited free time felt achingly empty. Her fault. As was this unspeaking impasse. But even if she could override her stubbornness, she'd no idea what she might say to heal the breach, or even whether she deserved to. 'Stark'll talk you through it. I'd better go get on to Family Liaison.'

Stark watched her go. 'Any chance of peace by Christmas?'

Marcus's eyes followed her too. 'Your guess is as good as mine.'

Stark leaned back on his sofa and let the tiredness in. Late evening sun reflected off the neighbouring building and in through his window, spotlighting dust motes in the air and warming his closed eyelids.

A buzz alerted him to a fresh email, chasing two earlier ones.

DEFCON-1.

He let out a long sigh. Another branch at the cross-roads. He could email back, but they were probably beyond that now, so he picked up his phone, with regret. Once Major Wendy Pierson had this new number, she'd never leave him alone.

'Hello?' Pierson answered.

'Hi. It's Stark.'

'About *fucking* time! Is this your new number?'

'No.'

'Liar. There's no getting away from me now.'

Maybe he'd change it again, and not tell his mum either this time. 'I'm impressed you haven't bombarded the sta-tion switchboard.' He resisted any of the standard *drop-short* jokes relating to her artillery speciality.

'The only reason I haven't banged on the bloody door,

like last time, is I'm far too busy and important to be dealing with your bullshit. So have you changed your mind?'

'No.'

'Change that to a yes, or I'll have you recalled to active service and court-marshalled.'

'That would get me out of all of it.'

'The satisfaction would be worth it.'

'For both of us.'

'Oh for the days when I could've had you shot.'

'I still wouldn't change my mind.'

'No wonder your mother despairs of you.'

'It's a broad church.'

Pierson huffed in disgust. 'You really are the most infuriating arse.'

Stark sighed. 'So I'm told.'

35

Another shitty morning in the life of Francine Millhaven.

Yusef Mohamed's father could hardly look at the remains. The sisters were too young. The mother stared at a cluster of moles on one shoulder and burst into tears. It would still take DNA comparison to put it beyond doubt, but the word '(Deceased)' was penned beneath his photo on the new board.

Killed for finding himself part of something above his pay grade, it seemed.

Fran stared at all four boards. She grudgingly conceded that Stark's handiwork had distilled chaos into order, but you had to wonder whether this was how his mind worked. It gave her the shivers. He could probably deliver the most complex recipe to perfection without ever tasting it. She preferred random ingredients, a glass of wine and her tasting spoon. One thing was for sure though – if the death toll continued like this, the damn boards would soon encircle her, with no door to escape through, Dixon lobbing food and water over to her!

It seemed madness that their search for Lucinda Drummond's killer was now focused on finding out exactly what had happened to a man she'd almost certainly never met, linked only by his possibly unwitting part in the murder of Nathan Goff, who she'd also never met, and the attempted murder of Adrian Fairchild, who might have killed her.

Degrees of separation.

Not what a police investigation needed. Nor any future prosecution.

Three in the morgue, and one a hospital-monitor flat-line away from joining them. Alex Zedani's name may sit appealingly central in Stark's triangular Venn diagram, but they were no closer to proving anything.

The river guy's expert had worked overnight to come up with some draft predictions of where the body had gone into the water, based on the assumption it went in after dark on the Wednesday evening after Yusef first went missing.

Factoring in tides, temperature, rainfall and a dozen other variables and assumptions, it gave a pattern from Purfleet up to Thamesmead, leaving hundreds of water-front properties where a boat might be launched, and dozens of piers, jetties and pontoons the body may have been dropped from. The report's map, which Stark was currently fixing to board four, showed the whole river in blotches of blue, through green and yellow to red, like a coloured contour map, but instead of the red being the highest terrain, it was the highest likelihood. In the centre of the map, and the greatest concentration of red, lay Erith.

'Could've told you that last night,' muttered Fran.

Stood behind her, Stark kept quiet.

'Well . . .' said Groombridge. 'Best not keep the Super waiting.'

The lift doors opened onto the top floor.

It didn't take a genius to guess why they were being summoned.

Groombridge hoped Fran could keep a level head, but

he was oddly more worried about Stark. The lad still had a foot in two worlds. His head too. When he'd first arrived here, fresh from injury and the traumas of combat, it was obvious his greatest struggle was seeing the difference between war and not. He was different now. Now he could see the difference all too clearly, but was torn as to where he fitted best. It may not take much to send him down a path away from them for good.

Cox's PA waved the three of them into the Superintendent's office, without preamble.

'Well,' said Cox, beckoning them to sit. 'Sorry I couldn't sit in on this morning's round-up. I've been on the phone with Assistant Commissioner Dunbar, among others. Any update on Adrian Fairchild?'

'Brought out of his medically induced coma this morning, sir,' said Groombridge, 'but hasn't regained consciousness, which apparently isn't a good sign. So far, no one has tried to finish him off in his hospital bed, but Haringey Uniform are maintaining their watch.'

Cox nodded, cheerlessly. 'I'm sorry to report that there's growing sentiment from above that if we don't soon demonstrate progress, this case should be handed over to the National Crime Agency.'

'What?' said Fran. 'Why?'

Groombridge jumped in. 'I think what DI Millhaven means, sir, is that plenty of murder cases get more complicated before they get less.'

'But this one seems to be gathering bodies like a rolling stone.'

Groombridge chose to leave the misapplication of that analogy uncorrected.

'Plus, the potential international interest,' continued Cox, 'should your theories about ancient coins prove true. Bringing in DC Swan from AAU bought us a little time there, but I'm afraid that time is running out. And then there's the added attention you bring,' he looked at Stark, somewhat apologetically. 'Welcome back as you are, while the press are clamouring for you, they're not letting up on the case.'

'I could step aside if it helps, sir,' said Stark immediately.

'With respect, I think that would send the wrong message, sir,' said Groombridge, hastily. 'Stark aside, we may *need* the press again on this one. Publicity has already helped us identify the van driver.'

Cox nodded. 'I said exactly that up-chain. But while AC Dunbar remains favourable, the unedifying departure of DAC Stevens left others exposed and jittery. We can't afford to get caught up in the Yard's political manoeuvrings again.'

While Assistant Commissioner Marjorie Dunbar had a fiery reputation, she'd once been DS to Cox's DI and remained an ally. But the deputy assistants below all wanted her job and more. Getting 'caught up', as Cox put it, had nearly seen the whole Greenwich force divided up between its neighbours by DAC Stevens, until Groombridge took the steps he'd felt forced to. Stark wasn't the only one with secret ties to Gwen Maddox. Groombridge had bet his career and reputation on her discretion. 'We'll lend our best endeavours to avoiding just that, sir.'

'Indeed,' said Cox. 'If we end up handing this over to

NCA, so be it. But let's make sure it's in the best possible shape, either way.'

More apologetic head shakes.

Stark stepped from the latest metal-clad box building back into sunlight. The day was getting hotter as it stretched languidly into the late afternoon.

He loosened his tie.

His feet were hot.

Comfortable footwear was nirvana to soldiers and coppers alike. Good patrol boots were your friends. Fran might look wearily askance at his choice of shoes worn with his CID plain clothes, but they'd pass muster while keeping his feet comfy, dry, and being grippy and robust enough to kick a door down. But they weren't designed for the heat, and he found himself missing the desert boots he'd worn for the last year.

A radio check confirmed the others' luck hadn't improved either.

He, Williams, Dixon, Swan and the three Ps had divided up to scour the industrial estate where Yusef was last seen, for private security camera footage. Tedious work.

Stark wandered back down the alley to the waterfront.

The tide was rising to swallow the mud banks, the water glistening in the sunlight, buildings on the far side eddying a little in the faint heat haze as boats chugged on their way or tugged at their moorings to be free. He closed his eyes, face to the nearest star, imagining himself far away.

A raucous disagreement ruptured his brief reverie. Squinting, he watched a cluster of gulls, bickering over some piece of flotsam at the water's edge. A large black crow sat atop a nearby timber, biding its time like a black hole in the spinning cosmos.

Tearing his eyes from it, Stark tried to picture how it all might have looked at night in last week's slim moon as a boat slipped out into the darkness to tip a weighted body overboard. The one thing that scene needed was a boat. There was an old slipway down into the water. It looked steep and slippery as hell below the high-tide line. Much easier to use a pier like the one jutting out from the adjacent aggregate depot. It was then he noticed the rundown sheds that shared its frontage.

There was no obvious entrance. No reception. No metal cladding, new or old. Just three large old timber sheds adjoined, or one larger one with a triple pitched roof.

There was a sign – *Coleman Brothers Boatyard* – in long-faded and peeling paint. The barely legible phone number beneath preceded the modern Outer London dialling code, probably by decades.

There was a security camera covering the gate. Its rust cast serious doubt about whether it was connected to anything. But the badly rusted gates sported a large, shiny new padlock.

'You're right,' nodded Ptolemy, sitting in the car, half an hour later, inspecting a photo of the padlock on Stark's phone, with an earnestly straight face. 'Deeply suspicious.'

'Better call in a SWAT team,' agreed Peters.

'You could always ask *him*,' said Pensol, pointing at someone in the distant background of the next photo.

Stark expanded the zoom with finger and thumb,

recalling the old man he'd seen creakingly sweeping a far corner of the aggregate yard.

'Yeah,' scoffed Peters. 'There's a keen-eyed lookout, if ever there was one.'

They were right, of course. And they were hot and tired too. Dixon and Swan were still trying buildings on the roads into the estate. Each of them had a collection of copied CCTV footage from dozens of buildings to look through, and many more to collect tomorrow.

Even so . . .

Stark checked his pocket for a remaining contact card and opened the car door, to general groans as the air con spilled out.

36

The aggregate depot had cameras, but none covering the sheds or their approach. The same proved true of other surrounding buildings or approaches.

Dixon found evidence that Coleman Brothers Boatyard had ceased trading in 1986, with the property sold to a development company that went bust in the 1991 financial crash. The property was auctioned off to a land-banking hedge fund, who probably hoped to package it up with the surrounding properties for swish waterfront flats, but they were then bought wholesale by a bigger fund that, in turn, went bust in the 2008 financial crash. Its innumerable properties were auctioned off in parcels or separately, largely to overseas investors, and finding out *which* was where a lowly DC ran out of headway.

'Boom and bust benefiting the Russian oligarchs, again,' commented Williams. 'If it's not football teams it's property. *Welcome to the Great British Sell-Off. Everything must go. Happy to help with all your grubby money problems.*'

Fran remained unamused. 'Surely this isn't the only suspicious property you've come up with.'

'Ignoring the possibility that any one of a dozen so far *un*suspicious buildings might be hiding our white Luton van,' said Stark, 'and that our perps might have used said van to drive Yusef's body anywhere from Purfleet up to Thamesmead to dump it in the river . . .'

'Don't let Cox overhear your resounding confidence,' she sighed.

'Why?' asked Swan. 'Is he getting pressured? Is this going to be passed up to NCA?'

'Don't worry, I'm sure they'll take you with it.'

Swan's face tightened at the slight. 'They treat AAU like a sick and distant relative they thought had already died.'

'Might get some publicity out of it though,' offered Stark. 'Boost your funding?'

'Which NCA would quietly syphon off for more gadgets and shoe polish,' riposted Swan. 'No, thanks. Sad as it seems, I'd rather bet on you lot.'

'Another resounding endorsement,' smiled Fran, grimly.

Gallows humour was better than none, at least, thought Stark. But that didn't get them any further forward. 'If we're not going to trace the owners for permission anytime soon, we're back to substantiating a warrant request or staking the place out.'

'Which would require an overtime request we probably *also* can't substantiate,' muttered Fran. 'I'll see what the Guv says.'

'I'll ask my inspector if we can add it to a patrol car route,' said Ptolemy.

Fran glanced at the wall clock: 5:30 p.m. 'And in the meantime, we'd better keep looking for something better than a shot in the dark.'

Williams, Dixon and Swan volunteered to stay a few hours more, but Stark sent them home. Tomorrow wouldn't be any easier.

He stayed though.

Work was better than dwelling on other things, like a missed call from his mum and her usual topics.

'You have lackeys for that now, you know,' said Fran, frowning around the door to the CCTV suite, where Stark was sitting alone with the stack of collected footage.

'Says the only other person here at eight p.m.,' he countered.

She looked at her watch. 'Damn these late summer sunsets.'

'DI stuff?'

'For my sins.'

'Don't you have lackeys for that now?'

'Useless sods go home or hide out in here.' She took a seat. 'Anything?'

He nodded. 'We've got the Luton van, heading out of and back into the industrial estate at times corresponding to the two Circular Way bike drop-offs. And I've found Yusef Mohamed going in and out on foot at corresponding times, but we always lose both a couple of streets in.'

'Anywhere near your nefarious-looking boatyard?'

'Not close enough to help with a warrant. We'll go looking for more footage tomorrow, I guess.'

'Any more luck tracing the owners?'

He shook his head.

She made a face. 'I need this bloody case closed without anyone else *dying*.'

She might want him to believe this was simply because of the additional paperwork but he knew better and kept his peace. Normally, at this point she'd offer something sarcastic, but she just checked her phone screen for notifications and sat there pensively.

'Nowhere to be?' he asked.

'Don't start.'

'What?' he feigned innocence. 'It's not like I asked you straight out about your love life.'

'I don't have one.'

'Or complications thereof.'

She scowled. 'One of your very few bearable points is that you value your own privacy enough to respect everyone else's.'

The same could rarely be said of her, but this didn't seem the time to point that out. 'Fair enough. My shrink always says it's much healthier to bottle everything up inside anyway.'

Fran gave him the look she'd likely have given Doc Hazel, were she here. 'She may have even fewer good points than you.'

'I'll make sure to tell her.' Stark leaned back in his chair to stretch his stiff back. 'Fancy continuing this mutual under-sharing over a pint?'

Fran weighed this up, but Stark's desk phone interrupted.

One of Maggie's switchboard minions, holding a call for him.

It took a long moment for the name to register.

The aggregate depot sweeper.

37

'So, to be sure I've got this straight,' said Groombridge into his phone, rubbing tired eyes. 'The old sweeper you spoke to earlier hadn't seen anything, but his night-guard colleague had. But the night guard doesn't speak much English, so with assistance from the sweeper and some good old-fashioned gesticulation, you believe that he's seen Yusef Mohamed coming and going from the boat-yard on foot and driving the suspect Luton van?'

'Yes, Guv,' said Stark.

'And you've typed this into a statement, which they both signed?'

'Yes, Guv.'

'And the guard understands what he signed?'

'Sweeper insists that he's interpreted accurately.'

'Because we couldn't find our own Bengali speaker at nine at night to corroborate.'

'Exactly.'

'And you're now sitting at the courts with Fran, waiting on the duty judge to consider a warrant.'

'While Dixon and Swan volunteered to come back in and go sit in an unmarked, with a view of the sheds.'

Groombridge nodded to himself, thoughtfully. 'And your warrant application – surveillance with option to enter?'

'That's the plan.'

'Okay. Use my name on the application.'

'Yes, Guv.'

'You already have, haven't you?'

'Yes, Guv.'

As soon as they had the warrant, Swan and Dixon withdrew. Unless they'd been making out, their stationary presence in such a secluded location was far too conspicuous. Stark was already concerned that the rusty CCTV camera on the gates might not have been as defunct as it was intended to look, and that the interest he'd taken in the sheds that afternoon might already have tipped off the bad guys. Fran offered Stark no soothing words. If the universe could spite you, it would. No sense in what-ifs.

Talking of which, the thought of Dixon and Swan caused Fran to wince. Anyone had to be an improvement on Commandant Tracy, but Swan . . . ? What John really needed was someone less wilful and above it all. It looked like he'd started sniffing around Constable Pensol, who Fran didn't know well but seemed a better fit. She sensed outside forces at work there. Perennial meddler, PC Peters. Maybe Stark too. At any other time she might have joined the conspiracy, but she strongly doubted Dixon had the courage to jump, and she was hardly in Cupid's camp right now.

Marcus had sent her a message last night. *Call if you want to talk. Miss you x*

Leaving it to her to pick up the phone, make the first move. Typical feeble man. Like it was her responsibility to sweep up the shards. Coward. Okay, technically, maybe his text was the first move, the olive branch, but someone had to be the emotionally un-stunted one here. Just because the argument had been entirely one-sided and her fault, she didn't see why he couldn't just man-up and tell her it was okay, that he understood, even if he didn't.

'You okay?' asked Stark.

'Why?'

'You're grinding your teeth and tutting like you're having some kind of angry internal conversation.'

'Isn't that what I'm always like?' she said, bluntly. 'Isn't that my reputation? Little Miss Irritable.'

'No one calls you little.'

Fran glared at him, but smiled inside, silently cursing Groombridge. *You need someone to counterbalance your yin with some yang, Fran*, he'd insisted, back when she was still complaining about Stark on an almost daily basis. Bastard. 'We can't see enough from here either,' she said, staring at the monitors showing a view of the sheds as seen from the third camera Bingo was busy installing for them outside.

They were sat in the cramped storeroom the aggregate depot manager had graciously offered up. Bingo was locating the cameras to give the best possible advantage, but the depot's curtilage didn't include anywhere with a perfect view. They had the gate and boatyard, but not the shed door. They'd have to look at getting something from over the road, but that building had no windows facing this way and installing a camera outside would be conspicuous.

Fran hated this. Surveillance. Sitting and waiting for something to happen, or not, when the second half of her warrant gave her permission to march over there and kick down the doors with a handful of firearms specialists at her back. There was every chance that even if this was the right place, the killers had abandoned it when they did away with their driver. Despite assurances, she wasn't at all happy that the night guard's nods at the photos of Yusef and the van were confident enough – but what else was there? It was the judge's job to give zero F's that they had the press and National Crime Agency breathing down their necks, so it had to be some kind of statistical anomaly that he'd come down on her side. The punchline being that she was now stuck playing the long-shot waiting game, while being on the hook for blame should it come to nothing. 'You know I'm going to blame you when this goes tits-up.'

Stark shrugged. 'What else are sergeants for?'

Fran inspected the contents of the pizza box, with a grimace. Even with 11 p.m. traffic, it had taken the moped driver too long to find the back of the depot, with consequent loss of heat. She'd have demanded a discount. Stark had paid in full. She lifted a slice, staring at the stretching tendrils of mozzarella like they were the creeping bony hands of the Grim Reaper. Her stomach growled, in hunger or horror. 'Didn't we agree we had lackeys for this shit?'

'You've got to let the plebs have the occasional night off, or they'll start to resent your boot on their necks.'

She tried a bite. It wasn't as bad as it looked. She actually quite liked pizza, and he'd deferred to her choice of toppings, but she wasn't about to admit that. 'I have never hated you more than I do right now.'

Stark nodded acknowledgement. What else was he for?

*

Stake-outs are not glamorous.

In both Iraq and Afghanistan, Stark had lain in wait for insurgent leaders for days in baking hovels or freezing ditches, with nothing to eat but dry army rations, drinking just enough to stay the right side of dehydration, without needing to piss back into the bottles too much – or worse, find somewhere to shit. Police stake-outs in cars were a holiday camp by comparison. A warm room, cold pizza and the availability of an albeit grubby toilet put this one head and shoulders above, but Stark opted not to share this observation with Miss Irritable.

Muttering discontent wasn't unusual, but her mood had turned worryingly dark this last week. This was the first time he'd seen her love-lorn, of course. Historically that had been her complaint about him, post Kelly.

She yawned, and summoned a weary glare at him.

Bingo, the on-loan techie, hadn't been able to get out of the room fast enough.

The other problem with stake-outs: manpower.

A minimum of two people. Rotating shifts. People not doing other vital work. Ptolemy had cleared it with his inspector for him; Peters and Pensol to stay attached, for now. There may be other uniforms happy for some over-time. But it was a costly, time-consuming punt. It could take days, or even weeks. It could come to nothing.

Which was probably why a change on the monitors took Stark by surprise. 'Movement.'

'What?' asked Fran, sleepily.

'Movement. There.' He pointed to the jetty, its dark bulk jutting out into the waters, silhouetted against the reflections of London's background light pollution.

'I don't . . .' Fran trailed off as the silhouette bulged and bent.

Something else was there . . . 'Boat,' said Stark.

A new, bobbing black shape on the water. Someone on board shone a red torch across the lower section of floating pontoon. Marking distance.

Then other shapes, merging with the pontoon, two, maybe three people, tying up.

They gave scale.

The boat was quite large.

And no more lights came on.

Stark checked his watch. Midnight.

'Now that,' said Fran, fully alert, 'is what I call suspicious behaviour.'

38

'Ready?' asked the Trojan commander.

'Whenever you are.' Groombridge fought the urge to whisper.

The last hour had been a farce of clandestine steps. Getting tactical support on board had been surprisingly easy. Getting everyone into position unnoticed was, as Stark put it, like tiptoeing through a minefield. He would know.

'Good.' The burly Eastender clicked his radio to transmit. 'Trojan Control Actual to Breach White. Status?'

'*Breach White, in position,*' came the reply.

'Trojan Control to Breach Black. Status?'

'*Breach Black, in position.*'

'Trojan Control to Breach Blue. Status?'

'*Breach Blue, in position.*'

In these moments, Groombridge always wished for a stopwatch or second counter. Time seemed to twist and groan, stand still and gasp. How many heartbeats, how long holding his breath? How many lives on the line?

'Trojan Control to Breach Teams. Standby, standby. Go!'

The crash of the big red key.

White light from inside ripped outward.

'*ARMED POLICE!*'

The interior echoed with overlapping bellowed warnings and demands for compliance.

Stark followed on the shoulder of the last man of Breach White, in through the front door – a passenger, wishing heartily for flash-bangs and an assault rifle. The specialist firearms officers in front of him had the Kevlar helmets and heavy vests with ceramic chest plates, so familiar to him. Stark's police-issue stab vest wouldn't stop a bullet. But if he came across an arsehole with a crowbar, his new ASP was going to have something to say about it.

'*DOWN ON THE GROUND!*'
'*HANDS BEHIND YOUR BACKS!*'

Stark saw a number of men on the ground around packing crates and detritus. Another frozen in panic, hands raised, before two SFOs encouraged him to his knees through a combination of shouts and gun-barrel diplomacy.

Some of Team White were already bunched around an opening leading through to the next shed area, in a cacophony of bellowed warnings.

Stark tucked in behind as they went through, confronting more panicked men.

One jumped to his feet right in front of Stark, something raised in one hand.

Stark blocked the guy's wrist upwards with his ASP and swept his legs from under him, guiding his weight semi-gently to the concrete, face down with a knee on his back, the thing in his hand skidding along the ground. A phone.

And suddenly the figures ahead were members of

Trojan Breach Team Black, forcing the final suspects to the ground.

And it was over.

In the near silence, radio traffic confirmed Team Blue had successfully captured the boat and three crew.

Stark took a deep breath to begin the adrenaline control.

Around him, SFOs worked to line up suspects on their knees with wrists bound behind backs, or slapped shoulders in congratulation. The headcount totalled thirteen suspects restrained. No shots fired. No casualties.

Stark stalked down the line of bound suspects, looking for the three crowbar-happy bikers, but no one stood out. All men. Various ages, colours, sizes and spectra of emotion, ranging from confusion to scared shitless. Few met his eyes, and none with any degree of defiance. A wolf might hide among the herd, but Stark knew the eyes of a predator. The Black Riders weren't here.

He cursed. Whether police holiday-camp pizza or combat-ditch rations, nothing stung after a stake-out more than coming away empty-handed.

And that now depended on the thirty-plus shipping crates lined up along the warehouse floor – unopened, perhaps indicating the contents were above these guys' pay grades.

A pair of sniffer dogs padded around them on leads – one for drugs, the other for guns, ammunition or explosives – excitedly surfing their handlers' adrenaline, but not barking. That ruled out having to wait for Narcotics or Bomb Squad, but they'd still have to wait for SOCO before they could investigate further.

Clicking his tongue in irritation, Stark turned away, looking for Groombridge and Fran, finding them peering at the back of the end shed.

Parked there were one white Luton van and three matching motorcycles, two black and one red. In the back of the van was a rusty metal chair, gaffer tape, bolt cutters and a lot of blood.

Comparison would likely show Yusef Mohamed's terrified final moments had played out here.

An hour later, and adrenaline control had well and truly crumbled into comedown, meets 2 a.m., meets standing around watching other people be busy.

SOCO had been standing by, several streets away. Standard procedure on an armed raid. Even if it was a bust, you'd need forensics to prove it so.

Now lots of earnest marshmallow people roamed the scene like a sped-up nature documentary of normally slow, globular creatures scurrying about.

But there was order in their efforts. Patience, and diligence. These weren't sworn officers any more, for the most part, but employees of a private service provider. But like Maggie's cohort back at the station, you couldn't fault their professionalism. The unflattering end of the policing world, from those answering the phones, often to desperate and scared callers, to those cataloguing evidence, often around a grisly corpse.

Tonight there was no corpse, at least. Just evidence of one in the making.

And the crates that Swan was clearly itching to get into.

She'd spent the last two hours urging the crime scene manager to hurry the hell up. But Geoff Culpepper was not a man to be rushed. Only when he was meticulously satisfied that all was in order did he consent to open anything.

They had their own brightly labelled SOCO crowbars.

The cracking and splitting of cheap packing pine was followed by the agonized squeak as the first lid was levered up. Inside lay what looked like a very old clay urn, around two feet high, carefully packed in foam.

'Oh my . . .' breathed Swan.

The next lid revealed another, then another. Varying sizes and shapes. And judging by the shock in Swan's eyes, some kind of Arts and Antiquities Unit jackpot.

But it wasn't just Swan who recognized them.

His mind went back to that baking-hot day in Basra. That poor man, sifting the dirt and straw, in shock. At the time, Stark could only guess what had been lost, so he'd made it his business to find out afterwards. They had been there to protect these people's heritage, to help find a new home for their priceless treasures – but a large haul had already been taken. Nearly forty ancient urns. Several more had been broken in the raid and left behind – lesser examples, apparently, discarded to make it look more like looting than a targeted raid orchestrated by someone in power. He remembered wondering why anyone would think these frankly unremarkable earthenware vessels were more valuable on the black market, to be hidden away in secret collections, than they were to historians and museum-goers. But apparently, they were. The odds that he, of all people, would be there in Basra, where they were taken, and here now, in a boatyard on the Thames, for their apparent recovery, boggled the mind.

Of course, that wasn't all that had been taken.

'Over here,' one of the SOCOs beckoned them to a smaller crate. It appeared to contain unremarkable and plainly modern machine-made crockery, but in a hidden section beneath, the officer had exposed an orange Peli case with a digital lock. They took an age, dusting for prints and swabbing for DNA, and ran the dogs over it for good measure, before one of the officers applied a jack tool to crack it open.

Swan peered inside, and breathed out two words. '*Holy fuck.*'

39

'Should get the Brass and National Crime Agency off our backs,' said Fran, with evident satisfaction.

Swan nodded, without appearing to hear. 'I still can't believe this.'

Stark stared down at the evidence tray too. 'Well, you did say we should be asking where the others were.'

Groombridge couldn't tear his eyes away either.

Twenty-two gold staters lay gleaming under the ceiling lights like imperfect little nuggets of antiquarian joy. The twenty-third, saved from the melting pots of Dosh4Gold days earlier, lay in its evidence bag beside them. How any of them had escaped the melting pots of post-war impoverished Iraq was a wonder in itself, and a story they might never uncover. But one had made its way to Adrian Fairchild for testing. He'd presumably declared it genuine to his shadowy benefactor, and now the rest had made their way upriver to a secluded London warehouse via a boat that had either come directly from overseas, or met a larger boat out in deeper water. Cargo this valuable would have required more care than simply being hidden in the back of shipping containers with 'Made in China' labels plastered all over it.

So far, none of the suspects had volunteered more information, but that process hadn't really begun. Initial interactions suggested a possible Turkish or Greek connection, but with none admitting to more than a smattering of English, definitive conclusions were premature. And that was just the start of the problems. The custody suite in Royal Hill Police Station had endured many descriptions over the years but capacious was not among them. Six cells, one generally kept free as the drunk tank, were not going to hold thirteen suspects, especially when you wanted them kept apart to prevent the cooking-up of stories. Erith's station was even smaller. But the warehouse-like building where Greenwich housed its vehicle fleet served as the hub for patrols and had been designed to double-up for mass detention. So the thirteen were now secured there in strict silence under the watchful eye of several uniforms. Interviewing them individually was the task ahead.

Right now, Groombridge resisted the need to stretch his aching back. He was getting too old for all-nighters. 'We're going to need a bigger lock and more insurance,' he said, looking around the station's cramped evidence room.

'I think this is the first time we've needed armed guards on the door,' agreed Fran, referring to the two firearms officers outside. Inside a police station, in the basement, as if Arnold Schwarzenegger was about to stare at the desk sergeant upstairs and say '*I'll be back.*'

The urns wouldn't fit down here, of course. British Museum staff had been called in to work with SOCO on carefully repacking them into their crates under the watchful eye of the firearms officers, who, rather than swanning off home for tea and back-slapping, had stuck around as guards – aware that this might be the haul of their careers, and certainly more unique than a drugs bust. Even Bingo the techie had been spotted grinning.

Outside now, dawn had done its thing, and those press that weren't loitering on the outer cordon around Coleman Brothers Boatyard in Erith, speculating their little hearts out, were doing the same before the front stoop upstairs, waiting for a briefing.

'Ahem,' came a circumspect cough behind them. Superintendent Cox, looking oddly cheerless under the circumstances. 'Well done, everyone, really, well done indeed.'

'Thank you, sir,' replied Groombridge, warily.

'Good. Good.' Cox's face spelled bad news. 'Now, there's someone upstairs you need to talk to.'

'Maxine Carver,' the stranger introduced herself. 'DCI, MO6 Special Liaison.'

Groombridge gave the faintest harrumph of incredulity. 'Home or away?'

Meaning, was she MI5 or MI6? Special Liaison covered a lot of sins, and Met Operations 6, Economic and Specialist Crime, covered a lot of ground. Stark had seen enough spooks downrange to know one in civvy street. Presumably, they were better at blending in when they weren't the only ones swanning around on a forward military base confident they wouldn't be called upon to defend it, or to step outside the wire to act on their so-called intelligence. But the biggest clue was the Official Secrets Act forms they'd all had to sign before she spoke to them.

This case just got weirder.

Fran looked about as trustful as a cat staring at the

smiling white teeth of a Rottweiler, although Maxine Carver, and Stark wasn't taking that name on face value, looked rather more like a panther. Raven-dark hair, aquiline nose, sleek, slim, graceful and dangerous. And good at ignoring questions.

'The press are gathering outside, so we need to keep this brief,' she began, without preamble. 'They will want to know what you found in Erith. You will not tell them.'

'Wait,' Fran sat up, indignantly. 'We're not allowed to tell them we just bagged the smuggling bust of our careers?'

'Or anyone else,' smiled Carver. 'Friends, family, colleagues. Strangers down the pub who you're sure can be trusted. No one at all.'

'Why the hell not? We should be on TV making ludicrous claims about street value.'

'Sign that form and I'll tell you,' replied Carver, nodding at the stack Fran had collated on the desk. Stark, Groombridge and Swan had signed. Fran, it appeared, had only pretended to. 'My colleagues are busy collecting forms from your DCs Williams and Dixon, your uniform friends and everyone that ever had anything to do with this case.'

'But why?' insisted Fran.

Carver stared at her and the forms. Truculently, Fran pulled hers from the stack and signed it for real.

Carver smiled. 'Because it would be contrary to the security interests of the realm.'

They all stared at her.

When no further explanation appeared forthcoming, Fran's face began to darken and Groombridge placed a hand on her arm to cap her venting. 'I think my colleagues might be hoping for more.'

Carver's smile didn't alter. 'I'd be amazed if you weren't.'

A few more seconds of silence were all Fran could take. 'You can't just come in here and gag us without saying why.'

'I have said why.'

'National security?' said Fran. 'Says who?'

'Says me.'

'But who decides?'

'Oh, that's easy,' smiled Carver, 'the powers that be. Look,' she went on earnestly, 'I can see how frustrating this must be for you, but I'm selected, trained and paid to put personal feelings aside, especially when they're not mine.'

Fran was coming to the boil. 'But what the hell have a few gold coins got to do with national security?'

'Ours is not to reason why, Detective Inspector.'

'A detective's *one job* is to reason why.'

'Your oath was to serve the Crown. In this case, wondering why falls secondary.'

'So we just do and die, is that it? Then what the hell am I supposed to say to the hacks outside?'

Carver wordlessly handed out a sheet of paper to each of them. 'This has been agreed with Superintendent Cox.'

Fran scanned it. '*Contraband?* What the actual fuck?'

'It has a pleasing ambiguity,' smiled Carver.

'Exactly,' cried Fran. 'And when I refuse to elaborate, they're going to chew my head off . . . unless I'm allowed to hide behind national sodding security too?'

'Just the words as typed, please.'

Fran scanned it again, finding nothing new to her liking. '*Being assessed?*'

'We'll wait a day or two before releasing news of the urns,' said Carver. 'Say we were waiting on expert authentication. But under no circumstances are you, or anyone else, to say anything about the coins.'

'But why not?' demanded Fran. 'This is bullshit! And don't you dare say you could tell me but you'd have to kill me.'

'Okay,' Carver nodded pleasantly. 'How about because, if you do, you'll be prosecuted under the Official Secrets Act and thrown in prison with all the nice people you've helped incarcerate over the course of your illustrious careers?'

40

So that was it.

Fran read the statement to the press. And they chewed her head off, to no avail.

Contraband. Being assessed. Further details to follow.

And the team wearily went about interviewing the suspects, reviewing the evidence, following leads.

Preliminary interviews had established the thirteen suspects to be mostly Turkish Cypriots, plus two Syrians, though without any documentation to back that up. Interpreters had been found and exhortations of innocent ignorance disgorged. None had yet offered details of any larger ship that may have ferried them to UK waters, a port of origin or the route taken. The Cypriots appeared too fearful to speak. The two Syrians, perhaps more senior, played dumb. Unsurprisingly, none of them had owned up to being one of the Black Riders. Stark remained convinced they weren't here. It was one thing to smuggle 'contraband', quite another to swing a crowbar at someone's head from the back of a speeding motorcycle. None of these men looked the part, plus there wasn't a size twelve shoe among them.

But the blood from the van was a type match for Yusef Mohamed. DNA would likely confirm. A perforated oil drum in the boatyard had seen service as an incinerator, containing plastic residue and the crumpled remains of what might once have been nitrile polymer gloves. But the melting point of aluminium is slightly higher than that of your average wood fire, and the long, charred zippers inside were very familiar to anyone with an unfortunate knowledge of anti-contamination gear. The Riders had silenced their driver in that boatyard warehouse – and yet, in Fran's words, *the bloody Brass seemed more concerned about national bloody security!*

Bingo had taken it upon himself to interrogate the phones found on three of the suspects, assumed to be ringleaders, for evidence of where they'd been. But all three proved to be burners, recently registered and with no signs of travel abroad. Calls between each other and one other number only, also a burner. With their citizenships uncertain, the judge had already approved Fran's application to hold all thirteen for a further forty-eight hours without charge, so the secondary interviews might reveal more.

While this was going on, efforts to establish who now owned the Coleman Brothers Boatyard had got no further. The Land Registry still listed it under the long-defunct hedge fund.

Reynolds, from Family Liaison, called to say Ryan Drummond was back from his sunshine diversions and getting antsy about their lack of progress in finding his mother's killer, so Fran decided palming the family off with her sergeant wasn't going to cut it this time.

'Sorry, she *what*?' demanded Fran, sparing an incredulous stare from her driving concentration.

With everything going on, Stark had decided to throw her something to divert her from more muttering rants. 'Eyes on the road, please, Boss.'

'She hit on you? Last week?'

'Only sort of.'

Fran rolled her eyes. 'I sent you round to tease out info with your Mister Smooth soppy eyes, not flirt with the victim's hot daughter!'

You sent me round because facing the victims of horrendous crime makes you so cross you think you come across as unsympathetic, thought Stark silently. 'I expect it was just her version of crisis avoidance, like the brother buggering off to the Balearics.'

'I think you're just a trouble magnet.'

'Can't argue with that.'

Fran cast him another glance. 'So what's going on with you anyway? You've had that mopey look about you these last few days. Do I take it Kelly wasn't waiting for you while you took off travelling?'

'Just worried about a friend of mine.'

'A girlfriend?'

'A girl friend.'

'With benefits?'

'Informal.'

Fran grinned. 'Worried how?'

'Worried in the way you worry when someone in a war zone fails to stay in touch.'

That wiped away her grin. 'War zone . . . ?'

Damn. 'Long story.'

'No, no, no. I've tried to respect your privacy, but if you left me in the lurch for a year to bugger off and play soldiers again, I'm done playing nice.' Stark had little option but to explain in as few words as possible, but brevity only seemed to exacerbate her increasing incredulity. 'And that's your idea of a sabbatical?'

'I suppose so.'

'And this friend . . . ?'

'One of the doctors.'

'They have medics here, you know?' said Fran, clearly alluding to Kelly, a physiotherapist. 'With all sorts of benefits.'

'I'm aware.'

'I'm just saying, most people wouldn't choose a war zone for a holiday. It's a long way to go just to get laid.'

'That wasn't really why I went.'

'Why did you?'

Stark opted against giving her the being useful line. Her patience had limits. 'Various reasons.'

'That you're likely to expand on?'

'Not really.'

'Okaaaay . . .' She pursed her lips. 'And Kelly.'

'Safely engaged to a handsome doctor.'

'Right . . .' She knew his tactics by now. A couple of truth bombs to stall her advance, then withdraw to high ground and dig in, counter-questions about Marcus kept in reserve as a deterrent. Mutually assumed distraction. 'Fun chat, as ever.'

Fragile détente having been re-established, they were greeted outside the Drummond family home by Sergeant Reynolds. 'Bit of an arse, this one. I've given the reality-check speech – *these things take time, no news isn't bad news, et cetera* – but it's always hard when we can't join the dots for them yet.'

Ryan's tan-less face and tired eyes suggested he'd concentrated more on Ibiza's nightlife than sunshine. Clubbing to forget, thought Stark, charitably, as they were met with his wall of discontent.

So much had happened that it was too easy to forget that this had all started with Lucinda Drummond's fatal fall. With the loss of a beloved mother. Stark let Fran join what dots she could. A narrow path that did little to appease her audience.

'Not good enough,' said Ryan, querulously. 'Mum's been dead nearly two weeks, Uncle Adrian is still in the hospital, and you're sat here telling us about some security guard and a warehouse.'

Traditionally, Fran nurtured a handy impatience for personal criticism, but there was a reason every copper started on the beat, learning the hard way that being the calm one in any altercation may not always defuse the situation but probably was the best way to avoid a punch in the face. 'These things are never simple –'

'And we're what,' interrupted Ryan, 'too stupid to understand?'

'I'm sure they're not saying that . . .' Libby attempted to dampen her brother's ire, having kept her own questions civil so far. With Fran and Ryan present, there had been no repeat of her previous advance towards Stark. Hopefully, she'd thought better of it, he mused with no small regret, but life was complicated enough.

'Not at all,' insisted Fran. 'I was only saying that it can take time, for *us*, to piece together the bigger picture.'

Ryan made no effort to mask his distain. 'My mother is dead and you're still pointing the finger at her oldest friend when he's been in a coma and can't defend himself, and patting yourself on the back on TV about *contraband*. You don't care. You're not even trying. You're worse than *fucking useless*,' he concluded, storming out.

Stark wasn't sorry to see him go, but in all honesty, couldn't help thinking the boy had a point.

Libby sighed, folding her hands in her lap, her face offering an embarrassed apology. Still as beautiful as her late mother, but more tired and sad than she'd been a week ago – in many ways, as stiff a rebuke as her brother's. 'I'm sorry, but . . . surely you're *not* still saying you suspect Adrian, after what's happened to him? I know he creeped me out, being . . . overfamiliar, but surely his stabbing and all these other things prove all this was someone else?'

Fran had opted not to tell them about Fairchild's dodgy offshore bank transactions and potential links to the aforementioned contraband. If he lived, there would be a case to build that she didn't wish to compromise. But withholding left her team looking bad, and clearly left a worse taste in her mouth than the curses released once she was back outside with only Stark to fume at.

There were no late-afternoon press or paparazzi visible outside his flat, but Fran dropped Stark off near the back way in, all the same. But as he turned the corner to go in through the rear bike store, a solitary figure looked up from her phone. 'Contraband. Are you f-ing serious?'

'And good afternoon to you too, Gwen.'

Gwen made a face. 'Not going to ask me how I know about your secret entrance?'

'Rudimentary deduction?'

'I was going to say cunning, but yes.'

Stark took out his key and indicated he'd like to get past her.

'Not so fast.' She stayed in his way. ' "Awaiting more detailed examination" isn't going to cut it. Fran knows that. What's really in that boatyard?'

Stark sighed. He really was very tired. 'You know all those times I've said no comment and you've said I was just being obstructive, and I've said I really wasn't at liberty to say and you've called me a git . . .'

'This is all ringing a vague bell.'

'Good. Then let's just skip all that to the bit where you go away unsatisfied but not one bit deterred from your noble quest for the truth.'

'I have a witness on record saying the boatyard was targeted because they saw Yusef Mohamed driving in and out in the white Luton van connected to the murder of Nathan Goff, which you've already hinted is linked with the stabbing of Adrian Fairchild and the murder of Lucinda Drummond.'

The night guard and sweeper. Maxine Carver's security edict hadn't covered that base, but she probably didn't care. They knew nothing of the crates. 'Is there a question coming?'

'Yes. What the hell ties all this together? Were Lucinda Drummond and Adrian Fairchild involved in the smuggling of stolen artworks?' Gwen maintained eye contact. 'I've looked up your newest team member. DC Sophie Swan of the Arts and Antiquities Unit . . . plus bigwig experts from the British Museum, plus a dodgy riverside warehouse no one seems to own, plus a seized boat . . . you can see where I'm going with this.'

'Not really.'

'Online, is where I'm going. With or without your confirmation. If all we can do is speculate, then I'm getting mine out there asap. A source close to the investigation would just be the cherry on top.'

'I'm sure it would,' he nodded solemnly. 'But this really is one of those occasions when I could tell you more, but someone might have to kill you.'

She looked intrigued but knew him well enough to recognize when she wasn't going to get more, and she changed tack. 'Saturday is your old pal the Queen's Birthday Honours List bash. I've still got time to shop for an unaffordable frock, if you're short a plus-one?'

The medal again. 'I promise you, I'm not on the list.'

Gwen scrutinized his face for signs of a lie. 'Okay, the VC-GC thing was always a long shot, I get that. But they can't ignore you completely after all the furore. At the very least, the Queen's Police Medal?'

'I'll be spending Saturday working, nowhere near Buckingham Palace. But right now, I'd offer you a brew, except I'm overdue some sleep. You're welcome to join me, if you promise not to get handsy. You look like you could use a nap too.'

'Pass,' Gwen smiled, and finally stepped aside. 'But the truth always comes out in the end.'

Not always, he thought darkly, letting himself into the

bike store. As he closed the door he heard her say, 'Contraband, my arse.'

Stark glanced at his own bike as he passed through. It was dusty, and the tyres were flat. Maybe a morning spin down to the Surrey Hills would blow the cobwebs off bike and rider alike, but right now all he could think of was his bed.

Closing the door of his flat, he placed his keys in the bowl and closed his eyes, soaking in the silence.

Strange how quickly the eerie emptiness of the place had been replaced with comforting solitude. A return to the norm. His norm, at least. Beyond the haunting reach of Kelly's warmth and the sweetness of Pensol's brief chaos.

He reheated some leftover takeaway in the microwave, washing it down with a beer, and fell asleep right there on the sofa.

When his phone rattled him back to consciousness at 3 a.m., he assumed it was Fran and was about to answer with a blunt remark when he saw it was the sat phone number. 'Gabrielle?'

'No, it's Jergen. I'm sorry, Joe, but something terrible has happened. Government jets bombed the hospital again. The damage is bad. I don't think there's any way back this time.'

Stark's heart went cold. 'Casualties?'

'No count yet. Some floors collapsed. There will be many dead. Three of the MSF staff missing – Sébastien, Luther and Gabrielle.'

Sometimes your worst fears circled back and materialized.

Stark's brain tripped into crisis mode. Questions,

suggestions, logistics – work the problem – but there was nothing he could do from here that Jergen wasn't already doing. The German promised to call when he knew more, but he had to go, leaving Stark adrift with nothing to do. He didn't even know Gabrielle's family contacts to phone her mother.

Turning on the BBC News Channel, it didn't take long to roll round to the story: a correspondent on a rooftop with a view of the collapsed hospital. Unknown casualty numbers. Libyan government denials, blaming rebel artillery – as if a hundred 105mm rounds could cause this much damage. Nothing of solace to Stark, but he couldn't take his eyes off it.

When his phone rang again, a couple of hours later, he snatched it up, hoping for Jergen with better news. But this time it *was* Fran.

'Adrian Fairchild,' she said. 'I'll be outside yours in twenty.'

41

When the message came for her to call the hospital, Fran's immediate thought was that Fairchild was dead. So she'd tried to pass that dread on to Stark by just saying the name, without explanation. But you didn't pick someone up at 6 a.m. to go see a dead man, so the sod got in the car without indulging her with questions.

'Get some sleep?' she asked.

He looked somehow worse than when she'd dropped him off. He was showered and neat as a pin, in his usual annoying habit, but his bearded jaw was set like stone. This friends-with-benefits worry was worse than he let on, she guessed. Most things were, with him.

'Some,' he replied gruffly. 'You?'

She had. The previous missed night, plus a large glass of Chardonnay, had proved equal to her worries, sending her into the sleep of the righteous. He'd obviously had less luck and looked a lot less likely to drop any truth bombs than yesterday, but right now she had more pressing thoughts. The one person who might unlock this case was finally awake.

The Whittington Hospital in Archway had no parking spaces for South London detectives on safari, but in Fran's worldview, blue lights and a DI badge made the 'Drop-off Only' zone, out front, fair game.

The two firearms uniforms on Fairchild's door checked

IDs, recorded names and patted them down over-thoroughly to signal their enthusiasm for babysitting duty.

Fairchild had finally been moved from the ICU to a secure side room, but from the look of him he might be rushed back at any moment.

He still looked pale, cheeks sunken. The only evidence of the replacement blood they'd topped him up with was the severe bruising to his face, with two black eyes now bridging a broken nose she'd not noticed while Stark worked to stopper the holes in his belly. The side of his head had been shaved to stitch a jagged cut, possibly from impact with the floor. And that didn't cover whatever surgical scars now lay hidden beneath his hospital sheets.

The duty solicitor already with him, somehow levered out of bed by the local force, looked barely old enough to shave. The Haringey DI assigned to the case had decided it was too early and sent his DS in his place. She seemed happy for Fran to take the lead, which saved Fran the effort of enforcing her will. A watchful nurse, present to ensure they didn't overtax her patient, plus the police recording equipment made the room extra cosy.

Fran clicked record, stated the location, date and time, listed all present, and read Adrian Fairchild his rights. *You don't have to say anything but withholding may harm your defence and will definitely piss me off*, et cetera. 'This is an interview under caution, Adrian. Can you confirm that you understand your rights as I've just read them to you?'

Fairchild nodded.

Fran kept her voice hard and pointed. 'For the tape, please.'

'Yes,' he croaked, clearing his throat with a cough. 'I understand.' His voice was high and raw. Dysphonia, the nurse had explained in advance. High-temperature smoke inhalation hurt the larynx as well as the lungs. Fairchild had spent longer in the burning house than Stark.

He licked dry lips now, reaching a trembling hand out to the clear plastic water cup on the wheeled hospital table angled across the bed. Splinted fingers didn't help, the ultra-cheap cup partially collapsing, spilling water down his gown. He almost looked like he might cry at his own helplessness, both physical and situational – he was sapped of the condescending authority with which he'd beckoned her into his subterranean museum labyrinth, along with his strength. Watching him clumsily sip was almost pitiful, but Fran was more worried about completing the interview without the nurse or lawyer pulling the plug and some future smarmy barrister arguing duress. 'Please confirm your name and date of birth for the record.'

He did so, again in cracking syllables.

Fran watched him carefully. Normally, she'd start with the friendly questions, slipping in a few more targeted ones, recap, reword, repeat, et cetera, getting less friendly, poking the sore spots, grating away at the suspect's patience. Hardened perps knew the ropes, but first-timers might buckle, and in Fairchild's weakened state this might be the best chance she'd get. If she pushed too hard the solicitor might claim duress, or the nurse might shut them down, but there was something in his eyes that suggested he might, just might, want this all over with.

'I'll be honest with you, Adrian,' she said, 'I'm not a patient person. I have lots of training and experience in how to slowly grind you down and get what I want, but I've had to wait a week for this conversation, and if there's one thing I hate more than being kept waiting, it's people wasting my time with lies. So I'm just going to lay it all out for you, and you're going to agree with everything I say and then help me fill in any blanks with complete and un-redacted cooperation – okay?'

Fairchild glanced at his solicitor, but nodded.

'Okay. Jump in if I get anything wrong. Which I won't.' Fran had been running it all through in her head as she drove. 'Seven years ago, two payments of twenty thousand pounds were transferred into your bank account from an anonymous account in Cyprus. My contact in the Met Police Arts and Antiquities Unit tells me this co-incides with the smuggling into this country via Cyprus of ten electrum staters stolen from a Turkish museum – coins you would be uniquely expert in authenticating – then lost to the black market.

'One year later, you were paid the same again, and six months after that, twin payments of *fifty* grand coinciding with the smuggling of a priceless stolen Mesopotamian dagger. Shortly after, you paid off your mortgage early. Then another forty appears. At which point you took a trip to the Cayman Islands, after which you transferred that forty to your *own* numbered Cayman account. A year later, you sold your house and along with two *hundred* thousand from your Cayman account, bought a much nicer house outright.

'We've checked your museum salary, of course, and it doesn't add up to three hundred and eighty thousand pounds over less than three years. Your tax return makes no mention of it either. But you've clearly been making yourself very useful to someone, and you're going to tell me who. But that's the least of your problems, because at some point before the night of the Queen's House exhibition opening, you came into possession of something rare even by your standards. The Nebuchadnezzar stater you told me was a fake – something you'd happily prove if I'd hand it over for a quick run through a mass spectrometer.

'Only it's not a fake, is it? Because you'd already scanned it, early on the very morning of the exhibition. In fact, each of the payments I've just described coincides with you booking time on the scanner in the wee small hours of the morning when no one else is around. And this wasn't any old stater. This was a prize of literally historic importance . . .' Fran paused. As she'd spoken, his already sallow skin had paled by degrees. Now he looked like a ghost. 'I'll take it from your silence that I'm spot on so far.'

More silence.

Fran nodded. 'For the record, the suspect has been offered the opportunity to refute, and has not done so. And this is where we get to Lucinda Drummond, Adrian. Because I have an account of raised voices, of a man showing a woman a gold coin, arguing, following her into the Tulip Stairs, and coming out alone.'

She watched his eyes flinch. 'I think you panicked and sought Lucinda's advice but didn't like what she offered. I think you tried telling her that you'd been strong-armed into authenticating those first ten coins, and that afterwards they used the indelible evidence of payments into your account to blackmail you into continuing. It's an old trap and you walked right in. But Lucinda wasn't sympathetic. She was outraged. Your oldest friend, the woman you'd loved since university, the woman who'd spurned you romantically and surpassed you professionally, threatened to turn you in. And so you panicked again and shoved her off the stairs to her death.'

'*No!*' burst out Fairchild, shaking his head in panic as the accusation drove home, glancing between Fran and his silent legal counsel as coughing racked him.

'Had she grown scared of you? Did she threaten to call out for help? Is that why you punched her in the stomach first?'

'That's not what happened,' he rasped, pleadingly. 'She was *alive* when I left, *I swear!*'

Fran let her eyes do the scoffing. 'Broken on the floor as the last of her life ebbed away?'

'*No!* She was *fine*. We argued, yes, but I'd never *hurt* her.'

The legal counsel finally earned his crust, placing a silencing hand on Fairchild's arm. 'My client admits nothing at this stage. And you've yet to offer anything more than conjecture.'

Damn. 'Then let me offer some more, Adrian, because as if things couldn't get any worse, here's where your life really turned to shit. Because while you were pacing up and down outside with an alleged headache, wondering how the hell you were going to get away with killing your oldest friend in a very public place, the person who'd seen you, a ne'er-do-well by the name of Nathan Goff, nicked your briefcase from the cloakroom.

'So now you're not only a murderer, you've lost the

priceless property of the criminals you've been working for. So when Goff calls you, offering it back for ten grand, you can't believe your luck. Only by this time he knows about Lucinda. So instead of handing over the coin, he punches you in the face, takes your money and says unless you keep paying, he'll tell the police you're the killer. I know this, because he was later arrested, drunk and disorderly, with a lot of money in his pocket, with serial numbers matching the ten-kay you withdrew from your bank that day.

'So now you've got no choice but to tell your employer. They break a couple of your fingers to test if you're telling the truth, then say not to worry, they'll get it back. The coin is in a nice orange box with a natty little GPS tracker. Maybe your luck is finally changing. But when they get to Goff's he's already posted the coin to Dosh-4Gold because he's an idiot. His visitors don't take it well. And now you're complicit in a second murder. Not some panicked staircase shove, but a really, really nasty one. And if you were shitting yourself before, it's crap-mountain now.

'And your employer, they get to thinking that you've become a liability. Our interview with you has painted a target on your back. And their next stop is your nice expensive house, where they impolitely ask for your passwords, delete your digital life, take away all your paperwork, stab you and leave you to burn, and then go use your ID badge to clean out your office too. Neat.'

Fran took a breath. 'So here we are. Thanks to this Good Samaritan,' she nodded at Stark, 'you're not dead. But you are deeper in shit than you ever could have thought possible. And your only chance of getting out of prison before you die of old age, or they pay someone in there to kill you, is to confirm everything I just said and tell me the one thing I don't know – who was paying you to sell out your life's work?'

The duty solicitor had been listening, fascinated, but had the wits to quickly interject. 'You don't have to say anything.'

Stark poured a glass of water and handed it to a grateful Fairchild, who sipped, looking sick.

He cleared his throat, and spoke. 'They did force me. The first time. A one-off, they said, or else. But after that first payment they had me and never let go.' He hung his head in shame.

The solicitor rolled his eyes, probably thinking he should cut down on the thankless pro-bono work.

'So it's all true,' Fran pressed her advantage. The terrible mistake, compounded with each reoccurrence. But Fairchild had *chosen* not to correct it. He could've gone to the police straight after, but he'd kept the money instead. She glanced at the camera. The red recording light was still on. Same for the audio backup.

Fairchild raised his head. 'Except Lucinda. That wasn't me.'

She shook her head. 'And why should I believe that?'

'Because I would never harm the mother of my child.'

Fran blinked. 'Your child? You mean, your godchild, Libby.'

Fairchild sighed and shook his head. 'Lucinda and I . . . reconnected briefly, about two years after she got married, after she found out Jeff'd been sleeping with his secretary.

I really thought I'd got her back, but Jeff always was a charmer, talked her round again within days, promising it was a one-off. Such a cliché. Lucinda laughed our indiscretion off as her revenge fling. She always was a pragmatist. I never suspected Libby was mine until years later, when I saw my mother's eyes in hers. Lucinda confessed she'd always suspected and organized a DNA comparison from Libby's hair. Scientists, you see, no hypothesis left untested. Libby doesn't know. I wanted to tell her but Lucinda wouldn't have it. Jeff's recidivist cheating had forced a divorce by then – and I don't believe either of them think much of him – but Libby had a father, and Lucinda didn't see any point opening new wounds. At least, that's what she said.'

Fran unfolded her arms and slowly placed both palms on her knees. 'Bullshit.'

'Quick word outside, Boss?' asked Stark.

Fran gave him a *not now* look, but his *now* look was stronger.

She paused the tape, slipped outside and waited until the door closed between them and Fairchild. 'What the fuck?'

'Pook's testimony never mentioned an impact,' said Stark, as if that explained it.

'What the *actual* fuck?'

'He said Nathan Goff had seen Fairchild follow Lucinda Drummond into the Tulip Stairs, emerge and take the briefcase to the cloakroom, and then came the scream. No impact. If he'd been loitering just outside the Tulip Stairs, he'd have heard her hitting the floor before Fairchild came out.'

Fran cursed Stark's memory. 'It's second-hand testimony. Chinese whispers.'

'Unless the impact happened while he was round the corner, outside the cloakroom?'

Fran cursed Stark in general. 'You *believe* him?' she asked, nodding through the vision panel at Fairchild.

'I'm kicking myself for not seeing it sooner,' he said earnestly. 'Libby has his *eyes*.'

'A feature that you committed to memory when she fluttered her lashes at you?' said Fran a little nastily, though Stark's memory was usually annoyingly faultless.

'Would he claim paternity otherwise, knowing we could easily test that ourselves?'

'Doesn't mean he didn't push the mother anyway.'

'Maybe.'

'*Urrrgh!*' growled Fran. Shoving the door open, she restarted the interview while Fairchild eyed her warily. 'Okay, bullshit or not, some would say all this only *adds* to your motive.'

He shook his head, sadly, tears running down his face. 'Some might, I suppose. But I *did* love her. I may be a fool. I may have betrayed my life's work. But I would never hurt Lucinda, or cause grief to my only child.'

'Now who's offering nothing but conjecture?'

Fairchild slowly raised his red eyes to Fran's, and nodded. 'Then how about that one thing you don't know, instead?'

Groombridge hit pause on the interview video after his second watch through, and sat back in his chair.

Fairchild should have hedged for manslaughter.

315

Solid chance the CPS might charge him with murder in parallel and settle for the lesser. The evidence that Lucinda may have been punched in the gut first was thin, but even if he admitted to doing so in panic, he could still insist she slipped over the handrail on her own. Full denial was a risk. Switching for manslaughter later would make him look shifty. He was going down for handling stolen goods anyway. Arguing coercion might help, but he'd hardly given the money away to charity. Guilty pleas across the board might cut his sentencing by a third, and full cooperation on the antiquities front would probably encourage a judge to allocate the sentences concurrently rather than consecutively. Instead of the rest of his life, he could be looking at anywhere between five to fifteen years inside. The more helpful he proved, the better for him. The legal counsel would have advised him that denying Lucinda's killing undermined his chances of leniency across the board. But cool calculation was easy when it wasn't you facing incarceration.

Fran had shown admirable restraint by her standards, channelling frustration into dogged repetition, as she'd been taught, but Fairchild stuck with his story — black-market antiquities, yes, murder, no. Either he was made of sterner stuff than it appeared, or he was telling the truth. Never an easy difference to spot, thought Groombridge, suppressing a sigh. At this point in proceedings, the attendant nurse had declared the questioning too taxing on Fairchild's frail health and shooed the detectives out.

They'd have to wait until tomorrow for another crack

at him. But if Fairchild was telling the truth, then Lucinda's killer remained a mystery.

Meanwhile, the one thing they could be sure of was that he'd exaggerated.

The secret copy of all his work on authenticating the various black-market antiquities, which he'd somehow had the balls to resist telling his attackers about, had been found where he described, stashed in a hidden floor safe beneath the charred carpet of his home study. It proved to be everything he'd promised, a treasure trove that lit up Swan's face. Photos, dates, mass spectrometer results, even serial numbers off any protective packing cases or any other clues he'd been able to note. The Arts and Antiquities Unit was going to be busy. And it went some way towards demonstrating that he had at least kept in mind the notion of the items being traced one day, even if it was after he'd enjoyed a lifetime of wealth.

But his claim of being able to reveal who had 'forced him' to work for them had proved less substantial. His employer wasn't stupid enough to meet in person. Why would they risk it? Like all higher-echelon criminality, dealing in priceless stolen artefacts required three things above all else – brains, money and balls. The rest you could buy, starting with brawn. And it was the brawn you sent to lean on people. Muscles, tattoos, facial scars and casual ex-military menace came as standard.

So, two such men would turn up, 'invite' him into their car and hand him a phone. A man with a gruff Eastern European accent would give him instructions, with a side order of threat. The men would hand him an orange Peli case and the four-digit code. Same two men each time, from the start. They never spoke, never saw what was in the case or heard what was said down the phone, but everything about them spoke of violent consequences, as if they'd had the words 'OR ELSE' tattooed on their calloused knuckles. Plenty of stick, balanced with dangling carroty assurances of continued health and prosperity.

Fairchild would carry out his tests, make his reports, lock the artefacts back in the orange cases, and hand them wordlessly back to the two men on their next appearance.

Until the Nebuchadnezzar stater. Perhaps it was the truly priceless nature of this object that demanded extra security, but there was a third man in the car. Sat in the back with one of the heavies. Fairchild was sat in front, as usual, and instructed not to turn around. Same voice as the previous phone calls. 'This one's special. We'll pay double. Don't get any sudden ideas about integrity. You sold that long ago. Never forget, we know everything about you.'

It was only when he opened the case afterwards that Fairchild understood quite how special, but that wasn't the trigger. That came later, when the key piece of the jigsaw fell into place. The piece that had Fran smiling like the cat that got the cream. Or perhaps more like the cat with the canary trapped behind her teeth like the bars of a jail cell.

The one thing better than Fairchild confessing to murder.

She'd wanted Alex Zedani in Interview Room One since the get-go.

Groombridge kept his counsel. He could tell her not to get her hopes up. Fairchild had no recordings, no video, nothing substantial at all to back up his finger-pointing. Only detailed records of his own side of the wrong-doings. Juries didn't always land on your side when it came to discreditable witnesses, and the CPS hated them.

42

Dying as she was to get stuck into Zedani, Fran conceded it was better to lead off with the bodyguard first this time round. The ideal approach would have been to interview them separately but at the same time, but the expensive-looking shark they'd turned up with insisted on sitting in with both.

Jan Zieliński sat opposite, with perhaps even less stone-faced charm than last time, and with exactly the same syllabic minimalism. Fran had suggested Stark break the ice, try tapping into shared history, though his wordless compliance hardly gave her confidence. He wasn't chatty at the best of times, and today he seemed to be in one of his darker moods, but he took it head on, as was his way.

He recognized Zieliński's Polish military unit, of course. It quickly emerged that they'd overlapped in both Iraq and Afghanistan, though by the latter conflict Zieliński had moved from military to mercenary. That was about as far as their camaraderie seemed to warm. If the ice thawed at all, it certainly didn't break. There remained a watchful tension between them. Fran half expected them to strip to the waist to compare tattoos and war wounds. She'd seen Stark shirtless and knew Zieliński would have to go some to come anywhere close on scar count.

Unfortunately, things didn't go much better on the main thrust. Which was Adrian Fairchild's assertion that he'd put a face to the voice. That during the preview tour of the Queen's House exhibition for their chief benefactor, Alex Zedani, the man's scary-looking bodyguard had taken a phone call, and Fairchild's blood had suddenly run cold. Same voice, same gruff tone he'd been living in fear of for seven years. It suddenly made perfect sense, he insisted. Wealthy patron of the arts was the perfect cover for wealthy purveyor or purchaser of illicit artefacts. Zedani had the logistical means to smuggle whatever he wanted across just about any border, and clearly the muscle too. And there he was – bold as brass, bronze, electrum and gold combined.

Fairchild claimed he'd already decided to confess all to Lucinda Drummond, but Fran suspected it was the sudden proximity and scale of the threat that spun him out. One for the barristers to argue over later. Her job was to lay it all out now, withholding Fairchild's name and the manner of the identification, though Zieliński would easily deduce his accuser. But the big man simply listened impassively and shook his head. 'Lies. Or mistake. Whoever tells you this is wrong. I don't know what they're talking about. I have nothing to do with any of this. I'm paid to protect, not bully little people into criminality, or kill women.'

'Your past suggests a more *mercenary* attitude.'

'You know nothing about my past,' he said.

Fran thought she felt a tiny bit of heat in his words, but hardly enough to work with.

'I do,' said Stark. He'd filled her in on some of the less savoury 'support services' companies like Temple Security offered in the grey areas of the Red Desert.

'Temple also provide a purely protective security capacity, at home and overseas,' added the lawyer. 'And if you go accusing them of otherwise, or digging for my client's service records, you can expect a more fearsome phalanx of lawyers than little old me.'

'Only he's not your client really, is he?' countered Fran. 'Your fiscal loyalties lie with Mr Zedani, and Jan here might find himself all alone, forehead-deep in shit, if the wind changes.'

'Jan here has no more to fear than you appear to have evidence to offer, and while my clients, plural, are happy to assist with your inquiries, if you continue to waste our time with baseless accusations, we'll soon find ourselves taking a less charitable view.'

He didn't use the word harassment. The big guns didn't waste ammunition. They were a long way from that stage. But Fran knew she'd need something a lot more concrete before she brought them in again. Perhaps it had been foolish to bring them in straight away, but she liked to see the whites of their eyes.

And next was the big prize.

'You've never mentioned being Russian?' Fran tried something new.

So far, the big prize had been far from giving. The lawyer had spent time 'conferring' with his clients between interviews – basically relating the accusation levelled at the bodyguard for the guardee to counter – which Zedani had done with understated aplomb, clearly far from intimidated by Interview Room One.

And while calmly answering all her questions, his

expensive lawyer sat there expensively saying nothing until calmly announcing that since she appeared to have run out of ways to reframe the same questions, over and over, perhaps she'd like to charge his client or let him go.

Zedani looked politely perplexed now. 'In what way was that relevant?' He looked to Stark, the way men always looked to other men when a woman confused them, as if the sense deficit lay with anyone else but them.

Stark said nothing. His default position generally, but in this case pre-agreed. One of Fran's earliest observations of him was of a disconcerting, geological stillness – that the world appeared to move around him, somehow bending to his fixedness or gravity. People too, and Fran would shamelessly apply any asset at her disposal in this room. Now, however, if you knew where to look, his silent scrutiny radiated the faintest heat of stoicism. His version of a screaming meltdown. His thoughts were never easy to discern, but he was definitely distracted today, and his distractions were always dark. Loyalty was another default position, and a friend in possible danger would be gnawing at him. Fran itched to know more, but for now had to settle for him avoiding the trap of answering for her. 'Alex*i* Zedani,' she read, emphasizing the new i. 'Born in Moscow.'

'Raised and schooled in Britain,' replied Zedani evenly. 'I hold dual citizenship.'

'Dropping the "i" help avoid the bullying in Eton?'

'Harrow. And no, it was just easier,' he smiled that smile. 'Like shortening Francine to Fran.' He'd done his homework too, and didn't look any more likely to budge than the bodyguard in the next room. 'Your so-called witness is Adrian Fairchild, I presume?'

Fran kept her face neutral. 'What makes you think that?'

'You asked about him the last time we spoke. And if you're saying all this is somehow linked to stolen antiquities, then I suppose Adrian might be a useful cog in someone's machine. Until he wasn't, and they stabbed him and left him for dead, according to the news. Did *he* kill Lucinda?'

'We're not talking about Lucinda.'

'I noticed, which is why I asked.'

'Is it? Or are you deflecting?'

'From what?'

'A witness linking you to illegal antiquities smuggling. Your transport company linking the Black Sea to the UK and beyond, with offices in Cyprus and a holding company in the Cayman Islands – leading world hubs for laundering dirty money. From the fact that Lucinda's determination to expose your black-market dealings would bring the legitimate side of Horizon Logistics crashing down with it – adding motive to your means and opportunity.'

'If your witness's fantastic assertions *were* fact, but they're not. Russian or not, I am a respectable business-man and philanthropist.' With powerful friends, he didn't need to add, having made the point on arrival that he'd cancelled several important meetings to 'assist' them today, and had a dinner at Mansion House that evening with a keynote speech by the Secretary of State for International Trade. 'Whatever Fairchild has got himself mixed up in is his problem, and he won't save his neck by desperately pointing a finger my way. And if it's as bad as you assert, then *he* is the one with everything to lose. So why not admit that you're going to charge him with Lucinda's murder, and be done with it?'

Fran preferred admissions to come from the opposite side of this table, but she knew when she was outclassed. She should pull the plug. Let him go. Let him stew while they built a real case, though she got the feeling that he was too clever to let dirt stain his hand-made shoes.

Two hours ago, Groombridge had said she looked like the cat that got the cream. If she still looked feline, it was the kind that was about to claw a face. Right now, she had nothing but a fistful of denials – and little inclination to believe any of them. The trouble was, she couldn't quite shake them either. As a sergeant she'd relied on her instincts, but inspectors had to rely on what they could prove. Someone had killed Lucinda Drummond. Odds-on favourite still had to be Adrian Fairchild, but Zedani and his 150kg ex-military security-for-hire bodyguard were back in the race.

So the next step would be to search Zedani's home and offices, dig into his empire to look for anything linking it to the black-market trade in gold coins or crappy old pots, but the way this was going, the judge might still not sign off on warrants. On the plus side, the investigation had a new direction now, and she just had to remember that, whatever the hard-done-by or smug intellectual superiority of the suspects, no one on earth matched her for unrelenting, obsessional determination to nail them to the fucking wall.

She smiled. 'I'm afraid you'll have to wait for the next thrilling instalment of the DI Millhaven press show, like everyone else.'

'You're wrong,' said Kat, firmly. She'd listened carefully to the anonymized summary of Fairchild's story, but the moment Fran linked it to her boss, Zedani, she'd begun shaking her head.

Fran shrugged to keep things non-confrontational. She was definitely feeling a lot less pleased with herself than a few hours earlier. Zedani and the bodyguard were a good fit for this, but she had to admit she didn't have it nailed down yet, and bringing them in felt less and less like her brightest idea. Interviewing the PA now felt like going through the motions, but in for a penny . . .

'But would you concede that he might have dealings you're unaware of?'

'No. I control his calendar and all his appointments.'

'Official ones. But not every moment of the day.'

'Of course not. What he does in his limited free time is his business, but there really isn't much.'

'And if his free-time business was black-market antiquities, how would you know?'

'You don't have to answer that,' advised the expensive lawyer, smugly sitting in on his third police interview of the day, with billable hours adding up nicely.

But Kat wasn't buying. 'Because I know *him*. And the idea is *absurd*,' she insisted. 'Alex is the kindest, most generous and honest person I know. And why on earth would he risk anything so stupid? He already has more money than he can give away.'

'I've never met a rich man who thought he was rich enough.'

'And how many really rich people do you actually know?' riposted Kat.

Good point, conceded Fran, in the privacy of her own head. And really, why *would* Zedani risk it? In her rush to accuse, had she really thought this through? Perhaps Fairchild really was just pointing the finger in desperation. Groombridge had cautioned scepticism, but then that was his default position. Maybe this new line of inquiry was a deliberate red herring, and she was being made a fool of.

Fran realized she was in danger of grinding her teeth on camera. It was her job to pose the questions, regardless. She forced a smile. 'Perhaps not that many. But I've lost count of the number of women who've sat in that chair and sworn blind I was wrong about their man. I don't know what's worse, the ones trying to deceive me or the poor saps deceiving themselves.'

'But he's not my man,' replied Kat, coolly.

'Maybe, but are you his girl?'

'We're straying worryingly close to a country 'n' western song, Detective Inspector,' interjected the lawyer. 'And all I've heard from you today is shoddy lyrics. I get paid by the minute, and even I'm beginning to lose patience.'

Fran ignored him. 'How about you, Kat. Are you losing patience?'

'Yes, I am.'

'Fair enough. Then I'll just leave you a few thoughts to take away and ponder in your own time. Perhaps you're right and Alexi is whiter than white, and this nice overpaid lawyer is here to protect your interests. Or perhaps, deep down, you wonder whether *I'm* right, and this shark-suit is here to keep you in check. Perhaps Alexi or Jan *did* slip back inside Queen's House around the time Lucinda Drummond was killed, and whatever reason they fed you wasn't so innocent after all.' Fran met Kat's all-too-beautiful eyes, trying to decide if she only imagined the flicker of doubt in them. 'In summary, Kat, if they were willing to murder Lucinda, and Nathan Goff, and Yusef Mohamed, and almost succeeded with Adrian Fairchild, to cover their tracks, then who are you really safer with . . . them or us?'

Kat's eyes flickered between her and Stark. A different kind of gravity. And if Fran found it annoying when men looked to Stark for sense, she found it almost as annoying when pretty young women looked to him for protection. The strong, silent, brooding type. Not hers, *God no*, but then she wasn't sure she had one. On paper, the silent subservient type, but that was even more yuck than brash and overbearing. The source of Marcus's hitherto longevity seemed to have been his blithe imperviousness to her wrath, which only maddened her more . . . and yet somehow didn't. God, she missed him!

That was twice she'd called on a non-existent deity in one daydream!

Kat and Stark were both staring at her, she realized, forcing her to pass her distraction off as an ominous pause, and call it a day.

'Nicely done,' commented Groombridge as they watched Kat being escorted out by the shark.

The limousine that had whisked Zedani and his body-guard away had returned for her. Assuming it was the same one. He probably had a fleet. Kat glanced back at them just before getting in. For a moment, Fran wondered if she'd see her alive again. 'I can't tell if I got through.'

'There was something there,' said Stark. 'Just for a moment, I thought.'

Groombridge nodded sagely. 'Assuming there's anything there.'

Fran sighed, irritably. 'Another long shot.'

'Sometimes that's all we have.'

'Don't I know it.'

'No one ever said this job was easy.'

'Ever thought of jotting down all your stirring pep-talks in a book, Guv?' she said. 'I'm sure publishers would queue up to snap up the only copy and burn it.'

Silence.

Fran was about to apologize for overstepping, before she spotted the glint of amusement in his eyes. Stark's too. Bastards. 'So, another crack at Fairchild?'

'Your call.'

Thanks. His sink-or-swim teaching style was as helpful as his uplifting aphorisms.

'At least it seems his sideways glances at Libby were parental rather than predatory,' suggested Stark.

'Who's to say they weren't both,' replied Fran, who generally took the time-saving path of assuming the worst in people, right up to, and in most cases, well beyond the point where evidence suggested otherwise.

Groombridge turned his eyes on her, reproach implied rather than expressed. 'You believe that?'

'Not entirely,' she confessed, reluctantly. Fairchild's faults were many, but in caring for his alleged daughter he appeared convincing.

'Boss,' said Williams, approaching. 'Something you should see.' He held out a printout. 'Just emailed to Fairchild's personal account.'

They all stared at the image.

Stark stiffened, like a tiger, eyes burning.

'Shit,' breathed Fran.

It was a photograph of Libby Drummond, crossing a street, digitally edited to encircle her head with blood-red cross hairs.

43

'Protection?' asked Stark.

Fran scoffed back down the phone line as she raced under blues to Libby Drummond's work address, doubtless with her usual scant regard for driving etiquette. 'The Super tried, but she's not a suspect or witness, and apparently the Met's not made of money.'

'Who knew?'

'Right. Best we can do is encourage her to move in with a friend, or sit a uniform outside.'

'After telling her that her creepy uncle figure is actually her doting biological father, but that he's also a criminally corrupt arsehole who's managed to pin a target on her back. Rather you than me.'

'Too right, since we can't risk you around damsels in distress,' scoffed Fran.

The fact that Stark was fighting a physical urge to rush to Libby's defence rather confirmed Fran's accusation, if for the wrong reason. He could do nothing to help Gabrielle, if she was even alive, making Libby the next worst thing. His good old saviour complex. The first step was acknowledging you had a problem, right?

There'd always been something in him, Doc Hazel postulated, even before the death of his father when he was a child. But that was the catalyst: a mother to support, a sister to protect. The police added fuel, but active combat lit the match, fusing everything with incandescent anger. Now that conflagration was down to buried embers, like a moorland fire smouldering beneath ground, threatening to burst upwards again at any lonely tree. Sometimes he wondered whether, should he eventually quench the heat, there would be anything left.

Fran may not fathom the full depths of all this, but she saw enough to send him to tell the corrupt father about his daughter becoming a target – an issue which, if Fairchild was half as doting as he declared, would all but guarantee his withdrawal of cooperation, and cast the investigation adrift once more.

'Question is, how did the bad guys find out Fairchild was her father?' mused Fran. 'Found it in his stuff, when they raided his home and office?'

'Or they knew already,' suggested Stark. 'Insurance, in case he got jumpy or needed additional persuasion?'

'*ARSEHOLE!*' bellowed Fran, which Stark attributed to some driver failing to get out of her way with sufficient haste. 'I hope you don't have as many *IDIOTS* on your route?'

He didn't tell her he was sitting in stationary traffic at roadworks, waiting for temporary traffic lights to let another two cars through before turning red again. His journey did *not* warrant siren and lights, though the result when he did arrive and update Fairchild would prove predictably and equally obstructive.

At first Fairchild demanded to withdraw or alter his statement, but when told it was already signed and filed, he started making claims about duress and medication, before calling for the nurse and demanding that Stark leave. Classic, thought Fran bitterly, fresh back from escorting Libby Drummond to the house of a work friend. One–nil, to the bad guys. Who ever said criminal menace didn't pay?

So their primary witness was off the table, statement on record but determined to refute it in any future testimony. His illegitimate offspring, morphed from grieving daughter to terrified pawn in hiding. Her brother, leaving stinking messages on Fran's phone. Three dead bodies and nearly a fourth, the press breathing down their neck, translating into pressure from politicians and the Brass.

Meanwhile, Zedani's name had appeared online as 'helping with inquiries'. That hadn't come from the police. Safe money was on the shark-suit lawyer getting ahead of the story and forcing Fran, as it did, to go outside and say the same words through gritted teeth. Not her best performance.

Superintendent Cox had suggested an early night for all. Fran was in no mood to argue, but no one seemed in a mood to leave. Or maybe it was just her mood that made them scared to.

Dixon had spent the day trying to find out who owned the boatyard while liaising with the three Ps who'd volunteered to trawl the CCTV from the surrounding streets to build a picture of comings and goings. Williams had been re-interviewing the boatyard suspects – all of whom claimed to be employed cash-in-hand by unknown powers, with no questions asked. They'd met a larger boat out to sea, transferred the crates, and returned to the boatyard. The larger vessel had covered its name, and you could bet it had its Automatic Identification System transponder turned off. It was clear this wasn't their first trip, but none would confess it explicitly. The most common theme was that the bossmen they met were big and scary, and wore ski-masks. The white van was often there in the warehouse, most said, but the motorbikes were new, and no one had seen any riders.

Their level of desperation was rising, but no one seemed sure what to do with them next. The overlapping options for charging them were hog-tied by Carver's national security information embargo, and with no UK addresses the mechanism for police bail had choked on its own red tape. For now they would be charged as illegal immigrants and held on remand – and as soon as this news was shared with them all cooperation had died.

A depressing amount of legwork lay ahead there.

DC Swan had decamped back to the AAU, determined to divert the attention of her depressingly few colleagues to testing the alleged link between the black-market trade and Alexi Zedani, undeterred by the fact that the source of that alleged link had withdrawn the accusation.

'What bothers me,' mused Dixon, 'is why smuggle priceless *contraband* on some old boat when you've got your own plane? I mean the big urns, maybe. But those coins . . . ? I wouldn't want to let them out of my sight. I know even private jets have to register traceable flight plans and everything – but make it a business trip, and who's to say it isn't? Didn't he just fly to Cyprus and back?'

'Even VIPs must have to go through some kind of air-port security,' replied Williams. 'Cartel leaders don't fly their own drugs.'

'Yeah, but they can just make more. Something priceless like this, irreplaceable . . . ?'

Williams shrugged. 'If you're just moving it for someone else, cargo is cargo. Depends how many times you want to risk it, I suppose. Deniability goes out the window if you're caught red-handed. What's he going to do – claim his PA packed his bag for him?'

Stark listened in silence. If Zedani *was* behind this, he'd let others take the risks.

'Okay,' declared Fran to the deafening silence around the room, close to pulling her hair out, 'you won't hear me ask this often but, ideas? Anyone?' Blank stares. 'This isn't about crappy pots and shiny pocket change, people. Lucinda Drummond is dead. The man we think killed her was stabbed and left for dead. Nathan Goff was tortured to death and Yusef Mohamed was dumped in the river. And the man most likely to be behind it all is just laughing at us!'

Her sentiments weren't lost on anyone, but the day had run out of hours while everyone ran out of steam. Predictably, it was Williams who summoned his courage first, departing for daddy bedtime-story duty. Dixon took Williams' survival as cover to slip away for whatever Commandant Tracy had planned, and Groombridge left for dinner with Alice. Leaving just Stark, with his head down in something, still not offering to expand on his worries.

In the spirit of things always being able to get worse, Fran took a breath to ask him straight out, but stopped herself. The fact that he was never in the mood was usually delightful, but not today. Today had been a chastening reminder of why she never let anything so foolish as *optimism* shine through the clouds of her better judgement. She'd been so eager to pin Zedani down that she let herself think this was the breakthrough. The only thing that hurt more than *looking* stupid was *feeling* stupid.

And conversations with Stark carried the constant danger of both.

Stark tried the satellite number but Jergen didn't answer. Starved of information, the knot in his stomach staved off any thought of food. And home. All that awaited him there was hollowing worry, and whisky. The pub would be too full of people. It had taken all his strength to make it through a day of them already. And Fran's sideways glances. If he'd had any premonition of how much worse Gabrielle's situation might turn out to be, he'd never have confessed his concerns to Fran yesterday. It was a testament to her own worries that she'd restrained herself from picking at him. Nothing to be grateful for there.

So he went nowhere. Just sat at his desk, trawling back through the case notes, as if anything new would jump out at him.

The desk phone rang in Fran's office and he wandered in to answer it. 'MIT.'

'Hi, er, it's Constable Barclay. I'm on front desk. Is DI Millhaven there?' Barclay was a good man, and the trailing question mark at the end of that statement spoke to a healthy trepidation in all things Fran-related.

'Hi, Duncan, it's Joe. No, she's gone for the night. Can I help?'

'Maybe. I've got a walk-in asking for DI Millhaven, but she dropped your name too.'

'She have a name?'

'Er . . . Katherine Hamilton-Smythe.'

Not someone Stark was expecting to hear from. 'I'll be right there.'

It was silent in reception. The brief calm between working hours and pub closing time.

Barclay nodded to their solitary guest.

Kat sat primly upright on one of the station's careworn reception benches. The kind of furniture that owed less to comfort or aesthetics than to its ability to resist damage – or use as a weapon or kindling. But that wasn't the reason for her discomfort.

Faint as it was, Stark recognized something in her expression from domestic abuse calls, back in his uniform PC days, and from the faces of bystanders or relatives on night-time incursions into the homes of Taliban bomb-makers, in his other uniform days. Frozen fear.

'I'm afraid DI Millhaven is unavailable right now. Can I help?'

She eyed him warily, his silence in their earlier interview leaving her little to judge him by. She looked ready to bolt, but instead silently held up her phone.

There was a photo on it.

Stark felt his anger rise again, like floodwater arriving unannounced downstream from some distant deluge.

Bracing himself against its force, fist curling, he stared darkly at the image.

Kat herself, outside what transpired was her apartment building, head encircled with blood-red cross hairs.

44

'They *did* go in,' said Kat. A deep breath came out shuddering, the words some kind of unwilling release of pressure. She wasn't trembling. Calm under fire, Stark supposed, was a high-powered PA prerequisite. But so was discretion, and those four little words were a betrayal that appeared to cost her something, deep down. 'Alex and Jan. They went back inside Queen's House, before Lucinda Drummond was found . . .' she gulped. 'To the toilets, Alex said.'

Alex said. A seed of doubt. 'What time, and how long for?' Stark probed.

'I don't know.' She dipped her head. A cup of sweet tea, courtesy of Constable Barclay, sat steaming beside her. Standard offering to the gods of late-night confessions. Kat hadn't appeared to notice it any more than she'd heard Barclay offer it. Stark had made sure to start the interview with confirmation of her acquiescence to it being recorded. Barclay was stationed the other side of the mirror-glass as witness. A lot could be riding on this.

'I stayed to complete a call . . .' she continued. 'Scheduling. I was on Alexi's phone. By the time I finished, they were back. A few minutes later, we heard the scream. We were all as shocked as each other, I swear.'

'But Alexi and Jan never appeared on the Great Hall

CCTV,' said Stark. 'The only way they could've reached the toilets was via the Tulip Stairs.'

Kat raised her eyes to meet his, still some defiance there. 'It wasn't them. It can't have been.'

Stark let that hang in the air un-contradicted for a moment.

'It can't have been,' she repeated in a quieter voice, with a hint of self-persuasion.

'Saying that's so,' said Stark, kindly, 'who else would have motive to threaten you?'

Someone was worried about what she knew, enough to threaten her life, so who else would she know anything about? The picture had arrived via email. The same anonymous address that had sent the similar image of Libby to Fairchild. Stark slid it in front of Kat now. There was no mistaking the message in either. *Say nothing, or else.*

'Adrian Fairchild received this earlier today.'

Kat's eyes widened in horror. 'Isn't that . . . ?'

'Lucinda Drummond's daughter. Someone Fairchild cares for.'

Kat stared at the image as if she couldn't tear her eyes away.

'We have Fairchild's statement on record, saying he'd been forced into authenticating illegal black-market antiquities for someone unknown, but that the go-between was Jan Zieliński. So I have to ask again, Kat,' he said gently. 'Who, other than Alexi Zedani, would have cause to worry about anything *you* might know?'

Kat was trembling now. She shook her head. 'He said . . .' Tears rolled unchecked down both cheeks, but she didn't look up, as if meeting Stark's eyes would make it all true. 'He said he loved me.'

'I told you they were shagging.' Fran didn't know whether to celebrate being right or bemoan the cliché. Either way, she was back in the station on a Thursday evening, dinner ingredients and an unopened bottle of Chardonnay abandoned on her kitchen counter back home, determined not to let this latest revelation stoke any more reckless optimism.

'She says it was true love,' said Stark. 'Or so she thought.' And enough of that thought seemingly endured that she'd barely nodded through his list of suggested safety precautions.

'Rich older man seeks hot young woman for up-close-and-personal assistance . . . ?' scoffed Fran. A classic power imbalance was no foundation for true love. But then, what did she know?

'Nothing like murder and death threats to take the shine off, either way,' said Stark.

'We haven't proved anything yet,' cautioned Groombridge. Fran had gone off the deep end once already today, and even she had agreed that they should try to build a proper case before they confronted Zedani and his lawyer with Kat's statement.

'We can place him in the vicinity at the time of death,' she said. 'If he overheard Lucinda arguing with Adrian Fairchild, or she confronted him straight after, that's opportunity and motive right there. You don't even need an ex-military-for-hire bodyguard to add means . . .' she spelled it out, appealing to his copper core. 'All his bullshit about giving money, credence and passion, when all he really wanted was *PR* – charity-washing, the glove puppet of legitimacy, to distract from his shady shit backstage.'

Proximity didn't prove connection, of course. A big fat coincidence could still just be that. But if Alexi Zedani was the puppet master behind all this, he'd finally made a mistake. With the threats against Libby, the offender would've known the police would be checking Fairchild's emails. They'd be relying on the cops to pass on the message. But the threat against Kat, that was risky. Fairchild was already in this up to his neck. What could poor Kat have to stay silent about, if not her boss? If she went to the police, and she had, it pointed a giant, flashing neon finger straight at him. It wasn't proof, but hopefully enough for Superintendent Cox to add his signature to a search warrant request. After that, it would be down to the duty judge.

'I'm not saying we don't act,' said Groombridge, 'only that we'll have to strike gold. The CPS would want every dot connected before they even thought about charging a highly respected mass-tax-payer with connections, currently rubbing shoulders with a government minister at Mansion House.'

'Killjoy,' muttered Fran. 'Just don't mention that last bit to the judge.'

'I'll pretend I didn't hear that.' Groombridge knew she was joking. If you wanted tomorrow's warrant signed, you didn't piss off the judge with selective disclosure today.

'Me too,' said Superintendent Cox, sweeping past into his office. 'Right,' he said, taking a seat. 'Let's have it. Mrs Cox gave me her very best withering look as I left, so this better be good.'

45

'Nothing so far,' confirmed Stark, staring at the fine wines in Zedani's temperature-controlled walk-in cellar. Not a speck of dust in sight. Just bottled affluence. He still couldn't quite believe the judge had granted them search warrants. Plural. Fran was currently outside the home of Jan Zieliński and had called to vent her impatience while the SOCO search team conducted the initial forensic sweep. He could hear her pacing. If they were going to miraculously find Lucinda Drummond's blood or DNA on her killer's clothes, it was more likely to be on the gorilla than the keeper. Fran's words.

The odds of finding any such thing were small, but of finding anything in Zedani's man-pad penthouse, vanishingly so – so Stark had drawn the latter straw. They weren't going to find anything incriminating here. No one was that stupid. Or maybe Fran just thought confronting this kind of opulence would make her too angry – not realizing quite how close Stark was to exploding right now, with all his thoughts a thousand miles away under a collapsed hospital.

Either way, with Superintendent Cox's added heft, the judge had narrowly decreed Kat's statement enough for a shufti around Zedani's life. Groombridge was back at the station organizing the man-power-heavy search of Horizon Logistics' offices, planned for the morning.

Everyone knew this was long-shot territory. Everyone was trying not to dwell on the political fallout, given Zedani's connections to people of power. His lawyer was standing with the building concierge out in the apartment's lobby right now, clocking billable hours with dark satisfaction – first among his legal threats being that, since his client would have no choice but to take refuge in The Savoy tonight, they could expect a five-star bill in the morning. Fran had scoffed in disgust at that one.

'Want me to accidentally break something really expensive and personal-looking while no one's watching?' Stark offered.

'And get another bill? Sod's got more money than the Met already. Get one of Geoff's crew to leave a floater in his toilet instead.'

'Do SOCOs eat? I'm not even sure the white onesies come off. How about I bag up the oldest bottle of wine in here for forensic testing at yours later? Want to know how much? I googled a few.'

'Go on.' He told her. She whistled. 'Christ. Bottles like that aren't for drinking, they're for showing off. Probably taste like piss.'

Stark rather doubted that. Everything about Zedani's home said he valued good taste above all else. While elsewhere, impoverished war-torn souls pulled at a mountain of debris with bare hands. Stark should be *there*, not *here*, with all *this* . . .

He stamped down hard on the surge of anger, but for a pin-drop he'd have smashed every overpriced bottle here to shards and gore.

No calls or messages from Jergen. Stark had tried the

sat phone again, but he'd be ripping at the rubble and marshalling rescue efforts – everything Stark couldn't do, because he'd flown home, because what … London needed another policeman more than Gabrielle needed him there? Because of his pointless deal with Pierson? His stomach twisted with guilt, and the room seemed to shrink in on him.

'You still there?' asked Fran's voice.

Stark forced some semblance of calm into his voice. 'Unfortunately.'

'Says the guy in the swanky penthouse. Though I have to say, Zieliński's place doesn't look half bad from the outside. I guess the whole private soldier thing pays well.'

'If only someone had told me,' muttered Stark, thinking about Tink's job offer.

'Well, don't get any funny ideas,' replied Fran pointedly. 'Gotta go. Looks like the Teletubbies are finally gonna let me in.'

Stepping back out into the sleek kitchen, Stark ground his teeth at the opulence all around. There were tasteful objets d'art everywhere you looked. The double-height seating area was dominated by two huge white leather sofas, designer armchairs and a TV bigger than most people's cars. Floor-to-ceiling windows overlooking the Thames. Palace View Apartments, on the Albert Embankment by Lambeth Bridge, lived up to its name. Shame the Palace of Westminster had been almost fully encased in scaffolding for years, but it still beat the hell out of the sliver of river visible from one end of Stark's own balcony.

His fingers flexed in the nitrile gloves.

For every thousand private soldiers out there with a half-decent pad, there was one smug arsehole in a place like this. But how many more non-combatants were out there risking their lives to save others for *free*? All he could picture right now were smoking ruins. The rubble forming a grave for so many, likely including one diminutive, huge-hearted French surgeon who'd just gone there to help.

He tore his eyes away from the mental image and back to Zedani's apartment. Forced his mind here, not there, but it was too late.

Rage boiled up in him again.

He stood welded to the spot, trembling with anger, fighting for breaths, fighting for control, searching for a point of calm to focus on, as Doc Hazel had taught him. He'd not had an episode this overwhelming for a long while. His eyes settled on the one object seemingly out of place in this museum to minimalism – a grey paper bag subtly emblazoned with the gold lettering of a boutique jewellery store, the kind that probably didn't stoop to anything so vulgar as a window display or price tags – neatly tied atop with gold ribbon, sitting on the kitchen island. Glaring at it, he gradually fought his way to control, half expecting the focus of his attention to burst into flames at the transfer of heat. The deep breaths slowly calmed. The fingers he'd not realized were digging into the worktop, eased, until he felt he was back within himself, the creature re-caged, if still prowling back and forth, hissing and with eyes aflame.

Another stupid, futile waste of energy and time.

Blinking, he blew out vestiges of anger in one long

breath . . . but not all. To let it all go would be to unfurl from spasm into despair, and despair was capitulation.

One of the nearby SOCOs was staring at him with worried eyes. Caught looking, she bustled away. More fuel for gossip. God knows what people must think of him, he sighed, returning his focus to the bag.

This whole place was for showing off. But there were no online images of a string of trophy girlfriends or ex-model-ex-wives. Zedani appeared to have it all, but who was he showing off to . . . ? A quick peek inside the bag revealed no apparent label. Where a few minutes ago he might've torn it asunder, he took care now not to spoil the wrapping. The warrant gave him authority to look inside, but despite his simmering anger it still felt like an intrusion.

Carefully extracting the small velvet box within, he opened it.

Glittering within was a fine gold chain necklace, with a heart-cut diamond pendant, three or four carats at least, bright white and clear. Stark let out a quiet whistle of appreciation. Money really *could* buy taste if bling was your thing. Perhaps there *was* a lucky lady out there after all, and Zedani simply preferred to keep his treasures under wraps. The SOCO photographer appeared at his shoulder to capture his find. Maybe it was the personal nature of the gift that induced Stark to rewrap it with such care. To a man of Zedani's wealth such treasure might equally be little more than a trinket of loose appreciation – something you send your PA out to buy for the mother you never call – but this looked more like the kind of gift you bought *for* the young PA who thought you loved her.

He wandered back into the large office, off one side of

the living space. If anything, the view was even better from here. As far as anyone could tell, there wasn't one scrap of business-related paper in the place. No printer, no filing cabinets, just a sleek desk and closed laptop.

Stark habitually lived neatly himself. Military deployment taught you to keep things simple and squared away, but it had been part of him before that, from the death of his father, taking up the mantle of responsibility, growing up early. Maybe before that too. Who knew? But it took real wealth to live *this* spotlessly. No unopened post, unpaid bills, shopping lists or takeaway menus. No dishes out, clean or dirty, or recycling awaiting transfer to outside bins. One employed people for the mundane stuff. But there were also no shelves of eclectic, unsorted books, music or films. No near-finished fiendish jigsaw puzzle or stamp collection. No life. Aside from the curated objets d'art, the only nod to the personal was the photo wall.

Now the SOCO photographer had finished capturing every square inch, Stark's eyes were drawn closer to the serried frames. Zedani in far-flung climes. Smiling with dignitaries, shaking hands or greasing palms, or both at the same time, cutting ribbons or gripping golden shovels in staged sod-turning ceremonies for various charitable endeavours, or grinning in front of a vast cargo ship.

Stark had turned away when something made him turn back, his eyes scanning for whatever it was that had triggered his attention.

One picture in particular.

Zedani, wearing desert slacks, aviators and an Arab-style shemagh headscarf, stood in front of a Mastiff armoured personnel carrier among a group of military types expressing varying degrees of smiles or disinterest. What immediately drew Stark in closer was that, despite their evident special forces weaponry and PPE, they wore no insignia of nationhood or rank. What they had instead on their Velcro patches was the subtle black logo of StoneTower.

And there, among the faces, stood Jan Zieliński, younger and slimmer but with the same hard expression.

The man Zedani claimed to barely know.

The man Fairchild had claimed was the missing link in all this, before the threat to Libby prompted his retraction.

A man who worked for Temple Security but made no mention of StoneTower?

But that wasn't what Stark was staring at now . . .

Because among the other faces, with one hand blurred as if in the act of shielding his identity, was the unmistakable broken nose of ex-SAS Staff Sergeant Douglas 'Tinker' Bell.

46

'Wait a second,' interrupted Fran, feeling her temperature rise. 'I thought you were *joking* about job offers!'

'I think you're missing the point here,' said Stark, down the phone line.

'Not really, no. I was *joking* about getting funny ideas. Now you tell me you've been plotting to sell out all along! How many pieces of silver are they offering?'

Stark told her.

Christ, thought Fran, incredulously. If that was the kind of offer they were up against, it was a wonder any ex-service people went into the police. 'Are you going?' she demanded.

'No, I don't think so –'

'You don't *think* so?'

'I thought I'd put that life behind me.'

'You *thought* . . . ?' Fran felt her expression darkening from incredulous to angry. 'Equivocate much, why don't you?'

'I think we're drifting even further from the point,' said Stark, an edge to his tone suggesting he was in no mood for her indignation.

Bit late for that! 'Which is that you're now wondering whether this Tink is working for Zedani too?'

'Exactly.' The three of them in one photo . . . ?

Fran rolled her eyes. 'I thought you said he was a friend?'

'The man beasted me up and down the Brecon Beacons and the jungles of Belize for months, making my life a living hell. So perhaps more of an inexplicable bond than friendship.'

'And you broke his nose.'

'I don't think I was the first.'

'What difference does that make?'

'He seems not to take it personally.'

'But if it's all brothers in arms bullshit, then why think he's joined the dark side?'

'While he was offering me a new job, he was asking me to tell him about my current one, in detail – not that I gave any.'

'Fishing for info on the investigation?'

'It didn't occur to me at the time, but now, I don't know. Him just turning up out of the blue . . . maybe this makes more sense than a job offer.'

Fran cursed. As if this damn case couldn't get any more convoluted!

The clock was about to turn midnight. Groombridge had told her to call with any significant developments. He'd probably still be awake. But while Fran thrived on the world's general disapprobation of her, her inner daddy's girl still ached for the approval of those few people she did respect – and the Guv'nor's wife, Alice, had cornered the market in wiltingly dry asides, particularly when it came to late-night calls before early starts. Plus, so far, Zieliński's plush apartment had turned up nothing they didn't already know.

Polish military, Temple Security. Photos from both, and family back home. No wife or children. None of Zedani.

None matching the photo of Tink's busted nose Stark had just sent to her phone. No mention of StoneTower. Their meagre hopes hung on the thin thread of laboratory forensics, and the off chance that one of the six identical suits, shirts, ties and shoes in Zieliński's wardrobe might have an invisible droplet of Lucinda Drummond's blood on them – as if a professional would be so stupid.

Fran sighed. 'Why are you such a pain in my arse?'

'What some call a gift, others name a curse.'

'And I don't suppose this Tink is the kind to buckle under questioning?'

Stark scoffed predictably. 'Not if my TQ training was anything to go by.'

'Well then,' she found a faint smile at the thought that Stark's night might prove longer than hers. 'I suppose you'd better do some digging before we kick in Horizon Logistics' door in the morning.'

Stark dug . . . starting on his phone while SOCO finished their search, then back at the office. Anything to take his mind off Tripoli. But after a couple of hours, his desk started to look appealingly pillow-like, and rather than wake to a crick in his neck, dribbling, still wearing yesterday's clothes, he forced himself home to a real bed.

Sleep came quickly but at the price of painful dreams. A flawless heart-shaped diamond glittering on perfect pale skin, his fingers reaching out in a warm caress, trembling, curled and charred in flame, soldiers' hands torn bloody clawing through mountainous rubble. A fine, ebony hand, unearthed, unblemished but for dust, soft but cold. The gut-sinking realization that you've failed, twisting you awake.

Not how every day started any more – but too familiar, all the same.

The only conscionable response, routine: on your feet, hit the head, shower, scran and square your shit away for inspection. A brief interlude of penitential physio on his hip and shoulder. Hard eyes in the mirror.

Parade-ready and first in, he was flicking on the office lights and firing up his PC when his phone lit up with Swan's name. 'Morning. AAU never sleep either?'

'Something like that.'

'You joining the raid?'

'Possibly not.'

'What's up?'

'Not sure. You got a minute?'

'Sure, fire away.'

'I mean downstairs.'

'You're here?'

'Yep, out front. And I can't help feeling that I'm in the middle of being kidnapped.'

Her voice sounded too strange for this to be dismissed entirely as a joke. 'Should I call the cops?'

'That's where it gets weirder. You'd better come down.'

Un-reassured, he did. But of all the people Stark expected to find with Swan, their suspiciously spooky Special Liaison hadn't even entered his mind.

Maxine Carver leaned with predatory feline noncha-lance against a blacked-out BMW 7 Series parked askew across the no parking zone. She looked him up and down, drawing deeply on a cigarette and breathing out a long stab of smoke. She was standing almost directly beneath a CCTV camera and signs declaring 'No loitering' and 'No smoking'. Such rules, it seemed, were not for the likes of her.

Swan stood beside her with all the apparent comfort of a lamb attempting invisibility beside a panther, and shrugged, with no words of explanation to offer.

Observing Stark, Carver took a final drag and ground the butt beneath her shoe with all the care she might take crushing dreams. 'Get in.'

Stark made no move to comply. 'That an order, DCI Carver?' They both knew that whatever rank she held, it wasn't a police one.

'As it happens . . .' She held up what was almost certainly a real warrant card, even if the ID was legendary. 'You'll both get a kick out of this, I promise.'

Swan got in the back.

It was only as he slid, perplexed, into the front passenger seat that Stark registered there was already another person in the back.

Someone whose shape in your peripheral vision screamed *threat*.

To call this triggering was an understatement. Not much more than a year earlier, Stark had been abducted from this very spot and driven away to what very nearly proved to be his death, and his heart virtually leaped out of his body now.

'Easy, soldier,' said Tink, hurriedly holding up his unarmed palms before Stark converted panic into action. 'We're all on the side of the angels here.'

Stark's heart stayed in his throat but didn't explode.

Carver eyed him warily; in case he proved as stupid as he currently must look.

Swan shrugged. 'Don't look at me. I haven't got a clue what's going on.'

'What the actual fuck?' exclaimed Stark, as soon as he could breathe.

He'd only just got his head around the idea that Tink might be working for the bad guys, but surely not Carver too?

'Your online trawling last night triggered a bit of a stir,' said Carver, unsmilingly. 'And risks blowing an asset in a delicate operation.'

Stark was too angry to care. 'For Christ's sake,' he glared at Tink. 'You're working for the spooks now?'

Tink grunted. 'I'm more of a . . . floating resource.'

'Even ghosts need a little off-the-books substance from time to time,' added Maxine.

Tink grinned. 'Rattle the odd chain. Stop the odd clock. Remind the world we're still hovering about in the shadows.'

Stark shook his head, biting down hard on his irritation. 'Home or away?' MI5 or MI6.

'Bit of both,' replied Carver. 'We're adaptable.'

'So, fishing for info on our investigation was for her, not Zedani?'

'Told you he was smarter than he looked,' said Tink to Carver.

She shrugged, as though it didn't matter that they'd messed him around. As if *nothing* mattered. 'Unfortunately, your web searches last night tripped some alarms we'd left in place. We'd really rather you didn't out Tink before we're ready.'

'And the whole StoneTower thing was bullshit?'

'No, I threw my fortunes in with them for a while, after the Regiment,' replied Tink. 'But then this lot came calling. StoneTower helps me keep up a front. They're very accommodating that way. I'd love to say the job offer stands. It's as much fun as you want it to be, with your kind of skill set. But you had to go and get all famous on us. Got to be the Grey Man, for haunting on the side.'

'I'm inconsolable.' That particular direction at the crossroads had looked both horrifying and far too appealing – but what did that matter now, with the road to Tripoli a smouldering ruin? 'But what has that got to do with Alexi Zedani?'

'He used StoneTower a few times for his wilder excursions. Our paths crossed. When Max started looking into his less PR-friendly activities, she tapped my shoulder. He was setting up his own firm, Temple Security, poaching staff from StoneTower, so I took both jobs. Double the pay cheque and I get to serve Queen and country again – what's not to like?'

'Zedani *owns* Temple Security?' And he'd known Jan Zieliński for years, poached him from StoneTower.

'All about the money, that one.'

'Less PR-friendly?'

'Let's just say that not all the shit Zedani ships is legit. And we're not just talking ancient pots and bling. Guns, drugs, whatever his clients need. But that's just the tip of the iceberg. His real currency is thin air.'

'Fake manifests, fake invoices,' guessed Stark. 'Money laundering?'

'In goes the client's dirty money and out it comes clean, funnelled back to them through offshore banks, transformed into UK accounts, investments and property, minus the laundry bill. Ain't life grand?'

'If you have evidence, shouldn't you be specially liaising with someone?'

'Hilarious,' Carver made a face. 'In my line of work we don't gather evidence, we develop leverage.'

'We're not in your line of work,' said Swan, firmly.

'Maybe not. But remember that little bit of paper you both signed?' Carver smiled like the Cheshire Cat, with everything else fading away to leave nothing but dangerous teeth. The Official Secrets Act was no joke. 'Well, this is where that gets real.'

'And why is leverage over Zedani useful?'

'Well, that's where this gets interesting.' She gunned the engine to life with a roar and pulled away, belting up as she drove fast through the busy streets with the kind of carefree speed that even Fran would only attempt under lights and siren.

47

'Where are we going?' asked Swan.

'You'll see,' said Carver, 'but I need you both to hand your phones to nice Mr Bell to turn off.' She didn't say please.

This really *was* starting to feel like a kidnapping.

Swan complied. Stark did not. 'I need to let DCI Millhaven know where we are.'

'Taken care of. I'm sure they can knock on Horizon's door without your help.'

'I'm waiting for an important call.'

'Not as important as this.'

'More important to me. Or you can just drop me off right here.'

Carver glanced at him. 'There are people on the ground out there. As soon as we know anything about your friends, you'll know.'

'What friends, where?' asked Swan.

They both ignored her. Stark handed his phone to Tink. 'If they call while that's off, I'm going to get much angrier than I already am.'

'Fair enough,' said Carver, overtaking the car in front with millimetres to spare. Stark gripped the door handle tight and tried to stop scanning the rooftops, cars and pedestrians with phones for threats.

'Relax, soldier,' said Tink. 'No one's shooting today.'

Stark popped open the glove box to reveal, as expected, a Glock 17 and spare clips.

'Just in case,' Carver conceded.

He flipped it closed. 'Aren't you supposed to keep that locked?'

'Fuck-all use if someone did start shooting.'

'Is it all right if I'm sick back here?' asked Swan.

Carver glanced in the mirror. 'Depends on whether you'd like to complete the journey in the boot.'

'Rude,' said Swan, quietly.

'Don't mind her barking,' said Tink, cheerily. 'Her bite's far worse.'

Carver steered the car north over Tower Bridge, through Whitechapel and Spitalfields and hung a left just before they crossed Regent's Canal into a street lined with warehouses – semi-industrial, multi-storey buildings in the process of gentrification into businesses or flats. Outside one was an unmarked car filled with the unmistakable figures of specialist firearms officers with MP5s.

Carver pulled up alongside and flashed an ID.

Stark didn't see if it said police or security services.

Another armed uniform appeared inside the gate and swung it open for them to drive through.

Once they were parked, Carver turned to Stark and Swan. 'What you're about to see falls under the category of state secrets you're not allowed to share with anyone – friends, family or colleagues.'

'Oh, come on,' said Swan. 'If this relates to our work in AAU, I have an obligation t–'

'To keep your trap shut until we say otherwise,' interrupted Carver. 'Same for you, Stark.'

'If it impedes a police investigation, you'll have to square that with my superiors.'

'I am your superiors.'

'Section Seven of the Official Secrets Act states that disclosure by a Crown servant is lawful if made in accordance with their official duty.'

'Oh, for fuck's sake,' she rolled her eyes. 'You've *memorized* the Official Secrets Act.'

'I don't sign things I haven't read.'

'Nerd!'

'Even so.'

'Okay . . . then let me put it this way,' she said, levelly, 'you're welcome to argue Section Seven from inside a jail cell without bail, for as long as we decide it'll take to come to court.' Carver held his defiant gaze a second, then softened almost imperceptibly. 'But I'll do my best to keep the compartmentalization from getting in the way for either of you. And with a bit of luck, this may even go public in fifty years.'

She climbed out of the car, as if everything were agreed.

Stark and Swan had little option but to follow her inside.

'I know this place,' said Swan. 'This is Franks House, an offsite storage facility for the British Museum. Or it was, before they moved everything to the swanky new building next to the museum itself.'

'Correct,' said Carver. 'Making this a handy spot to squirrel this lot away.' She swung open another door into the heart of the warehouse, populated with several people in white gloves, poring over a familiar set of earthenware urns in crates and a table with twenty-three gold dots laid out on black velvet. To one side was a fixed-chassis lorry and two high-end Mercedes E-Classes with blacked-out windows and Iraqi diplomatic plates.

A couple of men, with Middle Eastern complexions and sharp suits, observed closely.

One of them caught Carver's eye and jerked his head for her to follow into a dim side room. Inside, he eyed Stark, Swan and Tink with controlled suspicion. 'Is it wise, bringing him here?' he asked in crystal-clear English, gesturing to Stark. 'He attracts attention.'

'I'd trust this man with my life,' said Carver, to Stark's bewilderment.

The man raised his eyebrows slightly. 'But with your secrets?'

'In our business, that's the same thing.'

'And her?'

'Clueless and happy to remain so,' said Swan for herself.

The Iraqi gave the faintest reluctant nod, appearing to concur with her limitations.

Tink pulled a mobile hard drive from his pocket and handed it over.

'This is everything?' asked the stranger.

'It's enough,' said Carver.

They held each other's eyes a moment, before the drive disappeared into his pocket, and he left without another word.

Carver turned to Swan and Stark. 'I'll say this once only. And you'll never repeat it. That drive contains a copy of everything that dear Tink here and other associates have gleaned, tracing the path of your antiquities haul all the way back to Basra, via a senior and highly dodgy member of the current Iraqi government – a man we now have handy leverage over.'

'How senior?' asked Stark, not sure he wanted to know.

'Enough to be very useful in upcoming high-level talks when we are hoping to derail Iran's growing influence in Iraq,' smiled Carver. 'That man who's just left works for him and is also implicated up to his eyeballs. He will pass on the good news that they're both now assets for MI6.'

'So your mission was to ensnare them, but if you blow Zedani you blow everything?' said Stark. 'And he gets away with murder.'

'If that's what happened,' replied Carver, straight-faced.

'Hooking Zedani as an asset too.' Stark shook his head. There was little point bemoaning how the real world worked, but this was all closer to the shadows than he wanted to be.

'Wait,' said Swan, appalled. 'We're shipping everything we've recovered back to the men who stole it all in the first place? The coins too?'

'Don't worry, they know that if they try it again we'll feed them to their own side, or send in Tink.'

The granite Scot smiled like everyone's favourite uncle.

Stark didn't envy anyone that. 'So why are we here?'

'Aside from the gratitude of a grateful nation, it seemed fitting you be here at the end when you were there at the beginning. But mostly because you're a pair of nosey twits who'd probably ignore our threats and keep digging until you unearthed something we'd rather you didn't.'

'Fair enough,' muttered Swan.

*

Back in the warehouse, the Nebuchadnezzar staters were being locked into a Peli case while the urn-containing crates were being nailed shut.

One of the Iraqi men overseeing this grinned from ear to ear. Catching sight of them, he approached. 'Thank you,' he enthused. 'No words are enough. Truly. I never thought I would see this day.'

Carver smiled warmly. Hers was not a profession used to gratitude, but faking was right in her wheelhouse. 'You're very welcome. On behalf of Her Majesty's Government, it is our pleasure to see these historical artefacts returned to their rightful place.'

'Indeed,' he sighed, a sudden cloud appearing to dim his cheer momentarily. Whatever it was, he shook it off, eyes falling on Stark with a curious frown, his head tilting to one side. 'You seem familiar to me? Have we met?'

Professor Karim Mansour. Shock aside, Stark had already placed him from that baking warehouse, half a world away, in another life. 'That would be unlikely,' he demurred, and faded away as the man's attention swung back to the crates.

Outside, Carver lit a cigarette and made a call.

Tink caught Stark's eye, gesturing for a quiet sidebar. 'Murky waters,' he said quietly, staring straight ahead, as Carver paced up and down. 'A humble non-com needs to be careful. National security's one thing, but a nation's pride is another. You never know what actors are in play.'

Stark didn't know what to make of this, so said nothing.

Tink yawned. 'It's never all about the money. But,

brother to brother, the clever cash washes through property these days. All those nice riverside properties sitting half empty while their oligarch owners watch the values rise, leaving the rest of us staring at the mother of all scaffolding.'

'Where the fuck have you been?' demanded Fran. She'd arrived before seven to find his car in the car park, his desktop on but not logged in, and reports of him leaving via the front entrance around six this morning. Given his abduction last year, Fran had to fight the urge to check the front-stoop camera capture, until Cox passed on a dubious message that Stark was 'assisting Swan', of all people, this morning – without adding why or with what. Fran's two voicemails and three messages to Stark's phone over the last few hours had gone unanswered. And now he just walked back in, halfway through the damn morning, having completely missed the raid on Horizon Logistics' offices, and sat at his desk without a word!

'Can't say.'

Fran prided herself on intimidating double-takes, and this was a good one, but such things were usually wasted on Stark. 'I beg your pardon?'

'Granted.'

'I meant, what the bloody hell do you mean, you can't say?'

'I can't say.'

'Because wherever you've been is more important than finding evidence linking Alexi smug-face Zedani to three and a half murders?'

'Because a certain Special Liaison says I'm prohibited

from discussing where I've been by those bits of paper we signed.'

Fran stood agog, aware it wasn't a good look on her. 'Carver?'

'Her spooky self,' replied Stark, darkly.

Something had really got under his skin today, and now something had got under hers. 'Well, we'll see about that!'

'I expect so,' he said, checking his phone. 'She's waiting for you upstairs with the Guv, in Superintendent Cox's office.'

The next twenty minutes of Fran's life were ones she'd rather forget, being best described as fruitless and frustrating, intermingled with repeated uses of another f-word that she only got away with in Cox's office because there was no one junior for her to be setting a bad example for, and because Cox appeared to share her sentiments entirely.

'Not sure I've ever seen the Super go that purple before,' she said in the lift back down. 'Can't be good in a man his age.'

'He's barely ten years older than me,' pointed out Groombridge.

'Blood pressure must rise with rank,' she replied, unapologetically.

'I guess you'll find out.'

'Not me. I don't have the politics for higher office.'

'I used to say the same. The politics comes with the knocks.'

'Oh good,' she sighed. 'Something else to look forward to.'

*

Fran's day hardly got better.

When the lab quoted her a week for the search forensics on Jan Zieliński's clothes and belongings, she'd demanded expedition, only to be told the un-expedited date would have been double. A long time to wait just to have thin hopes dashed.

SOCO were still on site at Horizon Logistics, boxing up files and interrogating computers, while the forensic accountants began their work. Such things were not quick, and the worst thing they'd probably find was a decimal place missing off some tax form. Fran would leave all that to them and the Fraud Squad.

Maxine Carver had served up a copy of Temple Security's employee files – obtained God knew how – by way of apology, though Fran suspected it was more to stop her charging down there herself. But while there were dozens of ex-military, ex-police or simply ex-social types on the books from numerous nationalities, none she found matched faces from Zedani's photo wall, and Fairchild was no longer cooperating to help pick out the gruff Eastern Europeans he alleged had strong-armed him into authenticating antiquities. Both Temple and Horizon were probably as they appeared to be: the legitimate side of Zedani's life. The clever criminal kept their shady side in the shadows.

'Two adults?' asked the teenaged ticket vendor.

Fran held up her warrant card. 'I think we'll take the free tour.'

Stark held his up too.

The woman at the front of the line Fran had just jumped muttered something to her husband in German that Fran assumed was a commentary on the British reputation for queuing politely. Uncertain what to do, the ticketeer started talking about calling her supervisor, but Fran was already walking past.

The decision had been taken to open the exhibition. The show must go on, and Queen's House had glittering antiquities to show off. If she took her eye off him for a second, Stark would probably wander off happily for hours. But they weren't here for historical curiosity.

In all honesty, Fran wasn't sure why they *were* here, so it was a good job Stark hadn't asked.

The route signage and displays enticed visitors to take their time, but Fran wasn't wearing her tourist hat. The police tape sealing off the Tulip Stairs from the Great Hall had been replaced by a velvet rope curving between two brass bollards with a sign politely declaring 'No Entry'. This was no longer an active crime scene, but good taste prevailed. Visitors would have to leave this particular box in their sightseeing itinerary unticked for a respectful period, before the museum deemed it appropriate to cash in on ghost number two.

Fran gestured with impatient eyes for Stark to remove the obstacles, which he accomplished with wordless efficiency, lack of complaint honed to a fine point.

The exhibition coordinator, tipped off by the failed door-keeper, appeared round the corner at a trot, protest at the ready, until she recognized Fran from the night of the murder and, more importantly, recognized her expression. Choosing caution, she kept her distance but with head swivelling to ensure they weren't disturbing actual paying customers.

Fran stepped into the silent chamber, instinctively avoiding the central decorative tiling, as if the body of Lucinda Drummond still lay crumpled upon it. Not one spot of visible blood remained, even in the thin joints between tiles. There were experts for that kind of clean-up, if you had the money.

Her eyes followed the stone steps up around the cylindrical space. She was tempted to call the helix a spiral, if only to see if Stark could resist correcting her. Blue sky, visible through the circular rooflight lantern above, set off the blue paint of the ornate tulip-motif balustrade, while afternoon sunlight through the side windows cast slanting beams across the whole, spotlighting dazzling dust motes.

It really was stunning.

Maybe that was why she'd felt the urge to come. To remember that blood didn't always stain. That beauty could prevail, if you were willing to forget the rest. To dispel the picture of a terrified woman's final moments, cast into the void to her death. To ignore the ghosts.

Or perhaps she thought coming back to the beginning might somehow untangle the mess that followed. The boatyard. Ancient urns and gold coins. Witness intimidation. A stabbed academic. A disposable driver. A butchered thief. All starting with a successful woman in a man's world, and mother of two, cut off in her prime.

Loose threads everywhere.

Or a web. An arachnoid form, with Zedani's superficial smile, sat barely visible at the shadowy edge, sensitive to all her fumbling approaches. Fran couldn't help thinking every step she'd taken had been a mistake. And worse, that she'd find herself six months from now, no closer to a solution. There was too much money involved here. As soon as they put Kat's accusation to Zedani, his one shiny lawyer would multiply like bacteria. Give her a plain old crime of passion, greed or stupidity – she'd always got her man or woman. A rarity in the world of murder investigation, Groombridge had warned her, when she moved up to DI. Sooner or later, she'd fail, and gather her own haunting. Be forced to face the truth – that she didn't know what she was doing.

Stark didn't shuffle his feet or cough impatiently. He just stood, taking everything in, like a rock absorbing the warmth of the sun but radiating nothing back.

'Any news of your friend?' she asked him.

'Nothing good.'

'Anything I can do?'

'No.'

'Anything *you* can do?'

'No.'

Fran tried to be phlegmatic about things she couldn't change. It saved energy for losing her shit about everything else. If there was an opposite way, Stark's was it. The powerlessness must be eating him alive inside. She sought for one of Groombridge's inspiring aphorisms, but he wasn't any better at sugar-coatings than Stark was likely to swallow them. 'Bugger this,' she announced, with a deep sigh, 'I'm sure you owe me a coffee.'

Of course, trying to be phlegmatic wasn't the same as achieving it, and, being honest, she pretty much lost her shit about everything, to save time distinguishing. Even the good things; acknowledgement of which didn't stop her glaring at her phone screen, several hours later in the office, when it lit up with Marcus's name for the third time that day. She'd declined the previous two – message enough, for most people – but with only her and Stark left after another fruitless day's graft, maybe it was time to stamp this distraction down, once and for all. 'This about work?'

'No.'

Just that. No surprise at her actually answering, or her tone. Bloody man never could seem to get the hang of being intimidated. 'Then take a hint.' She hung up, but he called straight back. Fran went into Groombridge's office and closed the door. 'I don't want to talk to you.'

'Perhaps.'

'What does that mean? Are you saying I don't know my own mind now?'

'Perhaps.'

'I hate you.'

'I don't think so.'

'If you think calling me a liar will get you back on my good side, you need to *re*think.'

'I think we need to do this in person. Where are you?'

'Barbados.'

'If you *are* going to start lying, you should probably remember to disconnect me from your find-my-phone app first.'

'And if you're going to turn into a stalker, you probably shouldn't start with a police officer with anger issues.'

'Same goes for getting into a romantic relationship, I suppose,' he replied, 'but the world loves a fool.'

'No, it doesn't. And I don't want romance, or a relation-ship. Not with a fool. Not with anyone.'

'It is a damn nuisance, I'll admit.'

'And that's your sales pitch, Casanova? That I'm inconvenient?'

'But worth it.'

'Oh well, that's okay then. Save yourself the flowers and choccies, you had me at "nuisance".' She hung up, put the phone on silent and stomped out into the general office, only to find Marcus standing in the doorway with flowers, chocolates and what might pass for a sheepish smile, if he weren't so damned annoying.

'This is probably a bit awkward then,' he admitted.

On the plus side, he also had a bottle of Chardonnay.

48

'You shouldn't have,' suggested Stark, hastily logging off and plucking his jacket from the back of his chair.

'Probably not,' nodded Marcus, fully comprehending Stark's point that openly romantic gestures in Fran's place of work, even after hours, were taking the secret boyfriend risk to a new level.

Fran's face wasn't giving much away, which for her was not a good sign.

'Well, if your body turns up choked on rose stems, I guess we'll know for sure.' Stark gallantly left them to it.

He didn't pause to listen. There may not be a minimum safe distance from this one, but *away* was the only rational direction.

It was the *where to* that eluded him.

He made it as far as the car, but sat there, uncertain. Unwilling to go home when he was too wired to crash. He considered finding a bar, but his tolerance for a crowd was barely greater than for solitude right now.

The car's sun visor was down from Fran's outing to Queen's House in the earlier sunshine. Stark flicked up the mirror cover and met his own eyes.

'Have we met?' asked the familiar stranger.

How odd that he should come face to face with the old professor from that Basra warehouse, all these years later. That he should see some of those lost treasures returned.

Closing his eyes, he could still picture the dust and destruction, the shards, the man's silent tears, bereft even of anger. Feel the heat and sweat, and the stinging shame of his impotence to offer more than the most rudimentary help, fresh off the transport without even the smattering of Arabic he would afterwards seek. What wheels of fate had brought them back together. Stark imagined all the hands at work, the blood spilled, and for what . . . ?

It's never all about the money.

Tink was never one for idle asides. Stark had been replaying them all day.

It was certainly true that the clever cash did wash through property these days. The UK government talked tough on money laundering, but if you want to look like a modern, thriving economy, smart riverside developments were a must. And who better to pay for them than Jonny Foreigner and his nice liquid cash? It couldn't all go on football clubs. And if you were operating somewhere below that stratosphere, outfits like Zedani's could help spare everyone's blushes when the latest press upstart asked where all the money came from.

He'd done well out of it. Perhaps the whole 'patron of the arts' thing was his way of washing the blood and filth from his hands.

Leaving the rest of us staring at the mother of all scaffolding.

Twenty minutes later, Stark was sat at his home laptop, staring at the original developer's online marketing brochure for Palace View Apartments. Completed four years ago by one of the larger high-end development companies, boasting views of 'the Mother of Parliaments'. The units were all of a similar size, and all of them beyond affordable to anyone outside the top one per cent. The brochure spoke of basement parking, luxury mod-cons, exclusive pool, spa and gym, even shopping and cleaning services. Sales-tracing websites showed the penthouse being snapped up off-plan by Zedani through Horizon Logistics. A property company had swooped in to purchase the rest, selling them all on for increasing mark-ups, and keeping the overall freehold for the annual ground rents. Money made money.

Digging further, it seemed that the property company had grown from almost nothing by buying up three smaller ones. One of which had been a land-banking company specializing in buying up run-down industrial properties along the river. Properties like Coleman Brothers Boatyard perhaps, though Stark's online fumblings found no quick evidence of that. But Companies House listed the current property company's ownership as a holding company, registered in the Caymans.

Dixon and Williams had traced Temple Security's ownership to a holding company, also in the Caymans. Stark trawled the name from his memory. Different company. But ownership hierarchies got murky offshore. Horizon Logistics, for example. Also owned by a shell in the Caymans, which Swan's international colleagues had already suggested might be a placeholder for another in Cyprus.

Money sloshed around the world until anyone who might care about cleanliness had little hope of finding the blood-red sock that stained the whole wash. The oligarchs bought mega-yachts. The regular rich surfed the wave. Governments waved in 'investment' to make up the tax loss. The poor got exploited and everyone else got priced out. Trickle-up economics. Wheels greased by the likes of Alexi Zedani. Allegedly.

So Stark sat staring at the brochure, unsure what it was about it – aside from the colossal social inequality – that niggled.

He closed his eyes, mentally retracing his steps through every room in Zedani's penthouse.

And then he opened them again and picked up his phone.

Zedani didn't answer his buzzer.

The concierge, conceding that the warrant in Stark's hand was active for twenty-four hours, with one hour remaining, reluctantly opened the door.

He tried suggesting he should stay with them, even suggesting they sign in using the visiting tradespersons' book, but swallowed Stark's polite rejection and withdrew, almost certainly to call Zedani's lawyer.

'Is it too late to voice second thoughts?' mused Swan.

Groombridge was out with his wife. Fran hadn't picked up, so was either patching things up with Marcus or out burying his body. So Stark had tried Swan, guessing that after a day like today she'd be faced with the same dilemma as him – obsess or drink.

She'd gone with obsess. He needed a chaperone and she welcomed a distraction. And as distractions go, Zedani's apartment proved a banker.

The cleaners had been in. SOCO weren't known for leaving everything as they found it, even with Zedani's lawyer threatening to sue them for sheer effrontery, but you'd have no idea the place had been searched, top to bottom, yesterday.

Swan blew out a whistle of appreciation and envy. 'If I'd known this was the kind of life the black market offers, I'd have switched sides years ago.'

'Odds are this place wasn't paid for by antiquities. At least, not alone.'

He'd relayed his findings. If anything, her experience in such matters only made her more sceptical that they could join the Cayman-Cypriot dots to Zedani. 'So, you mentioned the wine store. We here to snaffle a ridiculously priced bottle or three?'

'Tempting, but no.'

'Then what is it we're looking for?'

Stark held up the brochure floor plan he'd printed out. 'Zedani had this place altered. The second bedroom was converted into his office, with this storage room fitted out as the wine store, but something's not right. The wine store isn't as deep. It's not obvious, but space has been lost.'

'Probably just the services, the air-con unit, or whatever.'

'Maybe.'

Swan stared at him levelly. 'You've dragged me away from a perfectly good evening of wallowing in self-pity to look for a secret cupboard?'

'I assumed if I told you that, you wouldn't come.'

She considered this. 'Depressingly, I'm not sure that's true. But it would be too small to hide much in.'

'Unless it leads somewhere else.'

'A secret *passageway*?' Swan looked justifiably incredulous.

'I was thinking more of a secret stair.' Tink's aside

about *half-empty* properties. The concierge had told him yesterday that they didn't have to worry about noise because the owners of the adjacent apartments were on holiday, and the people below lived overseas and never visited, but Stark's research listed the apartment below as still owned by the overseas holding company. Unfortunately, checking it out would require a second warrant that he'd have a hard time justifying to Fran, let alone a judge.

But the questions just kept forming . . .

What if Zedani wasn't just a businessman philanthropist? What if he wasn't just a smuggler and money launderer? What if he was a collector – the kind who could only show his exhibits off to himself, perusing his prize trophies in private?

What if the whole apartment below was his secret museum?

Swan actually laughed in his face. And then, when she realised he wasn't joking, did it again. 'You're a madman.'

'What's the harm in looking?'

'The harm is that I could be watching celebrity baking cock-ups on TV with a bottle of very cheap wine right now.'

'Where's the fun in that, compared to a treasure hunt?'

'I'm starting to understand why people keep shooting at you.'

'But we're here now. So . . .'

So they began in the wine store.

'You should've told me I'd need a coat,' complained Swan, over the faint hum of the refrigeration. The balmy summer night outside dictated shirtsleeves, while the wine store maintained a steadfast, shiver-inducing twelve degrees centigrade. There was an upright glass-door fridge keeping selected white wines even cooler for drinking.

What there didn't appear to be was any secret door or mechanism just the wrong side of cunning for them to find. Tapping on the walls just made them both feel foolish.

So they tried the big office instead.

'Oh,' said Swan, on seeing the bloody corpses. 'I guess we should've started here.'

49

Jan Zieliński had been shot three times, twice centre chest, once through the head, probably in that order – assassination style.

Two other men lay shot dead in identical fashion beside him. Heavyset, smart-suited. Stark recognized neither from the photos on Zedani's wall, but he'd not be surprised if both had the same Polish special forces tattoo, and he put money on them being Adrian Fairchild's black-market contacts/enforcers – if he got a chance to ask him. Because one thing was for sure, Team Zedani had come off second best against someone, and not long ago.

The blood pooling out across the floor was still wet and red.

Stepping carefully to avoid the gore, Stark felt Zieliński's skin. 'Still warm.'

Swan had gone white, but was already dialling her phone.

Stark hurriedly held a finger to his lips, and pointed.

In the far corner of the room, where the wall had seemed deeper than the wine store on the other side, a section of the apparently seamless vertical wood panelling stood ajar.

Stark quickly felt inside Zieliński's jacket, but his shoulder holster was empty. Same for the other two.

Swan spoke in hurried whispers into her phone.

Stark flicked out his new ASP baton, wishing it was his army Browning 9mm, and crept over to the secret door. Inside, a narrow stair ran down. All lined in the same timber, spotlit from above. The landing at the bottom disappeared round a corner. Stark caught the rumbling of a man's voice, but not the words.

'Wait for the cavalry?' whispered Swan.

The answer to that lay below. Whatever the hell was going on here, whoever was responsible had shot three armed guards dead before they could return fire. Stark could see no other telltale bullet holes. No shell casings either. The shooter or shooters had paused to collect their brass – a chilling sign of counter-forensic professionalism. 'One of us needs to creep down for recon,' he whispered back. 'Flip a coin?' The momentary surprise on her face was worth it, but he shook his head. 'If anyone but me comes up those stairs, slam the door and run.'

She nodded, grimly. 'I should've listened to the warnings about you.'

Leaving her to contemplate that truth, he slid silently down the stairs and peeped round the corner at the bottom, acutely aware that he was bringing a stick to a gunfight.

Another secret-looking timber-panelled door stood open a crack. A shadow flitted across it.

More male voices.

Stark had some basic French, a little German, a smattering of other NATO member languages he'd come across in his military years, and keys words in Pashto, but it was the Farsi part of his brain that lit up. But what would Iranians be doing here?

'Last chance, *kooni*,' said a male voice in accented but educated English. 'Tell us where it is.'

Through the crack in the door Stark could see the back of a man standing over someone bound to a chair. The seated man, wearing a grey suit with blood on it, began writhing against his bonds with muffled screams.

His tormentor slapped him hard, then pulled down the gag.

For a moment, Stark glimpsed the bound man's face. Alexi Zedani.

'Please,' he begged, coughing and spluttering. 'It was there. I don't understand.'

The tormentor said something in what Stark still thought was Farsi, delivering another hard slap, leaving Zedani lolling and whimpering.

Stark sympathized. He'd been in that situation, receiving punches.

'What you don't seem to understand,' said the apparent boss, in his accented English, 'is that I don't care about anything else in this room, including you. And we will break all these beautiful things into pieces, one by one, including your fingers, arms, legs, face and eventually your neck, until you tell us where the mask is.'

The mask? The Mask of Kings? But that was back with the Iraqis, thought Stark. They couldn't mean that?

'I swear I don't know,' pleaded Zedani. 'It was in that cabinet. It was *there*!'

'When? When was it last there?'

'Yesterday, I swear –'

Another slap cut off his protestations.

The tormentor reached down and replaced the gag, then efficiently snapped one of Zedani's fingers.

The muffled screams took a minute to sink into whimpers, as the gag was pulled down again. *'Please . . .'*

Stark was racked with indecision. There were at least two bad guys in there, discounting Zedani, but there might be more. And at least one gun, plus or including the three taken from Zieliński and friends upstairs. Stark's ASP baton wasn't going to close that gap without a whole periodic table of surprises. The wisest course of action was to retreat upstairs, update the cavalry, and wait for them to save the day.

A faint noise from back up the stairwell turned his head.

Swan was no longer peering down.

And that's when the door he'd been peeping through swung open and Stark found himself staring down a gun barrel instead.

A 9mm with suppressor. It looked like a SIG Sauer P226 but this was the Iranian knock-off, the PC-9 Zoaf. The man pointing it at Stark beckoned him to come out.

So much for any element of surprise.

The doorway opened, like the one upstairs, through a wood-panelled wall. The apartment's inner walls appeared to have been removed, leaving a wide, plush auditorium dotted with columns and glass display cases on white plinths like in a museum. Integral LEDs sparkled off the objects inside – an oriental vase here, a painting there, shiny coins that Stark was willing to bet were electrum staters. An ornate gold dagger and scabbard. And not just beautiful objects, but also ancient-looking, undecorated examples of pottery, statuettes, carvings.

An ill-gotten treasure trove of stolen and looted history. Zedani's dirty secret.

What drove a person to want such a collection – which they could only enjoy alone or with persons utterly trusted or complicit – was beyond Stark's comprehension, but right now he had greater concerns.

The gunman gestured for him to drop the ASP. Stark considered using it instead, but the man's cool eyes and professional posture convinced him to comply.

He was in deep shit. Whatever was going on here, the dead bodyguards upstairs had been deemed superfluous, and it was hard to see any way Stark wouldn't face the same conclusion long before help arrived. And that faint noise from above was worrying. He hoped Swan was okay and didn't venture down to see where he'd gone. But there was one display case in prime position, with a stand to hold something that wasn't there, and it seemed likely that events in this room were set to get uglier. 'I'm a police-man. And there's many more converging on this spot as we speak. Put down your weapons before the firearms team bust in here and your chances of survival fall through the floor.'

Maths update: four bad guys, three with pistols, one with a curious smile. 'And when will that be?' asked the smiler, apparently the boss. 'Before or after we kill you and take Mr Zedani with us?'

'Kill me and you're as good as dead.'

'Or,' said Bossman, 'we shoot you in the knee and take

you too.' He smiled. 'There are people in my part of the world who would be thrilled to lay hands on such a potent symbol of imperialist Western oppression, Sergeant Joseph Stark and his Victoria Cross.'

Fuck. That explained the smile. There had always been the chance that some jihadi nutcase would decide to target him for his profile. The bar for awarding VCs was so high that recipients mostly weren't alive to collect. If this man got his way, Stark's might just prove a delayed fatality.

'I suppose the first question should be, if your armed colleagues are still converging, did you come alone?' Boss-man jerked his head for one of the lackeys to go check.

The man slipped through the doorway and up, out of sight, gun at the ready.

'RUN, SWAN!' bellowed Stark at the top of his lungs, bracing for a bullet . . . that didn't follow. Only the muffled thump of a suppressed pistol shot, followed by a long silence.

The two remaining lackeys looked to their boss, who jerked his head with a word in Farsi.

A second lackey went to peer up the stairs – and the back of his head exploded all over the wall.

The body slumped in the doorway.

Stark reacted first, lunging sideways and forward, to attack the final lackey, shoving the man's gun arm up.

A shot sounded with a muffled crack but exploded into the ceiling, as they found themselves locked together, both wrestling over the gun, in a faint snowfall of dust and gunsmoke.

The man was strong.

Change of plan. Stark let go.

Just for a moment, triumph flashed in the man's eyes, before Stark grasped his lapels and dropped backwards, using his full weight and both legs to flip his opponent over him.

As a means of disarming someone, sending them flying was usually a good start. But the brief grunt of alarm was cut off by the noise of breaking bone, minus any sound of pain. Stark rolled onto his front to see the man crumpled, head first, into a structural column, bleeding heavily from the skull – which might've been survivable if his neck weren't so clearly broken. The last flicker of light died in the eyes. Another life to Stark's bleak tally, however accidental.

And that was pretty much where any control over events Stark still hoped for, ran out.

More thumps of silenced shots made Stark tear his eyes back to the room, where Bossman was unloading his pistol at the doorway, splinters of wood exploding off the surface.

Stark couldn't see who he was firing at, but he did see the pistol swing towards him.

Rolling sideways behind a wide display case, he heard two bullets impact on the far side without coming through, as the glass exploded above his head.

'*NOOOO!*' Zedani's panicked scream pierced the silence between the shots.

More thumps, and a grunt.

Peeking quickly, Stark saw Bossman stagger back and fall behind another case, before someone new ducked through the doorway, unloading an identical pistol on the way.

Floating spook asset and ex-SAS staff sergeant, his old pal Doug Bell.

'*STOP!*' Zedani was in full panic mode, rocking his chair wildly against his bonds.

Bossman leaned around his makeshift cover and unloaded a fresh clip in a wild spray, unsure of his target. Two display cases shattered. Zedani's panicked chair rocking ceased abruptly.

Stark reached for Lackey Three's pistol and snatched it back to his own cover.

Seeing this, Tink nodded and shouted, 'MOVING!'

Stark stood and unloaded suppressing covering fire into Bossman's plinth, while Tink advanced to closer cover.

'I'M OUT,' shouted Stark.

Bossman leaned round to fire in his direction, but the Zoaf held nine rounds, like its SIG progenitor, and Stark had kept one back.

Bossman twisted as the ninth bullet tore into him, and collapsed with a grunt.

Tink was there in an instant to kick the fallen pistol away, his own trained on the prone man.

He bent down and rolled him onto his back.

Stark stood over them both.

Bossman wasn't smiling now. There was blood on his mouth, but a cough brought up more. Lung shot.

From the look, Tink had already caught him in the guts.

Even as they watched, a death rattle presaged glazing eyes.

'Well,' said Tink, 'two to me, one to you, and we call this one a draw?'

50

Draws counted whole in Stark's ledger. Two more ghosts to haunt him. Later. Right now . . . 'At the risk of repeating myself, Tink – what the *actual fuck!*'

'You're very welcome,' grinned Tink, searching Bossman's pockets, finding a phone but nothing else.

'Where's Swan?'

'Lassie's having a wee kip upstairs. Didn't want her getting caught in the crossfire, and this way she can say honestly she didn't see a thing.'

'You knocked her out?'

Tink feigned horror. 'Hit a woman? What do you take me for? I choked her out like a gent.'

'For fuck's sake, Tink.'

'Your gratitude is lacking.'

'I'd say you're both right,' said Maxine Carver's voice behind them. She tucked her Glock into her waistband, behind her back. 'Not sure he's feeling the love either,' she added, nodding towards Zedani, slumped in the chair.

One of Bossman's aimless bullets had struck him in the back of the neck, exploding a hole through which half his blood must've pumped in seconds.

Tink shrugged. 'I guess it's zero for your custody sergeant, Joe.'

'And zero for your leverage,' said Stark, bitterly. None to interview, arrest, charge and incarcerate. None for Lady

Justice, and no one to help explain or account for this godforsaken mess!

Carver just shrugged. 'This lot tried to cut out the middleman then.' She looked around, and then at Stark. 'Give,' she said, indicating the pistol in his hand.

Taking a plain pack of wipes from her pocket, she diligently cleaned it. 'Prints and DNA gone. Wash your clothes when you get home.' She handed the clean pistol into Tink's grasp and turned again to Stark. 'Okay. You found the bodyguards dead upstairs. DC Swan called for backup. But one of the bad guys jumped her. Fortunately, heroic Douglas Bell arrived in the nick of time and in the tussle for the gun, the bad guy upstairs came off deader. Tink then fought and killed all the bad guys down here – unfortunately, not before one of them killed Zedani – while you, DS Stark, went back upstairs to look after Swan and never saw what happened down here or fired a shot. Clear?'

'Typical,' said Tink, grunting to his feet. 'I do the hard work and he gets the girl.'

Stark stared back. Adrenaline was still throbbing through his veins and he felt more like punching something right now than scene tampering. 'How did you get here so quickly?'

The old soldier smiled. 'Think.'

'Our phones?'

'You're welcome, again.'

Stark looked around the room, at the shattered display cabinets. Inside one, the bejewelled dagger lay strewn with bling made of toughened glass shards, but otherwise unharmed. There was a lot of paperwork ahead. And a lot of publicity. Better if his name wasn't on this at all. 'No. I've never lied on a statement before, and I'm not starting now.'

Carver made a face. 'Best if your name's nowhere near this.'

'Yours too.' Stark nodded to them both, sure their true credentials would avoid scrutiny. 'Officers working in liaison with the Arts and Antiquities Unit, then?'

Carver nodded with half a smile. 'DC Swan saves the day. Nice.'

'From a gang of Iranians?' asked Stark.

'Iranians?' Carver frowned. 'You mean these unknown criminals of possible Middle Eastern extraction that we may sadly never identify? We'll quietly offer their bodies back to their Revolutionary Guard pals in exchange for the next lot of hostages, but they'll decline.'

'National pride.'

She stared at him, curiously. 'Exactly that.'

You never knew what actors were in play.

She gave Tink a weary look. 'You tipped him off?'

'Not me, Boss,' he lied flatly.

'But if you had . . . ?'

'Hypothetically speaking, it might be because, sooner or later, Zedani would've run out of usefulness. And when that happens, too often it's people like me and Joe, and Jan upstairs, who get killed in the crossfire.'

'That's not your call.'

Tink nodded. 'Exactly.'

She held his gaze a moment – but British special forces selection was all about identifying individuals capable of making hard decisions beyond any option to seek permission, who knew that what *needed* doing was an ever-moving concept in loose orbit around what you'd been told to do by someone a long way away in clean boots.

The echoes of Stark's relationship with Fran were a little disturbing, but he didn't have the bandwidth for that right now. 'They were after a mask, but surely not the one I'm thinking of, unless . . . ?' His mind was racing. 'If the received knowledge that the coins had been melted down was bollocks, then you have to ask what else was.'

'Maybe you *are* smarter than you look,' nodded Carver. 'If the same Iraqi security minister who declared the coins lost was the same one who later went on TV declaring the mask recovered.'

'The same man behind the theft in the first place – the man you now have your hooks into?'

Carver made a non-committal face. 'And in the global industry of saving-face, the Iraqis and the Coalition Allies alike have a vested interest in seeing the Mask of Kings sitting in its nice glass box in the Lakeside Palace Museum. And any busybody antiquarian suggesting it might be a big fat gold-plated-tungsten forgery, might decide that saying so aloud could put more than his career at risk.'

'Professor Mansour?'

'Knows the limits of his power.'

'And in the global industry of saving-face, the Iranians have a vested interest in embarrassing the Iraqis and Coalition Allies,' said Stark. Christ, what a mess. 'Zedani wanted the coins and mask for himself – his prize exhibit – but gets caught in the middle.'

'National bloody pride,' nodded Tink.

'We've been tracking this team for a while,' confirmed Carver.

And given no warning to us poor dumb cops, thought Stark bitterly. 'And these aren't the guys that killed Nathan Goff.'

'They don't look the motorbikes and crowbar types,' agreed Carver.

'Or the kind of stupid gobshites to stab a man and not check he's dead before you torch the house,' added Tink.

Stark found his anger rising again. 'So the Black Riders were working for Zedani.'

'Maybe ...' Carver's face said she wasn't at all sure about that. 'But there are three key questions you should be asking.'

Stark was already there. 'How did these guys trace the mask to Zedani, if he wasn't planning to sell it on? And where is it now?'

'And ... ?'

The picture taking shape had a glaring hole in the middle. 'Who's the middleman?'

'Exactly.' Carver's face creased with wholly uncharacteristic uncertainty. 'Any ideas? Because this is about where my security service omnipresence truck runs into an impenetrable wall of what the fuck is actually going on?'

And that was when Stark realized who *wasn't* here. And the intrinsic issue with the word 'middleman'.

Gender.

51

Fran had been in a good mood.

After driving to her place in near silence, she and Marcus had talked a little, drunk a little, cooked and eaten a lot and drunk a little more, and were just getting to the fun bit of the argument when her home landline phone had rung.

It never did that.

Williams started with an apology and ploughed on before she could tell him what she thought of it, saving her the need to go on the offensive before anyone asked why her mobile was on silent. So now, after stewing in the back of a uniform car driven at speed, she was stood sober as a slapped face in front of the press at 11 p.m. reading a Carver-redacted statement – mood-wise, very definitely sub-optimal.

Alexi Zedani was dead, along with his bodyguard and two unknown henchmen, plus four apparent armed robbers. The AAU had probably never had a haul more applicable to their name. Stark was taking his recidivist position of ducking all credit, but she'd be damned if she'd let Lambeth CID take any of it. 'As I said, I can't go into the specifics at this time, but this was a joint operation between the Greenwich Major Investigations Team and the Metropolitan Police Arts and Antiquities Unit.' So the next person to ask about Joseph *bloody* Stark is going to receive a Fran Millhaven talking-to after school. 'A man in his early sixties, believed to be responsible for an illegal art collection, appears to have been killed, along with three men believed to be bodyguards, by four men attempting to steal it. Those four suspects were all shot in an exchange of gunfire with one or more firearms officers, and pronounced dead at the scene. One officer received minor injuries but has not been hospitalized.'

Swan's ego was as bruised as her neck, and to say that she'd *insisted* on staying to catalogue the collection was to skip the surprising and glorious string of expletives and threats with which she'd said it. She'd certainly gone up several notches in Fran's estimation.

'Can you give the injured officer's name?' called a reporter.

Fran wasn't surprised to see Gwen Maddox here. 'No.'

'Can you confirm the deceased collector was renowned businessman and philanthropist Alex Zedani?'

'No.'

'We're standing outside his building,' pointed out Maddox, helpfully.

Not of my choice, thought Fran, but the press had already swarmed around the blue lights here like flies around carrion, and delivering this statement to an empty pavement in front of the station steps would've suited no one but her. 'A number of people live here,' she replied, sounding lame. 'Rest assured, more information will follow. For now, investigations will continue into a wider spectrum of related crimes, with the assistance of Metropolitan Police Operations Directorate MO6 Economic and Specialist Crime, MO7 Serious and Organized Crime, the National Crime Unit and Interpol.' Not to mention a certain Special Liaison and her dangerous 'colleague' who'd given Fran only the briefest of statements, name-dropped the Official Secrets Act and evaporated, taking Stark with them. Handing all this off to Met-Ops ought to mean Fran should soon get time to reestablish diplomatic ties with a certain podgy pathologist, but she doubted it. 'I *can* now confirm that Adrian Fairchild continues to recover from his stabbing, and has been placed under arrest in connection with the investigation.'

'For the murder of Lucinda Drummond?' asked Maddox, annoyingly.

'Murder charges have not been brought at this time.'

'What about Nathan Goff and Yusef Mohamed?'

'As I said, events are moving quickly. We believe those responsible for Fairchild's stabbing and the murders of both Nathan Goff and Yusef Mohamed remain at large, and we are treating all of these crimes as connected.'

She snapped her folder shut and turned back to the taped-off building, but Maddox moved quickly to intercept. 'Fran!'

Fran raised an eyebrow. 'I didn't know we were on first-name terms.'

'Off the record only,' said Gwen. 'You know I wouldn't ask, but he's my friend too.'

'I wouldn't call him a friend. And it's hardly appropriate for you either.'

'Bollocks,' scoffed Maddox flatly. 'And we both know if there are bullets flying, he's usually in the thick of it.'

'And we both know that if that were the case here, he'd be a lot happier if your lot kept his face out of it.'

'But off the record, is he the injured officer?'

'No.'

The relief on Maddox's face was almost enough to raise her in Fran's estimation too, though calling her Gwen was a long way off. 'Was he here?'

Where the bullets were flying, thought Fran. 'I'm sure he'll tell you himself, you being so close and all.'

If you can find him, she thought, walking away.

Just as she was thinking this, a car came to a sharp halt right behind her with the faintest of skids. A big, blacked-out Beamer. The passenger window slid down, and Fran was just about to let loose a tirade of abuse when she saw who was behind it.

Maxine Carver raised both eyebrows with a shrug. 'He insists you get in.'

The *he* turned out to be Stark.

What, and why, went unexplained. Carver was in the front seat, on her phone. A dangerous-looking man with an all-too-familiar broken nose sat in the rear. In summary, getting into this car would only look more dicey if you threw in threats at gunpoint.

'In first, ask later,' called Stark, sharply.

Fran had many faults, but chief among them was her antipathy to backing down. She blamed her father's love of football. Being put in goal by your four elder brothers and peppered with walloping shots would make any girl cry, but with her father looking on, Fran's tears had been suppressed, in furious determination to earn their goddamn respect, long after they'd urged her to give up. Little girls could be afraid, or refuse to be.

She got in. 'Where are we going?'

Carver was talking rapidly into her phone but the dangerous-looking man to her right – whom Fran had to assume went by the name Tink – gave his fellow passenger a thoroughly disreputable grin. 'Your wee man's got a wild flighty idea, and the night is young.'

Stark said nothing, but indicated and pulled out into the traffic.

'Even if I thought you were right, we're not going to make it in time,' said Carver. 'We shouldn't have stopped for her.'

'I work for her, not you,' said Stark.

Fran felt her hackles rise at being discussed in the third person, but soon found her protests curtailed. Stark had many faults too, in her opinion, and chief among those she might hitherto have cited was that he drove like an old woman.

Opinions sometimes faced revision.

The Beamer erupted with blue lights, siren and roaring engine noise, and punched out into the eastward traffic along the southern bank of the river Thames, ducking in and out of and frequently entirely usurping an imaginary central lane in what some might call the very limit of text-book 'advanced police driving', a course she knew for a fact that Stark had not attended.

Clinging on to the door handle for dear life in the back, she found other words screaming in her mind, like demonic possession, and experienced a fond desire to be back in front of the press with a lame-arsed script to read out.

52

London City Airport was a minnow in comparison with its famous rivals, Heathrow, Gatwick and Stansted, or even Luton, but it held one key advantage in being the only one of them actually *in* London – its single short runway making use of the previously abandoned strip of land between two of the royal docks in the former marshlands of South Newham, on the Thames opposite Greenwich.

It couldn't take anything bigger than an Airbus A318 but did a roaring trade in domestic and North European hops, flight training and private jets, several of which stood lined up now in the apron lights like rock stars – gleaming playthings of the have-it-all, go-anywhere set, privately owned or charters for hire, should money be less of an object than convenience, or commercial first class be considered just too vulgar.

One polished jet stood fuelled and ready to go, the steward waiting to greet the happy flyers.

A sleek black minivan made its way towards it from the terminal building and slowed to a halt.

The driver got out, but before he could open a door for anyone, four people climbed out by themselves. Three large figures, wearing plain black baseball caps, jackets, trousers and biker boots – the largest sporting a bushy beard – each with a large black holdall slung across their shoulders and ladies, Louis Vuitton luggage in both hands. One small, in heels and ponytail, carrying a bright orange Peli case.

They were up the steps into the luxury interior in seconds.

'Close the door. Let's go,' Ponytail barked at the steward.

'Aye, we may have a wee problem there, lassie,' Tink grinned, impudently. 'I know the stick from the rudder and could give it a go, like, and your wee man up front's probably mad enough to try it, but his angry-looking boss is a bit of a killjoy. Just don't tell her I said so.'

Stark ducked out of the cockpit door with his warrant card raised, braced for trouble. But a seething Fran shoved past him with hers. 'Met Police!' she barked. 'Stay exactly where you are!'

And this was where life failed to follow the rules of TV crime drama, in which the culprits simply raised their hands in capitulation.

One of the large suspects bolted for the door. Tink thrust out a foot to trip him, sending him tumbling down the steps to the apron tarmac, condition unknown, but the second punched him hard across the face.

The bearded biker, largest of the three, launched himself out of his chair at Fran, barging her brutally aside and coming straight at Stark.

Stark had boxed in basic training – more obdurate than skilful. Boxers punched in a certain way; efficient and fast, but very different from the all-body, use-what-you've-got, win-at-all-costs techniques that dominated his later training. This guy was all boxer, so it was only some hindbrain recognition that swayed Stark's face out of the way of his massive fist by the barest whisker – and all training that drove his own left fist into the side of the giant's face.

As counter-punches went, it wasn't bad, but the guy's own miss had carried him off balance, meaning Stark's blow didn't land square. With a grunt, the big man rolled off the plush fuselage and plunged, shoulder-first, back into Stark, taking them both sprawling into the seats opposite.

Fighting his way free, Stark scrambled to his feet.

Tink was on his feet too, squaring up to Biker Two, blood running from an evidently re-broken nose, with a look on his face suggesting he might just take it personally this time. He carried a pistol holstered beneath his jacket, but was too busy grappling with a man half his size again, to be able to draw it.

As if in silent accord, both remaining bikers slid identical, familiar items out from their jacket sleeves.

Not this shit again, thought Stark, somewhat regretting handing the Iranian pistol off to Carver earlier. What kind of nutcase keeps a crowbar literally up their sleeve, even as they board a flight to freedom? Well, you're not on massive motorbikes any more, fuckers, he thought, flicking out his ASP baton.

Now things got ugly.

Stark felt the crowbar whip through his hair as he ducked Beardy's scything swing. The bar took a chunk out of the plush upholstery lining the fuselage. Good job this was Zedani's plane, or someone from a charter company was going to be compiling a hefty bill. Stark's counter-swing caught the huge man in the guts, but that was all muscle and no bone to break. With an even wilder grunt, Beardy swung back, but Stark was already swaying clear. This time, Beardy was ready for the counter and swayed clear too, but Stark adjusted. The ASP was a great weapon. People underestimated a good baton for incentivizing an opponent to call it a day with a broken arm or leg. Even more effective, if the skull wasn't out of bounds – but that was army, this was police. Beardy's crowbar was a little shorter, but with the added peril of a wicked hook and chisel ends and, in criminal hands, zero anatomical no-go zones. But what wild thugs like this guy – even boxers, who should know better – often forgot, was the efficacy of the jab. Twisting in his counter-swing, Stark thrust the tip of his baton into the man's ribcage. The popping sound told him he'd found bone. The guttural growl of pain told him it wasn't over. But as Beardy grasped his side and swung wildly in Stark's direction, Stark ducked and broke his assailant's kneecap.

Just because you had to avoid the head, it didn't mean you couldn't accidentally do some real damage.

The growl became a scream and Beardy went down.

Without the slightest compunction, Stark kicked him viciously hard in the face.

Lights out. Game over. Self-defence, Your Honour.

A glance showed him Tink standing over a similarly unconscious biker, beaming in triumph, teeth bloody, like a happy lunatic.

Fran had got to her feet and wisely left the boys to their scuffles.

But so had Ponytail.

Katherine Hamilton-Smythe – Zedani's evidently

disloyal PA – stood with the orange Peli case in one hand and a small pistol in the other, contained anger written across her perfect features. 'Get. The fuck. Off my plane.'

No one moved.

'Gonna fly it yersel', are ye, lassie?' asked Tink.

'No. You're going to get off my fucking plane, and send me a real pilot.'

'We can't all get off,' suggested the Scot. 'You're gonna need a hostage at least. Now I'm hardly worth shite, and the lady copper might be a bit fiery for ye, but your man Joe there . . . all shiny and famous – he's gotta be good for a bit of leverage, I ken.'

'Thanks a bunch,' muttered Stark, sure Tink was laying on the accent just for fun.

'Shut the fuck up,' barked Kat.

'Oh, hissy cat, this one,' chuckled Tink. The gun swung his way, and he held up his hands, backing towards the door. 'All right, all right, keep your crackers on, missy, you're the boss. I'm going. You too, Detective Inspector. I'm sure Joe'll be fine . . . right, lad?'

Kat spotted the heavy bulge beneath Tink's jacket and waggled her pistol at him. 'Go for that and you're dead.'

'Never crossed my mind, lass.' Tink backed through the door, lowering one foot to the top step, placing his hands slowly on the fold-out handrails.

Stark coiled, ready to lunge.

Perhaps sensing his intent, Kat swung the pistol towards him, threateningly. 'Don't even think about it, hero.'

'He can't help it, lassie,' said Tink, backing down the steps and out of sight. 'You'd best keep an eye on him.'

Kat positioned herself so she could cover both the door and Stark. 'Drop it.'

'Why did you do it?' he asked, dropping the ASP. 'Kill Lucinda Drummond? Did you overhear her telling Fairchild that she was going to blow your boss's sordid smuggling op wide open? Or was it because that threatened your side hustle with the Iranians?'

A momentary widening of the eyes indicated her surprise that he would know about that, but there was a ramrod self-confidence there too. She had the upper hand, and she knew it. 'Of course it fucking was. Stupid man, growing a conscience way too late. I couldn't believe my ears.'

'Biting the hand that fed him? But isn't that what you're doing? Nice necklace, by the way,' he commented, eyeing the heart-shaped diamond around her neck.

'Alexi?' she scoffed, feeling at the gem, with a sneer. 'I'm done living off scraps from his table or anyone else's.'

'Even after he lied to protect you? He knew you were inside at the time of Lucinda's death. You left him and Jan Zieliński alone outside.'

'And all I had to do was look scared and swear I'd just gone to the powder room to fix my make-up.' She fluttered her eyelashes at Stark. 'Men prefer not to think their arm-candy might actually need to piss. And Christ knows I've heard enough of Alexi's boring fucking phone calls. But what do I overhear on the stairs? Only Adrian *fucking* Fairchild spilling the beans, and Little Miss History Channel declaring she'll go public. I'd have killed them both if I could. If I'd known what fun it was, I'd have tried it years ago. One little punch and a shove. And the shock on

her face . . . even the sound of her hitting the floor . . .'
Kat smiled at the memory. 'I wonder what it's like with
a gun?' Her smile hardened, looking down the barrel
at him.

'No tears for poor Alexi, then?'

'What do you mean?'

'Your Iranian buyers tried to cut you out, and they
weren't happy when they didn't find what they were looking for. Alexi didn't make it, I'm afraid. Jan and a couple
of others too, if that matters to you?'

She must've known something was wrong. Maybe the
Iranians had gone dark on her. Maybe she'd seen Fran's
piece to camera outside Zedani's building. Either way,
she'd made a dash for the airport. If this update moved
her, it didn't show.

'Good riddance,' she said, with a tight smile. 'I was
never going to be just another jewel in his collection.
Alive or dead, I never want to think about his creepy old
hands on me again. Now, stop playing for time and get
my pilot.'

'And Nathan Goff? You sent these three after him, just
for that one extra coin. How much more would you get
for the full set? Have you any idea what they put him
through for your greed? Was it worth it?'

'It would have been.' Her voice stayed calm but her lips
tightened in growing anger. 'If you lot hadn't grabbed the
rest of them.'

'I expect that pissed off your buyers? Telling them
they'd only get what's in there?' said Stark, nodding at the
Peli case.

Another twitch of surprise.

'And Yusef Mohamed?' pressed Stark, pushing his luck. 'Your off-the-books gofer. Did he have to die just to cover your bloody tracks?'

'*Yes!*' Kat's porcelain visage cracked nastily. 'And if you don't shut the fuck up, you're next. Now get me my *fucking pilot*!' she shouted out the door.

'Excuse me,' said Fran.

Kat angrily turned her head, and got a faceful of police-issue pepper spray.

Stark was already driving her gun arm upwards as the shot erupted into the ceiling, sending a shower of padding foam and gun smoke rocking around the cabin in the concussed air. The force of Stark's blow, combined with the recoil, drove the pistol from her hand and bounced it off the curved wall, skimming it across the deep-pile carpet.

Kat staggered back, fingers scrabbling desperately at agonized eyes, only making them worse and, to add insult to burning injury, blinding her to the arrival of Fran's punch in her midriff.

Stark kicked the gun out of reach.

Fran stood over her prone and breathless victim like a vengeful angel. 'I really hate being ignored.' As mike-drop one-liners went, what it lacked in wit it more than made up for in venom, only slightly spoiled by her subsequent coughing in the pepper-tinged haze.

'I did warn you about the fiery one, lassie,' said Tink, grinning in the doorway, pistol hanging languorously in one hand. He gave Stark an encouraging thumbs-up. 'Still breathing, soldier?'

Stark rolled his eyes.

'Confuse and confound, lad,' Tink shrugged, unapologetically. 'Never doubted the pair of you for a second.'

Always control where the enemy is looking. Show them one danger so they miss the other. Stark imagined Fran would have a thing or two to say about being a pawn in the tactical mix, but she currently had her hands full.

Kat was still gasping from the combination of teargas and a gut-punch, but that didn't stop Fran cuffing her. 'Katherine Hamilton-Smythe, I'm arresting you on suspicion of murder, resisting arrest, firearms offences, impeding an investigation and *pissing me off*. You do not have to say anything, but it may harm your defence if you do not mention when questioned something which you later rely on in court. Anything you do say may be given in evidence . . . *Capeesh?* Good. Don't worry, you won't need any of that expensive mascara in prison,' she added darkly.

Kat used her first half-decent breath to ring out a chorus of charmless expletives and threats.

No one told her not to rub her eyes.

A quick glance outside confirmed that Biker One had made it no further than Maxine Carver and was now hogtied on the tarmac with two Transport uniforms pointing MP5 carbines at him. Stark rolled the two unconscious riders into as close to the recovery position as speed-cuffs allowed. Tink watched, amused.

'Reckon that was enough?' asked Stark, glancing at the tiny camera secreted at each end of the cabin. Courtesy of Maxine's Aladdin's cave car boot. Spotless audio, she'd promised.

Fran shrugged. 'That'll be down to the sharks.'

'And I suppose it depends on what's in that case,' added

Maxine, appearing in the doorway with a cordless angle grinder. No one asked where she'd got it.

She handed it to Tink. Dirty work didn't apply to her either.

Laying the Peli case on the tarmac in the headlights of the minivan outside, and skilfully removing both hinges, he cracked it open.

There had been a safe, discretely tucked away in Zedani's secret museum, found open and ransacked. From the cash and diamonds in the Peli case, Stark guessed Kat had helped herself to those along with the gift-wrapped necklace. But that wasn't the focus of everyone's attention right now.

Positioning himself to shield it from the eyes of any of the uniforms, Tink lifted something heavy from the case and pulled the black velvet drawstring bag off it.

'Now that,' said Maxine Carver, 'is *definitely* an official secret.'

Stark's head was both dropping and spinning.

Fighting for your life and arresting murdering thieves could only keep you going so long without sleep. Or distract you from stomach-twisting worry. The first twenty-four hours were the traditional window of hope in a missing person's case. It was now forty-seven hours since Jergen's call to place Gabrielle in that category, and this was far from traditional. Now Stark was concerned for Jergen too. The hospital had been neutral ground for the various militia that held only slightly less animosity towards each other than the government they were collectively fighting. With it gone, chaos might fill the vacuum. Now, at 2 a.m., with nothing but desk work in front of him for the foreseeable, exhaustion was threatening a coup of its own.

So he almost failed to realize that the ringing phone was his, and snatched it up only just before it cut to voice-mail. The sat phone!

'Jergen?' He blurted out, earning odd looks from his colleagues.

'*Non, chéri, c'est moi.*'

Relief flooded his being. '*Gabrielle?*' That earned a look from Fran, but Stark didn't care. '*Tu vas bien?*'

'*Oui, je vais bien,*' she sighed. 'But many are not. I was trapped with three patients for many hours, but others were not so fortunate. Sébastien and Luther, both killed. Others injured. And the security situation became bad, fast.'

'Is everyone else okay?'

'Some scrapes. The whole team flew to Geilenkirchen with the worst of the wounded. We've been too busy settling in the wounded to call.'

The NATO airbase in Germany, near the border with Holland. 'It's so good to hear your voice.'

'*Now* he worries.'

'I should've been there.'

'To hold back the aeroplane bombs with your will?' she said. 'If you'd stayed, you might be dead now.'

'Or stuck in Geilenkirchen with you. I can get a flight out today.'

'*Non, chéri.* You have your appointment with Major Pierson, yes? A deal is a deal. And I will be gone. Home to Paris for a while.'

'And Tomas?'

'*Oui*. He worries too.'

Stark let that settle in. Not everything was his fault or responsibility. Gabrielle did not need saving. It was enough to know she was okay.

'But then I think Aleppo,' she added. 'There is a team that needs more help. Jergen and some of the others are looking into it.'

'Syria?'

'*Oui*.'

'They bomb hospitals there too.'

'And each other, combatants and civilians. We go where we are needed.'

We. She wouldn't ask him to come. That wasn't how it worked among those who qualified as *we*. You either volunteered or you didn't. Judgement was for those who didn't know better.

'I haven't decided,' she said quietly, to his silence. A close shave was one thing. Death of colleagues was another. For all the horrors she witnessed, lives saved and lost, who could blame her if she chose Paris and Tomas for a while?

'Let me know.' He could say that she'd done her bit, done enough and more.

She could say the same to him.

But those were the decisions one made, alone, at the crossroads.

For now there was nothing left to say but *au revoir, chéri*, and nothing left to do but go home and sleep.

53

Fran gave up glaring at Maxine Carver.

It didn't seem to work, and her heart wasn't in it.

Her heart was, after finding Marcus asleep on her sofa in the small hours last night and him cooking her breakfast as she woke, more confused than ever. But she seemed to be taking an uncharacteristically positive view on that, which was clearly interfering with her glare mojo. Bloody man.

'So let me get this straight,' she said, to cover what had very nearly slipped into a smile. 'Katherine Hamilton-Smythe was actually born Katerina Kuznetsov to a medium-level player in the Russian mafia, here in London. And you think the Russians manoeuvred her into Zedani's employ to keep an inside eye on how honestly he was cleaning their dishonest money? But you didn't think to tell us any of this?'

'We didn't know,' replied Carver, curtly. 'You may have gone home for some sleep, but I've been up with my people all night working out how we missed this. And believe me, explaining it to my boss this morning was a great deal less pleasant than this little bunfest,' she added, eyes cutting to the plate of pastries Stark had turned up with.

After the adrenaline had crashed out of their systems last night, he'd looked ready to drop, but this morning he appeared transformed. Neat as a pin, as ever, but clean-shaven too, fading facial tan-line exposed. Over the year-plus since she'd seen his whole face, Fran had forgotten how handsome he was beneath, if you didn't mind the faded scars. But the true revelation was the pressure that seemed to have lifted from him. Good news about his friend, perhaps.

'She had us all fooled,' said Groombridge, which despite being true, irritated Fran, who felt that Carver should have known and *definitely* been more sharing.

'She certainly had her sugar daddy fooled,' she added, making a mental note that the power imbalance between a beautiful young woman and a wealthy older man could work both ways.

'Even my asset on the inside,' added Carver, with a barbed look at Tink.

He just shrugged. 'The Black Riders didn't seem Zedani's style. And Jan was never *that* much of a bastard. But I couldnae ken what was going on.'

'Leave it to him to see things askew,' said Fran, indicating Stark.

'Late in the game, but yes,' conceded Carver. 'Annoyingly.'

Stark said nothing, leaving Fran in the undesirable position of having to agree with Carver. 'You get used to it. So now what? You think what *was* going on is that sweet little Kat-claws got tired of being everyone's pawn and decided to try a little side deal of her own for the coins and the mask?'

'What mask?' asked Carver, pointedly.

Fran rolled her eyes. National security, as far as it had been explained to her, sounded a lot like saving-*bloody*-face. 'So Kat ropes in three of Daddy's heavy helpers and sets up a buyer – the guys Fairydust here conspicuously failed to arrest last night, the ones we're not allowed to call Iranian?'

Tink shrugged again. Carver nodded.

Fran frowned. Stark had said little about last night that wasn't already in his typically terse written statement, owning two of the dead. More fatality hearings. She put that aside for now. 'Only everything went wrong. Fairchild panicked, Lucinda Drummond threatened to go public, Kat overheard and killed her, and in the ensuing commotion the tester coin got pinched by Nathan Goff. The Russian heavies, using Zedani's secret boatyard as their base, got on their bikes to kill Goff and nearly took Stark's head off trying to get the coin back. Then when we ID'd the van and Yusef Mohamed on TV, they killed him too and left Fairchild dying for good measure. Then when we raided the boatyard, seizing the pots and coins, they decided to cut their losses and take off for mother Russia with the non-existent facial adornment instead?'

'That's about it, yes.' Carver's smile was too much like a teacher's beneficence to their pet pupil.

'And you can help us prove all this?' So far, Kat and her pals had said exactly nothing, and the lawyers that turned up had been dressed in suits so sharp they cut the air. Russian money would certainly fit.

Fran was hopeful that forensics would link the three heavies to the bikes and boatyard, and thereby the killings. One of them was already a match for the partial fingerprint lifted from the bike Stark had disabled outside Goff's flats, which tied them to the bikes in the boatyard and Yusef Mohamed's murder. And the lab *had* now managed to recover DNA from the print, which should put the match beyond question. Their large biker boots were a reasonable match for the blurred and bloody prints from there, as well as from Nathan Goff's murder scene, and there was always the chance that they'd been less than professional with their anti-contamination gear – if and when the labs ever processed their clothing, boots and crowbars for the victims' blood, DNA, hair, clothing fibres, et cetera . . . On top of which, the balance of the £10,000 in cash withdrawn by Fairchild the day after Lucinda's murder, and extorted from him by Goff, had been found on them, evenly split three ways – democratic but damning, when the serial numbers were examined.

All promising.

And confronting Kat with the secret audio-visual play-back from the jet last night was going to be fun. But she could still walk.

She'd proved herself an accomplished actress, and Daddy could afford a top barrister. Together they would reframe her confession on the plane as confusion and mis-understanding, claim she'd felt threatened, that she'd not heard them identify themselves as police and, fearing for her life, she'd have said anything to make her attackers think her capable of defending herself with the gun. Then they would set about portraying jealous and corrupt Adrian Fairchild as the only person with motive to kill Lucinda, not poor oppressed little Kat. And as for the rest, she could claim her scary boss, Zedani, had ordered her to take the box to Russia on his behalf, and she had no idea what was inside. She could claim the heavies worked for Zedani and, again, she'd had no idea, or even that she'd been kidnapped and coerced. Zedani hadn't the breath to contradict her, and the heavies – if they did work for her Russian mob father – might do their time in silence.

But right now, Fran's pressing worry was whether her case was about to get eviscerated in the name of national security by this bloody woman.

'Well, the plane footage goes a long way, so well done, Joe, for not mentioning the mask,' said Carver, 'but I think you'll like the contents of the laptop and burner phone you found in her couture-stuffed bling luggage even more.'

Both laptop and phone were covered in Kat's fingerprints, but a 2 a.m. call to Bingo hadn't filled Fran with hope of unlocking them anytime soon. Police couldn't force a suspect to divulge passcodes, passwords, or unlock devices through a fingerprint or facial recognition, and the big-tech companies would only comply when forced to by the courts. That Carver clearly wasn't bound by the same constraints was both worrying, from a civil liberties perspective, and deeply enviable.

'As I said, my team have been at this all night,' continued the smarmy cow, unnecessarily. 'There were records of calls to and from the burner phone found on the "unknown criminals of possible Middle Eastern extraction" who killed her boss. Emails, with photos, concerning the gold staters and a certain nameless facial adornment that we might have to redact a little. Calls and texts to and from the burner found on Joe's crowbar-wielding friend, including one containing Nathan Goff's home address in the hours before his death. Plus calls to and from another burner number on the call activity list you triangulated to

Yusef Mohamed's house. The second phone you say Yusef's sister mentioned, I'd suggest.

'Crowbar's phone was also the one used to call Dosh-4Gold,' continued Carver. 'But my personal favourite . . .' she paused, 'Kat's laptop still contains all the photoshopped building blocks and final images of both Libby Drummond and Kat herself in red cross hairs, plus the pop-up email account they were sent from.'

'She faked her own death threat to divert any burgeoning suspicion firmly at her boss?' asked DS Cox, redundantly.

'So it seems,' smiled Carver. 'But the pièce de résistance is probably this little text conversation from yesterday.' She read aloud from a transcript.

'Middle Eastern bad guy: *You have it?*

'Kat's burner: *I can get it anytime. But the police have the coins now.*

'Bad guy: *That's very disappointing. Without them, our offer drops to five.*

'Kat: *No way. It's worth ten times that to your rivals.* By this we assume Kat probably means the Iraqis,' explained Carver.

'He replies: *And who would you approach, in that chaos? And with the police closing in here. Five million sterling. Take it or leave it.*

'She replies: *Twenty or we walk. I have a Russian buyer.*

'He warns her: *Then fly away, little bird, but you'll never fly far enough that we won't find you.*

'She replies: *You can't threaten me. You know my connections.*

'To which he says: *And you know mine. Take the five and live, or run and die.*

'Several minutes pass,' said Carver, 'then Kat says:

Okay. He's home tonight, so I'll get it in the morning while he swims his laps. Five million. Tomorrow night.'

'Sounds like she's caving, but really she's buying time to pinch the non-mask and get out,' added Tink. '*They* think she's tipped her hand, and they try to get in ahead of her.'

It was now tomorrow, and the deal was off, either way, nodded Fran. The Iranians were dead, Kat and her crew in custody.

'We'll tell you what you can and can't use, of course, but there should be enough there to put Kat and her backing singers away for life,' smiled Carver, with maddening beneficence.

Fran looked at Groombridge, who shrugged, with a positive expression. 'We'll have to see what the CPS say, but it should be enough.'

Fran nodded. It seemed her unbidden optimism was affecting her contrarian mojo too. But with a fair wind, Kat was indeed done living off luxury table scraps from both her real and her sugar daddy, and should spend the next decades eating from a tray in prison. That had to be worth a warming ember of inner positivity.

A massive amount of work lay ahead. Eight dead and four in custody was a lot of paperwork, and that was just last night. Another massive Stark-induced mess to clear up, barely two weeks back on the job. How could she possibly still be crossing her fingers, knees and toes that he didn't bugger off again? She wasn't in such a strange mood that she'd say it aloud, but she needed him. Maybe a lightning rod was not a safe thing to be too close to, but it beat standing alone in the open.

*

'What happened to the beard?' asked Swan as Stark placed the drinks down. The Compass Rose pub was busy tonight, half the station turning out to celebrate a big win they'd never know the full truth about. If anyone ever did.

After Gabrielle's call, a few hours' sleep and a shower, Stark had, not for the first time, found himself disconnected from the man in the mirror. His desert gear was now cleaned and stowed away too. A few people had asked the same question during the long day's paperwork, but there was no simple way to explain truthfully.

'Forget that,' scoffed Fran. 'Who's Gabrielle?'

There was no simple way to explain that either. 'The friend.'

'She okay?'

'Narrowly, for now.'

'Hmm,' mused Fran. 'You likely to answer further questions on the topic?'

'Not today.'

Fran nodded, sure to revisit the topic as early as tomorrow. 'So what happens to the coins, pottery and other stuff?' she asked Swan.

'The coins and pottery are already on their way back to Basra,' replied Swan, sipping her G 'n' T. 'The rest, we'll work to return to wherever they should be.'

Fran raised an eyebrow. 'Thought the British Museum would nab the lot.'

'I think they try not to do that any more.'

'Not in much of a rush to send back everything they nabbed historically though.'

'I don't think my sergeant would sign off on *that* investigation,' said Swan.

415

'And what about the unmentionable?'

The Mask of Kings. Swan had been brought into the circle of knowledge to speak to authenticity, though she denied much expertise. Stark wasn't sure he'd ever seen anyone more shocked, angry and overjoyed all at once to discover a fake had been on public display all these years. 'Above my pay grade,' she replied.

'I'd like to know whose pay grade it *isn't* above,' mused Fran. 'Still, AAU came out of this shiny. Treasures recovered. International smuggling ring unmasked.'

'Might even get an office with a window,' said Stark.

'I won't hold my breath,' said Swan, but there was a faint smile there. So far Stark's name *wasn't* all over this – but she'd got the publicity the AAU needed, all the same. Win–win.

Fran took a long swig of her large white wine. 'Well, I'll be glad to wash my hands of the whole damn thing.'

Stark wordlessly sipped his lager. Claiming she wanted shot of the case hadn't stopped Fran bemoaning redaction all day, and that was before Met-Ops arrived tomorrow.

A silence descended on their table now. Awkwardness mixed with weariness. They weren't anywhere near washing their hands of it all – though Stark suspected that Carver would find a way to whitewash *him* out of it.

That was the difference between MIT and AAU, perhaps. Doubtless, the recovered antiquities each might tell a tale of blood, but in the Murder Squad a win was never a win. Every celebratory sip was tinged with tragedy. Even when the trail of blood led to the culprit, you never forgot where it led from. A woman who fell to her death, a young thief, a hapless driver, Alex Zedani and his bodyguards, not to mention the Iranians, all dead – for greed. The waste of it all tinged every celebratory sip with bitterness.

Williams had stayed for the first round and gone home for family and sleep. John Dixon was at the bar, chatting to Pensol, while Ptolemy restrained a grinning Peters from interfering. Few thought it likely John would have the courage to trade in Commandant Tracy, but Stark nursed a quiet confidence. Pity for Swan, but maybe now she'd had a glimpse outside the basement she'd seek a little sunshine too.

Fran let out a long sigh, eyeing Stark. 'I blame you.'

'Me too,' added Swan.

'For anything specific?'

'Everything.'

Stark could do little but shrug. 'My shrink says I'm to stop thinking everything is my fault or responsibility.'

Fran gave a harrumph. 'She gets paid for that crap. But she doesn't get to see you in action for herself.'

'I definitely should've heeded the warnings,' said Swan. She said it in jest, but the bruising around her neck spoke the truth of it.

Fran kept her eyes on Stark. 'So, you gonna pull another disappearing act now?'

'Want me to?'

She took a long moment to think about that. 'Would it make any difference?'

'You know how much I value your opinion.'

'Only too well.'

'Honestly, I was fifty-fifty on flying back out to Libya on Sunday, but the hospital I was working from just got bombed to bits, and Tink's fake job offer was never for me anyway. So maybe I'll stick around a bit longer.'

Fran scowled, shaking her head. 'It's your boundless enthusiasm for the job that warms my heart.'

Stark suppressed a smile. Maybe some things stayed *exactly* the same, after all.

'I must admit I was wondering if you only came back for this,' she said, fiddling with her phone to pull up the BBC News website, flicking past a headline – *PHILANTHROPIST'S DEATH LINKED TO ILLEGAL ARTS TRADE!* – to pictures of smiling recipients from the Queen's Birthday Honours List ceremony, held earlier that day at Buckingham Palace. 'No trip to Lizzy's gaff for you again this year? Guess that clocktower thing is old news.'

'Guess so.'

'Disappointed?'

'Less is more.'

If he didn't know better, he might say she looked almost disappointed on his behalf. The tabloid campaign to see Stark awarded the George Cross to go with his Victoria Cross had gained enough traction among the general public to filter inside the station and give rise to a form of collective pride that perhaps even Fran wasn't immune to.

At least there wasn't a *hero snubbed* strapline, he thought – until Fran showed him the various tabloid sites.

'Another round?' asked Swan.

Stark looked around the pub. Life went on, and that was that. 'Hell, yes.'

54

'You're sure about this?' asked Major Wendy Pierson the next day.

Stark had a huge amount of respect for the major, but their relationship was never going to be an easy one with this issue hanging over them. 'I've said I am.'

'Indeed,' she glared, 'but your long history as a massive pain in my arse forces me to keep asking.'

'And how often have you known my answers to change?'

'About the same number of times I've agreed with them.'

'Which your long history as a pain in *my* arse forces you to reiterate.'

'I'm serious. You're making a mistake.'

'It's mine to make.'

'You're still on the reserves list,' clucked Pierson, irritably. 'I can still order you to do what I want.'

Another reason he'd campaigned for his papers these last years. 'But you won't. That's what this is all about.'

'For you, maybe.'

His final act of compliance, and not at all what she wished. 'So we disagree to disagree, as ever.' She stood back and inspected his police dress uniform with a cool eye, searching for any fleck of lint, any button unpolished, any speck of dirt on his gleaming boots.

'Will I do?' Exactly what he'd asked her in this place, four years earlier.

The corner of her mouth twitched. 'You'll have to, I suppose.' She pulled out an envelope and proffered it.

His second stipulation of their deal. His long-overdue honourable discharge from Her Majesty's military reserves. 'That was supposed to come after.'

'Some things are too momentous to be traded.'

He could make a joke about accepting her surrender, but this was too momentous for that too. Taking the letter, he was no longer an army reservist. No longer a soldier. An ex-combatant. Free to be something else at last, whatever that might be, and no going back. He tucked it away, without opening it. An indiscernible weight in his pocket, but a mountain, he hoped, removed. 'Thank you.'

She nodded. She may never agree, but it was his decision to make. 'Well then, since I no longer outrank you, I might as well say, once only and with complete deniability, that I am immensely proud of you. And, since we're revisiting our previous exchanges here, stand like an *ex*-soldier and don't fuck up.'

Stark looked around the long, opulent Buckingham Palace Picture Gallery, thinking that, residents aside, few but the daughter of a brigadier general would dare drop f-bombs inside these walls.

Checking her watch, she knocked at the door halfway down and opened it.

There was no fanfare this time, no ballroom, just the huge Buckingham Palace Music Room with its gleaming black grand piano, five towering windows in the bowed bay, two enormous chandeliers and the diminutive figure of Her Majesty the Queen flanked by a Gurkha orderly, two Yeomen of the Guard and the Lord Chamberlain.

Stark's breath stopped.

Next to his mother and sister in their new dresses and hats, with awed smiles, stood another figure . . . wearing the same broad-brimmed cream hat and stunning sky-blue dress she'd carried off with such elegance four years ago.

Kelly Jones.

'You're welcome,' whispered Pierson.

If Stark had been capable of speech in this moment, he was beaten to it by the Lord Chamberlain's clear voice. 'Detective Sergeant Joseph Stark of your Majesty's Metropolitan Police Service, and Sergeant, Third Battalion, Princess of Wales's Royal Regiment, retired.'

Stark's legs carried him forward several steps.

'For valour in circumstances of extreme danger above and beyond the call of duty: the George Cross.'

Stark took more steps, bowed his head and stood to attention before his monarch for the second time.

She eyed him with a shrewd expression. 'Back again, Sergeant.'

'Yes, Ma'am.'

'Might I suggest you let someone else have a go next time?'

'Yes, Ma'am.'

The Queen fixed him with a penetrative stare, honed over decades of being no one's fool, perhaps wondering whether making that an order would have the slightest impact. An oath was an oath, and who knew that better than her? 'Quite right.' A warm smile lit up her face.

Taking the navy-beribboned silver medal from the plush cushion held out by the orderly, she hung it on the small brass hook secreted in the ribbon line above Stark's left breast pocket, next to his service medals and Victoria Cross.

She held out one hand in its long white silk glove for Stark to shake.

'Very good,' she nodded. 'Carry on, Sergeant.'

The palace photographer did their thing, but these photographs would not make the papers. As far as the press were concerned, yesterday's was the conclusive list of this year's Queen's Birthday Honours.

Stark's *principal* deal stipulation: that today's private ceremony would remain secret until after his death, something Pierson had threatened to arrange if he didn't behave, and to which the Palace had shown surprising sympathy.

Gwen Maddox had fallen somewhere between the two. Carver was ready to slap D-notices on any press that caught wind of the Mask of Kings, but Stark guessed Gwen wouldn't be thrown off the scent about today, and she deserved a little truth. Another exclusive he trusted her not to print. Unless he died, she'd reminded him.

Updating Doc Hazel was going to be interesting too.

On Pierson's signal, the visitors retreated through a side door into the White Drawing Room, where palace staff were waiting to serve them canapés and champagne in silver and crystal, leaving the Queen to whatever duties filled her Sunday afternoons.

Pierson held Stark back a step. 'She's right, you know,'

she said, quietly. 'Most people don't survive one cross, let alone two. You can't keep charging the guns.'

Stark wondered what she would say if she knew he'd stared down a barrel, twice, barely thirty-six hours earlier. 'Noted.'

Her look said she had little faith he would budge one inch. 'There's more to life, if you're done fucking up. Stand straight . . .' she said, and with effortless skill, herded his mother and sister aside with small talk, leaving him awkwardly face to face with today's surprise guest.

Kelly tilted her head, a quizzical expression inviting him to lead the dance.

All he could think to ask was, 'How are you here?'

'Long story. But it boils down to you being an idiot.'

'It usually does. I could use help narrowing it down.'

'It's what happens when you change your email and number and fly off into the sunset without giving a girl a chance to . . .' She took a deep breath. 'I don't know what. But let's stick with it all being your fault.'

'I still don't understand.'

'For probably the smartest man I've ever met, that does seem to happen a lot.' She held up her left hand, palm towards her.

No ring. 'You're not engaged?'

'No.'

'You turned Robert down?'

'Over a year ago. He popped the question that day, just after you conspicuously stepped aside – while I'm lying there in hospital, of all places,' she added, suggesting Robert's demonstrability wasn't everything a girl could wish for, after all. 'But I just couldn't . . .' A cloud crossed her expression. 'I guess what had just happened put things into perspective. What's really important, you know.'

'I daren't assume to know anything, right now.'

'No.' Kelly had a way of looking at him that could make him feel she was reading between his lines, off a script she had the only copy of. 'Robert wasn't sure what to make of it either. But he moved on and, it seems, found love again quite quickly.'

In all its blissful shallows, thought Stark, suddenly aware that he was free now to think uncharitably of the man. 'Then whose hand is online wearing the diamond?'

'Lydia. Early years teacher. Nice girl, I hear. And if your mother had bothered to look any deeper into Robert's profile, she'd have seen that for herself . . .' Stark watched his own thought processes reflected in Kelly's expression as they both came to the same suspicion. His mother was a lot smarter than she let on. '*Sneaky moo.*'

All Stark could do was nod. 'Sounds about right.'

Kelly visibly filed that away for later. 'Didn't work though. You still didn't call me. She should've known better. None of your business, you told her, am I right? Far be it for you to get in the way of Robert's happiness?'

Now all he could do was shrug. 'And yours.'

'Mine,' nodded Kelly, slowly. 'You seem to have a habit of deciding what might make me happy, or otherwise, without actually asking.'

Stark wasn't going near that one. 'So, how . . . ?'

'Louise, though I think your mum put her up to it. Then Wendy, of course.'

Stark glanced over and found the trio staring their way, his mother grinning, Pierson enjoying a smug smile, and his sister poking her tongue out at him. 'So, Robert is with Lydia, and you're . . . ?'

'Single. And you're . . . ?'

He thought about that. 'At a crossroads, I thought.'

'With someone?'

'Not really.'

'Complicated?'

Stark pictured Gabrielle scoffing at his hesitation. Laughing at him, telling him to forget yesterday, love today and let tomorrow bring what comes. 'Not really.'

Kelly's cornflower-blue eyes searched his. 'Ambiguity doesn't suit you.'

'Sorry. It's been a long few days.'

'It's been a long year,' she said, echoing words he thought he'd said too softly to be heard, in her car outside Royal Hill Police Station, on a hot day, what seemed like a lifetime ago. Her eyes softened. 'You look tired.'

'You look . . .' Radiant, he thought. Like dawn after night patrol. Like the home you dreamt of when you thought you might never see home again. The face you saw when you bled from consciousness, and your first thought when you came to. The hope you couldn't hope you deserved. But that was the soldier talking. And those days were behind him now. The other paths that had confused or confounded him seemed mere distractions now too, obfuscations, excuses. He wanted to tell her she was quite the most beautiful woman he'd ever seen, as he had the last time they were here, but this Stark, whoever he was, could find no words worthy of her. He wanted to tell her she was the only woman he would ever love, but her eyes told him that she already knew.

'There he is,' she said, taking both his hands gently in hers and peering deep into his eyes, smiling at his turmoil. 'I see you, Joe. The man you are, not the man you fear. So exhausted by duty, you can't believe that you deserve peace or happiness. But you do, more than anyone. And you can rest now, Joe, if you're ready?'

Something gave, deep within him. As if the dam that Doc Hazel saw in him had suffered one inaudible, fatal crack. He stood paralysed by the enormity of the question, as if even to breathe might bring the whole edifice down.

Kelly raised a hand to his face, thumb gently caressing something from beneath his eye.

After all this time, a solitary tear.

She smiled like warm sunrise scattering stormy night. 'I'll take that as a yes.'

Epilogue

Karim's chest swelled with pride. The emotion of exhaustion. He'd been at this for days on nought but naps, but finally the urns gleamed in their spotlit glass cases. Bullet proof and bolted down. Courtesy of the British Museum. A blessed partnership in the making.

He should sleep now, but there was so much more to do. So many treasures returned. It was almost enough to make a man think of prayer.

Sensing he was not alone, he turned to find a strange pair standing in the doorway. A native man in a suit too good for academia, too cheap for one of the corrupted political classes. The young white woman beside him, wearing a hijab, seemed familiar. It took him a moment to place her.

'I saw you in London,' he said in English, curious, and a little unnerved by her gaze.

'That would be unlikely.' She smiled – the bared teeth of a predator, bright and dangerous.

There was a strongbox in her hand. Chained to her wrist.

Stepping forward, she unlocked the chain and handed him the box. 'A friend of mine insisted you would want this back.'

It was heavy. 'Does this friend have a name?'

The woman's eyes held secrets, and humour. 'He would prefer to stay anonymous. He's a *backwards* sort of fellow.' She took out a small pad and pen, scribbled, tore off the page and passed it to him. 'The combination.'

Frowning, Karim placed the box on a nearby trestle table, typed the five-letter code into the digi-pad, and popped the clasps.

The object inside stole his breath away, gleaming golden in the light and in his heart.

When he could tear his eyes from it, he found the woman and her companion gone, as if they had never been. Passing phantoms. In their place stood his chief of security and two most trusted guards – men Karim had personally vetted and recruited.

'What is it?' asked the chief.

Karim could not speak. He looked from the Mask of Kings to the scribbled combination.

KRATS

Then he laughed. It was a *backwards* world indeed, but laughter, he decided, was better than tears.

Acknowledgements

Having not one but four books published is little short of a miracle.

In acknowledgement of this, my first thank-yous must go to my agent, Andrew, for seeing something in my early writings and for your encouragement and level-headed navigation through these rolling seas, and to Rowland for making my dreams come true with your continued faith in me and undimmed enthusiasm for Stark, Fran and the rest of the characters I love so much.

As with my previous books, the seeds of *The Woman Who Fell* took root in my mind long before I was free to write it in earnest. Like most authors, I cannot tolerate not writing for long, so whenever the current manuscript is away in someone else's hands, I will be working on the next, or ideas for ones after that. This book exploded out of the starting blocks long before the last was complete, somewhat laden with all the ideas I'd been storing up. Not long into developing it properly it became obvious that it was in fact trying to carry another whole book on its back, and having gratefully let that other idea dismount, the race to the finish was a thrill. That next idea is already in its stride and I can't wait to share the killer opening with you all – if enough of you buy this one. Spread the word folks! There is always so much more that I want to say than there is space in each book, and in helping me streamline this story to its beating heart I must again thank my editor, Ruth, for your saintly patience and gentle knife in excising the extraneous.

Thanks to my copy-editor, Shan, for your keen eye for style, continuity, wayward grammar and errant punctuation, to Nick for shepherding this book through the proofs despite my compulsive tinkering, and all the team at Penguin and Michael Joseph for everything you've done. You know who you are.

Somewhat sheepishly, my thanks must of course also go to her late Majesty, Queen Elizabeth II, for your dauntless service and inspiring grace, begging humble forgiveness for the temerity of placing you in the heart of Stark's life and motivation. I can only hope that you might have approved. Rest in peace.

Thank you to all who serve, in uniform and without.

My humble thanks to all you tireless reviewers, bloggers, book club readers and every one of you generous enough to offer kind words. Please continue to share the books you love with the people you love, and everyone else! I hope you find this one to your liking.

To all the publishers, booksellers and libraries for toughing it out through Covid and an ever-tougher market, and your sheer love of the written word.

As ever, my fervent appreciation goes always to all you wonderful readers, and those of you who have contacted me to say how much you enjoyed *If I Should Die*, *Between the Crosses* and *The Killer Inside*, and how much you are looking forward to this next Stark adventure – with fresh apologies for my tardiness. Writing around a busy family life and day job is slow, but my cup is full to brimming and my blessings daily counted.

And on that note, my most heartfelt gratitude goes ever to my beloved wife, three growing sons, parents, siblings, in-laws and all my family and friends — for allowing me time to wander in other worlds while never letting go of my hand.

I love you all.